Roman Elegy

ROMAN ELEGY

SABINE GRUBER

translated by
PETER LEWIS

First published in German as *Stillbach oder Die Sehnsucht* by Sabine Gruber
Copyright © Verlag C.H.Beck oHG, München 2011

First published in Great Britain in 2013 by
Haus Publishing Ltd
70 Cadogan Place
London SW1X 9AH
www.hauspublishing.com

Translation copyright © Peter Lewis 2013

Typeset in Garamond by MacGuru Ltd

Printed in the United Kingdom by TJ International

ISBN: 978 1 90832 310 1
ebook ISBN: 978 1 90832 336 1

This publication has been supported by the Austrian Cultural Forum London.

Non gridate più

Cessate d'uccidere i morti,
Non gridate più, non gridate
Se li volete ancora udire,
Se sperate di non perire.

Hanno l'impercettibile sussurro,
Non fanno più rumore
Del crescere dell'erba,
Lieta dove non passa l'uomo.

Shout No More

Stop killing the dead,
Shout no more, don't shout
If you still want to hear them,
If you're hoping not to perish.

Their murmur is imperceptible,
The sound they make no louder
Than growing grass,
Happy where men don't pass.

Giuseppe Ungaretti, translated by Andrew Frisardi

For Leo, Lorenz and Luis

2009

When the feeling of being alive fades, we still have the sky – for a fleeting moment, Clara caught sight of her own face in the window as the train entered a tunnel. She was startled by how blank and broad and detached it looked in the dim lighting of the carriage. Then the cloud faces returned, their surfaces and depths framed by thin, high wisps of vapour that looked like strands of hair. In the valley floor, espaliered apple trees stood in serried ranks, their branches tied to wires, while above them loomed cliffs of pink porphyry, overgrown with bushy scrub.

Once I'm dead, Ines had written, *I'll really bring the sky to life. I'll be white or grey, dark, light, red or orange-yellow, sometimes fat, sometimes thin, stripy, towering up like a cliff, or milky and lenticular, layered, like a veil, all ragged, or checked or shaped like a fishbone or beams of light, a crazy tangle of threads – yes, so then you can untwist me and plait me again – or one big, solid piece of cloth – then you can wrap yourself up in me! I'll be a broom-cloud. Or a hairlock-and-feather-cloud. A dense clump. Your ball of wool. Then I'll* – Clara slipped the page back into the folder and gazed out at the passing landscape, which they had once shared: a homeland-landscape.

Rows of elders lined the tracks, and behind them the odd walnut tree, and in the middle of a field, far from any habitation, she spotted a billboard advertising schnapps. Gradually, the sombre colour of the iron-rich rock gave out and the mountains took on a lighter hue above the apple orchards shrouded in their green and grey netting.

When Clara had taken the call, late at night, she'd been exhausted and so shocked by the news of Ines's death that she could scarcely collect her thoughts.

1

Ines's mother had asked Clara to travel to Rome to sort out her daughter's affairs. She couldn't think of anyone else, she said, and she herself was unable to go: 'After all, you were friends for years. It's what she'd have wanted.'

As the train approached Salorno, it seemed to Clara like a ship steering towards a green bay surrounded by bright, sheer cliffs. The apple trees grew more sparse and the houses poorer-looking and less solid; the balustrades on the balconies were no longer made of closely-spaced wooden slats, but airy wrought-iron railings, and more and more weather-beaten metal roller blinds began to appear in place of neatly painted *louvres*.

Once I'm dead – how grave those words which Ines had once so lightly jotted down now sounded.

When was it exactly that they'd last seen one another? Easter Sunday, or the Monday? The landlord of the inn in Stillbach had already turned out the lights over the bar, but they'd stayed sitting at the corner bench, far from the large table which, despite the smoking ban, still sported an ashtray with a little sign identifying it as the regulars' spot.

Outside, the unpainted crash barriers on the motorway were flashing past, rust-red like cattle trucks. The motorway maintenance workers' huts were that same rust colour. And the rails. And some tree trunks. And discarded drinks cans. Not to mention bridge girders, posts and gate latches.

Clara closed her eyes, stretched her arms and hooked her fingers into the luggage net above her head. She hung there, letting the net take her weight and enjoying this brief moment of calm in the still-empty carriage, which would start to fill up from Verona onwards, if not before.

She'd sat with Ines's aunt in the garden of the same inn in Stillbach. Some places on the chairs where the protective coating had been eaten away by rust blooms also had that same reddish colour. Ines's mother hadn't come along to the meeting. On the phone that time, Clara had noticed she was slurring her words. Perhaps she'd been drunk or taken too many sedatives. 'Dreadful business. It'll be the death of her,' the aunt had said.

On the left-hand side of the valley now, the high-rise buildings of Trento came into view, tower blocks deposited in a sea of green, looking forlorn and out of place. Here and there, washing had been hung out of windows to dry, some on lines rigged up on the concrete cladding of the balconies. The people there didn't mind airing their most intimate undergarments in public, unlike in Stillbach, where they were only ever hung out in backyards or attic spaces.

Hearing the guard approaching, she started hunting frantically for her ticket, only finally locating it when the man was standing right in front of her and watching as she rummaged through Ines's folder. The ticket had slipped down between the papers, little prose sketches that Ines had written by hand in the Eighties, when she didn't have a computer. Ines's aunt had given Clara a leather-bound organiser, the key to the Rome flat, the folder and Ines's mobile phone. 'I've no idea what these scraps of paper are', the aunt had said, 'but they obviously meant something to Ines. She asked me time and again whether I'd kept them safe.'

The roar of the air-conditioning came to an abrupt halt; the sudden silence seemed to slow the train down; Clara held her breath, but choked on her own saliva and started to cough.

Ines's aunt's hand had been shaking so badly that she had trouble lifting her cup of tea to her mouth. Looking at this frail old lady's hand, Clara was reminded of another one, made of marble, which served as a stoup in the vestry of the Dalmatian School in Venice.

Instead of changing in Verona and taking the train to Venezia San Lucia, this time I'm carrying on to Rome, thought Clara. How often she'd been invited there by Ines, but Clara had given all her spare time over to her work. As it happened, if Ines's death hadn't intervened, she would have been on her way to Venice right now, having already arranged with her husband that he should look after Gesine for the next fortnight while she finished her chapter on D'Annunzio. For months now, she'd been putting it off, preferring to concentrate on Rilke and Byron's dalliances in Venice rather than deal with this author, whose aristocratic airs and political opportunism Clara found just as unappealing as his habit of exploiting women and then summarily dumping them.

D'Annunzio had first approached Eleonora Duse in Rome, after her performance in *The Lady of the Camellias*, but the diva had shown no interest in this

Rapagnetta, to give him his proper family name. So he had tried his luck again in Venice. Basically, thought Clara, for all his posturing as a Renaissance prince or a Roman ruler, D'Annunzio had never really transcended the sense of his original name – 'little turnip'.

At Ala, the mountains closed in once more, as if huddling together at this point for one last time to signal their astonishment at the great plain unfolding before them. The houses in the little villages in this region were uniformly grey and beige, as though the sun were stronger here and had bleached out all the vibrant colours.

For Clara, Ala had always been the place where she could finally draw breath, where she felt her claustrophobia lifting and where her feelings of constriction were suddenly relieved, as cleanly as if someone had cut through them with a pair of scissors. The train shot into a tunnel that followed a gentle right-hand curve, emerging at the far end into the bright, wide expanse of the flatlands. The profusion of apple trees was replaced by peach trees, while the railway track here was lined with reeds, like in the suburbs of Rome.

But this time, the sensation of leaving the mountains behind wasn't liberating. For the first time, Clara felt adrift on the vast plain.

And suddenly, uncontrollably, she found herself in floods of tears thinking about Ines and recalling the smell of mothballs that had clung to her aunt's black dress.

Dozens of other women's bodies pressed in front of hers, and her hair was sometimes long, sometimes short, first straight, then wavy – not to mention all the different colours and tints that he gave her various hairdos. In this imaginary parade of wigs, Paul failed to settle on a clear mental picture of how she'd looked back then.

A few days before, at Ines's behest, he'd come to the Alberto Sordi shopping arcade. She said she'd got his phone number from a mutual acquaintance and had heard he was living in Rome again and conducting guided tours on the city's fascist and national-socialist past. Ines was already waiting at the café when Paul arrived at the arcade, twenty minutes late and beaded with sweat.

He couldn't put a face to her name at all and he wasn't able to call to mind any incidents or events from back then, although she'd already told him on the phone before they met up that they'd got to know one another at the Hotel Manente in 1978 and had even grown quite close. During their conversation, Paul had an image of that run-down hotel garden in his head and little by little, as if Ines's precise descriptions had somehow cut a path through the thicket of his forgetfulness, he dimly began to discern the outlines of a ramshackle little wooden shed, where they'd supposedly had two or three evening trysts.

Yet there was still a disconnect between the almost fifty-year-old face in front of him and the young Ines, though he knew from experience that some memories just needed time to mature. The night before, he'd even pulled out his box of old photos, but failed to find a picture of her.

Paul pushed away the empty coffee cup, left the Bar Oroglio behind the Piazza del Popolo, crossed the road and disappeared into the stinking corridors of the Metro. In actual fact, this Ines could just as well have been someone else, since everything that Paul associated with her also applied to any number of other women. His memory was so bad that he briefly entertained the idea that she'd fabricated this entire shared history of theirs, and yet the details that Ines related about the garden and Paul's student room in the hotel vouched for the fact that she was telling the truth. She'd remembered the name of the hotel cook and even the subjects he was working on for his exams then. Paul, on the other hand, found images of the present crowding in on him so insistently that after a while he simply gave up the struggle.

He'd been looking forward to this encounter, especially as he hadn't been in a relationship for over two years now, but her low, husky voice, which he'd found exciting when they spoke on the phone, was absent when they met face-to-face. Ines gave a brief account of how she eked out a living by giving private German tuition, doing occasional translation jobs and writing short articles, but she said that interest in German was on the wane and the translations and news-paper articles were less well paid than before. In her spare time, she was writing a multi-volume work.

Yes, she'd definitely said 'multi-volume', thought Paul as he got off at the penultimate tube station in order to take the bus in the direction of Forte Braschi. The name reminded him of the Palazzo Braschi in the city centre, not far from the Piazza Navona, where he'd gone to see a photographic exhibition a few months before. Pictures from the Eighties by Giuliana de Sio and Vittorio Gassman were on show – truly beautiful portraits that were at total odds with the associations that the name 'Braschi' otherwise held for him. And once again, Paul couldn't help but think of the *repubblichini* – the fascists – who had used the palace as an assembly hall. Even in the inner courtyard, before buying his entrance ticket, he couldn't dispel the thought that this place of art and culture, where he'd also seen an exhibition on Pasolini some years ago, had once been the scene of torture. Gangs of fascist thugs drove out of here to hunt down escaped Allied POWs, *carabinieri* who had remained loyal to the monarchy, anti-fascists and Jews. There was nothing in the building to commemorate these events.

Instead, the country now had a prime minister who'd called the fascist era a 'benign dictatorship' and who tolerated in his cabinet a tourism minister who had given the fascist salute at a recent *carabinieri* event. In Germany, thought Paul, this Signora Brambilla would have been dismissed from her post, whereas here you could count on the Prime Minister's backing even if you were a footballer who had a tattoo of the word DUX, proclaiming his allegiance to Mussolini, on his biceps and who had raised his right arm in the straight-armed salute, bold as brass, after a game.

On the bus, Paul tried looking at a city map, but gave up after failing to find the street he was looking for. He got off. The map he'd brought with him was sketchy, with lots of street names left out for lack of space. Paul couldn't make out where one street ended and the next began. He turned off Via Cardinal Garampi into a side street, figuring that there must be other streets in the area named after cardinals, just as there were entire quarters where the roads were named after Italian cities, provinces, or rivers. The woman in the tobacconist's hadn't ever heard of a Via Cardinal Sanfelice, but was kind enough to look it up on the Internet and informed him that he'd need to go back to the centre of Boccea; the street he was after wasn't far from the UPIM department store.

The return bus was heaving with pensioners weighed down with walking-sticks and bags. A Filipina girl was trying to help a woman sit down. 'Much too high, much too high,' the old lady was saying, shaking her head.

There were hardly any shops out here in the suburbs, so everyone had to travel into the centre of Boccea to do their shopping. For several kilometres, the number 49 bus route ran along the edge of a pine forest, which ascended a slight incline, so that Paul kept catching glimpses of the horizon through the tree trunks. Momentarily, he imagined that just behind the wood, the coast began. The light that day was so glaring, though, that it could just as easily have been a desert extending beyond the tree line. Stray dogs were roaming about here and there. Opposite the wood, multi-storey apartment blocks lined the far side of the road, nestling in lush vegetation.

Paul was still thinking about Ines, who had brought their meeting to an abrupt end, as though she found it distasteful spending any more time in the company of a man with whom she couldn't share her memories. He hadn't dared ask her whether they'd slept together in 1978. From the hints she dropped, he assumed they had.

The Via de Boccea was gridlocked. At the stop, two gypsy women were importuning passengers as they got off the bus; one of them offered to tell people's fortunes. 'No need: I'm sixty, in good health and I've got a job,' a man called out before stalking off.

After Paul had tramped round several blocks, vainly searching for the Via Cardinal Sanfelice behind UPIM, he tried the other side of the street. The people he asked for directions didn't even bother to stop but just walked on by, shaking their heads.

Again he found himself in a Via Cardinal something-or-other, but again it was the wrong one. Paul began to question what on Earth he was doing here anyway. What possible interest could he have in the life of this former *Sturmbannführer* and his followers? Paul had been surprised that Ines had asked about him – indeed, that there were still people around who didn't assume the ninety-six-year-old was already dead. She'd even known his alias, Otto Pape, and that he'd used a Red Cross passport to emigrate, via South Tyrol and Rome, to the Argentinian town of Bariloche, where he'd lived undetected until 1995.

It crossed Paul's mind that if only Ines had been a bit younger and less tomboyish, he'd have asked her out to dinner.

He walked round the block one more time and suddenly stopped in his tracks: here, one Via Cardinal merged into another, which explained why he hadn't found Via Cardinal Sanfelice straight away. And Sanfelice itself ran to a square that was named after yet another cardinal. How fitting, he thought, that the old man should have fetched up in this area of ecclesiastical street names; after all, Catholic priests had helped him and most of his fellow *Sturmbannführer* flee abroad.

An empty police car stood in the street outside the block of flats, a five-storey condominium. Paul found the policewoman in a bar across the road; she was leaning against the counter, deep in conversation with the bar owner and sipping an orange juice. Paul went in and sat down next to her.

An old man was sitting at a table reading the *Gazzetta dello Sport*. That wasn't him, he was easily a couple of decades older than this guy, as well as being thinner and having less hair. The last pictures Paul had seen of him showed a spry old ninety-year-old riding pillion on a scooter; his friend and attorney Paolo Giachini used to give him a lift into his inner-city practice until the protests against the relaxation of his house arrest grew so loud that the military tribunal was forced to rescind this privilege. The neofascist lawyer, who was well-known throughout the city and whose name sounded like *giaco* – a chain-mail vest – had put the old man up in his flat. The old Nazis who were clamouring for his release regarded him as some kind of glorious guardian angel.

Paul chose a seat with a clear view of the house. His plan was to wait until the policewoman stepped outside and then strike up a conversation with the bar owner. But what exactly was he going to ask him?

The windows on the third floor were all barred, with the blinds down.

Paul shuffled through the address book on his mobile, searching for Ines's number; after a moment's hesitation, he decided to text her to let her know that he was outside the block where the former SS officer Erich Priebke was being kept under house arrest. As he typed in the letters, different images of Ines came swarming into his head, so restless and fleeting that they meant everything and nothing to him at the same time. In the end, he deleted the message, amazed and more than a little ashamed at this sudden urge to communicate.

Clara wetted a tissue with saliva and tried to dab away the mascara runs from under her eyes before the people milling on the platform got on. She remembered that on her last visit to Venice, back in spring, corn poppies had been blooming between the tracks. When they were still girls, Ines had told her that the black spot in the centre of these flowers stood for love's sorrow. And when Clara had run into a wheat field one time to pick a posy of poppies, by the time she got home, they had all been just bare stalks; not a single flower had survived the journey.

Ever since Ines's death, incidents from their childhood and teenage years had begun crowding in on Clara. They'd gone to the same school, cribbed from one another and phoned each other up with the answers to maths problems. Together, they'd climbed over the fence of a German's holiday home and taken a dip in the pool when the owner had had to return home to Dachau for a few days. Now she would never be able to share those reminiscences with Ines.

The carriage filled except for one free space. Unnerved at the sudden proximity of so many people, she turned her head and stared straight out of the window, wishing she could transport her whole self beyond the crowded confines of the compartment.

Sometimes Ines would do a bunk when she came across acquaintances or friends on the street. She'd duck into house doorways and hide or dart into shops just to avoid having to make conversation. There were days when she couldn't stand being spoken to, or even have someone make a phone call within earshot.

'So why did you go and live in Rome, of all places?' Clara once asked her.

But it wasn't noise as such that bothered Ines. What she found intolerable was when anyone burst in on this *cloud language*, which she could only call up by withdrawing into herself; when they swamped what it was she was nurturing in her head with their prattle. At those times, she just wanted to be left alone and had no compunction about snubbing friends and acquaintances.

Clara recalled an argument with her husband, who'd often made disparaging remarks about Ines. 'Good job she doesn't have any children,' had been Claus's reaction one time – it was autumn last year – when Clara had been moaning about how unreliable her friend was; once again, Ines had failed to answer the phone. This had prompted Clara to try to explain to Claus the difference between authentic kids' language and common chitchat, and to defend Ines's habit of withdrawing into her shell: 'Remember how no-one was more devoted to Ines than Gesine when she was still very small? She could tell that Ines took her seriously. While both of us often underestimated her.'

With every kilometre that passed, Clara felt more and more empty. She couldn't find words to describe her state and kept staring out of the window for inspiration. *Part of my innermost being has been stripped away by Ines's death…* No, no, that's all wrong, Clara checked herself. *What a stupid cliché. I'm afraid that this long friendship might just disappear, dissolve into a series of anecdotes. What rubbish. It's already over and done with. And our Stillbach started to dry up long before Ines's death.*

Where was that passage? Clara leafed through Ines's papers. Somewhere, she remembered reading some remarks about their home village. Yes, there they were:

The stream was never still in Stillbach. Even where they'd channelled it into underground culverts, after several children had drowned in it, you could hear that incessant whooshing, that gurgling and bubbling sound that was audible pretty much throughout the small hamlet, faintly or clearly depending on how much rain had fallen. Even if there'd been a long dry spell, the water would still trickle down the valley in little rivulets.

In my mind, it's always summer there, thought Clara. *But my few recollections of the place will all seep away over time.*

She glanced at her fellow passengers' faces and pulled the organiser and Ines's mobile out of her bag. A local haulier who drove from Bolzano to Rome and back twice a week had brought a few of Ines's effects back to Stillbach. Over the last few years, he'd been employed several times as a kind of courier, carting packages and boxes to and fro, and had even gone out to eat with Ines in Rome on a couple of occasions.

This last time, the aunt explained, he'd refused to accept any payment. She – Clara – could give him a call anytime; he said he'd be happy, for instance, to transport any furniture that needed moving… 'He's a friend of the family, a good sort.'

Ines's aunt had been so grateful to Clara for making the detour from Vienna to Stillbach before going on to Rome that she'd held her hand and stroked her forearm for several minutes.

'But I know so little about Ines.'

'You must know more than me, in any event,' replied the aunt. She'd spent years trying to persuade Ines to come back to Stillbach. She'd been worried about *the girl* for some time. 'So thin – all skin and bones – and it's all my fault. It was me who put the idea of travel into her head. Ines's mother never forgave me for that.'

But Ines hadn't travelled, thought Clara, she'd been even more sedentary than her. Maybe the aunt thought that everyone who never returned to Stillbach or its environs led a nomadic life. The postcard of the Trevi Fountain that the aunt then produced, a dog-eared black-and-white photo glued onto a piece of card that she appeared to have carried around with her wherever she went, was from 1978. Even if there had been no postmark, Clara would have had no trouble dating it precisely: the outwardly unfussy handwriting, which still displayed some expressive flourishes, was unmistakeable.

In the final two years of grammar school, her and Ines's handwriting had affected a slight leftward-leaning slope. They'd both agreed that their political views should be reflected in the way they wrote. It was only when they read in a book on graphology that a left-sloping hand was a negative trait betraying an excessive degree of egocentricity that they opted for a rather more slovenly, loosely joined-up handwriting with upright letters that would, as they saw it, give a better impression of their personalities. Clara recalled that they'd both spent whole afternoons practising their new style.

All the stations – even the ones they didn't stop at – were clad in slabs of travertine. The benches on the platforms, the drinking fountains and the pillars supporting the platform canopies were all made of that familiar stone, which

Ines had loved so much. Even in the railway stations, she'd once said, you're reminded of the great showpieces of Italian architecture, the churches and basilicas and the amphitheatres and tufa fountains that you've come here to admire.

Clara stole another glance at her fellow passengers; she'd had nothing to eat since that morning and could feel her stomach rumbling, but nobody seemed to notice.

She replaced the sheets she'd taken from the folder and toyed with the idea of going to the buffet car, but dismissed it and opened the organiser instead. The aunt had cancelled a few personal appointments. And a colleague of Ines had already dealt with those relating to her work for the translation bureau. It was down to Clara, when she arrived, to inform Ines's private pupils about her death and to try to contact those friends whom the aunt hadn't yet managed to get in touch with. But what if she couldn't find the password for Ines's computer?

As Clara flicked through the organiser, which she was astonished to find contained any number of German, Austrian and Swiss service and emergency numbers but not a single one from Italy, her friend's handwriting evoked a painful intimacy. Clara tried to keep a grip on her emotions by staring into the face of the woman opposite, who was immersed in solving a Sudoku puzzle, but it didn't help.

Her friend seemed to have noted various details on places, names and times while on the move or in a hurry, with accuracy going by the board in her evident haste to jot things down; some information was almost impossible to decipher. Ultimately Clara could no longer tell whether it was her friend's bad handwriting that was making it hard to read what she had written, or the tears in her eyes. All of a sudden, she stood up, apologised to the man sitting next to her for brushing his knee, and squeezed past the other passengers' legs to get to the corridor. Pressing her forehead against the glass, she looked out at the landscape: an endless succession of cornfields, occasionally fringed with lines of poplars, with such vast skies spread out over the chequer board of fields that she felt dizzy. She forced herself to breathe very deeply and slowly.

Maybe she should get a bite to eat after all. She turned on her heel and made for the buffet car.

2009

*

After Marianne had gone off to live with Beppe, Paul stayed in Rome. He rented out his flat in Vienna and found himself a studio flat as a stop-gap. But rents had risen so much in the interim that he eventually gave up looking for a more spacious apartment. Whilst there was no new woman in his life, Paul saw no reason to move out of his one-roomed flat; it was on the Viale Trastevere, a few minutes' walk from Nanni Moretti's Cinema Nuovo Sacher. True, the flat was a bit dark, as both windows looked out onto the rear courtyard rather than the wide street, but Paul liked its proximity to the Porta Portese, where he used to mingle with the flea market stallholders early each Sunday morning, while Priebke, it was rumoured, took his regular constitutional in the park.

The policewoman, whom Paul had, after some hesitation, spoken to on the Via Cardinal Sanfelice, was friendly and told him that Signor Priebke was allowed out twice a week, that he was in good health and that he still had all his mental faculties. If Paul wanted to interview him, he'd have to get permission from the military tribunal. Priebke had no objections to people talking to him. Looking at the tall, portly policewoman, Paul wondered whether, with all those excess kilos, she'd be capable of chasing down suspects. Also, the surveillance of the detainee struck him as extremely lax; when the policewoman had been chatting to the bar owner, there'd been no-one keeping an eye on the front door.

Paul asked her whether she was there to guard Priebke. Sitting in her patrol car with the door open, she'd replied that there weren't enough police officers in the whole of Italy to keep a constant eye on all the people who were under house arrest. 'But a lot of Jews live in this neighbourhood,' she added, 'so that's why we've been posted here.'

In December 1997, when they first brought the prisoner to Boccea, the house had been guarded by ten *carabinieri*, two small police armoured cars, several squad cars and soldiers toting machine guns. The local residents had hung banners above the bar opposite and from their balconies, with slogans like *Buon Natale, assassino* – 'Merry Christmas, murderer' – and *Priebke vattene da casa nostra* – 'Priebke, get out of our house'. Living in the same building where

13

this Giachini put up the detainee were two cousins who had been transported by the Nazis and an old man who had survived Buchenwald. Yet the protests from people living in the neighbourhood, the Jewish community and the *Rifondazione comunista* all fell on deaf ears. Priebke had been released from custody on health grounds and transferred to the light, roomy 120-square-metre apartment, which Giachini had had fitted some while ago with window bars to keep out burglars. Behind the drawn blinds, the former SS officer kept himself trim on an exercise bike.

Paul was sitting at his desk; he leant back and linked his hands behind his head. In front of him were spread out various newspaper articles from the archive of the *Corriere della Sera*.

He'd spent an entire morning going to see where the old man lived and scouting out the house and its surroundings; what had he hoped to achieve? To catch a glimpse of him, perhaps? But he knew already what he looked like. If he hadn't known what he'd done, he'd even have said he seemed quite a nice old boy.

People like that, Marianne had once said, should be punished using their own methods. She'd only been able to say that because she had no idea what that particular gentleman's 'methods' consisted of. Paul knew all about the SS man's special interrogation techniques, and that during the first days of the German occupation he'd gained some useful hands-on experience in the basement of the embassy's Villa Wolkonsky, which he then put to good use at Gestapo headquarters.

'Mattei looks dreadful. He's awfully still,' announced Priebke's superior *Obersturmbannführer* Herbert Kappler after summoning him to his office. Fearing that he wouldn't be able to withstand the physical and chemical tortures he was being subjected to and might betray his comrades, the communist leader Gianfranco Mattei had hanged himself in his cell.

'*Spegni Via Tasso*. Put the Via Tasso out!' Other survivors, who'd been kept in permanent darkness in the notorious Gestapo prison, couldn't bear to see light ever again.

Paul got up and opened the fridge. It was empty apart from a piece of

Parmesan, three onions and a few small salad tomatoes that were past their best. Paul had even forgotten to chill the white wine. He popped a couple of ice cubes out of the plastic tray into a glass and opened a bottle of Pinot Grigio. As he approached the window, a neighbour opposite waved to him; her other hand held a watering can, which she was using to water her jungle geraniums. *Burning Love*, thought Paul, from the madder family. He'd once gone out with a botanist for a few weeks. They hadn't really hit it off. But Paul could still remember that there was a climbing plant called a Clitoria that truly lived up to its name.

After finishing his glass of wine, he flopped down onto the bed, unzipped his flies, pulled out his cock and rubbed it briefly. The usual fantasies didn't seem to do the trick, so he sat back at his laptop and watched a few YouPorn clips. When he was done, he tossed the used tissue into the wastepaper bin.

He really didn't feel like working. Ines hadn't got in touch despite promising to call him again. She said she had a few more questions for him about 1978.

What did she want to know? That, in the face of resistance from the Christian Democrats, a handful of reforming laws had been passed? That useless arrangements from the fascist period, whose sole purpose was to create posts for party functionaries, had been swept away and that the *equo canone*, a law against extortionate rent rises, had finally made it onto the statute book? That the *movimiento del '77*, the militant urban anarchist movement responsible for countless acts of sabotage and theft against shops and firms, had had its heyday then? That revolutionaries from this *guerriglia diffusa* had kneecapped critical journalists and politicians and members of the state security forces, leaving them traumatised cripples?

Why was Ines so interested in that period which Italians called the 'leaden years', the *anni di piombo*? Because the authorities then had thought they were restoring the human dignity of the insane by releasing them from psychiatric wards into the arms of their clueless and overstressed families? All very right-on and well-intentioned, thought Paul, but he'd known a girl student then whose brother suddenly turned up back at home and had proceeded to terrorise his whole family with his persecution mania. On one occasion, this young woman had spent four hours locked in the lavatory with her brother, because he'd grabbed the key from the lock and flushed it down the toilet. Basically, the asylum had been transferred to the parental home. As so often happened in Italy, absolutely no support structures had been put in place to back up the legislation.

Paul poured himself some more wine and paced up and down the room. Water was running from the base of the neighbour's flowerpots, pattering down heavily onto the corrugated iron roof that covered part of the courtyard. Paul listened to the fast, regular dripping, the intervals between the drops growing steadily longer until the noise finally ceased altogether. The tin roof belonged to a small garage specialising in scooter repair, mainly of vintage Vespas and Lambrettas. Paul wondered how the young mechanic who ran it could possibly make a living, as this *officina* surely couldn't be much more than a hobby. It wasn't unusual for the workshop to be closed for days on end; then, suddenly, Paul would hear music drifting up from it again and catch the whiff of cannabis smoke.

In the autumn of 1978 Paul had got himself a used Lambretta and sold it on a year later, because he was going back to Vienna. Today, it would be worth quite a bit. How come he could vividly recall the white Lambretta with its red cockpit and the two separate beige-coloured seats set one behind the other, but couldn't form a clear picture of Ines back then?

At the café in the arcade, she'd wanted to find out whether anyone had known Priebke's whereabouts in 1978. What was her interest in the old man?

Though Paul knew a good deal about Priebke, he could only guess. On New Year's Eve 1946, he and another officer and three NCOs had escaped from the British internment camp at Rimini-Bellaria and fled to South Tyrol, where, from January 1947 to October 1948, he and his family had lived on the Bahnhofstraße in Sterzing. There, it was thought he'd received help from his fellow SS officer and former colleague from the Gestapo detachment in Bolzano, Rudolf Stötter, who had arranged safe houses in his hometown or hideouts in the surrounding mountains for other former Nazis on the run. Disguised as a stateless ethnic German from Latvia, after the war Priebke applied for a passport under the assumed name of Otto Pape.

Ines had found it incredible that the Franciscan monastery in Bolzano, whose school had turned out the region's élite for over two centuries, had been an important way-station on the Nazi war criminals' rat run. After a brief interim stop in Sterzing, Adolf Eichmann had also spent some time at the Bolzano monastery. Unlike the SS concentration camp doctor Josef Mengele, whose family owned a thriving agricultural machinery business, Eichmann couldn't afford to stay in expensive hotels in South Tyrol. Nor could Priebke, whom the Bolzano brothers put up in the old infirmary while he was making his escape plans. In the summer of 1948, in the nick of time, Herr Pape received a crucial letter of recommendation from the Pontifical Commission for Assistance in Rome and applied for a passport so he could emigrate to Argentina.

Another passenger on the *San Giorgio*, the ship that carried Pape and his family from Genoa to Buenos Aires, was the South Tyrolean Cornelio Dellai, who ended up running the Hotel Catedral in Bariloche, where Pape found work as a head waiter. A year after his arrival in South America, the Latvian Pape had once more become the German Priebke, who was able to live undisturbed in Bariloche until he was discovered by a journalist from the American ABC network in 1995. In 1954, Priebke had secured a permanent post in the town's Hotel Sauter; he became renowned for his punctilious personnel inspections, regularly checking the underlings' fingernails, shoes and trouser creases; in the hotel kitchen, he was alleged to have described in detail the massacre at the Ardeatine Caves. In the early 1960s, he bought a sausage shop in Bariloche. He sat on the board of the German School there, which made sure – as a sacked teacher later revealed – that Hitler's *Mein Kampf* wasn't removed from the library shelves, while the works of Heinrich Böll were banned.

The official word was that nobody in Germany or Italy knew anything about where Priebke had fetched up, though the relevant authorities must have kept tabs on him, Paul told Ines. During his time in Argentina, Priebke had travelled to New York, Paris and South Tyrol and had even spent a few days in Rome in 1978 and 1980, meeting an old comrade who had been active in the secret service.

In August 1980 a female grammar school teacher who had lived on Via Rasella as a child recognised him and spoke to him. She reported that Priebke, who was accompanied by a blonde woman and sporting a summer hat in the blazing midday sun, had sat down on the steps of a house in the street.

'So we may even have crossed paths with him in the city back then,' Ines said.

That could still happen nowadays, he had replied. All she would need to do would be to take a stroll in the garden of the Villa Doria Pamphili on a Wednesday or Sunday at 9 am sharp. Leaving the old man out of the reckoning, though, he'd still recommend a walk around this park, set high above the city and with a profusion of shady pine trees.

Ines hadn't responded to this. Instead, the deep furrows on her brow had given her such a glowering expression that Paul imagined for a fleeting moment how she might look after a facelift. Recently, late at night on one of the channels owned by the Prime Minister, he had seen a report on facelifts and correcting droopy eyebrows. The surgeon had removed a strip of skin from his patient's buttocks and grafted the trimmed dermal implant into her lips to plump them up. He wondered whether the premier's face also contained skin grafts from his bum.

Pretty soon, Paul thought, 'arse face' won't rank as an insult any more. He went to pour himself some more wine, but the bottle was empty.

There was a blast of cold air on the back of Clara's neck. After eating one sandwich, she ordered a second, and although she hadn't enjoyed the overpriced red wine, she asked the barman for another small bottle. Maybe because of the fierce air conditioning, the buffet car was sparsely populated.

Clara rang Claus to check if everything was OK at home.

Claus told her that Gesine was spending the coming weekend at a girlfriend's and that he didn't have much planned. Then he lapsed into silence.

'Don't you want to know how I am, then?'

'I'm waiting for you to tell me,' he replied.

'You're really not interested, are you?'

'Spare me the histrionics, Clara.'

'How come you never call me?'

'I was going to this evening.'

'You always say that.'

Clara's gloom lifted for a while after the call. She composed a reproachful text message, but didn't send it. Claus had been working at the hospital until half an hour before she rang, he must be tired. Anyway, he would never change now.

Desires seek us out, not vice versa, thought Clara. And they don't diminish with age.

Had she got that from Ines, or from a book?

It suddenly struck her that she'd left D'Annunzio's novel at home. She'd be able to get hold of the Italian original in Rome if need be, but that was no good, as she needed the quotations in German. Perhaps Ines would have a copy of *Das Feuer* on her bookshelves? Not very likely. Unlike Clara, who had started reading Italian authors in German translation while she was still in Stillbach, it had never even crossed Ines's mind. She wouldn't even have deigned to read the novels of Italo Svevo, whose Italian was notoriously difficult, in German.

At Florence, the engine was switched to the other end of the train and they left travelling in the opposite direction, so Clara got up and switched seats. She now found herself studying the delicate facial features of a man who from behind had looked like he did a daily workout with dumbbells and exercise bands to strengthen his shoulder muscles.

She called to mind that other head, which Brecht had once described as 'looking like it was made out of yellow wax' – the 'turnip head' of the greyhound-breeder Signor Rapagnetta/D'Annunzio. No, there was nothing for it but to include the four-year relationship between D'Annunzio and Eleanora Duse in her Venice book, even though the relationship had been so one-sided. Nor did Clara warm to the almost completely undisguised portrayal of the artist couple in the novel. Why did Stelio have to be a much-vaunted poet/composer, while his lover Foscarina was, naturally, a devoted and submissive old actress, whose very name betrayed her melancholic disposition?

All the same, there was no denying that when the two had met up again in Venice, Duse was no longer in the first flush of youth. Rather than stay in one of the city's famous hotels, she'd opted instead to take up residence in a small *palazzo*, far from the prying eyes of inquisitive guests and passers-by. Even there, to avoid being bothered, she came and went by the rear entrance and ate in her room – the very antithesis of her poet lover, who went out of his way to court publicity, postured as some kind of genius and loudly proclaimed the virtues of God, Art and the Fatherland. As far as he was concerned, she was just another woman to add to his collection.

Clara vaguely recalled a letter from Duse that she'd skim-read on the Web shortly before leaving Vienna; in it, the actress had spoken about two different kinds of love – the kind that turns out happily and the kind that saps a person's will and reason. Duse saw the latter as the truest yet at the same time the most destructive form. She must have been completely in thrall to D'Annunzio, to whom she represented nothing more than a couple of rungs up the career ladder. Only this could explain why she'd allowed him to move into the Palazzo Barbaro Wolkoff and sponge off her for months. It was she who had chased around looking for opportunities to stage his mediocre, embarrassingly pathos-laden dramas, and had even funded the stage sets with her own money. She was a delusional fool, for whom he felt nothing but contempt, as indeed he did for all women.

Ines had never lived beyond her means. When money was tight, she'd made do with *pasta in bianco* or *risi e bisi*. She wore the same clothes for years, until they became threadbare and shone in the sun.

One time, Clara had offered to lend her friend some money, but Ines was worried about not being able to pay back the 2,000 Euros and didn't take her up on it. What Ines found even worse than Clara offering her money was the pity implicit in the 'doctor's wife's magnanimous gesture,' as she put it. All she said to Clara was: 'You can't go around doling out Claus's cash to me'.

One tunnel after another and in between that, a painterly landscape of rolling hills, studded with lines of cypresses and pines. The white dots in the distance were flocks of sheep on the move.

Gazing at this picture-postcard landscape made Clara feel sentimental. She hated it when kitsch tugged at her heartstrings; that was something she and Ines had always had in common.

Clara was pleased that she'd left D'Annunzio's novel behind. It wasn't just that she found its one-sided depiction of Foscarina/Duse as a deluded and self-sacrificing *slave of passion* deeply off-putting. She also really didn't have the stomach for its evocation of the melancholic atmosphere of decay pervading Venice in the late autumn – D'Annunzio would instantly turn a simple wind-chime into a *silk-bedecked bundle of nerve fibres*. Even so, she was forced to admit that the *poeta* had a talent for describing colours, sounds and tactile forms. But at the same time, he was incapable of writing about anything that he hadn't experienced first-hand; he seemed to have a compulsive urge to reveal the most intimate details of his life. The repercussions didn't bother him.

She opened Ines's organiser once more. Over the first few months of the year, the name Francesco cropped up time and again; sometimes there was just the letter 'F' – shorthand for Francesco, Clara presumed. She dimly remembered a telephone conversation with Ines, in which her friend had talked about the son of that Stillbach woman who had gone to Rome some time before the war to look for work and had stayed there. Emma was her name. Did she have a son called Francesco? Clara wasn't sure. In any event, for months on end the two of them had met every Wednesday, until suddenly the relevant slots in the calendar were left blank. Had Ines withdrawn into her shell again, sealed up the windows, plugged her ears and gone to bed at night with one pillow under her head and another on top? *Small talk makes me gag, like I'm getting too little air or breathing a bad atmosphere*, she'd written to Clara a year before, *so please don't be angry with me if I don't come to your birthday party*. Had Ines been on dates with this Francesco? Had she grown tired of his company? Or that of his friends? That herd instinct among Italian men? 'If you get one boyfriend here,' she'd once joked, 'before you know it, you find you've got ten.'

Her friend seemed to have kept her private life secret from her family, because Ines's aunt didn't have a clue about any of her relationships. Clara had hoped to glean some useful information on this score in Stillbach. Evidently, the aunt had been expecting exactly the same thing from Clara.

Then again, maybe she hadn't had a private life.

Clara flicked back and forth through the planner, finding repeated doodles of palmettes and rosettes, swirly scroll designs and spirals; these patterns were so familiar to her and suddenly she thought she caught a whiff of that unique mélange of smells: BO, chalk dust and break-time sandwiches. Out of sheer boredom,

at school Ines had covered whole blank pages of exercise books with her scrib-
blings, putting into the various curlicues and floral patterns the initials of the boys
she fancied at the time. Arno, Peter, Thomas – within a couple of years, the names
of the lads she was besotted with, with bum-fluff on their upper lips, had changed
to Fritz and Rainer. Clara was amazed she could still remember all this stuff.

Her heart thumping, she turned to the page containing the date of Ines's
death. Who was the last person she'd met? There were no entries for the day
itself. But four days earlier, she'd noted an appointment with one Paul Vogel, in
the Galleria Sordi; she'd even jotted down his mobile number. Clara made a
mental note to call him.

For a while, the railway line ran alongside a narrow country road, where
workmen were mending the surface, then it was back to meadows and fields.
Drifting between wakefulness and fitful sleep, Clara happened to glance out of
the window and instantly caught sight of a man, naked from the waist down,
leaping out from behind a bush. He seemed to have judged his distance from
the railway track perfectly: too close to the line, and the passengers wouldn't
have seen his erect penis at all; too far away, and they'd have missed all the gory
detail. Clara burst out laughing, but the irritated looks of her fellow buffet-car
passengers, directed at her rather than out of the window, told her she was the
only one who'd seen him.

'A naked man,' she explained, jerking her thumb towards the window.

The man with the broad neck swivelled round to face the direction they
were travelling in – far too late, though; no sign of anyone out there now –
raised his eyebrows and went back to his newspaper.

In the total silence that descended on the carriage, Clara herself began to
doubt what she'd seen. Had she nodded off and woken suddenly from a dream?
She couldn't have given an accurate description of the man; all that stuck in her
mind were his red T-shirt and his cock, which had been a fair old size. Maybe it
was a fake one? She really couldn't say whether he'd been old or young, dark-
haired or fair. Everything was just happenstance.

Clara had happened to look out the window, whereas the others hadn't.

Ines happened to be dead, whereas she was still alive.

That afternoon, Paul was busy taking a group of Austrian archaeology students round the former Gestapo HQ, which now housed the Museo storico della Liberazione. The young people, who'd really wanted to see Nero's Domus Aurea, were disappointed to find it closed. The site had been damaged by repeated water seepages after heavy rain. The last time Paul had been to the 'Golden House' was with Marianne; that was five years ago now. She'd told him all about the sliding ceilings made of ivory, through which flowers were strewn and fragrant oils sprinkled. One of the ceilings – the largest, above the octagonal dining room – was even said to have revolved like the Earth to reveal day and night scenes.

Paul tried to dispel his recollections of Marianne, but even the effort of doing so put him out of sorts.

The museum in the Via Tasso was empty. In less than thirty minutes, he reeled off his standard patter, briefly sketching in some of the historical context and answering questions at the end. Most of the high-ranking Nazis, he explained, were billeted at that time either in the Villa Napoleon, the Vatican delegation's main residence, or in the German Embassy's Villa Wolkonsky. No sooner had they moved in than they wrung the necks of the peacocks that lived in the garden and roasted the birds over a camp fire. 'Poor birds,' Paul heard the same girl say who had asked where 'the bigwigs' lived.

He wondered for a moment whether to tell them about the Italian soldiers who had wandered the streets after their country's surrender starving and begging for somewhere to stay, but decided against it and left the students to their own devices. Let them spend their whole lives grubbing around for fragments of bone and potsherds, documenting, conserving and archiving every last little thing they found, he thought. He left the museum, which looked for all the world like an ordinary house, and lit up a cigarette on the pavement outside. When he'd finished, he wandered back in and followed the young woman who'd asked where the leading Nazis lived and was now standing in one of the well-preserved detention cells. Reading an inscription on the wall, she was muttering under her breath: '*É facile saper vivere / grande saper morire*'.

Moving to a display case, she asked Paul what the words *corraggio amore baci* meant, and when he told her that a family member of one of the inmates had stitched 'Chin up, love. Kisses' into a pair of socks for him, her expression changed. She stayed by Paul's side and got him to translate all the graffiti on the walls and asked what had happened to Rome's Jews and about the people murdered in the Ardeatine Caves; Paul had already forgiven her for her crass remark about the peacocks when she suddenly asked him whether he had anything on that evening. She said she'd really like to go out to dinner with him, just the two of them, 'without the annoying group'. Before he had a chance to reply, she stuck a card with her contact details into his jacket pocket and left the room. He reckoned she must be in her mid-twenties – she had on a kind of beach dress over her thin linen trousers, which hid her bottom, and was also wearing some elegant sandals and carrying a matching handbag.

One of the men, evidently the person who had organised the archaeologists' trip, then buttonholed Paul, quizzing him about the Italian premier and the concept of 'coming to terms with the past' – for which there was no word in Italian. After all, it wasn't like the Germans had introduced evil to the city, the man continued. It seemed to him that the Italians were trying to hide their own fascist crimes behind those of the Germans and were retrospectively trying to present themselves as victims of the German invasion. The man clearly wasn't stupid, but his declamatory tone – he kept glancing round the room like he was looking for an audience – got Paul's back up, while his observations about the Prime Minister really didn't amount to much more than the usual boring diatribes about his totally apolitical outlook. Even so, the guy had some hard facts and figures at his fingertips – that the acceptance of neofascist ministers into the Italian cabinet after the 1994 general election made it the first European country to break a taboo in place since the war, and that in marked contrast to Austria, which became a political pariah six years later following the formation of the 'Black–Blue' coalition between the Christian Democrats and the Freedom Party, it didn't have to fear any EU sanctions, and so on, and so forth… Paul half switched off – he knew these arguments off by heart, he'd had countless discussions in Vienna with Marianne and his other friends about Jörg Haider's party being in government, had gone on demonstrations against racism and xenophobia, and even contributed some articles on the subject. So he just kept nodding at the right junctures, all the while keeping an eye on his young archaeologist, who was standing outside in the corridor reading her Baedeker.

In profile, she looked a bit like the botanist he'd dated; he'd been thinking about her a lot lately – especially the walks they'd taken in the pinetum. With her, he'd visited places that hadn't reminded him of anything, neither historical events nor painful private recollections, while her enthusiasm for butterflies and wild orchids had been infectious and had done him good. But in bed, she'd acted like she was at a photo shoot; she kept going on about how unattractive she was.

The young woman glanced up from her guidebook and gave him a smile. Paul guessed there must be more than twenty years' age difference between them. When he looked down at his liver-spotted arms, it struck him that he was himself some kind of archaeological find. It would be stupid of him to take her out to dinner.

The man was still talking. He spoke a few snatches of Italian, had grown up near the border in Carinthia, and was going on about his childhood, explaining how he'd always supported the Italian football team. When he started rhapsodising about what a great player the goalkeeper Gianluigi Buffon was, Paul couldn't restrain himself any longer. Buffon, Cannavaro, De Rossi – all those star players had strong links with the far right. He recounted how Buffon had not only sported a T-shirt bearing the fascist slogan *Boia chi molla* – 'Death to traitors' – he'd even appeared in a number 88 jersey. He'd tried to laugh it off by claiming he'd chosen the number because it reminded him of four balls and that you needed balls to play football: 'But,' Paul went on, 'I suppose you know that 88 is Neo-Nazi code?

'HH – Heil Hitler,' answered the man quietly.

'After the 2006 World Cup win, Buffon did a lap of honour holding an Italian flag with the fascist Celtic cross emblazoned on it; while at Real Madrid's Champions League victory in 2007 he waved a Mussolini-era flag, complete with the *fasces* symbol, in front of the cameras.'

Paul refrained from mentioning that De Rossi had links to the far-right *Forza Nuova* party – by now, the man had already lapsed into silence, plus Paul's iPhone had started to vibrate in his breast pocket.

'Hello – No. – Yes, that's me. – A few days ago. She was supposed to call me again. – Oh no, surely not… I'm so dreadfully sorry.' Paul opened the door to the stairwell and stepped outside. 'No, I didn't know her well. We'd only met once recently. – That's terrible. – Of course, anytime. – Yes. – Yes. – So soon? – Yes. – Sure. – All the best to you, too. – 'Bye.'

He leant against the wall, looking at the display on his mobile. Top of the list of recent calls was an Austrian mobile phone number. He stored it under the name *Clara Burger*, took a deep breath, went back into the museum and asked the group to assemble at the bus in ten minutes. Then he disappeared outside again, quickly, before anyone had a chance to latch onto him. Two streets away, he could see workmen laying some new tarmac across an entranceway; the black asphalt continued steaming as the roller flattened the surface.

Ines was dead. Frau Burger, who had called him, was on her way to Rome, as Ines's mother had asked her to settle her daughter's affairs. Ines's body would be transported from Rome back to South Tyrol today, and the funeral had been arranged for next week.

As always happened when someone in Paul's circle of friends and acquaintances died, his immediate surroundings suddenly seemed unbearably loud and hectic to him. When he was younger, he'd imagined that there was some sort of machine that accelerated time, a god, who after every death tried to claw back the time on this Earth that the deceased was now missing by manipulating the mourners' perception.

Paul sat down next to the coach driver, relieved that he didn't try to strike up a conversation.

It took them half an hour to drive from the Via Tasso to the Via Ardeatina, a journey of barely five kilometres that should have taken ten minutes in normal traffic.

Paul wouldn't truly miss Ines – their meeting had been too brief for that – but even so he felt something akin to a pang of grief. He'd meant more to her than she had to him, so much had been clear that day they'd met in the Galleria Sordi, but although he hadn't felt drawn to her, he'd still been flattered by her interest in him.

His mouth felt dry. There was no bar at the Ardeatine Caves. But just another hour to go and the working day would be over. Mentally, he started to run through his stock presentation: *The monument is comprised of a plastered stone slab raised a metre off the ground on eight circular supports, under which lie, in neat rows, the tombs of the victims, along with one more sarcophagus dedicated to all the other patriots killed during the liberation struggle…*

'Excuse me, can I ask you something?' The young archaeologist, who'd sat down right behind him, had stood up and was now leaning over Paul's seat, her breasts at eye level. A sequence from the last YouPorn clip he'd watched flitted into his mind.

Yes, he replied, there were toilets here, and yes, this visit was the end of the tour. The girl sat down again and the film clips evaporated. A moment later, the bus drew up outside the entrance to the memorial, an ugly gate made from a latticework of bronze thorns, flanked on the left by a monumental group of sculpted figures so large they could be seen from some way off. Paul had never quite understood why a sculptor whose work was still firmly rooted in the fascist idiom had been commissioned to make a piece for this location.

The archaeologists assembled on the Piazzale Martiri di Marzabotto, leading to the caves. The name of the square recalled another massacre perpetrated by the Germans in the autumn of 1944 at a small village in the Apennines near Bologna. Paul delivered his lecture and then sat down on the low wall around the square. Some members of the party wandered off into the caves, while the others went to look at the simple monument, which in contrast to the brash sculpture of the prisoners was the very epitome of dignified silence in stone. Only the young woman hung back, indecisively, on the gravel-covered square, waiting until the others had disappeared. Then, smiling, she started to make for the sandstone caves before veering off at the last moment to the entrance to the toilets. Paul popped a piece of chewing-gum into his mouth, stood up and followed her.

He pulled the door shut behind him. 'Let's cut to the chase. Do you want to come to bed with me?'

'It – it's all a bit sudden for me. I didn't mean it like that.' She turned round to the washbasin and started to rinse her hands. 'How did you mean it, then?' he asked.

For an instant, she glanced up and caught his gaze in the mirror before looking down again, shrugging her shoulders and turning off the tap.

'OK, I see,' said Paul, 'I must have got the wrong end of the stick.'

Outside, he took up his perch on the wall again, studied the chrysanthemum-like pink and yellow blooms in the earthenware pots behind him and listened to a donkey braying somewhere in the distance.

She could have taken a taxi directly from Termini station to the flat and saved herself the cost of a hotel, but Clara simply couldn't face it. The idea of sleeping in a dead person's bed. And of taking the mug from the holder above the washbasin, which Ines had used just a few days before.

But even in the hotel room, she was haunted by the thought of all those who'd been there before her, leaving odours behind them that no cleaning agent could ever erase: lovers, bickering couples, insomniacs and sleepy-heads. But at least Clara hadn't known these people.

After she'd swiped the plastic card through the lock three times, the door opened. The room was quite small and the floor creaked as she walked across it. She started to push her suitcase along with her foot but then picked it up, worried that the dirty castors might leave a mark. Particles of grit could get inside the little plastic wheels and work their way loose, scratching the carefully polished parquet flooring and lino.

She made straight for the window. She had to drive the others out of here, all of their sleep smells, the aromas of what they'd eaten, the cold stench of smoke that had lodged in the curtains, the faint whiffs of sickly-sweet shampoos or aftershaves. She wanted them gone from her head: the tourists with their rash expectations, the newlyweds, the pilgrims and all the others whose business here she hadn't the faintest idea about. Clara needed sole possession of the room. She required fresh air and no memories. She didn't want to think about anyone.

Leaving the suitcase in the middle of the room, she flaked out on the bed, her arms and legs splayed wide, and lay there for a while, listening to her own pulse and breathing. She tried to focus on herself, but couldn't stop her thoughts from sweeping ever onward; labyrinthine streams that all flowed into the same river, the River Ines.

No-one lives on in our memories, thought Clara. The dead are swamped by the storm-surge of our thoughts. All that remains of Ines is a little scrap washed up to the surface, one specific sentence, one particular gesture – the rest has nothing to do with her or with her life.

Before Clara arrived in Rome, she'd phoned this Paul; she had no idea who he was. It was clear she'd caught him at work, as he'd been quite curt in his responses; on the other hand, though, he had offered to help.

If only someone would relieve her of some of these phone calls. The elderly lady she'd just been speaking to had been on the verge of a nervous breakdown. It seemed that Ines hadn't simply been her private tutor, but also some kind of all-round therapist. Another woman was struck dumb on hearing the news, so that Clara had to ask several times whether she was still on the line. Another student didn't utter a single word of sympathy, merely announcing that he'd let his parents know.

The air conditioning wasn't working and it was close and stuffy in the hotel room. Clara got up, shed her clothes and took a shower. She yearned for the hard mountain spring water she was used to in Vienna; what came out of the taps here was soft and stank of chlorine. Even so, she lingered long under the shower – almost too long, as the plughole was blocked. Looking down at her feet, she suddenly noticed water lapping at the brim of the shower tray.

She wrapped herself in the hand towel, and being at a loss for what to do next, lay back down on the bed and closed her eyes. Whenever I'm somewhere else, she thought, Claus becomes an irrelevance, perhaps our relationship only really operates on the level of the daily humdrum. She didn't miss infatuation or grand passion but just the sense of curiosity, of someone listening attentively to her and taking an interest in her. She'd never had any time for all that 'I'm unfaithful because I love you' stuff. With D'Annunzio, it had been sheer vanity, self-affirmation, an artistic compulsion.

Gesine was just about to sit her school-leaving exams and not for the first time, Clara asked herself whether she should go back to her 'ordered life' or make a fresh start. 'A fresh start' – how seductive that sounded to her in her played-out existence, which had left its marks on her skin and hair. It occurred to her that she could take over Ines's flat.

You'll never leave Claus, she could hear her dead friend saying. Cowardice on her part? Or just a lack of options?

Clara had hoped that the hotel might be neutral territory, but such a loss permitted no neutrality, and grief seemed to permeate everything. Perhaps that was why Ines could never bring herself to visit cemeteries or graves; you never found the dead at home, instead they were everywhere and nowhere at the same time.

'I don't want to be buried,' Ines had once confided in Clara, 'if I outlive Mum and Aunt Hilda, which I suppose I will, I want you to spirit my corpse away with as little fuss as possible'. Clara wasn't able to carry out her friend's wishes. The aunt and mother insisted on having 'the girl' brought back home to be with them. To be interred in hallowed ground in Stillbach.

Clara got her laptop out of the bag and booted it up. Her publisher's reader had got in touch, saying how much he'd enjoyed her piece on Rilke, but that he'd liked to have heard more about the poet's encounter with D'Annunzio and Eleanora Duse. It'd be intriguing to know what impression the Diva had made on Rilke. Wouldn't that make a wonderful lead-in to the chapter she was working on right now? And could he expect that from her sometime soon?

Side-shows and tittle-tattle, thought Clara. So did they want her to write, say, about the excursion that Rilke took with Duse and that Princess of Thurn und Taxis-Hohenlohe, when a peacock's shrill call had given the Diva a fit of the vapours?

By contrast, the reader had found her treatment of the Venetian poet Gaspara Stampa a bit overwrought. Fair enough, the passages on the *poetessa*'s unrequited love and her mésalliance with the Count Collaltino di Collalto and the story of how, in 1548, she had followed him all the way to France, where he was on campaign with King Henri II, and been humiliated by his infidelities – all that material fitted well in the context, but Clara really ought to cut all the textual references. It wasn't important to know that Gaspara had written 203 sonnets.

Tear me to pieces, Love, torment me, take away from me the man I'd like beside me always—take him... the reader seemed to be oblivious to the fact that Rilke couldn't conceivably have fallen in love with those lines of Gaspara Stampa in isolation from their author, that he was most likely besotted with both the poetess and her work, even though so little was known about her after 350 years. A love story involving no sex just wasn't viable. No, what Clara really should have done was turn the clever Gaspara Stampa into a courtesan, make the unhappily infatuated poetess a literary groupie. After all, common *cortigiana* were the muses who'd sparked the creativity of Titian, Tintoretto, Ariosto and Pietro Aretino, weren't they? Not to mention sparking the reader's interest. Women as idealised creatures, as eye-candy, as figures of fun? No problem – shovel them into the book. But as poets, serious authors worth reading? *Tear me to pieces...*

The laptop was churning out so much heat that Clara shifted it off her knees onto the bedspread. Sitting awkwardly, she skimmed through the rest of her e-mails, deleting invitations, petitions and junk mail.

There was a message from Gesine, asking if she could borrow Clara's little black dress. Did Claus know there was a party planned at Gesine's friend's house that weekend?

One of the last e-mails was from Francesco Manente. *Subject: Ines.* How had he got hold of Clara's e-mail address?

Dear Frau Burger,
Ines's death has really hit me hard – I owe her so much.
    It would be a great comfort to me if I could get to know you. Ines told me lots about you. My mother originally came from Stillbach, and Ines used to go and visit her in the care home; I'll never forget how kind that was of her.
    If you come down to Rome, please look me up.
With deepest sympathy,
Francesco Manente

Why hadn't Ines ever mentioned these visits to see old Mrs Manente? And what exactly did Francesco owe Ines? Clara Googled his name, but got no hits.

He didn't seem to be on Facebook either. But when she typed in the name of the woman from Stillbach, she got a link to a hotel in Via Nomentana. *Questa pagina è in allestimento. Vi chiediamo un po'di pazienza.* – 'This page is under construction. Thank you for your patience.'

Though Paul had thrown open all the windows, the heat in the room wouldn't dissipate. He stuck the fan on the small, white-varnished table in front of him and weighed down the sheets of fluttering paper with an ashtray, failing to notice it was full of butts.

On his way home, he'd dropped in on Lorenzo and sunk several glasses of white wine, but hadn't stayed for dinner. The family atmosphere oppressed him.

The bus back had been freezing, like a cold-store. Plus the driver had suddenly veered off on a detour; Paul didn't catch the reason – some head of state or other visiting the premier or the pope.

His neck ached. That bloody draught from the fan. And the bottle was empty, again. Paul sat sprawled on the sofa and gazed at the door, as though a woman had just entered, put her bag down by the coat rack and was walking towards him.

And again he felt that scratching, like there was someone else inhabiting his body, like somebody was walking around inside him. 'There are too many dead people in your life,' Marianne had once told him, 'They'll come back to haunt you.'

Paul got up, put The Kinks on the CD player and uncorked another bottle. *You really got me. You really got me. You really got me.* As he went to pour himself another glass, he missed the target, slopping a mixture of wine and cigarette ash over the tabletop. He dragged off his T-shirt, mopped up the mess with it and flung it toward the living-room door but missed, hitting the wall.

Down in the courtyard, someone was singing along to Paul's CD; the young mechanic had a girlfriend round; he was gyrating to the music with his arm round her waist. 'You really got me. You really got me.' Peals of laughter, and a waft of sweet-smelling smoke.

The phone rang; Paul waited, then turned up the answering machine to listen to the message. It took a while for the tape to start. A new commission. Things are really looking up at the moment financially, he thought. He'd found a niche market and wasn't forced, like Lorenzo, to take package tours round the Colosseum. He had Marianne to thank for that, too – she'd sent him on that chamber of commerce seminar: *Helping you identify niche markets. Specialise and individualise to gain a competitive edge.* Ha, ha. Only in his love life had he remained a generalist. An idiot. And now here he was with the archaeologist's business card in his trouser pocket, but what use was it to him?

Ines came into his mind again; he wondered how many men she might have had. Marianne would have corrected him here: 'Loved, not *had*!' Women always loved, she maintained. Even if they didn't love a man, they loved his world.

My world – Paul mused – war crimes, massacres, torturers. He pulled out the archaeologist's card.

Desire grows thicker and more viscous with every day that passes until it clogs you up, blocks all your veins and arteries, he thought. What had got into him and lodged fast inside him couldn't be rinsed out, either. If only he could talk to Marianne. 'Please, Paul, just leave me alone.' Granted, he hadn't been exactly sober that night, but had repeated this sentence to himself so often since that he felt obliged to obey it to the letter.

Marianne was in poor health; she was having dialysis. Still, when they'd last spoken, some months ago already, that hadn't prevented him from keeping her on the phone for an hour at three in the morning. Time and again he'd tried to get her to change her mind, as though rational argument could rekindle love. This Beppe bloke was good for her. He was there for her. Cared for her. Why didn't Paul leave her in peace?

He'd been there when they'd been together – but not for her: his thoughts had usually been somewhere else. 'Sooner or later, you'll get bored with that interior decorator,' he told her.

'Sooner or later, I'll be dead, too,' she'd replied, 'and until then boredom's the least of my problems'.

Paul slipped his iPhone out of its case and looked at his e-mails. Twenty-four bits of junk mail and a notification of a forthcoming event. No texts. The Kinks began to get on his nerves, so he turned off the CD player.

It had been a mistake to speak so bluntly to the archaeologist. He should have known that women of her age still set some store by courtship rituals. What had she expected? For him to gyrate around in front of her like a peacock, putting all his rivals to flight with an impressive display of the shimmering eyes on his fanned tail feathers? For him to dance attendance on her? To bill and coo? Or maybe change colour like a salamander? All that palaver was ridiculous at his age. Anyone could see that his hair was greying and that his skin had lost its youthful glow. Let others fight over who had the strongest breeding genes – they could count him out of that particular contest.

He lay there on the sofa for quite some while, his feet up on the coffee table. 'You really got me. You really got me' was still coursing through his head. Everything carries on relentlessly, he thought, even when there's a switch to turn it off. The connection was automatically restored someplace else. And that 'someplace else' was in his own head.

Somewhere he could hear a couple making love. The mechanic and his girl-friend, maybe. He stood up and closed the window. There was a time when the sounds of copulation hadn't bothered him, in fact they'd even turned him on. What was wrong with him? 'Nothing makes a man feel lonelier than someone laughing softly in another person's ear.' If only it was just soft laughter in this case. Who was it who'd said that? He couldn't ask Marianne for an answer anymore.

He decided to get out of the house again and pulled on a new T-shirt and brushed his teeth. This Burger woman must be in Rome by now; she'd been on the train when she called him. She wanted to look though her friend's papers before the funeral and contact a removal firm.

As Paul descended the staircase, he suddenly realised he was gripping the handrail. He needed a strong coffee. And lots of mineral water.

A tram drew up right outside just as he emerged, so he jumped on it and rode to Largo di Torre Argentina. He'd once read somewhere that Anna Magnani had set up a cat sanctuary in the vaults below street level here. Now, every time he visited the busy square, teeming with traffic, or was waiting there on a bus, he couldn't help but think of the actress. In turn, this recollection prompted other, involuntary associations; he hated his memory for being so predictable. And whenever he called Magnani to mind – whom he'd found beautiful precisely because she'd not been afraid to appear ugly on screen – he inevitably recalled her jealousy and the fact that she had once tipped a plate of pasta over Roberto Rossellini's head after learning about his affair with Ingrid Bergman.

Paul would have loved to follow her example, but instead his pride had condemned him to three years of a *ménage à trois*. Ultimately, only Alitalia and Austrian Airlines profited from his pig-headedness, and Marianne and Beppe remained an item.

He had no idea what to do with the rest of his evening. After getting off the tram, he crossed the square and looked at the window display in the Feltrinelli bookshop. He bought a North African cookbook from a black guy at a stall, containing such unpronounceable dishes as *Chakchouka*, *Mogrhrabi* and *Mahshi*, although he almost never cooked. In his present mood, though, he'd have bought used glass eyes.

It can't have been louder than this, he thought, in Dante's Inferno; even the screams of the damned would be drowned out by this incessant roar of traffic and wailing of sirens. He walked along the Corso Vittorio Emanuele but before reaching Palazzo Braschi turned off into Via del Governo Vecchio. Despite his resolve to drink no more that evening, he ordered himself a spritzer in the Cul de Sac bar and wandered back out onto the street to have a smoke.

As usual, there was a lot of activity going on around the Pasquino statue; tourists snapping away and young Italians reading out loud to one another the satirical verses pasted on the plinth. Most of the readers had that look of spiteful amusement on their faces that people adopt when fun's being poked at a familiar hate-figure. Paul wouldn't have put it past the prime minister to have the daily diatribes and scurrilous verses directed at him and his cabinet colleagues scraped off the statue. He was amazed that this last 'talking statue' still existed at all. After Pietro Aretino had used it as a place to publish his mordant poems attacking Pope Adrian VI and the Curia, the statue only just escaped being thrown into the Tiber. And the fact that the Nazis took no action against Pasquino must have been down to their poor grasp of Italian, with events from Hitler's first visit to Rome in 1936 onwards spawning a rash of polemical verse.

Paul pulled out his iPhone again – no new messages. He flicked his cigarette butt away and rang Frau Burger. Rather touchingly, she recognised his voice instantly. And he hadn't even given his name, just wished her a good evening.

She wasn't in good shape at all, she said. Ines's death had really knocked her sideways, but then again some distraction might help.

A group of bare-chested men pushed past him, so close he could smell their sun cream. English, thought Paul.

'I can come and pick you up if you like.'

Really no need, she'd order a taxi.

Before setting off for the Campo de' Fiori, Paul drank a double espresso in the bar across the road, then washed his face and hands in the bathroom. The feeling of freshness was all too brief; on the way he was overcome by a surge of weariness and his limbs felt stiff.

As it turned out, a rendezvous on the Campo de' Fiori was a bad idea. The square was heaving with young people meeting up after dinner before going on to films or parties. There were no free tables, nor even any standing room at the bars. Paul thought about where they might move on to, but in the meantime positioned himself – as arranged – under the statue of Giordano Bruno, keeping an eye out for a tall brunette with long, wavy hair.

Trouble was, every other woman here had hair fitting that description and Italian girls seemed uniformly tall to him with their high-heeled sandals. Repeatedly, he found himself making a move to accost some woman or other, only stopping at the last moment when she didn't return his smile.

She shouldn't have come down to catch a taxi. In Vienna, you could hail a cab on any street corner, but here they either failed to materialise or sailed past you. By now, though, Clara had got so far from the hotel that she thought she'd rather wave in vain at the yellow cars than tramp all the way back to the lobby and ask the receptionist to order her a taxi.

She could still hear Francesco's voice on the telephone, a curious blend of standard German intonation and the familiar cadences of the Stillbach dialect. She had answered his e-mail straight away and he'd called her up. Their conversation was awkward and halting at first; he was making every effort to speak perfect German, which he did indeed manage for long stretches. But occasionally, he groped about so long for the right word that it set Clara's teeth on edge. They spoke only briefly about Ines; presumably, they both wanted to avoid piling on the pain by trawling up memories of her. Francesco had got to know Ines at the old people's home; she'd taken an interest in his mother in the wake of an interview she'd given some years before, when things were going better for her, to a woman historian from Rome. Their conversation was published in a university journal that dealt chiefly with oral history. In the same issue, a study had quizzed Francesco's mother and several other domestic servants about their experiences during the fascist period and the German occupation of Rome. 'Mum really became a kind of grandmother substitute for Ines, a little bit of Stillbach far from home.'

Only when Clara asked Francesco in Italian how his mother was and how she'd fared as a German speaker in Rome at the end of the 1930s did he switch to his native tongue and start speaking naturally about his *mammina*.

A classic domestic servant's tale, thought Clara, but with an unexpected ending. The chambermaid pregnant and desperate. The man who put her in the family way sees her sitting in the garden, her eyes red from crying, takes pity on her and asks her to come to the hotel kitchen with him and make him a cup of tea. All the while, she doesn't utter a word and in her distraction, brews him a black tea with lemon and salt. Whereupon the young man exclaims: 'Right, that's enough – how much salt can a person take!' And saying this, he gently prises the tea-towel from her hand and uses it to dry her tearstained cheeks. Still she says nothing, but takes heart, realising that she's something more to the hotelier's son than just another chambermaid from the North, and that he won't leave her in the lurch.

'And that's literally where I came in, amid all that salt,' said Francesco. Another week went by before his mother plucked up enough courage to spill the beans. His father then went straight back to Trevignano to tell his parents. The family owned a holiday cottage there on the shore of Lake Bracciano. Barely a month later, the wedding took place, with just the immediate family in attendance. No relatives travelled down from Stillbach. It just wouldn't have been feasible in all the upheaval at the end of the war.

'Taxi! Taxi!' In her anxiety, Clara almost ran into the path of the oncoming cab. The driver made a gesture signalling she must be crazy and drove on.

So, this Emma Manente's still alive; she must be over ninety, thought Clara. She'd once heard her parents talking about this woman from Stillbach, because someone from her family, a sister maybe, had died. That time round the dinner table, Clara's parents had wondered aloud why Emma hadn't left Rome; up till then they'd assumed she must be ill or maybe even dead.

Mammina, Francesco told her over the phone, couldn't be budged. He'd even offered to go back to Stillbach with her, but she'd refused. After everything that had happened, he understood why she didn't want to have anything more to do with 'them up there', but on the other hand a new generation had long since grown up who didn't think every Italian was a workshy Lothario with Mafia connections. There'd even been leftwing and Green politicians like that Alexander Langer who'd worked tirelessly to bring about reconciliation between the various ethnic groups.

'He killed himself, mind.' Clara had interjected.

In the distance, she caught a glimpse of something yellow and started waving frantically at it, even though it was at least ten cars back.

No, not everyone could endure the labour of Sisyphus that opposition politicians 'up there' were condemned to, she thought as she stepped out into the road.

At last – Clara opened the taxi door, told the driver where she wanted to go and, after he'd nodded in assent, settled in the back seat. As she did so, he noticed he was looking at her in the rear-view mirror.

'Pardon me,' he said, 'but you look familiar.'

'Well, you don't ring any bells with me,' she replied. She thought of a friend of hers who was so much the spitting image of President Bush that he'd once given a Munich taxi driver a really nasty shock.

'Got it – you were one of my fares last week, weren't you?'

'Impossible – I was in Vienna then.'

'Oh, so you live in Vienna?' He was driving so slowly that Clara looked at her watch twice in the space of just a kilometre.

Francesco had kept on talking and talking, and Clara didn't have the heart to cut him off and now she was going to be late for her meeting with Paul. What did she care about those stories of Francesco's mother and her friends who'd come down to Rome from South Tyrol in the 1930s? Anyway, the long and short of it was that his *mammina* had stayed in Rome, Francesco was at pains to point out, while all those other women had gone back to their villages in time.

Clara asked him what he meant by 'in time'.

The women had all thrown their lot in with the Führer, he replied, they'd opted to become members of the German Reich in the nick of time.

'Married?' asked the driver.

Why can't this bloke leave me be, thought Clara: 'Yes, for the sixth time, plus I've got five children by four different men… Can you step on it a bit?'

He laughed and pumped the accelerator. 'So how come you speak such good Italian?'

'Four of my ex-husbands are Italian.'

'Clearly a woman of taste.'

'If I was, I wouldn't be divorced from them.'

That gave him pause for thought and he slowed down again. On the dashboard next to the driver's seat, she noticed some photos in a metal frame. Only the face of the smiling, white-bearded Padre Pio was familiar, the Capuchin monk with the stigmata; he was flanked by pictures of two children.

She was still amazed at the way Francesco had dived headlong into his story. Despite having had nothing to do with one another before, he'd insisted on giving her a blow-by-blow account of his mother's past. So now Clara not only knew the exact date when Emma had upped sticks and left Stillbach – the anniversary, coincidentally, of D'Annunzio's death – but also that she'd first gone to work in Venice, but had fallen foul of an especially pernickety and mean mistress there and so decided to try her luck in Rome.

'You're having me on,' said the driver; keeping his left hand on the wheel, he rootled around in the door pocket with his right hand, producing a bag of toffees, and passed them back to Clara.

'OK, I'm an Italian,' she said, 'but with German as my first language.'

'From Bolzano Province?'

Here we go, she thought, I'm about to be treated to a lecture on rightwing extremism in South Tyrol. But instead the driver launched into a paean of praise for her homeland, its stable economy and its almost full employment. Did she know the per-capita GDP for Bolzano was twice that of Sicily? He'd been holiday-ing in the Dolomites for years and there was nowhere to match its cleanliness. 'The South's the problem,' the man continued, 'without those cousins of Africans' – the precise phrase he used: *i cugini degli africani nel sud* – 'we'd be far better off.'

'Aren't we all related?'

'Signora, the whole world's related, that's the problem. You've got to sort the wheat from the chaff, then the bread will taste good again.'

'But you only eat cake, right?'

Clara recognised the Area Sacra Argentina, and realising she was fairly close to Campo de' Fiori, asked the driver to pull over.

'I can get you closer, though.'

'Thanks all the same, I feel like stretching my legs.'

He didn't see her at first, because she came from the opposite direction he was expecting. The taxi had dropped her off on the Via Arenula and she had walked up the Via Giubbonari. As Paul stood scanning the heads and bodies of all the women criss-crossing in front of him, she came up from behind, touched his shoulder lightly and said 'Excuse me!' – so startling him that he flinched.

'Paul Vogel?'

'That's me. – How did you recognise me so fast?'

'That wasn't hard. You're the only middle-aged man here.'

Paul felt oppressed by the hubbub on the square; Clara's voice was drowned out by all the young people's noisy *Ciao*s as they greeted one another, which *en masse* sounded like a chorus of miaowing cats. It hadn't escaped him that she'd called him a 'middle-aged man'. The phrase hadn't just slipped out, nor could he put it down to naïvety or thoughtlessness on her part – she gave every impression of being a thoroughly serious and deliberate person. Her dark clothes were elegant and well-tailored, and her long hair freshly washed, brushed back severely from her forehead and held neatly in place with a hairclip.

This was the first time in years she'd been to Rome, she said, spinning slowly on her heel to take in the sky above the rooftops.

'Unless, that is…' – here she paused and looked him straight in the eye – 'you count watching Rossellini's *Roma, città aperta*. I saw it a fortnight ago, after Ines had talked about it several times on the phone. We just happened to have a DVD of it at home.'

Paul pricked up his ears at the mention of 'We'.

Without discussing where they were heading, they wandered out of the Campo de' Fiori, walked in the direction of the Palazzo Farnese and, at her request, sat down on a stone bench in front of the building. 'This is always what comes to mind first whenever I think of Rome', she said. She waved her hand in the direction of the palaces, her wrist making a circular motion. Paul couldn't stop looking at her arm. Her hands look so young, he thought, younger than her facial complexion.

She was from Stillbach, where she and Ines had been at grammar school together, and had gone on to study *Lingue e Letterature Straniere* in Venice. For her part, after leaving school Ines had moved to Austria and enrolled on a German Studies and Art History course. After graduating, she took up a post in Rome for several years as a university foreign language assistant.

'We never lost contact,' Clara told him, 'despite the fact that Ines was living in Innsbruck and then Rome, whereas I left Italy after doing my doctorate.'

Her skirt had ridden up her thighs, making her long legs look even longer and her skin was so clear and pale that Paul was afraid she'd get sunburnt, even though it was evening by now.

'Ines was my daughter's godmother.' She suddenly closed her eyes and lapsed into silence, with her head resting against the wall of the palace. For a moment, she seemed oblivious to Paul's presence beside her. Her chin trembled slightly and Paul noticed that tears had welled up under her eyelids; her lashes were wet and shining. It seemed inappropriate to take her hand, so he just touched her lightly on her shoulder and waited for her to carry on.

'There'll still be butter in the fridge,' she said at length, 'and the laundry will still be in the wash basket.' Paul liked the sound of Clara's voice and was only sorry she didn't speak a little louder. She sounded a bit husky, possibly a result of choking back the tears, or maybe she was a smoker.

'The thought of the empty flat really spooks me.'

'I... I can come with you, if you like.'

She looked up.

A group of tourists had stopped in front of them and their guide began talking first about the façade and then the famous gallery inside the building, decorated with paintings by Annibale Carracci.

Paul took the opportunity to distract Clara. '*The Triumph of Love Over the Universe*', he whispered in her ear, pointing up behind them, 'the frescoes on the first floor'. Instinctively, Clara turned round to look up. 'The gallery's only open to the public very occasionally,' he added.

She rummaged in her bag for a tissue and blew her nose. He carried on telling her all about the paintings, the portrait of Bacchus crowned with vine leaves and ivy and the voluptuous Ariadne, her body wrapped in a toga, whose triumphal chariot was drawn not by horses but by big cats that looked like tigers. But when she didn't respond, he let it drop; he didn't want to come across like some obsessive nerd.

'We saw one another twice, maybe three times a year, generally on high days and holidays in Stillbach,' Clara continued, 'but we still remained close.'

Paul tried to remember the name of the artist who'd painted the other, later fresco of *The Triumph of Bacchus*, which showed the god surrounded by drinkers, but it wouldn't come to him.

'I'm so sorry it turned out this way,' he said, putting his hand on her arm again, 'did she have anyone here?'

'You mean a man friend?' Clara balled the tissue up in her hand. 'I've no idea. Ines didn't have much luck with men. She did have a relationship here in Rome with another woman for a while, but it didn't last. Maybe there was the odd lover, too. I wouldn't put it past her.'

'And you?'

'Me, I'm married and have a daughter who's almost grown up now.'

'I envy you that.'

'Really?'

'Absolutely. Finding the right person and settling down, that's true happiness, right?'

She gazed straight ahead and furrowed her brow. '"Happiness is good health and a bad memory", according to Hemingway. Can anyone be happy after almost twenty years?' she said quietly. 'But I have to travel a lot for work, so that makes everything a bit easier and more bearable.'

Right now, she explained, she was writing a book about famous lovers in Venice. Unlike normal city guides, which were just cut-and-paste jobs from earlier ones, in her book she was trying to blend literary history with anecdotal material, but to present it in such a way that someone with no interest in literature would still find it engaging. 'It's really a book for lovers, for honeymooners.' As she spoke, Clara narrowed her eyes a little. The creases running from her nose to the corners of her mouth took on a half-moon shape, softening her face. Looking at her, Paul was fleetingly reminded of Marianne. He couldn't put his finger on exactly what aspect of Clara's appearance had prompted this recollection, though. Maybe it was their mouths that were similar?

With Marianne and me, he thought, it was more like a combination of bad health and a good memory – no wonder we were always at each other's throats.

He stood up and looked at Clara. 'Shall we go and eat?'

She remained seated. 'I had a couple of sandwiches on the train,' she said. But the end of her sentence dissolved almost into unintelligibility; Clara, who up till then had managed to keep a lid on her emotions, was now sobbing uncontrollably, her shoulders heaving.

Paul sat back down beside her and put his arm round her. He didn't know what to say, didn't even have a tissue to give her. She smells good, he thought, the perfume was a new one to him, it wasn't like anything else he knew.

'You were really fond of Ines, weren't you?' he asked.

In response, she simply nodded and, diving into her bag, pulled out a vanity mirror and quickly checked her face. She didn't apologise or say how embarrassed she was about breaking down in public, but just looked up at him after a while, wide-eyed, and attempted a smile.

There was a candidness about her that irked Paul, yet this unaffected naturalness surely wasn't, as it had been with Marianne, the result of a life-threatening illness, which necessarily concentrated the mind on the things that really mattered, but rather must have always been an integral part of Clara, like her dark, shining hair.

'It's not just Ines I'm crying about,' she said, standing up, 'but that's another story'.

Paul saved the question of what this 'other story' might be for later. He suggested they stroll over to Trastevere, where he knew a good *panetteria* that'd still be open at that time. A slice of pizza would do him and then Clara could decide what she wanted to do with the rest of the evening.

On the Ponte Sisto, a woman latched onto them, begging for her fare home, but when Clara asked her where she lived, she stuck out her tongue and walked off.

As Paul stood waiting in the queue outside the La Renella bakery, Clara leant against a house wall in the narrow alleyway outside and watched the passers-by. Now and again, she glanced up to look for Paul in the queue; when they caught each other's eye, she didn't smile but shot him a serious look, as if her thoughts were elsewhere.

When he emerged and asked her whether she'd like a taste of his courgette pizza, she took several bites of the hot bread, like they'd known one another for years. And when he revealed that he'd bought her a bag of chocolate-coated biscuits too, she was so delighted she planted a spontaneous kiss on his cheek for his 'kind gesture', though she still kept using the polite form of address to him.

This show of exuberance took Paul by surprise. He walked behind her down the narrow street, hemmed in by cars and oncoming pedestrians. On the Piazza Santa Maria in Trastevere she asked him to come with her to Ines's flat.

'I want to get this over and done with.'

'What, right now?'

'Yes, the sooner the better.'

Clara was now of an age where one didn't fall in love at the drop of a hat anymore, because her hopes for the future were already a bit past their sell-by date and because the true happiness she'd once thought she'd find had never really materialised. Even so, there were moments this evening when she felt like she was on holiday with a new man, causing her, temporarily at least, to forget her grief and her family. She was amazed at how little distraction one needed to be happy.

And as she walked along with Paul, she started musing again on how it would be to simply stay here, to take over not only Ines's flat but her private tuition students and her translation work as well, while completing her book on lovers in Venice. One of Claus's colleagues had done just that apparently: left his family in the blink of an eye and acted as though his previous existence had never happened. When visiting his girlfriend in winter, to give himself an alibi, this colleague had even gone so far as to dangle his coat inside a pub for a spell so that it smelt of cigarette smoke when he got home. But ultimately, he didn't leave his wife for his lover – it turned out she was just a convenient springboard for his leap to freedom and he left her in Vienna along with everything else. Instead, he upped sticks and went to Africa to work for an aid organisation.

Happiness is like a door that has been left ajar or unlocked. Over time, you stop paying attention and you don't notice that the door has slammed shut and that someone else has turned the key. In her married life in Vienna, thought Clara, even the windows were locked by now. Only the books that she lived and breathed afforded her a view of the wider world. They were the cracks in the roller shutters, the missing slats in the blinds, the crack in the curtains that lets in a chink of light.

Ines, too, had always preferred buying new editions to new clothes. And she'd been glad to get away from Stillbach, as well. This urge for new experiences had begun in her flat, where she kept shifting the furniture around, rearranging things to try to create a totally different sense of space. One of her boyfriends – was it Claudio? – couldn't take this upheaval anymore and ended their relationship after he'd come home late one night and ended up sprawled on the tiled floor. Not wanting to wake Ines, he'd crept through the living room in the dark and crashed out on the leather sofa, without realising that Ines had moved it to the far side of the room.

So what exactly had Ines been working on, asked Paul, lighting up a cigarette as they walked.

'Why, did she tell you she'd started writing again?' *I'm chopping words and sentences. Firewood for the memory*, was what she'd written on one of the sheets Clara had read on the train, but those were notes from an earlier period.

'Yes, that why she asked to meet me. She wanted some background information about the events around 1978,' Paul replied.

'I'd no idea. We weren't in contact much latterly. I once made the mistake of making a negative comment about something she'd written and she never showed me anything ever again.' The postcard Ines had sent to her aunt was from that same year, Clara recalled, which meant she must have been in Rome herself that summer. Unlike Clara, as a girl Ines had had to take on weekend and holiday jobs to fund her school and university studies.

'All I associate with 1978 is Aldo Moro, his body stuffed in the back of that red Renault R4.'

'Wasn't it beige?'

'No, definitely red. I remember it vividly. I had a red R5 myself later on.'

Paul pulled Clara smartly aside as a car swung round the corner. She felt the pressure of his hand and looked briefly into his eyes. 'They still don't know who was responsible for his murder. It's likely that Gladio and the P2 masonic lodge had some involvement and possibly even the KGB and the CIA...'

'They all had a common interest in preventing the communists from getting into government,' Paul agreed, 'One thing's for sure, the *Brigate Rosse* weren't working alone.'

'Maybe that's what she was writing about.'

'She also asked me about Erich Priebke, though.' Paul cut across a busy street, with Clara hard on his heels.

Priebke – Priebke – the name rang a bell for her.

It was so loud that Clara couldn't catch what Paul was saying. He suddenly sprinted to a taxi, overtaking a man who started protesting, quite justifiably, that Paul had cut in front of him and that he'd been waiting here ages for a cab. But Paul simply ignored him and pulled Clara into the taxi. 'Otherwise we'll never get away from here,' he explained.

Clara felt Paul's thigh against hers but rather than move away, she stayed pressed up close to him.

'Priebke was Herbert Kappler's second-in-command,' Paul said.

'It was Kappler who…'

'Kappler organised the deportation of Rome's Jews and ordered 335 hostages to be executed in the Ardeatine Caves in reprisal for a partisan attack on a Gestapo police unit – five more victims than prescribed, what's more. He was sent down for life for that. As it turned out, though, he only ended up serving a couple of years, while Priebke spent fifty years in Argentina and is now living in a comfortable apartment in Boccea.'

'He's still alive? What, here in Rome?' Clara smoothed down her skirt and noticed that Paul was looking at her hand. 'I can still remember the television report about Kappler's escape from the military hospital. I always imagined his wife had smuggled him out in a suitcase. He was such a thin, emaciated little man.'

'He had cancer. Poetic justice, you might say. Rarely happens.'

How true, thought Clara. Ines had been one of the vast majority who didn't deserve it.

'I should have told Ines about that Karl Hass too, but it didn't occur to me when we met – she left so soon, something must have put her out of sorts. She claimed that we knew one another from the Hotel Manente in 1978. I was living there as student then, but with the best will in the world, I can't remember whether I… whether we…' Paul hesitated and looked out of the window. 'It's just sad that she's no longer around.'

Had Clara heard him correctly? So they'd had an affair more than thirty years ago? But I'd have known about it, surely, thought Clara. In those days, Ines confided in me about everything. It bothered her that Paul had dropped this hint, but more than that, it troubled her that she was troubled by it. 'So who was this Hass?' she asked quickly.

'Do you really want to talk about that now? There are plenty of nicer subjects.'

'But I'm really interested.' She'd also have liked him to explain why he couldn't remember about Ines.

'Hass was another member of the execution squad in the Caves. In the late Sixties, he played an SS prison guard in Visconti's film *The Damned*. At the time, he was wanted for war crimes in Italy.'

'So you're telling me that all the time these images of Hass were being screened he was a wanted man? — There must have been influential people pulling strings to make sure he wasn't arrested,' said Clara, 'just like with Moro. Some people knew exactly where the terrorists were holding him, but they didn't lift a finger to save him.'

'Hass worked for the Americans, the Germans and the Italians,' replied Paul. 'he wasn't some top agent, just middle-ranking, but even so as a former Nazi Party functionary he was clearly useful in the fight against Communism.'

Paul was really getting into his stride now and in short order Clara was treated to every last detail about the life of this man from Kiel. He'd tried to escape at the end of the war, but was detained several times, including once in South Tyrol, but always managed to get away. Italian fascists like Giorgio Almirante and Pino Romualdi, who later founded the neofascist MSI party, provided him with false papers. Those two sent Nazis who were on the run to Hass's house, and it's thought that he helped fund their escape to Argentina.

'But even while he was helping other Nazis escape justice, he was on the wanted list himself. He was described as having close-cropped dark hair with a centre parting and a dark complexion – a typical Aryan, then,' Paul said, laughing, 'plus he spoke with a lisp and was a heavy drinker.'

The motion of the cab rounding a bend pressed them closer together; Clara kept looking straight ahead at the street.

'By 1947, Hass was teaching Maths and English at a monastery school in Ascoli Piceno and after that he went on to work for the American counterintelligence services at a forces broadcaster in Linz. It was his job to get officers in the East to defect to the West. Several did, and some were even sent back across the Iron Curtain as spies. But when it transpired that some of the supposed defectors were actually communist double agents, the whole operation was wound up. Hass simply moved on to his next assignment. He was sent as 'Agent Giustini' to Rome to counter the Italian communists. – Best if you turn left here,' he said to the taxi driver.

'And what happened next?'

'Well, in the early Fifties his wife in Germany used the missing persons law to register him as deceased and in 1962 the Italians officially closed the files on him too. In justification, they claimed all attempts to track him down had proved fruitless. Yet just a few years later, there he was, working as an actor and an extra, not just on *The Damned*. Have you ever seen the film?'

'No. I don't recall it.'

'He doesn't have many lines in it: just a couple of sentences that must have been second nature to him.'

'Such as?'

'"Face the wall! Face the wall!" He invariably played SS men. Actually, 'played' is the wrong word, isn't it?'

'Sounds like an echo from the Caves.'

'Later still, he was employed by the German War Graves Commission on Sicily, and under his real name, what's more. Around the same time, he registered himself as alive in Germany again, in order to claim his pension. And if Priebke hadn't been exposed in Argentina and extradited to Italy, Hass would have been able to enjoy an undisturbed retirement. But Priebke cited him as a witness for the defence, not only because he'd been present at the massacre, but also because, unlike Priebke, he'd got off scot-free. – But that's not the end of the story. Before the Priebke trial here in Rome, which Hass was subpoenaed to appear at, he jumped out of his hotel window and broke his pelvis, probably in an attempt to avoid having to give evidence.'

'And was he convicted in the end?'

'It was commuted to house arrest, as usual,' said Paul.

'So is he still alive? – No, that's impossible; I've just done the maths.'

'That's right. He died a couple of years ago in an old people's home here in Rome.'

As they got out of the taxi, Paul offered Clara his hand. She grasped it, not wanting to let it go. If Ines had been interested in the events of 1978, then where did the Nazis fit in?

The key jammed in the lock; only after several attempts did Paul finally manage to force the door open. Clara had passed the bunch of keys over to him without more ado: 'I can't manage it. I haven't got the patience.' She told him about a girl-friend's house key, which suddenly stopped working after three years. Nothing at all had changed: it was the same key and the same lock as ever.

He began to worry that she'd start going on about some supernatural force stopping her friend – and them now – from gaining entry, but Clara said nothing. When they finally got in, she just stepped into the narrow corridor and fumbled for the light switch.

It smelt in the flat, Paul couldn't say of what.

Clara made her way straight to the small kitchen and started looking for plastic bags to put the shrivelled houseplants and the wilting cut lilies in. As she poured the stagnant water from the vase down the sink, she began to gag at the stench. Paul flung open the window and sat down on the only free chair, next to the old sideboard. He felt tempted to look in the fridge for a bottle of wine and down a glass. On top of the stove was a pan with the remains of some risotto; mould had grown on it right up to the lip. Clara slammed the lid back on the pan and stood, leaning against the window frame, her back to Paul.

He noticed that she was shaking. When he stood up to see what the matter was, she turned away from him.

'I can't stand it,' she said, brushing her fingertips across her eyes.

'Just leave it. Let me deal with it.' He scraped the pan clean and rinsed it out. All the telltale signs pointed to Ines having lived on her own. Or if she did have a lover, he can't have been round here much, Paul thought.

'A year ago, my cousin was killed in a motorway crash,' Clara began, 'that was bad enough, but this thing with Ines is far worse. – It's like my youth has died with her. – Now she's gone, it feels like I've lost myself, like a part of me's been torn away, because she and I can't reminisce together anymore.' Clara put her head out of the window for a moment and looked down into the street, before turning back to face Paul. 'Have you ever lost a friend?'

He shook his head. 'I know what you mean, though. You're losing a person you shared experiences with.'

'Shared a whole life with, more like,' said Clara. 'All of a sudden, you've got no foil anymore, no…' – she pondered for a second – 'no-one to give you your cue.'

'You mean, all your memories have no focus any more…'

'Yes, perhaps that's it.' Clara's hand brushed against a page-a-day calendar pinned up by the window, on which no pages had been torn off since Ines's death. Noticing what it was, she took it down and dropped it into one of the plastic bags with the dead plants. A dusty imprint remained on the wall.

'When memories lose their focus, it's like –' here she hesitated, turned to the washbasin and washed her hands, '– like a bit of you has died. As a kid, I always used to think there must be worms in our heads that eat memories and thoughts just like maggots eat a person's body.' Finding no tea towel, she shook her hands dry. 'I thought forgetting was like having part of you eaten away.' She opened the fridge, scanned its contents, closed it again and then, shaking her head, opened it once more, as though she'd just remembered what she was after. 'Do you want a drink?'

Paul had the choice of an open bottle of Prosecco, a Martini, or some sticky elderberry liqueur. The sparkling wine had long since gone flat, but he still quaffed a glass of it, then checked himself from pouring another, though he'd happily have polished off the small amount left in the bottle.

The apartment measured about ten to twenty square metres larger than Paul's *monolocale*, but being divided into several small rooms gave it the impression of being pokier; against every free wall, there were bookshelves up to ceiling height.

Paul leant over Ines's desk, while Clara rummaged in boxes and leafed through files in search of the rental agreement, bank statements and other papers. Squatting down to pull some photos out of the bottom drawer of an old wooden chest of drawers, her hair fell forwards and Paul caught a glimpse of her neck, a part of the female anatomy that he'd always found attractive. The botanist was the only woman he'd ever known who hadn't responded to having her neck kissed and stroked. All she did one time when he bit her gently on the neck was to liken him to a cat. She went on to inform him that cats used the neck bite for three things: carrying their young, gripping a female during copulation and killing their prey. Hadn't he ever noticed how kittens fell into a kind of paralysis when their mother grabbed them by the scruff of the neck and carted them off? And didn't that give him pause for thought? There'd been no sign of paralysis with Marianne and all the other women he'd known, thought Paul.

He forced himself to tear his gaze from Clara and began leafing through Ines's books on the desk, attempting to decipher the scribbled notes in the margins. Clara handed him a photo showing Ines in the 1970s. Paul's initial reaction was that he was looking at a picture of the young Clara – the similarities were striking – but then he began to make out traits of the tomboyish woman he'd met just a few days before at the Galleria Sordi. He looked at the back of the photo for a date, but there was nothing. Clara could only guess roughly when it was taken, leaving Paul with no idea still of what Ines had looked like in 1978.

He was surprised by the titles that Ines had been consulting at the time of her death; at least he assumed that the books lying around on her desk had something to do with the 'multi-volume work' she'd mentioned: *Rome 1943–1944; Nazis on the Run; Mussolini, Hitler and Haile Selassie*. The books were full of Day-glo yellow and pink Post-it notes with names like Priebke, Schwammberger, Eichmann and Hudal written on them.

He'd dearly loved to have snooped around in the desk drawer, but how would that look to Clara? Schwammberger, Schwammberger – Paul gazed fixedly out of the window – Josef! Yes, that was it. He was that South Tyrolean who'd run various SS labour camps in the Krakow district of Poland. Paul recalled having read somewhere that when he'd first been arrested, before he managed to flee to South America, they'd found jewellery on him worth 50,000

Reichsmarks, which he must have stolen from inmates. The jewellery, lots of which had names or initials engraved on it, was immediately confiscated and auctioned, so that it could no longer be used in evidence against him.

Clara had taken a pile of photos over to the sofa with her and begun sorting through them. She told Paul that Ines had once supplied the words to accompany a volume of photographs by a well-known German woman artist: 'I always liked that text of hers. I can't remember the exact words, but she talked about that searing sense you get that you're seeing something completely unique when you look at a picture of a dead person. She wrote "The photo freezes the subject for all eternity", or something like that.' She passed Paul a picture of herself and Ines; in the background was a small mountain lake with water lilies growing in the shallows.

'Stillbach Mere,' Clara explained. She spread the photos out on the table. 'I can't bear to look at all these snaps. They drown everything else out.'

Paul noticed her eyes were moist again and sat down next to her.

'Ines's mother's devastated; I couldn't say no. But I'm finding this all too much for me.'

'I'd be happy to help you,' Paul said, 'I'm only taking one tour tomorrow, but before that…'

'What can I do with all the books? Who on Earth wants German literature down here in Rome?'

'The Pope, maybe?' suggested Paul.

He followed her into Ines's bedroom, which contained nothing but a large bed with a single mattress and a clothes valet made of chrome-plated steel. Two clothes rails contained a jumble of T-shirts and jeans, with two hats perched on the end knobs – a black felt hat and one made of white velvet. Clara grabbed a T-shirt and buried her nose in it.

Paul prised it gently from her hand: 'Now then, that won't help.'

'The summer hat was a present from *me*.'

On the bed were a pile of books and a sheaf of papers, along with two red exercise books and a felt pen.

Ines evidently took work to bed with her, thought Paul. He called to mind his own bed, half of which was covered with papers and magazines most of the time. A wave of desire swept over him. He could maybe try the young archaeologist again, send her a text at least. It still wasn't too late. He glanced at the clock.

'Do you need to be off, then?' Clara had picked up a manuscript and was flicking through it.

'I suppose I should do some preparation for tomorrow,' he replied.

She put the manuscript in her bag. 'Do you really not mind if I bother you again?'

As they were leaving Ines's flat together, they arranged to meet outside the apartment block at eleven the next morning.

Clara was scarcely out of sight when Paul texted the archaeologist: *Even if you didn't mean it like that, perhaps we can try another way? Fancy a drink in the Centro Storico?*

He got on the number 77 bus and rode to the Piazza San Silvestro terminus. During the journey, Paul reached for his mobile three times, but the ringtones were from other people's phones. As he was getting off, a young man barged into him and although it was most likely an accident, Paul snapped at him: 'Why don't you bloody look where you're going?'

Now and then, he'd had bust-ups with Marianne, but never serious ones; they both used the little spats to work off something or other that was bugging them – and afterwards everything went back to normal again. But things were different now. Nowadays there was no point of friction for Paul to vent his excess energy on. So he walked, sweating, all the way home from the bus stop.

He was right outside the front door when his mobile rang.

'I just wanted to thank you again,' said Clara.

'No need, really.'

'Guess what – she was working on a novel.'

'Oh, right.' The *multi-volume work*, he thought.

'You feature in it, you know.'

1978

1

Ivy had wound its way up the tree trunks, sunshade poles and stones, entwining itself round the table legs and the cracked marble slab that had been left propped against the wall, and turning everything green. Under its lush carpet, even the piles of garden furniture stacked away in the far corner looked like hedges. It had rambled over the abandoned bicycle and the wine bottles in their straw baskets and even where there were no boards or other supports for it to gain a purchase on, it clung fast to the ground. It was rampant, spreading relentlessly and attracting a growing army of bees, wasps and hoverflies. Only a light blue plastic tarpaulin stuck up out of the sea of green ivy, defying its tenacious suckers, as if trying to assert itself against nature in the midst of all this luxuriant, all-enveloping foliage.

Fetching a cushion from a serving table covered in Campari ashtrays and sugar shakers, Emma Manente sat down on the chair next to the door. She'd just cast an eye over the terrace, checking the position of the individual tables, shifting chairs around and securing the odd tablecloth clip that was in danger of falling off. Only then did she allow herself a breather, resting her head against the wall and stretching her legs so that just her feet were in the sun.

That morning, while doing up her double-breasted blouse in front of the mirror, she'd suddenly been struck by indecision: were women meant to button from right to left or the other way round? In the end, down at reception, she'd noticed from the left-to-right buttoning of her male guests' jackets that she'd been right all along. She was clearly all at sixes and sevens at the thought of the new girl arriving this afternoon, which would disrupt the usual routine. Yet another one she'd have to show the ropes, explain everything to and keep an eye on the whole time.

She recalled how she herself had once stood in that Venetian family's kitchen and been forced to sing out loud while making pastry. Even taking long pauses to catch her breath was viewed with suspicion. '*Canta, cara!* Keep singing, dear!' the mistress used to call out. Signora Scabello claimed to be interested in German folk songs and girls from South Tyrol. She preferred them to Italian girls. Emma hated having to sing songs like *im Frühtau zu Berge wir zieh'n fallera* with her fingers all sticky from making shortcrust for the *crostata*. Back then, she'd never have dreamt of eating bits of leftover pastry – she thought uncooked flour could give you worms.

The Scabello woman used to tot up every last expenditure, waiting at the kitchen table whenever Emma came back from buying groceries and going through all the individual receipts with her. 'Shopkeepers are always trying to pull a fast one and so are my girls,' was her constant refrain.

For the first few weeks, Emma had made a point of approaching the market from the Rialto side, to avoid passing the vaulted building housing the fish market, with its writhing mantis and spider crabs. She couldn't imagine why they were being offered for sale alive; after all, the butcher back home in her village didn't sell twitching rabbits. And then there was the smell. Signor Scabello was friends with one of the fishmongers and usually went to fetch all the fish and seafood himself. But one time he'd sent her on an errand to the fish market because he'd forgotten the *granceole*. Carrying back a sack of these spider crabs, Emma got the feeling it had taken on a life of its own. In a moment of panic, she dropped the bag and stood frozen to the spot. One of the monsters' knobbly red carapaces had half slipped out; Emma was at a loss how to get the crustacean's spindly legs back inside and was too embarrassed to ask anyone for help. So in the end she had just bent down and, holding open the neck of the bag with one hand, kicked the spider crab back in.

The Scabellos' place was a small *palazzo*. Emma slept under the main staircase in a windowless cubicle that had once been some sort of store cupboard, and where mops and buckets were now kept. During the daytime, she had to fold up her camp-bed, as the cubicle was also used as an interim storage space for food deliveries or demijohns, so that by the evening it always smelt of vinegar, onions or tomatoes. Whenever the Scabellos had guests, Emma had to stay up, sometimes 'til two in the morning. She would sit for hours on call in the kitchen, even when there was nothing more to be done and all the dishes had been cleared away. Only the nanny, the *bambinaia,* was allowed to go to bed; she was a woman from Burano in her mid-forties, a matronly lady with years of domestic service. Many was the time Emma had caught her polishing off the children's leftovers behind the Signora's back, even though there was always plenty to eat at the Scabellos. Later, in Rome, at the Church of Santa Maria dell'Anima, where she went every Sunday to meet up with other German-speaking servants, Emma had got to know a parlour maid who'd had to live for weeks on a diet of white rice and semolina, and who'd taken to secretly gnawing scraps of meat from the bones put out for the dog.

Emma heard the palms rustle and the tablecloths flap as the wind caught them. No, it was actually a good job that the new girl was coming today; she could use an extra pair of hands. She'd had enough of helping the chambermaid and mucking in around the kitchen.

The girls from Stillbach and the surrounding villages had always been reliable. They lived on site, so didn't have to commute in to work every day. Plus they could speak German.

Over the years, word had got around that German-speaking guests wouldn't encounter any language problems at the Hotel Manente and that the place was spotlessly clean and well-run. The tourists came mainly from Bavaria and Baden-Württemberg, and were besotted with old Rome – never more so than when, at the end of an arduous day spent dodging reckless scooter and moped riders, they could sit in the hotel's quiet garden or, after riding on a hot, packed bus, flake out in a deckchair and order a pot of the weak filter coffee they so liked. Then, screened by the walls and the ivy-covered chain-link fence, they'd compare notes on the latest results from the German football league.

Emma's eye was caught by an elderly guest who'd set up his chair in the shade of the magnolia. He was sitting with his back to her and reading. Hermann Steg was one of her regulars. Every year without fail, he booked the same room for the same period. Round midday, when most of the other guests were out and about, he'd repair to the garden, while in the evening he kept to his room. He was a taciturn man, who didn't even break his silence to greet people; instead, he'd just respond with a brief nod of his head. Emma knew virtually nothing about him, except that he'd been a teacher at a private school and had a nice little nest-egg of a pension that allowed him to spend a fortnight in Rome every year followed by three weeks in Ischl. She'd noticed that Steg moved his lips when he read and that he had covered his books with homemade newspaper jackets – presumably less to protect them than to stop anyone from seeing the title and engaging him in con- versation. He sometimes forgot to change his shirt and his trousers were always hopelessly crumpled for the first few days' stay because he packed his suitcase badly. He didn't have a wife or lady friend in tow. Emma hadn't managed to find out whether there'd ever been a Frau Steg. One time she'd spotted him gazing intently at the contents of his handkerchief after blowing his nose; Emma had craned her neck to try to catch a glimpse of what was so fascinating…maybe he had some lung disease and was coughing up blood? But Steg had suddenly sensed he was being watched and turned round to look at Emma, who promptly darted back into the hotel doorway.

Steg reminded Emma of Signor Scabello; they both walked like their knees were slightly stiff. Scabello had also preferred to hole up in his studio rather than talk to his children's friends. He didn't get involved in his wife's business, either. Emma came to realise that his reticence was mostly just a front for cowardice. 'I'll see what I can do about getting you some better accommodation,' he'd said to Emma when she'd voiced her astonishment at having to sleep under the stairs. But of course he hadn't stuck up for her, out of fear that his wife might misinterpret his motives. Signora Scabello was of the firm opinion that girls from South Tyrol knew nothing about beds anyway and thought the storeroom must be really cosy for them after the bales of hay she imagined they normally slept on.

In fact, at home Emma and her two sisters had shared a bedroom, with windows looking out over fields. She'd even had a feather duvet and pillow; there'd never been enough money for a mattress, though. Instead, she'd slept on a straw sack filled with corn-cob leaves or wheat straw.

Emma dozed, relishing the warmth of the sun on her feet. The silence was occasionally broken by Steg coughing or turning a page of his book. She was just on the verge of nodding off into deep sleep. Not long ago, she'd had a daydream so vivid the boundary between sleeping and waking had blurred. She felt like she'd gone back to the time when they'd blown up Johann. In her dream, they were no longer separated, and as her reverie continued, it took her to a place where Johann was still alive. Behind her closed eyelids, his body and facial muscles were still animated and even kept on moving long after Emma had opened her eyes. They'd set in motion the leaves on the hedges below the terrace, and the entrance door, which slammed shut for no apparent reason, and the curtains and the fringe on the tablecloth; even the air that flowed into her nostrils was composed of his exhaled breath.

From inside the house a faint clanking sound drifted out onto the terrace; it seemed Antonella was still scouring the pots and pans. Just from the noises they made, Emma could tell what tasks were being performed; she could sometimes even identify individual guests from the sound of their footsteps. The elderly, with dodgy hips, tended to waddle like ducks, while teenagers, impatient for dinner, shuffled up and down outside the entrance dragging their feet sulkily and children skipped along. Emma squinted at the serving table. The girl had forgotten to refill the sugar shakers. The oleanders hadn't been watered first thing, either, and there was a huge pile of ironing waiting in the laundry room. Feeling the left side of her neck starting to tense up, Emma tried shifting position and as she did so brushed against the edge of the table, knocking the tablecloth clip off. A lizard flitted to the far side of the terrace. Steg sat up with a start and twisted around momentarily before returning to his book.

2

There was a small, single-storey outhouse of three or four rooms in the hotel garden; all its windows were shuttered, only the door was open. Through it, I spotted a large washing machine of the kind I'd only ever seen in launderettes, a metal spin-dryer shaking and rocking to and fro, and to the right of the door a trough mounted on bricks, which must have once been used for hand-washing. The instant I saw the laundry block, I felt sure my room was going to be there, but in the event I was wrong.

The woman who'd come to fetch me at the gate and asked me to wait outside on the gravel path by the fountain for the proprietress had disappeared somewhere in the garden. I stood there for a while, then began pushing gravel into little piles with one foot and instantly smoothing them out with the other. Then I started to count the windows of the hotel – they were high double windows and wouldn't be easy to clean – and finally decided, after no-one had emerged and come down the entrance steps to greet me, to leave my suitcase on the path and explore a bit.

In the fountain, the goldfish had gathered under the cool water inflow; in amongst the yellow, red and orange fish, I spotted two shubunkins, whose white dorsal fins looked like they'd been nibbled. Both were smaller and squatter than the other fish and didn't seem able to tolerate being directly under the inflow; one of them kept apart from the main group, and seemed to be having problems with its swim bladder, as its tail kept bobbing up.

Above me loomed an ornamental fountain sculpture, a figure with a porous stone face eroded by time; it seemed a much later addition to the slender, moss-covered column, presumably replacing the topmost bowl, which had been damaged beyond repair. The water gushed out of a makeshift opening under the figure's feet into an overflow basin and from there into the main collecting basin, at the far end of which was a pipe, bent at right angles and with a stopcock, which supplied the fountain with fresh drinking water. At the opposite side of the basin, excess water flowed out through a hole covered by a grating. No doubt the metal grille had been put there to stop any goldfish from being accidentally sluiced down the outflow and falling into the drain at ground level.

I thought of the two fish that, as a child, I'd brought home from the Luna Park fair in a clear plastic bag, much to the annoyance of my mother, who felt sorry for the poor creatures. To begin with, we kept the fish – one was orange, the other black – in a dark bucket; only some weeks later did our neighbour donate an aquarium, the size of a pressure cooker and with coloured gravel on the bottom. We put it on top of the washing machine in the corridor; and every time the spin cycle started, the water surface would crinkle like a strong gust of wind was ruffling it. One time, the orange fish jumped so high that it flipped out of the tank and landed on the washing machine, then slipped onto the tiled floor. I was playing at the other end of the corridor with my doll, whose back you could open and put a miniature music disc in. As I recall, I was listening to the Cat Song – *Quarantaquattro gatti* – which little Barbara Ferigo had performed with the magician Zurlì when she won the *Zecchino d'Oro* TV talent show.

Flapping frantically, the goldfish disappeared under the boiler; I didn't want to touch it, so I yelled for my mum, who'd gone round to the neighbour's for a cigarette. My screams were so loud and piercing that they brought my mother and her friend and the other two neighbours as well running out into the stairwell. Mum got hold of the fish and dropped it back in the tank. It recovered, but a few weeks later had the misfortune to be near the bath plughole when my mother, who was trying to catch the other fish to put it back in the cleaned aquarium, snagged her rolled-up sleeve on the chain and accidentally yanked out the plug. The sudden vortex sucked the fish, which was weakened anyway by its earlier ordeal, into the outflow. As for the black fish, though he never jumped, he still only outlived the orange one by a couple of months. I'd noticed that he found it increasingly difficult diving and was trailing long streams of mucus, and then one day I found him floating on the surface, belly-up and lifeless.

I dipped my right index finger, then my whole hand, into the fountain, until it suddenly occurred to me that I'd be meeting the owner any minute and that when I shook hands with her, she might think the dampness was caused by nervous, sweaty palms. I wiped my hands on my skirt, but was horrified to see that the water left ugly stains on the fabric that wouldn't dry out in time. So I twisted my skirt round, only to discover that the seat was all crumpled and a bit threadbare from too much sitting down.

Behind the fountain, the gravel path opened out onto a part of the garden hidden from the hotel entrance, which was surrounded by low palm trees and shrubs. Hearing the front door creak, I immediately turned back to the fountain, but it was only a guest, a young man in dark clothes and with the air of a priest in training, who nodded briefly at me and headed for the gate.

I looked down and, seeing the sticking-out back pockets of my skirt, which were now at the front, was trying to twist it round again when I heard my name being called. The back and front of the skirt were on my hips and there was no chance now of putting the worn patch back where it belonged.

The proprietress had materialised silently from behind the bushes and was standing to my left in front of the broad marble steps leading to the main entrance.

'How was your journey?' she asked, and without waiting for an answer, added: 'I don't want to see you with your hair down, understood? Either you put it up or get it cut. Didn't they tell you that?'

I began to explain that I hadn't started work yet, but that of course I'd follow the rules to the letter, etcetera, but she cut me off; 'In fact, you're looking a bit of a mess generally.'

And, without glancing in my direction, she started up the steps; I followed, dragging my heavy suitcase. I was relieved that I wasn't going to be living next to the laundry and began to imagine a nice little room overlooking the back courtyard, but the proprietress swept on past reception, heading for the cellar steps, ignoring the old wooden lift waiting with its doors open in the lobby.

'Your skirt's all skewiff,' she said, without turning to look at me.

She waited at the top of the staircase to the basement for me to catch up, nodded curtly at me and, descending a couple of steps, waved her hand in the direction of the corridor at the bottom: 'The ironing room's at the end; you go through it to get to your room. I'll come and fetch you in ten minutes.'

There were various baskets in the ironing room containing creased tablecloths, pillowcases and tea towels. It smelt of bleach and starch. The two windows were at head height and looked out into the garden; but bushes and trees planted close to them meant that no light came in. On the ceiling were four irregularly spaced strip-lights. The garden framed in the windows put me in mind of a painting by Arnold Böcklin, *The Isle of the Dead*, which had hung in our living room at home for years. I'd found the tall cypresses in the picture really threatening, even more sinister than the towering cliffs with windows cut into them. The sight of that island always filled me with a sense of foreboding and the heavy frame that my mother had the print mounted in – painted to look like gold leaf – only set it apart more starkly from the rest of the décor and made my dark imaginings all the more vivid.

I put my case down next to the large ironing machine used for smoothing out linen tablecloths and opened the door to my room.

Here, as in the previous room, you could only reach the windowsills by standing on tiptoe, while the windows could only be opened by climbing on a chair pushed up against the wall. There were two chairs, both covered in clothes, magazines and half-eaten packets of biscuits. Even on the unslept-in bed, someone had left their red cardigan, a flower-pattern skirt and a pile of T-shirts. There was a large wardrobe in the room, too, with posters of Vasco Rossi and Suzi Quatro stuck all over it.

I was at a loss what to do. Unpack? Clear the stuff off the bed? Put the clothes that weren't mine in the wardrobe? A few minutes had already passed, the proprietress would be back any moment now. On a narrow table under the windows I found a portable radio–cassette recorder. I opened the dark grey plastic lid and just had time to read *Massachusetts* on the cassette when I was startled by someone walking by just outside the window. A man's legs in suit trousers. I snapped the lid shut and went to get my suitcase. It was made of brown, grained leather, which had split in several places. 'There's no way I'm buying you a new one,' my mum had said.

The room smelt strongly of starch, but also of varnish. I eased open one of the windows and listened. The man's footsteps had receded, he was on the gravel path now. I found the crunching sound under his feet calming somehow. I thought about the gravel and roadstone quarries on the outskirts of the village and the workings that over the years had been left to fill with ground water and become nature reserves. This was my first summer away from the gravel pits, away from the rumble of dumper trucks and the clatter of conveyor belts. I'd fought tooth and nail to swing myself this holiday job in the South, I'd brought this semi-subterranean room down upon myself, this room with its all-pervasive varnish smell whose source I couldn't trace.

The door flew open and a young woman rushed across to the

wardrobe, then dashed out again without introducing herself. 'Catch you later!' she shouted as she vanished out the door. All I had time to take in was her shoulder-length hair, dyed blonde, a fringe that was a bit too long and stuck out too far, making it look like a porch, and her chipped red nail polish. I noticed this when she'd held the wardrobe door open for a couple of seconds, diving inside before emerging clutching a pinafore and leaving the room as precipitously as she'd entered.

I realised that my palms really were sweaty now and that I was short of breath, and I suddenly regretted having won the battle of wills with my mother. I could hear her now, objecting that I was too young and that the job was too far away and worrying aloud what might become of me, and I pictured her in her tiny kitchen, anxiously wringing the tea towel as she spoke, or breaking up tinned tomatoes with a wooden spoon, bashing down ever more insistently on the base of the pan: 'And don't whatever you do come back pregnant.' I thought of the kitchen window, which Mum had covered with coloured cellophane so she wouldn't have to look down into the yard where, less than a year ago, a woman from the estate had committed suicide. She'd been sitting there all night long in her lemon-yellow Fiat 126, which she'd parked right opposite our window, but nobody had taken any notice of her, because the car was often left in our yard overnight by the woman's husband, who was having an affair with our neighbour in the flat above at the time. Our neighbour hadn't been at home that evening, otherwise she'd surely have recognised the car.

Mum had gone into the kitchen first thing to get herself a glass of water and caught sight of the woman with her head slumped on the steering wheel.

3

Emma Manente managed to intercept Antonella just in time before she walked into the dining room wearing a grubby pinafore. Emma called to mind how, when she first came to Rome, she'd not only had to wear a crisp snow-white apron, but a little maid's cap and cuffs as well, all of which she needed to keep spotlessly clean by hand-washing them in the hotel basement; the only thing she was allowed to send to the laundry were the starched collars of her blouses. In those days there'd been a kind of compost heap in the hotel garden, between the bushes and the moss-covered back wall, where the stray cats used to congregate. Emma had never seen so many scrawny, mangy animals. Whenever she had to take the leftovers down to the garden, generally in the evening when it was already dark, the cats would always spook her. Catching wind of the food, the creatures would mob her, miaow-ing and smooching round her legs and jostling to get at the bucket, setting it swinging with their outstretched paws. Sometimes the cats would lose their grip on the rim of the bucket and make to jump up again and Emma had to shield her legs from their claws by stepping back or leaping to one side, or shooing them away with a tea towel or a broom. The beasts fought over the fish heads and the gnawed chicken bones, spitting and hissing and slashing at one another. The really poorly and weak ones grew even sicker and thinner, with their coats full of scabs, their faces scarred and their eyes gummed shut with pus. They smelt awful. No-one in the hotel looked after them. In Stillbach, stray kittens were taken away from their mothers at birth and either drowned in the stream or had their necks wrung. Back home, misery was quickly tidied away, no smells were permitted and efficient countermeasures were taken against the urge to procreate.

The new girl wasn't Stillbach born and bred. Although Emma's links with the place had dwindled to a dozen or so phone calls home a year, Stillbach was such a small world that she still had her finger on the pulse of the place. Her cousin would have rung her straight away and told her whose daughter was coming to work for her. All Emma knew was that this Ines was the niece of the parish secretary, but she didn't have any more details, as the secretary had only moved to Stillbach a year ago. On the phone, her cousin had said she didn't know the parish secretary personally, or her sister for that matter, but she'd heard that the sister had been widowed some years before and had a teenage daughter. I hope the widow's daughter is here of her own accord, thought Emma. Widows' daughters whose mothers make them earn their keep usually weren't good workers. Emma's favourite girls were those who longed to come to Rome, who expected something from Rome and who saw their work at the hotel as the price they had to pay for being in Rome. She really warmed to girls who thought of Rome as a gift, as a gift implied some obligation, it required gratitude, and Emma knew how to exploit that, demanding punctuality and hard work in return. Emma was convinced that giving was a reciprocal arrangement, otherwise there was no public spiritedness about it. She had Rome to give and in return the girls gave themselves. She liked girls who were prepared to do anything, girls who – just like her all those years ago – hadn't seen much of the world.

Emma had arrived in Venice wearing a summer blouse buttoned right up to the neck and with long sleeves. Her mother had been adamant: 'I don't want you coming back home with one of those blokes from down there in tow.' Before she left – it was the beginning of the week – her mother had stuck her in the washtub and given her back a good scrub, although baths were normally reserved for Saturdays, with the one tub of warm water having to serve for her and all her brothers and sisters too; even then, her mother would scrub woollen socks clean in the used bathwater with curd soap. With her soap-softened fingers, she'd then plait Emma's hair into pigtails. A short haircut for a girl would have been a scandal in Stillbach and Emma only learnt what a bathroom was when she got to Venice; all they had back home was an outside privy. Only much later – she had left home by then – did her parents get a washhouse, with a washing trough that always reminded her of the coffin-like trough for blood and offal in the courtyard of the local butcher's. As kids, they used to lie in it and play at being dead; the bereaved, standing around the edge of the trough, prayed for the deceased. The game was blasphemous, sinful, but at least it gave them something real to own up to when they were forced to go to confession on Sundays.

The new girl didn't look like she'd been to confession once in the last six months. Maybe she wasn't even a widow's daughter. Some women claimed to be widows to avoid the stigma of being known as mothers of illegitimate children. In any event, the new girl was a bit of a risk. Emma didn't know enough about her. She didn't like that long mane of hair for a start – a real come-on to men, if ever there was one. The parish secretary was an incomer who was always done up to the nines, her cousin said. When Emma had fetched up in Rome, no-one had asked her where she'd come from. In those days, lots of women from Stillbach and other villages, young and old alike, had gone begging up and down the valley, after mortgage debts and increased taxes had put lots of families on the breadline. Emma had had no choice but to look for work elsewhere, in her own, foreign country, where, unlike Switzerland or Germany, you didn't need a residence permit. The *Catholic Sunday News* was full of small ads. Plenty of Italian families were looking for *ragazze tedesche* – 'German girls' – who had a good reputation for being fit, efficient, honest, clean and well brought-up. At the same time, the paper warned its readers to beware of girl-traffickers, who it claimed were often of Jewish extraction. Her father had ringed the article and passed it over to her at lunch one day. He'd run across it in the village pub and torn the page out. Emma had never met a Jew, at least not to her knowledge, and the Lady General, as they called her – the local agent for jobs in the South – definitely wasn't a Jew, although she did deal in girls. She met young women at the bus station and took them home with her to interview. Emma had only been in her flat once, but had a distinct memory of the crucifix in the little shrine and the dusty palm fronds with most of their leaves missing. At that time the Lady General hadn't struck her as particularly pious, but at least she wasn't Jewish, that was for sure – or was it all just a cunning disguise? The Lady General passed on prospective employers' addresses to girls and gave them some handy tips, and even read out a couple of passages from a housemaiding magazine called *La brava domestica*. Emma hadn't really taken any of it in; she was overawed by the beautiful flat and the lovely things in it. She was also too ashamed to tell the Lady General that she'd walked most of the way from Stillbach and tried to hide her broken fingernails and her bare feet in clogs.

Emma's clothes may have been shabby, but unlike the new girl at least she'd taken care not to get any stains on them. Emma had tied up her pigtails and made herself look as smart as she could in front of the Lady General, sitting bolt upright on the soft, green velvet-covered chair. Her hostess had served them tea in dainty little glasses in silver filigree holders. Emma could clearly recall their big, looped handles. Years later, she'd bought herself a similar set of glasses, but somehow the tea never tasted as fine in them as it had back then. The two girls from Stillbach who'd come with Emma to see the Lady General were a bit older than her and had already worked in guesthouses. Maria was fed up with cooking from morning till night for an annual wage of 200 lire, especially after hearing that you could earn 130 lire a month in Rome, while the other girl just dreamt of getting some better food:

'No more polenta and nettle soup, that's all I ask!' she exclaimed as they were leaving the Lady General's flat together. She was so delighted she waved the slip of paper with the address of her new employers in the air like a flag.

Emma was standing in the dining-room doorway watching Antonella. The girl wasn't clumsy, but she was slow and she wasted too much time on unimportant things, rearranging the cut flowers in their vases instead of changing the water, or folding serviettes into pretty shapes but forgetting to put out dessert spoons. Emma preferred her to stick to the kitchen, it bothered her when Antonella spent more time than strictly necessary in the dining room. She just didn't cut the right figure there, coming across a bit like some would-be suburban hooker. Her brother and minder was a strapping, good-looking lad, whom Emma was sure would steal the gold chain from around his mother's neck given half the chance. She found it hard believing that this Mimmo earnt a living working in the bakery that used to belong to their late grandfather. Mimmo wasn't remotely like the baker in Stillbach , who had a paunch so big it looked like his own dough was rising in it. His hair had all fallen out prematurely and he sweated buckets. Quite apart from the fact that Emma's family hadn't been able to afford bread back then, Emma was always revolted by the thought of the baker's sweat dripping into the loaves. She was relieved to find that the *filoni* here in Rome didn't taste salty and had a dense, dry crumb to them. All of a sudden, she remembered that there weren't enough *rosette* for dinner, that she needed to check the number of drinks crates that had been delivered at midday and that she hadn't called the travel agent back yet to find out when the next consignment of guests from Germany were due to arrive.

4

The room had had a fresh coat of paint not so long ago. The previous occupants must have stuck pictures or posters on the walls and then taken them down, stripping off the new paint with the sticky tape and leaving a cluster of little dark patches at eye level. I was still unsure what to do, but on the other hand I had no choice. If I demanded my own room, I'd get on the wrong side of the proprietress on day one. I'd never have got the job in the first place without Aunt Hilda's help and she would be the first to learn that I'd blown it. Mum had set her face firmly against my trip to Rome. All journeys made her feel deeply uneasy anyway; she had a dread of open spaces, saying she felt like a marble that couldn't stop rolling the minute it encountered the slightest slope. Since the advent of farming, Mum maintained, Man had been a naturally settled creature, and she had only ever left the village under duress. It was bad enough that her own parents had been forced to move seven times. If Hitler hadn't lost the war against the Soviets, she was sure the family would have been forcibly resettled in the Crimea. She'd got fed up with people calling her an 'Eyetie pot-maker' when she was a kid: then, to crown it all, she said, 'all they did was re-pot us – one minute we were despised for being Italians and the next for being Germans.' Aunt Hilda had burst out laughing when I told her this: 'Your mother should have gone to live in China,' she laughed, 'then she'd have felt nice and safe behind the Great Wall.'

It had taken several attempts to persuade Mum that there was nothing dodgy about a holiday job at the Hotel Manente and that I was a grown-up now. Besides, I'd learn some Italian and earn myself a bit of money, and after studying Latin at school for four years, I'd finally get to see Rome. Aunt Hilda weighed in on my side, reassuring my mother that she knew Stillbach, and that Mrs Manente came from there – as though the village name alone guaranteed the character of its occupants, even acting as a seal of approval for those who'd long since moved away. Mrs Manente, my aunt claimed, was a feisty old bird who looked out for her girls and was utterly trustworthy – *una persona affidabile*, she added, as if tossing in an Italian phrase would somehow clinch the argument.

I opened my suitcase and started putting my T-shirts and jeans away in the wardrobe, which smelt of patchouli oil. In one of the drawers, I found a box full of change: ten-lire, fifty-lire and hundred-lire coins, even five-lire ones, plus some deutschmarks and Austrian schillings and even a few dollar coins; there were also some others I couldn't identify straight away. Was this the other girl's money box? Were they tips?

Even Aunt Hilda wouldn't have approved of this basement room. The mirror on the back of the door had the imprint of a big lipstick kiss on it, bright red, beside which was stuck a newspaper photo of a woman called Gina Loris, who looked like Gina Lollobrigida. There were traces of my roommate everywhere. In the bottom drawer was a stack of women's magazines and some tattered Mickey Mouse comics. I tried to make some space on one side of the wardrobe, put the magazines with the hand towels and stuffed the rest of my things – a few paperbacks, undies and my sponge-bag – into the drawers I'd cleared. When I'd finished tidying things away, I had a pang of conscience, because I'd found a few handwritten envelopes among my roommate's magazines, which I'd bundled together and shoved in her underwear drawer.

I was just looking for somewhere to stow my suitcase when I heard footsteps; a moment later, I saw a pair of legs framed in the window again, only this time they weren't in suit trousers but drainpipe jeans.

'Antonella!' came a voice. I hid behind the wardrobe door and kept stock-still.

The man called her name, quietly, a few more times; I also got the impression he bent down to see whether she was in the room but finally, after shoving a scrunched-up piece of paper through the open crack of the tilted window, he went away again. It landed at my feet. I could hear my own breathing and crept out from my hiding place. At that moment, there was a knock at the door; I scooped up the note and tucked it into my waistband.

'Right, let's see if we can find a pinafore to fit you,' said the proprietress.

Suddenly, I longed to be back in the cavernous ticket hall of the Termini station, where I'd arrived barely an hour ago. Its curving roof had none of the boxiness of this hotel, or of the harsh angularity of its owner's face.

'Well, what size are you?'

'I'm not really sure', I replied. I didn't dare pull in my stomach to look slimmer, or the note would have fallen out.

'What, you don't know your own size?' We were standing in front of a fitted cupboard in the ironing room, which she'd just unlocked. Pulling out a pile of pinafores, she gave me a quick once-over before selecting one and handing it to me: 'This'll probably do.'

I grasped the pinny and glanced about me helplessly. There was nowhere private for me to change. Should I just strip off in front of the proprietress? She stood there waiting impatiently. 'Don't worry, I've seen plenty of girls' bodies in my time', she reassured me briskly.

All the same, I turned around and tried to slip out of my skirt without letting the note fall out. Easing my skirt down with one hand, I pressed the note firmly against my stomach with the other and managed to slip it, unseen, under my clothes as I deposited them on the ironing board.

The pinny was a bit tight around my bust.

'Turn around.' As I gave a twirl, the proprietress smoothed her hand over the back of my pinafore. 'Just leave the top button undone for the time being,' she said, 'we'll search you out something better tomorrow morning.'

I was just about to do up the lower buttons when she leaned over and handed me my clothes. The note fluttered to the floor.

It was close in the ironing room; I only realised now that I was sweating. The proprietress put my clothes back on the ironing board and picked up the note. She glanced round the room like she was looking for other signs of untidiness to explain this scrap of paper, but everything else was neat and tidy, the floor was as clean as a whistle with no pieces of broken buttons or cotton threads lying around and the dried washing was all in the proper baskets.

I grabbed my clothes with one hand and made to take the note back with the other. The proprietress didn't respond. Instead, she looked at me coolly and, without a word, started to unfold the paper.

'I was just about to throw it away when you…'

'So, did you meet him on the train, then?' She was pointing at something scribbled on the paper that I couldn't decipher from a distance.

'I've no idea what the note says.'

'Oh, really? You're not even here a day yet and already you're making assignations? I've taken on responsibility for you. If you don't want me to put you straight back on the next train, you'll forget about him right now.' She tapped the paper angrily with her index finger a few times and then screwed it up in her meaty hands, like she was kneading dumplings. 'And you can put that grubby skirt of yours in with the dirty laundry. I'll show you where.'

Aunt Hilda had told me that Mrs Manente had spent the war in Rome because she'd got pregnant. Not by a soldier, but the hotel proprietor's son. By some lowly Italian, in other words. While the other women from South Tyrol living in Rome had all, almost without exception, opted to go and live in the Third Reich and drifted back to their home villages to join their parents and siblings for the trek across the border, the young Manente girl had decided to stay put in Rome. Down in the South, Aunt Hilda explained, Emma Manente had been the *porca tedesca,* the German slag, while back in Stillbach, she was seen as a traitor. But she'd got a child, and a husband. And later she got the hotel too, after the death of her husband. Exactly what he died of, even Aunt Hilda, who made a point of knowing everybody's business, hadn't been able to find out. It was Aunt Hilda, then, who'd got in touch with the proprietress's cousin, the only relative in Stillbach Mrs Manente was still on friendly terms with. She'd fallen out with her brothers and sisters and hadn't been back to the village for ten years, Aunt Hilda said. That was when her mother died. Emma had attended the requiem mass and joined the funeral procession, but hadn't spoken to anyone.

I followed the proprietress; she was a heavily-built woman but with a slight stoop. The South wasn't made for women like her, even the ironing board was far too low. No doubt all the furniture in the hotel had been acquired by her mother-in-law, one of those dainty little Italian women, condemning the proprietress to a lifetime of bending down to get at things.

From the ironing room, a long corridor led down towards the kitchen; in-between were the stairwell and the life. The laundry bags and various appliances were stored behind a curtain underneath the stairs, as there was a little overspill dining-room next to the kitchen that was used by guests.

I was introduced to the cook, Ada Cocola, who'd come to fetch me at the gate. She looked like a rough draft of the actress Anna Magnani. Her hair was tucked up under a white cloth whose ends she'd knotted together on her forehead. She was tight-lipped and came across as unfriendly. She reminded me of my maths teacher at the grammar school, whose mood you could read from her look even before she spoke. My roommate stood beside Cocola, peeling apples. Apart from Antonella, there only appeared to be one other kitchen helper. His efforts to try to make himself look older than he really was only succeeded in emphasising his boyishness. He was wearing sand-coloured suede sandals with thin soles and a huge shirt collar stuck out from under the bib of his blue apron. Shaking my hand, he announced *Piacere!* – 'My pleasure!' – which was greeted with hoots of derisive laughter from the others. 'We're not at a conference, Gianni,' Antonella said. Cocola disappeared into the cool room and the proprietress, who had been lurking by the door and saying nothing the whole time, pulled the screwed-up note from her pocket and summoned Antonella. 'What's the meaning of this?' she asked her, all the while keeping her gaze firmly fixed on me.

Antonella spun round to face me. Gianni plucked nervously at his apron. Ada Cocola came back carrying a huge piece of meat, which she slammed down theatrically on the marble-topped table; it sounded like a slap in the face.

'Haven't the foggiest,' said Antonella, shrugging her shoulders. 'Who's it supposed to be from, anyway?'

'So, playing dumb, are we? Just like your colleague here. Just you wait, I'll get to the bottom of this.' Saying this, she took a couple of steps out into the corridor, then stopped in her tracks and came back in: 'And another thing – the shakers on the terrace table need refilling.'

5

Towering summer clouds swept over the city, casting shadows as they went. Emma had always loved dramatic skies with billowing clouds like the ones back home in Stillbach, which shrouded the mountaintops and ushered in nightfall, a time when all the farmyard animals grew restless.

One moment, Emma was way down in the base of the valley, with the cloud-capped mountains looking like their peaks had been broken off, and then in the next instant, she was swooping over the grey-white sea of cloud, with the mountaintops rising out of it like islands. She tossed and turned fitfully from one side of the bed to the other. Now she was looking at a workman laying paving, who was using his hammer and chisel to trim down a recalcitrant stone that wouldn't fit into its allotted space. He was kneeling on the ground and had a roll-up stuck in the corner of his mouth. Occasionally, he'd pause and look up at the lowering clouds, then turn the stone in his hands, appraising its form, before laying into it once more; in the brief moments when the sun broke through the clouds, she could see his neck glistening with sweat.

Woken by a sudden noise, Emma glanced around the bedroom, in the dim light cast by the lamp on her bedside table. What were those mountains she'd been flying over? Had she heard someone knocking at the door, or imagined it from the hammering in her dream? Was it just the paver banging home his troublesome stone? In her mind's eye, she still had a vivid image of the little man, dressed in shorts and bending over the sand bed where most of the paving stones had already been laid, arranged in a herringbone pattern. But when Emma tried dragging over a bucket of cement screed for the workman to brush into the joints, it turned out that the pattern wasn't complete and that some stones were missing. Time and again, he patiently removed the stones he'd already laid and prepared a new sand bed for them, seemed finally to complete the job and then…

Was there a thunderstorm brewing? Emma got up and went to see whether there was anyone at the door of her flat. She stopped for a moment in the stairwell and listened. The hotel was deathly quiet. Outside, a wind was getting up.

She went back to bed, but found she couldn't sleep anymore. There were an increasing number of nights now when she'd find herself wandering aimlessly round the room, flicking through a newspaper, or just staring at the pattern on the wallpaper, unable to get to sleep. Who did that paver look like? Johann? Mimmo? Hermann Steg? Franz, whom she hadn't heard from in over a month? Her late husband? Or even the pusillanimous Signor Scabello?

The first time she'd travelled to Venice by train, the other passengers had peered in through the compartment windows and pointed at her crude shoes. If only they could see her now. Outside Venice Santa Lucia station, there was a group of men hanging round the canal whose trousers had been trimmed roughly at the bottoms and which were held up by pieces of string instead of belts. Their clothes were no less shabby than her brothers' back in Stillbach, who worked as day-labourers for various farmers in the neighbourhood.

Emma was terrified that no-one would come to pick her up from the station and that the address the Lady General had given her was wrong. She waited there over an hour for Signor Scabello. Several men approached her, even the father of a family who'd just put his wife and two children on a train and doubled back to chat her up, murmuring obscenities in her ear. She came within an ace of simply jumping on a departing train, no matter where it was headed, just to get away from this station.

A gust of wind shook the palms outside her window. The neon sign outside the Esso filling station opposite suddenly went out, flickering a few times behind the red lettering before it finally gave up the ghost. The power failure had plunged her room into total darkness, too. Emma got up again and felt around in the bedside cabinet for a torch.

When it came, the thunder sounded like the distant rumble of artillery. Her father had served in a rifle brigade up in the mountains and had been able to look down through his binoculars at the far side of the valley and see the cornfields around Stillbach ripening and becoming ready for harvesting. But there were no men left there to harvest it. Her mother had worked out in the fields all day long and tended the livestock – a few hens and three goats – first thing in the morning and last thing at night. Her two older brothers lodged with and worked for local farmers, like they were foster children, while she and her sisters were shut up in the house during the day. What was her mother supposed to do with them, after all? When the big guns started firing, Emma and her sisters used to creep under the bench by the stove.

Emma still hated the sound of thunder, although here in the South it was less threatening, because there weren't any mountains for it to reverberate off. She switched off the bedside lamp so it wouldn't suddenly light up when the power came back on and wake her up again. She had to stop thinking about Stillbach. But sleep just wouldn't come. Somewhere on the upper floors, the shutters kept banging against the wall in the wind. Emma had specifically asked Antonella to secure them. Now that the new girl was there, they could finally get on with cleaning the blinds. Especially the blinds on the ground floor, which were in full sight of the guests, and needed years of dust and spiders' webs wiping off them.

Lightning lit up the room at ever-decreasing intervals. Emma lay rolled-up tightly on her bed and gazed at the bedside table, where she'd put the small collection of framed photos her cousin had sent her over the years. Illuminated by the lightning flashes, the pictures looked like someone was taking them all over again and momentarily Emma even got the feeling that, in the black-and-white portrait done at Gugler's Studios, her mother was trying to force a smile. The photo of her father was hidden behind her jewellery box.

Even through her tightly shut eyelids, Emma could still see the flashes. There were no storm warnings down here, nobody climbed up church towers and rang the bells to signal the approach of a thunderstorm. And nobody prayed for the hailstorm to miss their fields and orchards and spare their maize from being flattened or their fruit from being ruined. Emma dragged the sheet right over herself and when that didn't work she buried her head under the pillow. But this only made an abyss open up behind her closed eyes and her breathing sounded so sonorous that she sat up with a start.

Sitting there bolt upright in her bed, she felt suddenly exposed. Not even Franz was there for her. Especially not him. She stayed frozen in an awkward position, with her legs stretched out and her back hunched forward.

After the war, she hadn't experienced many more thunderstorms in Stillbach. At the beginning of the 1950s, in an attempt to patch things up with her family, she'd travelled up to see her cousin. Emma's meeting with her mother that time had lasted just half an hour. Her mother had sneaked out of the house to come and see her and was fearful lest Emma's father should hear about their rendezvous. Or her brothers, for that matter. Her mother had looked careworn and over-worked; her hair, once so thick and luxuriant, had thinned and her eyes had disappeared almost entirely behind swollen, droopy lids; they looked like two tiny, black buttons, as lifeless as if they'd been sewn in place. 'It's no good, love,' she said wearily. They'd refrained from hugging one another. All Emma could manage was to squeeze her mother's shoulder awkwardly, just the once, suddenly jerking back her hand in alarm when they started firing loud anti-hail rockets up into the thunderclouds from the outskirts of the village. Her mother took the opportunity to tie her headscarf on and dash off, leaving Emma to wonder what she'd been more frightened of – the approaching storm or the grilling she'd get at home. Shortly afterwards, the heavens opened.

Once, towards the end of the war, her mother had sent her a letter in Rome, penned in her formal handwriting; the two pages were riddled with grammatical errors but written in impeccable old German black-letter script. The loops on the capital letters were so regular they looked like they'd been printed; her mother must have laboured over the letter for days. In it, she listed every last bit of livestock they owned. And all the villagers who'd passed away: the traitors and the loyalists, the deserters and those who remained true to the Reich. And she talked of Johann, whose father had been devastated by the loss of his eldest son. '*How can you stay there, in the place where they murdered him?*' she wrote. '*Come back home. And if there's no other way, bring the kid with you, too.*'

But there was another way. Emma couldn't envisage living at home anymore and she certainly couldn't imagine living as a single mother with a child that already had a father. And there were the father's parents to think about, not to mention his promise of marriage, even if at that time she still believed he'd only said it as a way of defusing the situation. Plus Emma had been allowed to remain at the hotel and not been banished like other servants in trouble – that gave her some cause for hope, for believing that she really did belong here, or at least that the family thought of the child as one of their own.

There was a huge thunderclap directly overhead. Emma had clasped her hands together like she was physically trying to keep a grip on herself. The Esso sign rocked violently back and forth and the palm trees were bent double in the gale, bending almost to the ground and then springing back up. Emma counted the seconds between the light-ning and the thunder, but there must have been several thunderstorms raging concurrently, for even while a thunderclap struck close by, in the distance she could also hear the kind of faint rumbling that normally only set in once a storm had passed.

In Stillbach, she'd even been able to hear thunder in stereo as it bounced back off the mountain slopes. But then everything in Stillbach came at you from at least two directions, Emma thought. Anyone whose hearing was well enough attuned didn't just pick up the echo. Take the Aryan lineage certificate that her cousin had spirited away from Emma's mother's bedside table to give to her own son, a budding historian – stuff like that showed that it was impossible to pigeonhole things neatly. Emma had been gratified to learn from her cousin that, even in her family, Italian names predominated from as recently as the second generation. *Only those who are of German blood can become an Aryan comrade.* As soon as Italian blood began to seep in, the entries in the family tree abruptly ceased. Emma's father maintained that a fire in 1860 had destroyed all the documents, making all further investigation pointless. To dispel any lingering suspicions, he'd been one of the first people to join the Party and later had even disowned his own daughter. He'd let it be known to Emma that it was inexcusable for her to have taken up with some yellow-belly Italian. When the going had got really tough, the spaghetti-eaters had simply quit the war. 'We could have won in Russia if only they hadn't meddled in Greece and had sorted out their own dissidents once and for all.' He wasn't about to welcome some back-stabbing partisan into the family. He'd always been against Emma leaving Stillbach in the first place.

Time and again the room was lit by lightning. Emma flinched, rummaged in the bedside table drawer and popped another sleeping tablet out of its blister. When enough saliva had collected in her mouth, she swallowed the tablet. Wrapping herself in the bedclothes once more, she caught herself murmuring a prayer to her guardian angel, imploring him to keep the hotel intact – and, of course, the poor in their shanty-towns too, with their wooden and corrugated iron shacks and dented cars. The storm was so violent that the angel had trouble folding his wings. He was flying with his back to the light, and as he was caught by a strong gust and swept away, all he could do was shake his head at all the junk being blown around.

6

The pinkish stone, interspersed with bushes, unfolded before me, the trees in the apple orchards with their propped-up trunks and the towering poplars marking the beginning or end of a plot. I could hear Aunt Hilda's voice and feel Mum's hands, and tossed and turned from one side of the bed to the other. What relief I'd felt when the valley finally narrowed towards Salorno and the ruins of Haderburg Castle came into view. The keep on its towering rocky outcrop stood there like an abrupt caesura in the line of hills. Soon after, the train swept through the gorge and I was released from that claustrophobic, enclosed landscape; I'd passed through the airlock separating the places where Austro-Bavarian and Italian are spoken. The mountains grew brighter and before me unfolded the Piana Rotaliana, at whose apex the Valle di Non begins – the valley from which my great-grandfather, a day-labourer dressed in rags, emigrated into the lowlands through the Gola di Rocchetta.

I closed my eyes, but it did no good. I couldn't block out the sound of rustling paper: Antonella was reading a *fotoromanzo*, flicking back and forth through it like she was looking for a specific page. So for the time being, I was condemned to replay in my head a confused welter of immediate impressions and memories from my journey down to Rome. The squashy mattress and the all-pervading stuffiness of our shared room did nothing to improve my mood. I sniffed the fabric of my nightie, which smelt of home and still somehow retained, pressed into its creases, Mum's hand movements as she ironed. As I breathed in the scent of the familiar washing powder and fabric softener, I fancied that the mountain air had impregnated the cotton. In my mind's eye, I could see the washing flapping in the breeze on a line tied to a walnut tree – truth was, though, all we had at home were a fold-out rack on the balcony and a communal drying area up in the loft.

I'd really been looking forward to my summer in the South, to the plants with their heady scent, whose leaves grow fuzzy or waxy to cope with drought, and their spiny stems and the gnarled tree trunks, but down here in the basement all I could think of was the lush grass of home, the moss and the waterfalls, which from a distance looked like chalk lines scribbled on a slate. The picture I conjured up was of the tarmac car-park behind our block and the vegetable allotment with a chain-link fence round it to stop the neighbourhood dogs from getting in, and my mother's black hands as she pulled up carrots.

There was a rumble of thunder in the distance. Antonella switched off the bedside lamp. I could feel a tightness in my chest I knew only too well from school, just before taking an exam, and realised that my breathing was constricted. This sensation only grew when I thought of our estate and the council flats that had been built to tackle the post-war housing shortage. From my poky cellar room, the simple state-subsidised workers' apartment blocks seemed positively bright and appealing. Even the scathing term 'Fanfani boxes' that Aunt Hilda applied to them made me think of 'fanfares' rather than the Italian employment minister who'd started the whole scheme.

Antonella had come to bed after me and immediately launched into a diatribe against Mrs Manente, her obsession with cleanliness, the way she bullied all her staff except Cocola, who behaved like she was secretly the real owner of the hotel. Ada Cocola came from a fascist family, Antonella knew for sure, and she and the Manente woman were as thick as thieves. 'That's why we get so many German guests,' Antonella continued, 'they're among friends here.' As she said this, she gave me a look which implied that she numbered me among the German fascists; she seemed to take my silence as tacit support for Manente. I began to feel embarrassed that I'd put my things away in the wardrobe so tidily.

Antonella shed her pinny, took off her bra in front of me and laughed, most likely because I'd turned my face away, or maybe she was just amused at the neat arrangement of my clothes in the wardrobe. She didn't like Germans, because they'd deported her grandfather. 'They rounded up all the men on the outskirts of the city, herded them into the grounds of the Cinecittà film studio and carted them off to forced labour camps. Of course,' she went on, 'that's not your fault, but you're one of them all the same.' Her grandfather had been put to work in a chemical factory, handling dangerous salts and acids. 'When he came back, he was red all over like he'd got scabies, and coughed up blood for the rest of his life.'

She couldn't remember the name of the factory: 'Sickert… Scickert, was that it?' In any event, she said, they'd made chemical weapons there. The works were in a narrow valley that shielded them from air raids: 'It's all narrow valleys where you come from, too, isn't it?'

'Actually, from Stillbach you can see the whole of the valley,' I replied, even though I wasn't from Stillbach.

No, come what may, I was *one of them*. What could I say in my defence? That I had an Italian passport, that my father – an Italian – had never given a toss about my mother and me? That my grandmother was called Annesi on her mother's side? But what good would it have done to reel off names, when there were people up in South Tyrol who had Italian surnames but still peddled German nationalist propaganda? Or if I'd added that it wasn't just that castle on the border between the two cultures that had been the subject of bitter quarrels and fighting, but that down the ages the entire region had been one big bone of contention between bigots with a chip on their shoulder?

In the meantime, Antonella clearly thought I'd nodded off, since just a few minutes after she'd switched off the light, I heard a soft whistle outside and the slats under her mattress creak as she got up and tiptoed over to the window. She stayed there motionless for a moment, presumably to make quite sure I was fast asleep.

The kitchen had been the scene of a fierce argument that evening, about the crisis facing the government and the forthcoming presidential election. Antonella was sure Sandro Pertini could count on the votes not just of the far left but Bettino Craxi's socialists as well; Cocola had called her an ignorant Commie stooge. 'That'll look just great, won't it, having some partisan bitch as our First Lady?' she called out from behind the larder door while putting leftovers away on the shelves.

'And a partisan as President!' Gianni chimed in.

'All your lot can do is kidnap judges and assassinate politicians,' Cocola went on. It was the first time I'd heard her utter anything more than a few terse orders.

Many of the names they bandied about as they argued meant nothing to me. At the time I had no idea who Sossi was, or what Sindona had done, but later learnt that he'd been involved in banking fraud, Mafia dealings and the P2 masonic lodge, and that he'd ended up being poisoned in prison by cyanide in his coffee to ensure his silence.

'The Christian Democrats didn't lift a finger to help Moro,' retorted Antonella, 'The fact is, your lot were getting mourning posters printed even before the Red Brigades killed him: *Aldo Moro: Victim of Murder – He Lives on in Our Hearts* – Ha! They're the heartless bastards; they were all too happy to sacrifice him.' Antonella, who was standing behind the table, flung the bowls used for mixing salad into the washing-up water so violently that oil and vinegar splashed all over the tiles behind the sink and the wall above. Mrs Manente, who came into the kitchen at that moment, told her to take the bowls out of the sink and put them back in again, only this time with 'some decorum'. She also made Antonella clean the tiles and the wall at the end of her shift, standing over her until the work was done to her satisfaction.

I heard the low whistle again, followed by the whisper of a man's voice, unknown to me, though I suppose it might just have been the softness of the tone that made it unfamiliar. Was it the same guy who'd dropped the screwed-up note through the window?

'I've got the key,' he hissed.

Antonella got dressed; I sneaked a quick look, but immediately closed my eyes again. Not much light from the street lamps shone into the room, because the garden on this side of the building was surrounded by a wall about two and a half metres high. In the darkness, I could just make out Antonella's silhouette and saw that she was bending down to lace up her trainers. She left the room straight after.

At last, I could switch on my lamp and didn't have to pretend to be asleep any more to get some peace. In the hour and a half that Antonella had been in the room, I'd not only picked up a whole string of Roman insults, but also learnt that that *fija de'na mignotta* – 'whore's daughter' – Manente was a widow and that she didn't believe in coincidence but thought that everything was ordained by God's will. As far as Antonella was concerned, she didn't reckon God possessed free will. I also learnt that the Italian Communist Party had clean hands, but that Cocola's and Manente's hands had decades of dirt clinging to them. Antonella hadn't shown much interest in learning anything from me. Finally, she asked me whether I'd ever heard of the *indiani metropolitani* and, without waiting for my reply, pulled her stack of magazines out from under the bed.

I glanced over at the wardrobe; our pinafores sagged limply on the hooks like hanged men. When I closed my eyes again, all I could see were three-dimensional, coloured forms floating around a vast space. I had no idea where these coloured patterns came from. Was it just my tiredness? It was humid in the room and still reeked of varnish. I wrapped myself tightly in the sheet; as I moved, the bed rocked like a small wooden rowing boat caught in the wake of a large passing ship. Although I'd closed my eyes, I could still make out a sort of flickering; I sat up in bed, thinking that someone might be flashing a torch into the room. Only then did I hear the rumble of thunder. To try to get some sleep, I decided to put the mattress on the floor and switched off the light.

I woke up again around four. Antonella's bed was still empty. It had rained in the night; I could smell the wet earth and thought of the stream behind our estate where the primary school teacher's kid had drowned, which became a torrent after thunderstorms, strong enough to sweep boulders along. Just after I'd left home on my trip, the locals got together for a group photo, but posed in such a way that there was always someone missing, or bending down, or hidden behind someone else.

7

A tour party from Stuttgart was milling around reception, a dozen impatient new arrivals with cases so massive that Emma double-checked the register, unable to believe that they were only staying a week. Most of their luggage was secured with padlocks, while two leather suitcases also had zip-up nylon covers. One of the women wanted an attic room, while another, who wore her hair in a topknot and a dress buttoned up to the neck, asked for a ground-floor room as she was scared of heights. Yet another insisted on giving a blow-by-blow account of her knee replacement; Emma was able to reassure her that the hotel had a lift.

'So, you're going to trust that rickety old cage,' said her husband, who in the few minutes since they'd arrived had already gone up and down several times in the lift between reception and the first-floor landing. 'If you get stuck in there, it'll take days for anyone to get you out.'

Emma, who'd started to enter the guests' names and passport numbers into the register, was about to say that at least the lift's open metal cage meant there'd be no problem breathing if it got stuck, when the phone rang. It was Franz. Emma couldn't make out what he was saying. The new arrivals were making too much noise, laughing at a lift joke someone had just cracked, talking about which rooms they wanted, like they already knew the hotel, and discussing their plans for the evening.

'Now's not a good time – call me again in about quarter of an hour,' Emma said to Franz. The woman with the topknot nodded in agreement and rolled her eyes when Emma ducked down under the reception desk to try to hear a bit better. The only things she was able to catch were *Ferie d'agosto* and 'I can't make it any earlier'; the rest was drowned out by the hubbub of the Germans and by the roar of traffic at Franz's end. He was calling from a public phone box; Emma could hear him feeding in tokens and then saying to someone 'Oh, shit! I'm running out of coins.'

All at once, the solitude and panic of the previous night came flooding back and the conscious effort she'd made that morning to pull herself together suddenly evaporated. As she watched, the new arrivals became puppets, teetering to and fro like they were subject only to the laws of pendular motion and the force of gravity. The knee woman's husband, who'd launched into a lecture about how unsafe Italian lifts were, suddenly looked as though he were made out of painted papier-mâché and his gesticulating arms were being moved by unseen strings.

The line went dead. Emma noticed that her writing hand was shaking and that a patina of sweat had formed on her face. She hailed the new girl, who'd appeared in the stairwell: 'Come here and take down the guests' details, will you? The names go in the left-hand column, then the passport number and date of issue, and on the right you put their home addresses.' It was all that Emma could do to hand over the room keys to the couples and the single woman. The smart aleck reminded Emma of her own father when he was young; she hadn't had the opportunity to get to know him when he got older. Apparently, over time he'd grown less irascible and turned into a lugubrious couch potato, but after downing a couple of glasses of red wine, he'd come out with long, beautifully constructed and complicated sentences, which astonished the rest of the family. No-one could fathom where this new-found eloquence had come from all of a sudden. And they weren't Nazi diatribes either, her cousin had said.

The first time Emma had gone back to Stillbach from Rome, wearing an altered dark red dress that had belonged to her mother-in-law but was now too big for her, her father had snatched it from her room that same evening and cut it to ribbons on the chopping block. There was no reasoning with him. Her mother had told her she'd better leave again straight away. Only the money that Emma had earnt in Rome was welcome back home.

Even though most of the new guests were only staying on the first floor, almost all of them took the lift. They all, it seemed, wanted to experience a *frisson* of danger; one of the men rattled the elevator cage to see how secure it was.

Emma flopped down on the leather sofa in reception and looked at the new girl, whose neck and cleavage were covered in red blotches. Ines was still bent over the register, writing in the details, but suddenly looked up, staring straight at Emma. 'May I ask you something, please?' she began, pausing to swallow hard. 'Would it be possible to have my own room?'

'What's wrong with the one you've got?' Emma shifted her position, leaning forwards slightly.

'Nothing; it's just that I'd rather be on my own.'

'Listen, you're here to learn Italian, aren't you? Antonella's a good girl. You'll get used to her. I did, so you can.'

Emma was still sweating; she wiped her forehead with her palm. One of her colleagues from back then, whom she used to run into at the Church of Santa Maria dell'Anima, had had to sleep in the kitchen in a collapsible box-bed. Another spent her nights on a camp-bed in a corridor, in full view of her employers, who had to squeeze past her whenever they went to the toilet in the night. That girl hadn't even had her own wardrobe and had been forced to store her personal belongings in the broom cupboard. Emma had really fallen on her feet in Rome and not just where accommodation was concerned; all the time she'd worked for the Manentes as a chambermaid and kitchen help she'd been well treated. She'd even managed to amass loads of cigar and cigarette butts that she'd squirreled away and sent to her father. She'd brought Johann a handful one time, too.

Ines didn't reply. She went straight back to the register, only glancing over at Emma now and then. Emma stayed put, fearful lest Franz should ring again. She had no idea where he was right now. Probably busy making speeches at political meetings ('Don't ask – you wouldn't understand anyway'). Remo's death eight years ago had drawn a line under the endless wrangling between father and son, the constant arguments about political affiliations and where the country was headed. Emma had hated the way they bickered endlessly, but at least back then she'd been able to glean some information on what Franz was up to from her husband's recriminations and accusations. The *Feste de l'Unità* rallies that Francesco had been attending for years were just designed to fund the Communist Party and its newspaper, Remo had complained. 'If Francesco isn't studying, he should be working in the hotel,' he insisted. Remo never referred to him as *Franz*. He sometimes called him *Franziskus* when he was trying to make the point that Emma and her son were cut from the same cloth. A few years back, Emma had gone to one of the rallies. She'd actually enjoyed it. The formal debating sessions were boring, but the talks by writers and actors had been interesting, and there were some nice bookstalls and snack bars. In the end Franz had grown impatient with her, though. He couldn't be looking out for her the whole time, he said, and whisked her off home again. She would have loved to stay on for a bit, watching the old couples who came out in the evening to dance to Italian folk music. The men were usually small and emaciated-looking and clung on to their plump wives like children who tug at their mothers' skirts when they want something.

The new girl finished filling out the register and Emma let her go on her break, but not before telling her what needed to be done later.

'And get yourself a piece of cake from the kitchen if you want,' Emma called after her.

As she walked away, Ines made a point of drawing herself up to her full height; it seemed like she was consciously holding her head in the air.

Emma sat there, hunched over, with her eyes shut and her hair plastered to her temples. Large sweat stains had formed beneath her armpits. She was thinking of the alpine meadows above Stillbach, the mountain mere that you came to after a walk of almost two hours, and the refreshing coolness of its waters after the rigours of the climb. She was always so eager to reach the little wooded lake that she pushed herself hard on the walk. She'd never swum there, because swimming was looked upon as a sin in Stillbach, but she had dabbled her hands and feet in it. Only her brothers and Johann and a few other boys had been bold enough to jump in. The black water of the mere made it look large and dangerous, an impression even the fragrant water lilies couldn't dispel.

Then Emma had travelled to Venice for the first time and gone to the Lido with the Scabellos; she was amazed to see that everything in her field of vision was water – salty, limpid water, which grew darker near the horizon and appeared to stretch as far as the eye could see and then some. On this beach, her beloved mountain lake seemed little more than a large washtub.

Emma had been lent a bathing costume by Mrs Scabello, but hid in the bathing hut for ages, not daring to step outside and show her milk-white skin. She felt naked. And once she did venture on the beach, she kept constantly on guard, looking round every which way as surreptitiously as she could, until she suddenly realised that Stillbach was many hours away from Venice and that she was completely incognito here. Because she didn't know how to swim, she had nothing to do, so just sat in a deckchair and gazed out to sea. It reminded her of a vast cloth that someone kept tugging on to smooth out the wrinkles, but however hard they tried new and bigger ones kept appearing, while the breeze gusted into the striped sunshades just like it did in the trees at home, setting them flapping.

Four decades had passed since then. Back then, the war hadn't yet started, Emma's family were all still living in Stillbach and hadn't yet had to opt for staying in Italy or crossing the border to follow the Führer.

Emma sank deeper into the leather sofa; her eyelids felt heavy. When Remo was still alive, she'd sometimes taken Franz down to the beach at Ostia. She'd sit and watch him swimming backstroke; he always had a very determined expression on his face, with his chin pressed hard against his chest, and with his toes turned inwards so that even his feet, which were on the large side, looked smaller and more dainty. He had a powerful kick and would have made a good lifeguard.

Why hadn't he called again? Didn't he even have enough money these days to phone her? And how come he hadn't found himself a wife yet? When that film director had been murdered in Ostia three years ago, Franz had wept openly. Emma was shocked at his display of grief and for weeks after she'd been plagued by the thought that Franz might be gay, but hadn't plucked up the courage to ask him. Then, at Christmas, he'd turned up at home with a woman, that rather blowsy, curly-haired girl from Trieste, who'd left clothes lying all over the place and insisted on having breakfast served up in her room. Even so, Emma had been so relieved that she'd brought her espresso and fresh croissants in bed, in person.

'Long day?'

Emma hadn't noticed that Hermann Steg had come up the marble steps and was now standing framed in the main doorway. She sat up with a start, crossed her legs and folded her arms. 'So, how was your day?' she responded.

It seemed like he was about to slope off without answering and Emma was relieved she wouldn't have to make small talk. But then he suddenly doubled back and came and sat down on the sofa next to her. 'I went to look at some fragments of Roman sundials,' he replied. *'God created Time, but He said nothing about Haste.'*

Steg looked at her in astonishment.

'It was an inscription on a sundial on a house in the village where I grew up,' she said. 'It never told the right time, though.'

'Roman sundials were never right either, apparently. Most of them were brought back as plunder from cities in the far south of Greece.'

Steg had crossed his legs as well and Emma looked at both of their right feet, at her and Steg's toes, as they jiggled to the same rhythm.

8

Loretta Goggi's *Ancora innamorati* was blasting out at full volume from the tape recorder. Antonella was lying on the bed, with her arms folded behind her head, staring at the ceiling. I cleared a chair of clothes and sat down, unbuttoning my pinny. After last night, I was hoping that Antonella might be catching up on lost sleep, but she was captivated by the song, even attempting to sing along, which she managed for a while before losing the thread and lapsing into humming the tune; in the chorus, she struggled to hit the right pitch. I longed for some peace and quiet and wanted to read, but was forced to listen to the music. Antonella belted out the line *chi sara più forte di noi due* – 'Which of us will be stronger?' – at the top of her lungs. I asked her to turn it down a bit but she ignored me. Once I'd made myself comfortable on the bed, though, she shot up and switched off the tape player. 'Spoilsport,' she sulked.

No sun penetrated the room, and no dry air either, as Antonella had closed all the windows so no-one outside could hear her music. I didn't dare ask whether I could have a window open, just a crack to get some fresh air. Outside, birds were twittering and the breeze was wafting the smell of jasmine and blowing the leaves outside the windows, allowing dappled light to twinkle through – but inside it was dark and humid.

'Trouble is, there's no music in your language,' said Antonella. 'You can't bear it that down here we can all sing – doesn't matter whether we're rich or poor, young or old. The only people who sing up your way are perfectionists and drunkards.'

I thought of the German women's choir I'd seen on the beach at Rimini on my last holiday with Mum and Aunt Hilda: they'd sung Schubert's setting of Goethe's *Heidenröslein*. Behind the choir, kids had been chucking sand at one another; there wasn't a rose in sight. As the tide came in, it lapped round the women's feet, but in the burning midday sun, they'd kept on singing all the same, assailed by the wind and waves. Their fleshy bodies, clad in bikinis and swimsuits, quivered to the reverberation of their powerful voices. The women had let the straps of their bikini tops or one-pieces dangle down, or had tied them round the back, to stop them leaving white lines on their tanned cleavages. All their swimsuits, almost without exception, had a bold flower pattern.

We didn't sing much, it was true. We only joined the church choir before we got married. We learnt the notes and just kept quiet when we weren't familiar with the repertoire. I heard this 'We' like an echo in my head.

'So who do you mean by "You"?' I asked. I knew plenty of songs by Antonello Venditti, Fabrizio De André and Lucio Battisti, some of them off by heart, but I didn't go around bellowing them out. I loved the everyday voices at the beach, embedded in the sand and water, the anonymous hubbub of children yelling, whistles and mutterings; I loved the hum of telephone wires, which sounded almost melodic when there were houses nearby for the sound to bounce back off and the cooing of doves on the windowsill, the raucous cawing of seagulls and woodpeckers. 'And you,' I replied evenly, 'drown out everything with these schmaltzy *canzonette* by Goggi or Cocciante or Eros or whatever they're all called.'

Mum had once told Aunt Hilda why she'd fallen for my father. She said that Italians had a reputation as great lovers because they'd learnt how to use smoke and mirrors to hide all the unsightly stuff. 'Love's all about pretence,' my mother explained, 'and they're real past masters at that game.'

My father soon got bored of keeping up the pretence, though; as an employee of the state railway, he was transferred to Brescia and went back to live in his home village of Manerba del Garda, where he took up with his former girlfriend again – Mum had only learnt about her existence when she was four months pregnant. Ultimately, his ducking and diving had come as no surprise to her: 'Give an Italian a piece of cloth, no matter how small, and he'll make a lovely job of folding it to whatever shape you want,' she'd once said.

These were the same people who painted the stucco on church columns to look like marble, or who, like Antonella, put nail varnish on the light bulb to create a sexier ambience when she was entertaining boyfriends. Red nail polish, I learnt on my first day at the Hotel Manente, was the poor person's version of a dimmer switch. Antonella didn't seem to be bothered by the overpowering smell it produced.

'I mean *you*,' replied Antonella, '*i tedeschi*, the Germans.'

'There was a picture of President Giovanni Leone hanging in my school's classroom.'

'Well, they'll be taking that down now, for sure. Leone pocketed millions from a deal for military transport planes. He was a bad bet right from the off. He'd never have become president in the first place if it hadn't been for the votes of the neofascists. But I'll bet you've still got a picture of Scheel hanging there, too.' She pronounced it 'Skeel'.

'No, my president is your Leone – who incidentally, unlike Walter Scheel, hasn't got a good singing voice.'

'*Our* Leone, my arse!' Antonella rolled her eyes.

I tried explaining all the ins and outs of South Tyrol, but she kept interrupting me and insisting that, even if I wasn't, then at least Manente was a German, without a shadow of a doubt. You could even hear it when she spoke.

It was true. Whenever Mrs Manente got agitated, the soft Italian

'C', which was pronounced like a German 'K', came out as a guttural 'Ch' sound. Even after four decades, then, Stillbach and its proximity to Southern German dialects still came to the surface sometimes. She'd even occasionally mangle Cocola's name into 'Kchokchola'.

'So, if you're not a German,' demanded Antonella, 'then what are you?'

Truth is, I wasn't sure what I was. I never had been. And the more people wanted me to tell them, the less idea I had. To lots of Italians, I was a German, while to most Germans I was neither an Italian nor a German. I'd once heard an old Italian guy say about Austria: 'Does it still exist, then?' As a kid, I'd always thought that that eagle with the cricked neck that appeared in wrought iron above gates or carved on the façades of houses had something to do with the Italian city of Aquila, not with the emblem on the coat of arms of Austrian Tyrol or the old Austrian monarchy. Yet I distinctly remembered us having to draw this red bird on a white background after we'd been on a school trip to Tyrol Castle and seen the original fresco of the region's emblem in the chapel there. I don't know where this tendency to explain everything as having Italian origins came from. I could only conceive of the eagle as an *aquila*, that is as a live, dark brown feathered bird of prey and never as a red heraldic device of the nobility. How absurd, I'd thought as a child, to paint it the same colour as a cranberry. In my eyes, they'd turned this majestic king of the Tyrolean skies into a crimson hot-air balloon floating up towards the sun, rather than swooping down in its camouflaged plumage to seize its prey.

'When all's said and done,' said Antonella, 'Manente's a German nationalist but doesn't dare show it openly for fear of her son.'

'But he's not here.'

'Still, that doesn't make her worry any the less.'

I saw with relief that Antonella was opening the window.

'Francesco's one of us,' she said, 'he supports the cause.' She didn't say what cause that was. As Antonella continued, I learnt that Mrs

Manente had been engaged to a Nazi, but had got herself pregnant by Francesco's father.

'Maybe she was made pregnant,' I suggested, 'against her will.'

'No, she got her feet nicely under the table here and even managed to provide for her family too. She used old Manente's money to support those Italian-haters up North.'

'She worked hard for that money,' I objected. 'You can't feed an entire family from one potato field, not even if you top it up by selling door-to-door or doing seasonal odd-jobs.' I was parroting Aunt Hilda's words. Her parents had grown up in the same valley as Mrs Manente, but the two families had never met. Aunt Hilda once told me her father had been made redundant, but that the few jobs that came up in factories had all gone to Italians. Women had an even slimmer chance of finding work.

'But they'd only employ Italians in the factories back then,' I said.

Antonella chewed at a hangnail. 'We're to blame, then, are we?'

'You're counting yourself with the fascists?'

Her only riposte to this was that I was *strana* – weird – so I'd be bound to take the side of the *stranieri*, the outsiders and foreigners. I let that one ride, then asked, 'Aren't you tired?'

Antonella fell silent for a while; she seemed to be mulling over whether I'd noticed her little night-time excursion the previous evening. Then she burst out: 'If you say a word to the boss –'

I could hear a cat miaowing somewhere outside. A guest must have gone out to the garden to have a snooze in a deckchair. Miaows like that were only ever directed at humans; left to their own devices, all the cats did was growl and hiss at one another.

So where had Manente got the note from, Antonella wanted to know. I told her about my accident with the skirt, but she didn't seem to believe me.

She grabbed one of her *fotoromanzi* from under the bed and flung herself back on the mattress. I only knew these photo stories, which were made to seem as true to real life as possible, from the German teen magazine *Bravo*.

'Isn't he dreamy?' she said after a couple of minutes, holding up the magazine and showing me a picture of a man whose eyebrows joined in the middle. Despite the designer stubble on his chin and his prominent nose, there was something effete about him. 'What, don't you recognise him?' Antonella asked. 'I don't believe it! Everyone knows who he is – it's Franco Gasparri!' She jabbed her finger at the photo. 'His birthday's the same day as my brother Mimmo's. Call yourself an Iranian?'

Gina Lollobrigida and Sophia Loren had begun their careers as *fotoromanzi* stars, she went on, she supposed I didn't know that either. '*La stella nella polvere* – ring any bells?' She chuckled to herself as I tried translating the phrase: 'Star in the dust?', 'Dust-star?' I found the phrase more appealing in my own language.

There was no denying this Franco Gasparri was attractive, but I didn't go for his light-tan suede jacket with a fringe over the breast pockets, *à la* Easy Rider.

It suddenly crossed my mind that my father might look like Franco. I only had some very old photos of him. Whenever I tried asking my mother about him, she changed the subject. And when I tackled Aunt Hilda, she just referred me back to my mother: 'I'm not even your real aunt, you know,' she said, 'it's up to your Mum to tell you about him.'

9

Emma stood in the dining room looking at the cake slice on the sideboard where the desserts were served. It was a kind of spatula in the form of an elongated, gently tapering trapezoid. Emma ran her finger along its leading edge and felt the engraved flower pattern on the blade. Nobody in Stillbach had owned such a grand cake slice. Then again, Johann had lived in Stillbach. And Stillbach was always wreathed in the beautiful, shimmering green of the larch trees.

Emma had even managed to meet Johann in Rome a couple of times. Secretly, of course. She told the Manentes she was going sightseeing with one of the priests from the Anima. It was the only way of getting away from the hotel for a whole day. Even before Johann was transferred to Rome, she'd gone on excursions to Palestrina and Ostia Antica to see the remains of temples, theatres, forums, granaries and mills. But rather than meet Johann in the chaos that was Rome in those days, she'd preferred filling her time with memories of Stillbach. In her daydreams, she could accompany him time after time on a walk up to the mountain mere, or catch his gaze as he stood with his friends in the little square outside the church after Sunday mass. These quiet and meaningful looks could never be recaptured during their brief encounters in Rome. Johann, thought Emma, might have noticed that she was already getting to be quite at home in the unfamiliar city and that she'd begun to show more interest than was absolutely necessary in it. But in all likelihood, it had never even occurred to him to confront her about it because he realised that Emma would never admit to it. Everyone knew he and Emma were an item, and even though there'd scarcely been any intimacy between them, the promise of marriage necessarily implied that they'd return to Stillbach.

There were cobwebs dangling from the chandelier, moving as if in slow motion in the faintest breath of wind. Emma also found some dust balls on the floor. Straight away she summoned Antonella and bustled around the room, pointing out things that needed cleaning. She caught sight of herself in the mirror behind the buffet; it made her look dowdy, she thought, and made her movements seem somehow distorted.

'I can't rely on you, can I, Antonella? It just won't do.' But at the same time, Emma knew it would have to do. With a hotel full of guests, she simply couldn't afford to lose any staff. All of a sudden, she could see Remo's mother standing in front of her – what must it have been, thirty-five years ago? – showing her how to fold napkins properly. A few deft hand movements and, hey presto! the old lady instantly transformed a square piece of linen into a sailing boat or a water lily, while Emma was still fumbling about deciding whether she should be folding up the entire triangle of fabric or pulling just the tip of the square down to the bottom. Old Mrs Manente had just finished explaining the difference between damask and linen when Remo came into the dining room. His face and arms were streaming with blood and he was covered in dust, and hard on his heels came the laundry maid, with her hand held up to her mouth in shock, who'd opened the garden gate for him. 'Water, quick – fetch me some fresh water and towels,' Emma heard old Mrs Manente say; she was amazed his mother wasn't in a shrieking panic but instead was taking it all so calmly and level-headedly, just like Emma's own mother back in Stillbach. The three women set about treating Remo's wounds – lacerations which in some places were bleeding profusely but which were for the most part only superficial. Remo had been visiting a friend in

San Lorenzo when the sky above the apartment block had suddenly turned black. Just as Remo began to make his way home, a shower of debris and shards of glass rained down on him. Allied bombers had targeted the railway marshalling yards but had also hit several residential houses, the university campus and the Campo Verano cemetery. 'Now they're even trying to kill the dead,' Remo joked, shaking his head very slowly as though the pain was retarding his movements. This was the first time – or so it seemed to Emma – that he treated her not just as another member of staff, but as a woman; for her part, as she wiped the blood from his forearms with an alcohol-soaked cloth, she forgot for a moment that he was the son of her employer. As she tried to pick muck and glass out of one gash with a pair of tweezers, Remo noticed she was trembling; he caught hold of her arm and gave it a squeeze. By this time, everyone had rushed into the dining room to see what all the fuss was about. Remo seemed to be suffering from shock because he kept on going on about the cemetery and the churned-up graves. Hundreds of bombs had fallen on this quarter of the city and there were rumoured to be more than one thousand dead, but for days after, all Remo could talk about was the dead people who'd been killed twice and Pope Pius XII's family vault, which apparently had sustained some damage.

That very same day, the Pope had been driven over to San Lorenzo to view the destruction for himself. It was the first time since the outbreak of war that he'd left the precincts of the Vatican. He visited the Basilica of San Lorenzo fuori le Mura, in which a bomb blast had ripped a deep crater. The populace had really appreciated the Pope's visit, especially as he had a reputation for avoiding people, even requiring his own gardeners to hide behind bushes when he took his daily constitutional in the grounds of the Vatican.

'Thank you,' Remo said, and after a short pause in which Emma took the opportunity to look into his eyes once more, added; 'Emma'. Old Mrs Manente immediately twigged what was going on between them and ordered Emma off to the laundry with the dirty towels. That put her in her place alright. Just like Remo would never be accepted in Stillbach, so Emma was left in no doubt that if she changed sides she'd never truly belong either.

Emma could smell the fat of *prosciutto crudo* melting in the heat. Someone had brought the *antipasti* into the dining room too soon; the guests hadn't even come in yet.

The bombs had fallen from a height of twelve angels. How many feet that was Emma couldn't remember, but the angels as a measurement of length had stuck in her mind.

Everything goes too fast in wartime, Johann had told her back then. 'You hang around for ages waiting for something to happen, then when it does it's gone in a blur and you're left dealing with the consequences for the rest of your life.' Nowadays, Emma could recall the exact husky tone of Johann's voice; back in Stillbach, she'd thought it came from smoking, or an inflammation of his airways, or a bronchial constriction. But even in Rome, where cigarettes had long been in short supply, he kept on coughing as though he needed to clear his throat before every new sentence.

'The Po basin always gets me down. That endless, flat expanse.' When was it they'd talked about that? After Sunday mass at Santa Maria dell'Anima? The end of '43? As he'd said this, Johann had mimicked the action of smoothing over a tablecloth. Emma had never seen hands like his since. His nails had no white flecks on them and no furrows either, and his fingers were long, regular and hairless. Remo's nails had been more round than long and had a pronounced arch. A guest, a beautician from Regensburg, once told her that Remo's nails had a condition called 'clubbing'. She'd insisted on giving Emma's nails a manicure. 'What well-defined half-moons you have,' she'd exclaimed, 'and such nice red finger pads!' There were some guests who couldn't stop working, even on holiday. They found it impossible to sit there doing nothing, so went about clearing cups and plates off the terrace tables and taking them to the kitchen, picking up fallen leaves, or making their own beds. One time, a young couple from Stillbach had spent their honeymoon at Hotel Manente and argued incessantly; the husband, an apple-grower and forester, spent most of the time weeding the hotel garden. If he'd had the chance he'd have planted it up with fruit trees; he couldn't see the point of ornamentals.

Emma watched Ines putting out water carafes and taking bottles of wine, marked with the table number, to their correct places. Though Ines had only loosely tied up her long hair, her upright posture made her look quite presentable nevertheless. Some of the women who had come to the Anima all those years ago still wore their hair in plaits, even though they'd been in Rome for over a year. Some were afraid of what people back home would say and didn't have the courage to break with tradition. Others kept this hairstyle because their employers liked it that way. In Venice, Emma had coiled her braids up around her ears, but in Rome old Mrs Manente packed her off to the hairdresser after a guest had summoned her with the words: 'Hey, Heidi!' She didn't want Emma looking too rustic, but nor did she want her to look too pretty, either.

Because Emma was afraid of how her father would react, she spent the first Christmas holiday in Rome. She didn't even tell the women at the Anima her real reason for staying, claiming instead that she was required to work over the break. Only after she'd confessed to her mother about her new short haircut and got a letter back telling her to take the evening bus when she next came home and to arrive in the dark, so people in Stillbach wouldn't see her looking like that, did she venture home again for a few days. But her father had got to hear about her short hair anyway and although he was unfriendly towards her, he didn't take it out on her physically. Almost in passing, he let slip the remark that he'd got himself another son. On the evening she arrived, her mother had sprinkled her with holy water – she only looked at her properly the next morning. She conceded that the new haircut was practical, but she still didn't like it.

'You can clear Table Eight: the couple there have gone off to Naples for the day and won't be back for dinner. By the way, you've forgotten the ice-cubes for Table Two.'

Ines disappeared into the kitchen and sent Antonella back out with the ice. Emma watched her, saying nothing but waiting for Ines to come back in the dining room. When she did reappear shortly after, carrying bottles of orangeade, she took the dish of ice-cubes from Table Three and put it on Table Two. Good girl; when she delegated a job, she checked it was done properly. That pleased Emma. She also liked Ines's dignified but modest bearing as she moved between the tables.

'And tuck your hair up properly, will you?' Emma said.

10

I'd have given anything to have Manente's mouth stitched up, like the Inquisition had done to Giordano Bruno when he was burned at the stake, to stop him addressing the crowd. She dogged my every footstep. I had to make a conscious effort to think of what my mother had told me: Stillbach's a one-horse town and women from Stillbach generally don't make much of themselves. So the very fact that Mrs Manente had made a clean break with the place was reason enough to respect her. I was already sick and tired of kowtowing to her, though.

I was standing at the kitchen table and putting salad in individual bowls. My eyes were still red after slicing onions for a whole hour. Cocola made sure no-one was ever short of a job. I'd barely finished peeling and cutting the onions when she looked at me and nodded in the direction of the string of garlic hanging from a nail on the side of the kitchen dresser. After just quarter of an hour spent scraping the papery skin off each clove of garlic, my fingertips were so raw and sore that I had to hold them under a running tap to dull the pain. Cocola picked out a wilted salad leaf from one of the bowls and laid it on the chopping board. 'Who washed the salad?' she demanded. Gianni vanished into the larder; Antonella made a face. At that moment Mrs Manente came in and slammed the platter with the *prosciutto crudo* down on the table. She had a good mind, she announced, to deduct the price of a half-kilo of Parma ham from each of our wages, so we'd learn to keep an eye on one another. 'If one of you is too stupid to do a job properly, then at least the rest of you could stop them from making a public display of it.'

Cocola bodily shoved the whole set of salad bowls to the far end of the kitchen unit, making them clink together alarmingly.

'Are you sweating?' she asked Antonella once Mrs M had gone back to the dining room.

'It's July,' answered Antonella, 'why wouldn't I be?'

'Exactly – so that's why the ham was sweating, too.'

The sticky garlic juice gummed my fingers together and burned in the cuts I'd given myself with my clumsy onion-chopping technique. Making a huge effort not to burst into tears in front of Cocola, I thought of the shubunkins in the garden and of the handful of gravel I'd dropped into the water. The fish had immediately mobbed the sinking stones, thinking they were food.

'Remember, the underplate stays where it is.' Manente was hovering at my shoulder once more. I was to approach guests from their right whenever I cleared away finished plates, she instructed me, whereas serving portions out of platters or bowls was always done from the left, and prepared plates of food had to be served from the right. I didn't dare tell her that I'd always had trouble telling my left from my right and that I had to look at my palms to work out which was which: I knew my left hand was the one with a tiny black birthmark. But that ruse wouldn't help me if my hands were full of dirty plates, or glasses and cutlery. I looked for any distinguishing marks on my forearms, but failed to find any; they looked like identical twins, as plump as one another and tanned just the same. There wasn't a biro to hand, either, so the only thing that occurred to me off the top of my head was to give myself – after quickly checking the birthmark again – a deep scratch on my left forearm.

The first guests started drifting into the dining room and soon I was dashing from table to table, doling out the salad bowls and baskets of bread, all the while glancing down at the red weal on my arm to make sure I wasn't approaching a diner from the wrong side. Over and over, I repeated to myself: 'Ladies first. Age before youth,' and kept a fixed smile on my face, greeting people, checking everything was OK, memorising 'one bottle of mineral water, one Cola, two beers for Table Nine; two glasses of the house white for Table Seven', and serving the first course. I got a nasty surprise when the party from Baden-Württemberg entered *en masse* and began demanding my attention all at once: 'Waitress!' they shouted, 'there's no salt on our table!' or 'Where's my spaghetti?' or 'We'd like some more bread, please!' In the end, I had no idea who'd had the *antipasti*, who was still waiting for their pasta course and who had already been served their main. I could feel little strands of hair that had escaped from my headband starting to tickle my face and my feet began complaining from too much standing up in the kitchen and from scurrying around the dining room. The burning pain in them wasn't unlike the garlic I'd just had under my fingernails. I carried stacks of full plates into the dining room and empty ones out again, brought through seconds and pieces of tin foil for guests to wrap big bits of meat in for later. Mrs Manente didn't help me; she was standing around chatting to guests in German that sounded like she lived in the Federal Republic but had never quite shaken off her Austrian background. But although she appeared to be engrossed in conversation, she kept a beady eye on me all the time, clocking all my movements, which only unnerved me more. As a result – the scratch marks on my forearm had long since faded and I had lost all track of which side I should be serving what from – I managed to accidentally assault two ladies from Stuttgart who were sitting next to one another and chatting by lunging between them to get their plates. I bumped one of them on the bridge of her nose; she jerked back with tears in her eyes and, as she put her hand up to feel her nose, a spot of blood appeared on her finger. 'Well, I never!' she exclaimed angrily. Mrs M sent me off to fetch some ice.

When I came back, all eyes in the room were trained on me. Even the young man I'd seen in the garden on the day I arrived was staring at me. For a second, I thought he winked, but when I looked again he had a straight face and had returned to his food. This time he was dressed in jeans and a white T-shirt; no hint of the trainee priest about him now.

Mrs Manente wrapped the ice cubes in a napkin and dabbed at the woman's face. Although I'd said sorry myself twice already, she kept on apologising for the unfortunate incident. Outside, in the corridor, she took me to one side: 'Never, ever wave your hands about like that again in front of a guest's face.'

After the accident, though, I found serving a whole lot easier. As soon as they saw me coming, the guests made sure to get out of my way fast. The young man even cleared his own plate and knife and fork away and took them to the kitchen. He waited in the doorway for me to squeeze past him carrying the next pile of plates, but again said nothing, just smiled at me.

'That's Paolo,' Cocola called out from the far end of the kitchen, 'our student.'

'Paul,' he corrected her and nodded a hello at me. Cocola, who was busy scraping leftovers from pots into storage bowls, paused, wiped her hands on her apron and came over to the door. 'There's some cake left, if you'd like,' she cooed at him, 'or some fruit if you prefer. Grapes? Or medlars, maybe?' She steered me away from Paul: 'Herr Steg's dinner's on that tray there: Room 34,' she said, before turning back to dance attendance on Paul again.

In the lift, which ascended in jerky lurches, I set the tray down and lifted the plastic cover to peek at the contents. The scent of the honey melon whetted my appetite; I ran my index finger over its juicy, greenish-white flesh and licked it clean. A whole missing slice of melon would be too obvious, so I settled for swiping a piece of Parma ham from the plate. It was mild-tasting, slightly sweet even. To restore the symmetry of the starter plate, I took another bit of ham from the other side of the melon and artfully rearranged the remaining slices. I suddenly heard voices in the stairwell, so I covered up the tray again. It almost slipped off the narrow bench in the lift where I'd balanced it, but I caught it in the nick of time.

Steg was sitting at the open window, reading. There were books all over the place, on the bed, the floor and even the radiators.

'So, you're from Rio Silenzio, are you?'

'You mean Stillbach?' I shook my head and, thinking of the ham I'd just eaten and worrying that the smell would be on my breath, kept quiet.

Steg got up, went over to the table, took the cover off the tray and thanked me. I was concerned he might spot the missing slices of *prosciutto*, so I didn't really pay close attention to what he said. It sounded like *pullata* – 'Where's my *pullata* today, then?' – or something like that. The farmer's wife next door to us at home had always got her chickens in at night by calling: '*Pull, Pull, Pull!*' Maybe that's what he meant, I thought: he'd ordered chicken. 'There's no chicken on the menu tonight, I'm afraid,' I replied. Steg looked at me, taken aback; he clearly thought he'd misheard me at first. Then he answered: 'But – nobody ordered chicken, what gave you that idea?'

On the table was a postcard showing the Palazzo Montecitorio and its obelisk, which was crowned by a small metal ball with an arrow sticking out the top of it. The sky on the postcard was as blue as the swimming pools among the apple orchards, which I'd seen from the train, glinting in the sunlight, on my journey down to Rome, still not quite two days ago.

Steg pursued me to the lift. He kept his distance, but I still got the impression that he touched me lightly.

'I hear you're still at school,' he murmured.

I fled to the safety of the lift cage.

'And bring me some more ham, will you?' he shouted after me.

As the lift clattered down, I was struggling to remember a line from a work by a Roman poet, which we'd had to translate at school. *Sed non...* I couldn't get the final word: I came up with *satis*, but that wasn't it. But that in turn made me think of 'satyr'. How appropriate: 'Randy old goat,' I muttered under my breath.

11

The pilgrims from Baden-Württemberg had left and only a handful of new guests arrived. Steg had extended his stay by a fortnight. The guesthouse in Ischl was being renovated, he explained. In truth, Emma hoped that she was what was keeping him in Rome, for Steg had taken to sitting down next to her quite often whenever she went out to the table beside the terrace door to have her lunch and cast an eye over the paper.

Aldo Moro had been dead for two months now and Sandro Pertini was Italy's new President. Emma couldn't stand carnations. Wherever the President went, he was handed a bouquet of these red flowers, whose blooms always looked to her like someone had been picking bits off them.

One of the first stops on his itinerary was the Ardeatine Caves, Emma read. She noticed her back was aching and bent forward to try to get more comfortable. No wonder she was feeling her age: thirty-four years had passed since then. She was twenty-eight when it happened. A victim on the wrong side. Love blown away in an instant. And the family in Stillbach lost forever, because everything panned out differently after that. Remo instead of Johann.

What did she care about this Kappler bloke, or that Don Juan who'd bed-hopped his way round the boudoirs of the fascist bigwigs in the swish Parioli district? Priebke, that was his name. Ernst Priebke. No, Erich; she'd become so forgetful of late. One of the women at the Anima had even seen him face-to-face once, briefly. 'An absolute picture of a man,' she swooned during an Advent service, 'steely blue eyes and so handsome in his uniform – just immaculate!'

As Emma leant back, a sudden stabbing pain in the small of her back made her gasp. A visit to the doctor was long overdue. A trapped nerve maybe, or even a slipped disc?

There he was, then, the new President – and alongside him the defence minister Ruffini and a clutch of other well-known politicians. Emma was just about to put the paper down when her attention was caught by the caption under the photo. Apparently, a partisan by the name of Maurizio Giglio, who'd been taken to the caves on a stretcher from Gestapo HQ because he couldn't walk anymore, had remained steadfast to the last. Before the firing squad got to work, SS-Obersturmbannführer Kappler – Emma read on – supposedly asked him where Pertini was hiding, but the 23-year-old Giglio just shook his head – *un ultimo no*, one final defiant 'No' – even after they'd ripped out his fingernails and toenails in the Via Tasso.

Emma winced, massaging her back with her fingertips. Pertini, the carnation-president. Partisan rabble, the lot of them. Even so, she did feel genuinely sorry for the young Giglio boy.

The wind sighed in the trees. A flickering, light-dappled shadow spread across Emma's body. She was keeping a sharp look-out for Hermann Steg. A wasp landed on her espresso cup, sipping the foamy milk residue. The bougainvillea in the corner of the terrace looked a bit bedraggled – perhaps the girls weren't watering it enough. Its mauve flower heads were all drooping. Only the oleanders, though planted in small tubs, were spreading vigorously.

Emma got up and went to stand in the doorway. She thought she'd heard noises in the stairwell. That morning, Steg had spoken to Ines again, but Emma hadn't picked up what they were saying because she'd got embroiled in a conversation with a married couple from Munich about how variable the prices of pizza were. All she wanted to do was chuck 2,000 lire at them and have done with it. For most of her guests, it seemed even cheap food wasn't cheap enough. At breakfast, they always asked for extra rolls, spreading them thickly with butter and piling them high with slices of ham and cheese to save themselves the cost of buying lunch. It wasn't unheard of for them to forget about rolls that they'd squirreled away in their bedside tables, leaving the chambermaids to find mouldy remains in the drawers after they left.

Steg had looked relaxed, almost happy, when he'd been chatting to Ines. It struck Emma that he'd never been that happy around her.

Johann hadn't laughed much, either. I should have gone back to Stillbach earlier and not waited for him to be posted here, Emma thought. On that fateful day, he'd just come back from target practice out at the Forum Mussolini. And just 24 hours later, Eleven Company was due to be relieved by Ten Company. It was his last day of training. If only they'd planted the bomb a few days later, Johann would have survived. Then maybe Emma would now be a landlady in Stillbach instead. Or a farmer's wife in Nörderhof. And she'd be getting along fine with her brothers and sisters. And her father wouldn't have... her mother would have... and all those other countless 'if only's.

Emma folded the newspaper and stuck it in the waste bin next to the serving table. She started counting the sugar shakers. All present and correct. But a few ashtrays were missing. Things were always disappearing. The guests helped themselves like the hotel was some sort of free souvenir shop, drying their hands back in Tuttlingen or Reutlingen on Hotel Manente towels, or stubbing out their fags in Memmingen and Meiningen in Martini or Campari ashtrays. People like that treated everywhere like it was their own backyard. One time, Emma had thrown a man from Rankweil in the Vorarlberg out of the hotel after she caught him stuffing bed linen into his suitcase.

A gust of wind caught the tablecloths, sending one of the clips clattering to the ground. Emma made no move to retrieve it.

She wouldn't have turned a hair if the partisans had bombed the brothels round the Piazza del Popolo – the haunt of plenty of Germans that one could happily have done without. That's exactly what they were planning, in fact, but they shelved the idea for fear of killing too many civilians. Johann was just a simple policeman, responsible for papal guard duties; by rights, the SS should have been the target.

Emma chewed and tugged at a protruding hangnail until a spot of blood welled up. She looked at her fingers and was startled to see that her hands were trembling. If only Franz were there. Not that she could ever have spoken about all this with him, but he did take her out of herself. Also, she saw something in him that was part of her, something deeply familiar that reminded her of her brother – at least of the way he'd been when she'd set off on her journey south, to these rust-red and orange palaces, which looked for all the world like they were on fire as the sun went down. Between the tenement blocks here, people laid out little vegetable plots and fenced them in with old iron bedsteads.

During the German occupation, old Mrs Manente had been afraid to let Emma out of the house. The city was crawling with partisans, she said, and Emma was a big girl now, too big to pass herself off as an Italian. 'And whatever you do, don't open your mouth,' she urged her, 'they'll hear straight away that you're not from around here.' The way Emma said the letter 'Q' would give her away. Even now, she still habitually pronounced it 'Kv' – *Kvando torni?* 'What time are you coming back?' – a sound she produced by resting her incisors on her bottom lip. Only occasionally, when she was concentrating, did she manage to make it sound soft, forming her mouth into the shape of a brief kiss: *Dimmi quando,* 'Tell me when'.

She'd never had any problem keeping quiet, she was used to it from Stillbach. There, mere looks were often enough to give you a guilty conscience. When you asked her father a question you got no reply, just that 'How-dare-you-even-ask' look. Emma found it hard to believe the story that he'd started speaking volubly in later life.

She touched her throat, feeling for the string of pearls that were constricting her neck. She didn't seem to be getting enough air. She checked her erratic, racing pulse, which simply refused to calm down, shouted first for Antonella and then for Ines, but neither girl heeded her call. They must have been down in their room, or maybe they'd already gone out for the afternoon.

No sign of Steg. Had he changed his routine? Perhaps she'd spoken out of turn and unwittingly offended him?

Time was when Emma would retire to take a nap after lunch, or sometimes she'd go into the city centre to visit some church or other or just stroll along the Via Nomentana for a stretch, to the Basilica of St Agnes, in the left aisle of which lay the entrance to the Catacombs. Emma and the Manentes had once taken shelter there during the bombing raids. Afterwards, the family had decamped to Trevignano for the duration of the war, where they felt safer, while Emma stayed behind at the hotel to look after the place. Whenever she heard the slightest rumble, she'd dash down into the cellar, pressing her hands tightly to her ears. Emma was especially fond of the garden in front of the church and of the Baptistery of Constantia, which was just a few steps away from the basilica. Latterly, the rotunda of the Baptistery had become a favourite location for weddings and baptisms, which surprised Emma, as the building hardly contained any Christian symbols and even the mosaic decorations on the ceiling, which Remo had once told her were among the oldest in the city, only showed plants, flowers and birds. Emma hadn't been there for some years now; she'd got fed up of being crowded out by wedding parties, the women darting about taking snaps and the men with their Super-8 cine cameras, taking endless footage of every last family member.

Emma had just the one photo of Johann. His memorial picture. *Dear Lord, grant him everlasting Peace.* It wasn't her Johann, though, the boy who'd dived into the mountain lake. Or who'd tried to dissuade a friend of his from Stillbach from sporting his feathered Tyrolean hat on Italian Unification Day. 'They'll banish you,' Johann warned him.

Emma happened to be standing nearby after the church service and saw an Italian fascist snatch the hat from Johann's friend's head during the singing of the fascist anthem *Giovinezza*. Johann picked up the hat but didn't keep a tight enough grip on it and the friend snatched it off him and put it back on. This deliberate act of provocation – in 1935, or was it 1936? – cost the young man three years' internal exile.

The memorial picture showed Johann as a police recruit. He'd complained to Emma about what a disreputable state his uniform was in when it was issued. He'd spent the first evening in the barracks trying to patch it up as best he could. 'I'm being posted to Rome to guard the Pope. Imagine how smart I'll look in *these* trousers, though.'

'No, you're not exactly one of the Swiss Guard,' Emma had conceded.

Johann was convinced that his war would be over when Italy surrendered in September 1943. But he'd reckoned without the Germans. They'd just been waiting for the moment when they could march into Italy and co-opt people like him for their own ends. Hitler or Mussolini? Johann had never asked himself this question. He didn't much care for either. But after the bomb attack, Emma recalled, everywhere you went you heard talk of baying mobs, armed to the teeth, roaming through the streets singing, and of rabid Nazis under the command of that Kappler. Sure, some of the Germans in the city then may have fitted that description, but not my Johann.

Emma's heart was racing again, but her hands – at least, so it seemed to her – weren't shaking any more, possibly because she was pressing her palms down hard on the tabletop.

It just wasn't true that on the day after the revenge killings in the Ardeatine Caves Romans had been numb with shock. Or that they'd spoken in hushed whispers and tugged their hats down low to hide their faces. Emma could clearly recall that she'd run into people on the street who were furious that the bread ration had been cut from a hundred and fifty to a hundred grams. Prices were their sole topic of conversation. There was talk of a public meeting in the Appio district to protest against the rises. People were complaining that the cost of cooking oil had gone through the roof. Before Christmas, Emma had still been paying 500 lire a litre, but a few days before the attack, the price had shot up to 900. Emma had cashed in her monthly ration tokens and planned to go on to the Anima but had run out of time.

Most people were pretty indifferent about the death toll, too, either from the bomb attack in the Via Rasella or in the Caves the day after. All they'd thought about was their own bellies and their stick-thin children. The only person to react at the time was the Pope, who'd branded the partisans as 'irresponsible elements'.

It was years before Emma could bring herself to visit the place where it had happened. She gave this place of death and destruction a wide berth. Whenever the bus turned off the Via Nazionale to enter the Umberto I Tunnel, she always turned around to avoid seeing Via Rasella, which was on the right as you emerged from the far end. Here and there, the pock-marks caused by grenades and gunfire had been patched up after a fashion, but many façades in the city still looked like they were suffering from some incurable skin condition.

12

For a moment, I thought I heard the proprietress calling me, but when I tilted the window to make sure, all I could hear was the chirp of cicadas. I never actually saw one; apparently they're so well camouflaged they blend right into the background.

Antonella wanted to go into town to meet her brother Mimmo, so she'd cleared off as soon as our afternoon break began. I read for a bit, had a snooze and wrote a letter to my mother and a postcard to Aunt Hilda. On it, I wrote that I'd already visited St Peter's, that Castel Sant'Angelo was closed due to staff shortages, that I'd almost broken the nose of a woman from Stuttgart and that I was sharing a room with a Roman girl, who – no, on reflection, better not tell her this – who secretly slipped out of the hotel at night and got clandestine messages from men.

When I went out onto the terrace, I saw Mrs Manente bending intently over one of the tables. In the midday light, her hunched shoulders made her look like an old, powerful man. On the table was a piece of chipboard, no larger than a metre square. Emma Manente's finger movements were like those of a pianist hammering away incessantly at the same key. Presumably, she'd never learnt to play, even though her hand movements seemed to suggest that she knew a thing or two about music. In front of her lay neat rows of jigsaw-puzzle pieces, arranged by colour. Steg had waylaid me that same morning and poked fun at Mrs M; her passion for jigsaws had, it seemed, begun some years ago with 100-piece puzzles and progressed to a stage where she was now tackling 5,000-piece ones. Had I noticed, he asked, that they were invariably pictures of scenes from the immediate environs of Stillbach – photos of Lake Resia or Mount Ortler? Innsbruck and Munich also came into this category. Last year, he'd seen Emma complete a puzzle of the Golden Roof in Innsbruck and one showing an autumnal scene in the wooded South Tyrolean foothills, both of them with 5,000 pieces. 'Now that's what I call *lignam in silvam ferre*,' he whispered to me, jerking his thumb at a pile of jigsaw boxes stacked on a chair. I didn't understand what he meant. As he said it, he brushed my shoulder with his other hand, as if by accident.

Mrs Manente was so engrossed in what she was doing that she didn't notice me at first. She'd started by assembling the edge pieces, concentrating on areas of clear blue sky. In one corner of the chipboard square, she'd set aside some bits of the puzzle with an unusual colour or shape. She'd already fitted some of them together to reveal a far-off mountain peak glowing in the evening sun.

'What are you doing here? Why haven't you gone sightseeing in the city?' she asked, finally noticing me.

'I thought you called me.'

'That was quite a while ago.' She ran the tip of her tongue over her top lip.

The constant drumming of her fingertips on the chipboard didn't suggest that Mrs M was enjoying the puzzle. Quite the opposite, she seemed even more agitated than usual. Perhaps her powers of concentration were on the wane and she'd realised she was no longer capable of memorising all the details of the individual pieces or, as she once had done, of quickly homing in on a particular piece she was after. On a couple of occasions, I noticed how she absent-mindedly shook her head and removed a piece that she'd mistakenly thought belonged with another. Another time, she tried so hard to force two pieces together that the layer of paper the image was printed on began to detach from the cardboard backing and stuck up awkwardly.

'Well, what are you waiting for?' she asked. 'Get yourself off into town and look round the Piazza Navona or the Pantheon or wherever. Make use of your free half-day, for heaven's sake!'

Although I didn't like going into the city centre on my own, I got on a bus, alighted in the lower reaches of the Via Vittorio Veneto, crossed the Piazza Barberini and, after following the Via del Tritone for a while, turned off into one of the small alleyways that are less choked with traffic. In the meantime, I began to feel less anxious; it was stiff with tourists here and I had nothing to fear. I avoided return-ing pointed stares and ignored guys calling out and wolf-whistling. Anyhow, in this scrum they were hard to pinpoint and could just as well have been directing their attentions at other girls. Only once was I absolutely sure a man was following me. *'Bella'*, murmured a voice behind me, *'bellissima'*. I latched on to an English tour party, whose guide was pointing at the entrance to the Quirinal Palace and telling her group that the name of the alley where they were standing came from that of the palace's own bakery. The young man stalking me had also stopped and positioned himself behind the tour guide, in my line of sight. I reckoned he was in his early twenties. His jeans were so tight he must have put them on wet. It didn't seem to bother him in the slightest that I didn't return his glances. I kept in step with the English ladies as they ambled on, taking care not to tread on their toes. Most of them were wearing Dr Scholl sandals. The heels of the woman directly in front of me were solid masses of rough, calloused skin, cracking in several places.

A sound of clattering cups came from a bar as we passed, followed by the noise of coffee beans in a grinder. I glanced quickly into the dark interior to see if it had a toilet. The white-haired barman whacked the filter against the wooden counter edge below the espresso machine to knock out the old coffee grounds. He was wearing a cream-coloured apron which fitted him so well that it seemed tailor-made. With a couple of deft hand movements, he twisted the cleaned and newly charged filter unit back into the machine. I ordered a *caffè macchiato* and squeezed past cardboard boxes, drinks crates and cleaning materials to get to the loo, which, as it turned out, didn't have a locking door or any toilet paper. I hoped my stalker had lost patience and moved on. In trying to brace the door shut with my foot, I performed such contortions that my first jet of pee missed the bowl entirely. One leg was soaking wet. I swore in Italian and instantly thought of Aunt Hilda, who didn't speak a word of the language, but who still couldn't bear it when people used profanities like *porco Dio, porca puttana* or even *santo cielo*. I rubbed my leg dry as best I could with my hand. The tap on the basin released a trickle of light brown fluid when I turned it on.

The barman had pushed my coffee to the far end of the counter, next to a good-looking woman in her mid-forties with a rasping voice that would have scared off the most persistent dog. I cast a cautious look outside: the young man was over on the far side of the street, leaning against the wall and smoking a cigarette. He waved at me. Two men came into the bar, greeted the barman behind the counter with a handshake, got their coffees without ordering them and didn't pay for them either when they left soon after. By this time, my cup was empty; I cast around for a reason to linger in the bar a while longer. I rummaged in my shoulder bag and thought about buying a *ciambella* doughnut, but they looked rather desiccated and most of the icing sugar on them had soaked in. Their surface looked like a snowy wood that had been hit by a storm.

Then my eye fell on a telephone mounted on the wall in the corridor leading to the toilet. I changed a 500-lire note into *gettoni* and dialled my mother's number. Above the phone hung a framed photo of Enrico Berlinguer in a blue suit and tie. Dressed like that, I couldn't picture him leading the mass strikes at the Fiat works in Turin, which he'd supposedly been instrumental in organising. First thing that same morning, Antonella had been rhapsodising again about her Sardinian working-class hero, telling me about a speech Berlinguer had given at the *Festival nazionale delle donne comuniste* in Arezzo, where he'd put clear blue water between Eurocommunism and Moscow. 'It's down to him that we've got Pertini as president and that we're shot of that swindler Leone,' Antonella said. After a pause, she added: 'You're not really interested in politics, are you? But just remember this: without the communists, we'd never have had the right to get divorced or have an abortion. Do you realise that?'

Mum wasn't in and Aunt Hilda wasn't answering either. I paid for my *macchiato* and left the bar. Mr Nuisance had disappeared.

I let myself be swept along by the tide of tourists. Soon, I found myself in front of the Fontana di Trevi, though I was being carried relentlessly on, jostled and shoved. I took refuge on the far side of the fountain, where the crowds were thinner, stepped down and sat on the edge of the basin. The noisy splashing mingled with the shouts of the street hawkers; I caught snatches of English, French and Spanish. All around me, couples were holding hands, standing with their backs to the fountain and tossing in coins.

The basin was alive with the sparkle and glitter of the thrown money and I wondered whether the lack of coins that people were always complaining about all over Italy wasn't down to this kind of extravagant gesture. Aunt Hilda thought that the Swiss and the Japanese were to blame for the coin shortage; the Swiss melted down our cheap lire to make their watch casings, she claimed, while the Japanese made buttons out of them. Mum just shook her head at 'that load of nonsense', preferring the theory that Italians were simply too lazy to empty all their coin-operated machines and minted too few coins in the first place, and that was why customers now were being fobbed off at the till with sticks of gum, toffees, or even those mini-cheques, which crooks had started to counterfeit as soon as they came out.

Our currency wasn't actually the lira, Mum went on, but that kind of chewing gum that, if you chewed it long enough, you could blow bubbles that burst on your face.

I kept my eyes peeled for my stalker; I was intrigued to know if he'd found a new victim. There were several single men hanging about who clearly weren't tourists. One of them was fiddling with his car or motorbike key fob, another, in platform shoes, was casually cradling his groin and looking around like he was waiting for someone. The steps behind me were crammed with schoolchildren who'd shoved their rucksacks down between their feet. 'Watch out for your valuables,' their teacher was telling them.

Suddenly, I thought I glimpsed Antonella. Could it really be her, of all people, sitting there on the edge of the fountain – she who avoided tourist haunts like the plague, because she couldn't stand *stranieri*, foreigners? Had she arranged to meet her brother here?

I moved nearer and was on the point of calling out to her, but one last twinge of doubt made me check myself. Her face was half-hidden by a baseball cap, plus she had sunglasses on, which I'd never seen Antonella wear. She seemed to be clutching something in her hand, I couldn't make out what. I ducked behind a French tour party. The girl took a couple of steps in my direction, then turned back again. After a while, she sat back down on the edge of the fountain, dangling one hand in the water and making a motion with the other as though she was pulling on a string, but there was no string to be seen. I moved a bit closer. That clinched it: it *was* Antonella and she was pulling something out of the water which glistened as it slipped through her fingers. In an instant, I realised it was nylon fishing line. So, she'd tied a magnet to one end and was fishing coins out of the fountain. All that loose change I'd seen in the box in her wardrobe wasn't tips then, but the money that tourists threw into the fountain to bring themselves good fortune and ensure that they came back to Rome again one day. Witnessing this petty larceny made me feel very uneasy. Best that

Antonella never knew I'd seen her. Perhaps she had to provide for her family and the wages she earnt at the hotel weren't enough.

Before I left, I chucked two coins of my own into the fountain, not because I wanted to come back to Rome twice, but because I'd heard it would guarantee you'd fall in love.

13

Steg did eventually turn up, but went to sit at the far end of the garden with a book. Every so often, Emma got up and, after checking to make sure no-one was looking, stood on tiptoe to get a better view of him. Sitting down, all she could see was the crown of the tree he'd put his deckchair under.

Earlier that morning, Emma had toyed with the idea of giving Antonella the day off and cleaning some of the rooms herself, to give herself an excuse to go into Steg's room. But how would that look? In the end, she settled for conducting a tour of inspection with Ines and Antonella, checking if the mirrors and taps were clean, if they'd missed any limescale stains or toothpaste smears and if fresh waxed-paper liners had been put in the wardrobes and the radiators dusted. In one room, Emma found rubbish still in a waste bin, while in another the ends of the toilet roll hadn't been folded over, plus the carpet runners weren't back in their proper place by the bed and the bathroom tooth-mug smelt of mouthwash. Sometimes Emma had to crouch down to check whether the floor had been mopped under the beds as well. She also ran her hand over every shower tray – on no account should there be any trace of wetness.

In Steg's room, although the double bed had been made properly – Emma couldn't find fault – she did notice that both sides appeared to have been slept in. Was he really that restless? Or had someone spent the night with him? With the girls in the room, Emma didn't have a chance to snoop around.

When she'd worked as a chambermaid herself, she'd sometimes lingered longer than necessary in guests' rooms, sniffing bottles of perfume and marvelling at the gorgeous fabrics of some of the women's clothes. Most Romans in those days went around in rags. They didn't even have shoes, but tied makeshift scraps of goatskin round their feet instead.

The day Emma last saw Johann, she'd walked past a bakery not far from St Peter's. There was a knot of children outside with sunken cheeks and stick-thin arms. They were hanging around in the hope that someone would buy bread and tear them off a hunk. Just like in Still-bach. But the woman who came out of the shop at that very moment hadn't been able to afford any bread, as it turned out. Emma could vividly recall her mass of wild hair and the dark shadow on her top lip, wispy hairs that were almost a moustache. 'Four lire's what I used to pay for a large loaf and now half a loaf costs four hundred! And it's all hard and mouldy, as well!' the woman shouted. She was beside herself with rage and needed someone to vent her fury at. 'The Germans control all the food supplies, it's an absolute scandal! All they're worried about is their own soldiers. And meanwhile my pupils are starving.' Emma just nodded and moved quickly on, fearful the woman might engage her in conversation and hear her German accent. In Stillbach too, during the First World War, the farmers had been forced to hand over all their food to the troops. Emma had been born during that war. All the grain and the eggs – the soldiers had commandeered the lot. Her mother had recounted all kinds of stories about how desperate they'd been for food. Like how they'd hidden their last three chickens – the only things left to eat in the house – from the troops. Or how several children in the village had suffered brain damage from malnutrition and the faces of the women had become drawn and taken on a deathly pallor. Mothers and daughters alike had iron deficiency, and girls who wanted to find a husband slapped their own faces or surreptitiously pinched their cheeks during Mass to make themselves look healthier.

The first time Emma saw rouge was at Mrs Scabello's, in a flat powder compact the size of her palm, with a blooming rose engraved on the lid.

Emma stood on tiptoe again and looked over directly at Steg. He didn't budge. Crestfallen, she retired indoors and started leafing through the address book at reception: *Spaccamonte. Stagno. Staub.* Ah, there he was: *Steg.*

What had she expected? That the date of Steg's birthday might suddenly and miraculously have shifted in her favour? No, he was still born in 1918, making him two years her junior. Johann had been a little older than her, and Remo almost ten years her senior. Now it occurred to Emma that Steg had never once thanked her for the Christmas cards she'd been sending him all these years. Franz had always teased her about that. And he found her habit of sending birthday cards to the older guests even more absurd. 'They're all going to pop their clogs soon, anyway. You're wasting your time trying to promote the hotel to them!' Franz was always loafing around in the sun and the more he did so, the less Emma felt she could afford to take the weight off her own feet.

She grabbed the duplicate key for Room 34 and stepped into the lift. Upstairs, she took a quick look out of the window. Steg was still in his deckchair; all he'd done was shift it round to keep in the shade. The gap between the chair and the side table where he'd put his notepad and pen had grown wider. A spot of light was playing on Steg's shirt and Emma quickly dodged back, worried that her watch or pearl necklace was reflecting the sun.

With trembling hands, she opened Steg's door, having first strained to listen for any sounds of movement from the other rooms. But only three rooms on this floor were occupied. The guests from number 30 had gone down to Ostia Antica and wouldn't be back before the evening and the people in the other one had been talking about going to two of Rome's best vantage points they hadn't yet managed to visit: the Giardino degli Aranci and Monte Mario.

Emma hadn't been up to either of those places for years. Why would she? Those panoramic views of the city usually only made her feel sad and her melancholy was grotesquely at odds with the 'oohs' and 'ahs' of the tourists as they snapped photo after photo and picked out the domes of the basilicas they'd already been to, or the ones they still meant to visit. This precipitous roofscape of houses and palaces looked like a mottled, uneven flagstone, Emma always thought. Remo had never understood what she meant by that, nor her claim that this view down on the city from the surrounding hills only made her think of other, far higher perches, places that made you feel you could soar into the air and drink in the sky. On the Stillbacher Horn, Emma had been alone with nature. Here, up on the Gianicolo, the Pincio or Monte Mario, she was hemmed in by people and the places where they lived and just felt stifled by their cares and woes.

Steg had closed both windows and the room was stuffy. In the bottom of the wardrobe lay his dirty laundry: underpants and shirts, hankies and socks, all jumbled up. Steg had bought himself some new shirts, presumably because he'd run out of clean old ones. Why didn't he just send his stuff to the laundry? Emma had offered enough times. Had he gone out and bought the shirts to impress someone?

Emma's eye lighted on some postcards on the table by the window; she turned them all over. Only one had been written, addressed to a Frau Professor Thuile, no doubt a colleague of his. A volume of Juvenal peeped out from under a sheaf of typewritten pages, and next to it a tattered map of Rome. Between the Vatican City and the Colosseum, Steg had placed two aspirin tablets, presumably to mark particular locations. No sign of anything suspicious in the room. The blue Pilot-brand ballpoint that Emma had lent Steg was stuck in a dictionary as a page marker.

The bathroom window was shut, too, but the smell in there wasn't unpleasant. Steg, it seemed, consistently hit the target when he peed – either that, or he hadn't gone to the loo since it was last cleaned, using the toilet downstairs between the dining room and reception instead.

The bidet was full of a stack of old newspapers, which Steg had expressly instructed the chambermaids not to throw away. On the shelf underneath the mirror, Emma found a bottle of aftershave called 'Old Innsbruck', with a stylised image of the Golden Roof on the label, and behind it a silhouette of the Nordkette mountain range. It was a jumbo-sized bottle, more like the sort you see in the hairdresser's than one for personal use. Emma unscrewed the cap and put a dab of the scent on her neck.

Steg had never felt so close at hand; she now smelt a bit like him, the cooling mentholated aftershave wafting her some of the mountain freshness she so missed here. All at once, she was back on the footpath that led to the mere above Stillbach, and from there further on up to the alpine pastures just below the Horn. She felt herself breathing more deeply, like she was climbing a steep hill. She quickly put the bottle back in place next to the tooth-mug and sat down on the edge of the bidet. The bristles on Steg's toothbrushes were pointing in all directions, like the branches of Scots pines or stone pines. Emma sat there for a while gazing at the floor tiles and, holding her perfumed finger to her nose, imagined herself as a chamois, clambering up over rocks and roots to reach the heights. Far off in the distance, she could hear the sound of children. In the forest? On the street? Then foot-steps, moving ever more slowly. Please go on past, she thought. But there was no time for her to work out what to do next; the footsteps stopped abruptly and she heard the sound of a key turning in the lock. First one way and then, when the door failed to open, the other. Now you've locked it, Emma thought to herself. The door rattled before it finally opened. Emma held her breath. Gingerly, she slid down off the edge of the bidet onto the floor; she heard her knee-joints crack and a rustle as she brushed against the pile of newspapers. A jolt of pain shot up her back. I'll never manage to get up again, she thought ruefully.

The curve of the bidet bowl stopped her from getting into a comfortable position. She tried to lever herself off the floor and prop herself against the wall; the key thing was not to make any noise. Maybe, if Steg had just nipped back up to the room to get another book, he wouldn't notice her here in the bathroom. She could see limescale streaks on the underside of the bidet. Those girls simply weren't thorough enough, not even the new one, whom she'd cut too much slack just because of where she came from. But what if Steg did come into the bathroom? She heard him open one drawer, then another. Was he worried that someone had broken in, on account of finding the door unlocked? Was he checking that everything was still there? A sigh came from the next room, unsettling in its suggestion of exhaustion. I'll close my eyes and make out I was suddenly taken ill, she thought. But Emma was far too nervous to close her eyes, she couldn't stand the darkness and preferred gazing at the porcelain of the bidet. One time, when she'd not yet been in Rome two months, one of the Anima women had tried to convince her that you could flush out the sperm after having intercourse. Emma hadn't believed this for a second but even so, after going with Remo, she'd fled in a panic into one of the vacant guest rooms and squatted over the bidet inlet until her inner thighs were red and raw. There was no way she could have a child by Remo. And so soon after Johann's death. *Come back to Stillbach,* her mother had written, *otherwise they'll kill you as well. We don't need your money anymore.* But before she knew it, Franz was already due, and her marriage to Remo had all been settled by his parents.

Why didn't Steg leave the room? He'd obviously sat down on the chair; Emma could hear its backrest creaking. If he didn't clear off soon, her excuse that she'd had a dizzy spell wouldn't wash any more. If he found her now, he'd be bound to call a doctor. By now, Emma was sweating. With the full weight of her body resting on it, the hand she was using to support herself started to tremble, so violently that she began to wonder whether the shaking wasn't running through the tiled floor and spreading out in waves into the adjoining room. Wouldn't it be better if she simply called out for him, feigning a fainting fit? 'Herr Steg,' she began, but all that came out was a faint croak that blended in unnoticeably with the sounds from the next room. But, as it happened, Steg had stood up and approached the bathroom door. Perhaps he'd just got up to consult his dictionary. Emma didn't hear him press down on the door lever; the only thing she did register were steps coming ever closer. She closed her eyes.

'Heavens above!' she heard Hermann Steg exclaim, 'what are *you* doing there?'

14

I'd turned into the next street and could still hear the distant splashing of the Fontana di Trevi mixed with the clamour of tourists' voices when someone tugged at my sleeve. My first reaction was not to turn around, as I was fearful my stalker had found me again, but then I heard Antonella's voice: 'You saw me, right? Admit you saw me. You're just making out you didn't see me.'

Her firm grip on my arm prevented me from getting away. Her hands were still wet from fishing coins out of the fountain.

'I didn't want to disturb you,' I told her.

Antonella was out of breath. She took off her baseball cap and ran her fingers through her hair. 'They just chuck money away. Day after day.'

'It's not meant for you, though.' The place on my upper arm where she'd had hold of me was damp and felt cold. I stepped aside from the stream of tourists into a house entrance.

'Surely you don't believe all that rubbish –' Antonella sat herself down on the seat of a Vespa parked in the entrance. 'Or are you superstitious? You realise the money goes straight to the city council?'

'And to people like you.'

'What's so wrong with that? It's my city too.'

'What'll you do if they catch you?' I asked.

'I'm not doing this on my own, you know – do you think I'm stupid? We split the proceeds.'

'Who, you and Mimmo?'

'No way, he'd be dragging me back home by my hair if he knew what I was up to.' She hopped off the Vespa. Behind me, someone opened the door to the house and a blast of *varechina* wafted out. Or was it *candeggina*? Or *nettorina*? By the time I got back home two months from now, I'd know every last Italian word for bleach and disinfectant plus a smattering of Roman slang and precious little else.

Antonella squared up to me. 'So? What now?'

I shrugged my shoulders. 'How often do you do it?'

'What?'

'Steal coins.'

'Steal?' She laughed. 'I'm not taking anything from anyone. I'm not even robbing them of their illusions.' Her gaze was caught by a young man walking past the entranceway. He looked at her and she waved back. 'See you tomorrow,' she called out, before turning her attention back to me. 'Listen – I need 200,000 lire. I want to get myself a *Ciao* scooter, right? I don't get to keep any of the money I earn at the hotel; I have to hand most of that over at home.' She probed the crack between two paving stones with the toe of her left sandal. One of its cross-straps had broken, so much was evident from the makeshift black thread that had been used to sew it back on. 'Lucky for me people have taken to throwing money into the water, anyhow – time was when they just took a sip from the fountain.' As she said this, Antonella made a face, as if the very thought disgusted her. 'No way they could do that now – there's so many tourists they'd drink it dry.'

'All in the name of good luck,' I added.

'I dunno whether I'd call it good luck to come back to Rome – or fall in love with a Roman, for that matter.' Here, she paused, taking off her sunglasses and rubbing her eyelids with her index finger. 'It would have been better for all of us if Manente hadn't, for a start.'

Right in front of us, someone passing by bit into a club sandwich and licked mayonnaise off their finger with the tip of their tongue. I caught a fleeting glimpse of hands with dirty black-rimmed fingernails and a sunburnt face.

'She just doesn't belong here,' Antonella continued.

'So where do you reckon she does belong?'

'Dunno, somewhere in the North. Austria, maybe.' I noticed she had damp patches on the back pockets of her denim skirt.

'So, not even Stillbach, then?'

'Wherever,' she replied.

'But that's in Italy.'

'Not really,' she said, shaking her head.

So did the people who forced the region to Italianise also belong in Stillbach, I wondered, but kept it to myself. There was no point arguing with Antonella. She was proud of being a communist. Two days ago, she'd shown me her party membership card. But at the same time she clearly thought Italy was exclusively for the Italians.

'The only person Manente ever loved was her Nazi,' Antonella went on, 'she should never have married the boss.'

'But she was pregnant by him.'

'That's a lie. She conned him. The only thing she was interested in was the hotel.'

I found myself walking along beside her, though I'd no idea where she was heading. She turned into a street at whose far end loomed the dazzling white bulk of the Victor Emmanuel II monument. The Altar of the Motherland. The Wedding Cake. The Typewriter. Now I'd got my bearings again. I'd been here before.

'How could you possibly know that?' I asked, tripping over a broom that a street sweeper had left propped against the wall of a house. The bloke was some distance away down the street, leaning against his dustcart and having a smoke. Maybe my words got lost in the traffic noise, or Antonella shrugged without my noticing, but in any event she didn't respond.

To the left and right, all along the Via del Corso, the mannequins in the shop windows and the passers-by seemed to merge into one. Someone with an old man's hoarse voice was hawking lottery tickets.

Abruptly, Antonella stopped in her tracks. 'I'm off to meet Mimmo. Want to come along?'

A few minutes later we were boarding a bus back in the direction of the hotel. It smelt of sweat, deodorant and perfume. The windows rattled; every time the driver changed gear, it put me in mind of a tractor. The noise was out of kilter with the smart appearance of the driver, who wore a suit and tie. Also, he was sitting a foot or so above the level of the passengers, making him look even more dignified. When we got off the green ATAC bus, I could already make out in the distance the pink-coloured buildings in the Umbertine gingerbread-house style, but Antonella set off in the opposite direction to the hotel. We got to a public park, where we sat down on a bench to wait for her brother. Antonella lit a cigarette; in the pauses when she wasn't dragging on it, she used her front teeth to chisel the varnish off her nails.

'I just need to hand the money over to him, then we can go,' she announced.

'What money, the coins?'

'No, no – I told you, he doesn't know anything about that.' Antonella linked her hands behind her neck and stretched luxuriantly. 'We've all got to help out at home, or else we'll lose the bakery.' She paused. 'My Dad's just like them,' she said, nodding in the direction of the park entrance, where some men were sitting smoking on a low wall. She'd already hinted that she couldn't stand her father; she hated the fact that he loafed about doing nothing – though he didn't drink because he feared the wrath of his mother, whose husband had been a real hero, one of the partisans. 'Sometimes Dad goes and visits Mimmo in the bakery and deliberately gets flour on himself to make it look like he's been helping out there.'

'How much did you fish out today?'

'You're not back on that again, are you?' Antonella crossed her legs.

'Look – you know nothing about it. Or maybe you're just jealous I've got this job.' In the interim, she'd nibbled every last fleck of nail polish off her index and middle fingers.

Job? – I shook my head in disbelief.

'I've made two or three thousand already. There were too many people there today, though. But you don't want too few, either. One time, this German wanted to report me. He started yelling blue murder like I'd stolen his wallet.'

'So what did you do?'

'I legged it,' said Antonella.

'And the others working this scam, do you know all of them?'

She didn't respond but turned her head away and pointed at an approaching figure. 'There's Mimmo now.'

He was taller than Antonella and stopped in front of us, with his shoulders hunched and his hands buried in his trouser pockets. His white trainers had a light brown trim.

'This is Ines,' began Antonella, 'remember I told you about her already – she's our new German girl.'

Mimmo's face was shiny with sweat, or did I flatter myself he was looking flushed for another reason? He gave me his hand. A smile was playing round his mouth and eyes – but not just there; every facial feature, and even his shirt and the way in which he bent down to greet me, was one big beaming smile.

15

Emma had the image of Johann before her now; he was marching in step with all the other recruits along the Via del Babuino, but overhead all the windows were shuttered and the balconies empty of onlookers. Nor were there any flags to be seen, or girls eagerly waving. Emma could see his head, held proudly high, and his fair complexion and his mouth opening and closing in unison with the rest – yes, that was her Johann singing all right. The German troops always sang on their way back to barracks, or rather that Lieutenant Wolgast – who they called 'Lieutenant Vollgas' behind his back – ordered them to sing. So there was Johann, belting out the song *Turn, My Darling* with all the others, in time to the steady crunch of their boots on the cobblestones. For all that, he was completely unmusical; in church in Stillbach, he'd just gone through the motions of singing, silently miming the words. All Emma could see before her now were choirboys' mouths and, among those wide-open orifices, Johann's mouth too. Involuntarily – she seemed unable to stop the images flickering past – in the very next instant, Johann had turned into someone else and was grasping her by the shoulders.

'Come along, I'll help you up.'

But a vivid picture of the recruits still floated before Emma's eyes as they approached the tunnel that had been drilled through one of Rome's seven hills, towards that gaping hole in the middle of the city, which reminded Emma anew of the rough-hewn tunnels through the hillsides on the mountain road above Stillbach. She didn't understand where these images came from, showing her fiancé and all his singing comrades, with their machine-pistols at the ready as they marched relentlessly onward, all the while getting closer and closer to the underpass beneath the Quirinal Palace, this bolt-hole right in the heart of the city, where the homeless and people who'd been bombed out of their houses took refuge for want of anywhere else to go. And in that moment, Emma too was at a loss what to do next, for she'd seen something which of course she hadn't actually seen on the day it happened – the soldiers wheeling left just before the mouth of the tunnel into the narrow, gently rising Via Rasella, where only a rubbish cart and a road sweeper were standing. And in the midst of the recruits tramped her Johann, who probably had nothing on his mind except his imminent leave, the end of his training and the handover to the troops of Ten Company. He'd have been wondering about his new guard duties and perhaps thinking to himself: 'Not long now, just up the Via Rasella and at the end of the street right into Via delle Quattro Fontane as far as the Interior Ministry's Viminale Barracks,' and no doubt daydreaming of her, his Emma, and their next tryst at the Anima, and going back to Stillbach one day, when the Germans had finally managed to bring law and order to this open city and finish off the communists.

It was warm. Wearing his steel helmet and his heavy munitions belt, Johann must have been sweating, just like Emma was sweating now. What should she do? Not daring to open her eyes, she quickly ushered her Johann – *Turn, my darling* – out of the ranks of his fellow soldiers and into the tunnel, so he could emerge at the far end – safe and sound.

'It's nothing, really,' Emma heard herself say. Clutching the proffered hand, she pulled herself up into a sitting position.

'Should I call an ambulance?' Steg pressed his palm to her forehead for a moment. 'Well, you don't seem to be feverish, at least.'

Emma could still feel the bidet poking into her back, but it wasn't painful any more, as Steg felt her wrist to take her pulse. She focussed on the gentle pressure of his index and middle fingers and hoped that he didn't manage to find her pulse straight away.

When she finally opened her eyes a crack, all she could see was her own chest, rising and falling. 'I – I just wanted to check…to draw the blinds.'

If only he'd stay here. But the recruits were on the move again and they weren't going into the tunnel, but turning into the Via Rasella instead, where that man in the blue road sweeper's uniform and the blue-black peaked cap had already positioned his rubbish cart in the middle of the road outside the Palazzo Tittoni, so that the platoon would have to march around it.

'…twenty-one, twenty-two, twenty-three…' What was being counted? Heartbeats? Steps? Seconds? The victims? For the second time that day, Emma felt a searing pain in her back. The rubbish cart exploded, disintegrating in a fraction of a second. The blast tore a huge crater in the stone wall of the Palazzo and another in the road. But the tiles beneath Emma were still smooth; Steg was standing beside her and next to him was Johann, whom she'd sent into the tunnel to save him from being blown to smithereens. She'd chased him into that hole so he'd remain complete, every inch still her Johann. So he wouldn't be atomised. Entrance closed: Johann was safe under the hill. Safe in her personal air-raid shelter, her *ricovero di fortuna,* as they called it in those days.

'Frau Emma, open your eyes. Emma?' Steg wasn't his usual taciturn self. He was talking as if he feared that silence might be a harbinger of death and that he had to do something to combat it, yet it was only in total silence that Emma was able to see Johann. It was good that Steg didn't smoke. He smelt of aftershave.

The road sweeper had a pipe in his mouth. Emma knew that he'd stood next to the rubbish cart smoking. In fact, she knew more details about the incident than anyone who'd actually been there. After all, each of them only had the witness of two eyes, whereas Emma had her own and that of all the others who'd ever looked into it. For years after, articles about the bombing kept appearing in the newspapers and continued to do so. *L'azione partigiana.*

The man had lifted the cover of the rubbish bin and lit the fuse with the embers in his pipe. If only there'd been a build-up of ash in the bowl, he'd have waited in vain for a spark to catch the fuse and someone would have noticed that this road sweeper wasn't all he appeared to be. But the platoon had other things on their mind; they were busy singing the song that Lieutenant Wolgast had ordered them to sing, and were oblivious to everything else. They swung round the corner, relieved to be getting closer to the barracks with every step. Meanwhile, in the rubbish cart, unseen by the marching troops, the fuse had started to fizz. The bomber shut the lid and placed his peaked cap on top as a signal to the other partisans involved in the attack that the device was now primed.

Fifty seconds to go.

Meanwhile, the singing column of recruits had filled the entire road.

'Feeling a bit better now?' asked Steg.

A whirlwind of shrapnel, plaster fragments and stone shards, thought Emma. She steadied herself on the edge of the bidet and, taking hold of Steg, levered herself upright. 'It's just this heat.'

His arm felt strong, like he did some manual labour now and then. On that afternoon, the street sweeper had set off 18 kilos of TNT, an explosive that expands at a velocity of several thousand metres per second. She'd got that fact later from the newspaper. In the aftermath of the explosion, they'd had to go round picking up chunks of human flesh and the shoes of those who'd survived the blast.

From outside came the drone of a light plane's engine, interspersed with the yowling of a cat.

'The girls are always reliable, I just wanted to...'

'Have a little lie-down on the bed while I fetch a doctor.'

'No – no doctors,' said Emma, squeezing his hand.

Steg helped Emma over to the bed and she lay back with her feet touching the floor. She fancied she could smell the newspapers that Steg stashed in his room and the dust that clung to his books.

Steg went back into the bathroom for a damp cloth, giving Emma the opportunity to inspect the bedclothes more closely. She couldn't find any evidence of a woman's hair and the pillowcases were clean, too – no traces of make-up or lipstick. Then Steg came back, bent over Emma and patted her forehead with the cloth.

Only now did it occur to her that she hadn't made any effort to spruce herself up and that here she was, lying next to Steg with her hair all messed up and dressed in a blouse that she'd been wearing for the past seven or eight hours.

'I'm sorry for putting you to so much trouble.'

Steg looked at Emma but said nothing. He made a face like he'd only just noticed – now that the initial shock at finding her slumped in his bathroom had worn off – that there was a woman lying on his bed. Unable to hold his gaze, she closed her eyes.

At Steg's side, Emma would chance one last trip back to Stillbach. She wouldn't have to book in to a guesthouse as a single person, under her own name, which a few people in Stillbach would doubtless still recognise. No, as Frau Steg, she'd be able to stroll across the church square, her features concealed by dark glasses and a hat, and enjoy being a stranger for a while, an Austrian tourist. Incognito, she'd watch her siblings and her former friends who'd never moved away from Stillbach for all those decades growing frailer, fatter, balder and wearier. Only now and then, when there was talk of Rome or the Pope on one of the RAI channels or elsewhere, did they pause to remember Emma, and then instantly forget about her again. Perhaps they also thought of her when they passed the war memorial in the village cemetery and read Johann's name: *Died 23rd March 1944 in Rome.*

Emma knew from her cousin that that the gossip had died down pretty quickly and that the last time she'd been the talk of the village was when she'd come back for her mother's funeral and refused to walk directly behind the coffin with her brothers and sisters, but instead had mingled with the other villagers right at the back of the cortège.

Steg brushed Emma's hair from her forehead and for an instant she dared to hope it might be some token of endearment, but he only let his hand rest there for the briefest of instants.

16

When Antonella and I got back to the hotel, the garden gate was ajar; Cocola was standing by the rear entrance with a serious expression and talking to an oldish man, who was just taking his leave. It was so quiet in this part of the garden that you could hear the man's footsteps as he crunched down the gravel path.

Antonella went on ahead; she was in a rush and wanted to change before going out again – where to, she didn't say.

I walked over to the fountain and looked for the goldfish; one of the shubunkins was missing. Probably the one whose tail had kept bobbing up. I thought about Mimmo as I scraped some moss off the column with the figure. The fountain ornament looked a bit like a gnawed bone. But behind its heavily eroded surface, you could still see it was some kind of female statuette holding a cornucopia in her hands.

Mimmo had invited me to come and see where he worked and bake some bread with him. But because Antonella hadn't felt like visiting her family, I'd ended up going back to the hotel with her instead. I hadn't felt bold enough to go off on my own with her brother to the outskirts of Rome; mainly, I was worried that I wouldn't be able to find a bus back from there into the city centre after a certain hour and would be totally reliant on Mimmo for transport. During our brief encounter in the park, he'd rattled off one question after another: How come I spoke Italian so fluently? What kind of music did I like? Was

I enjoying Rome? Was I an only child? When he wasn't bombarding me with questions, he'd showered me with compliments on my hair and eyes.

The old Italian blarney. Their love of flattery. Their deep, smouldering looks.

'Don't fall for their spiel,' Mum had warned me. And what about Mrs M – had she fallen for it and got herself ensnared by some attractive hotel owner's son? Or had she, as Antonella insisted, deliberately hooked up with Remo so she could stay in Rome and take over the hotel? Or was she so shocked by the death of her beloved 'Nazi' that falling in love with Remo Manente brought salvation, a new beginning for her, a welcome distraction?

I hadn't been to Stillbach very often. The only things there are a church, a cemetery, an inn and a primary school, which also doubles as the parish hall. About fifty houses cluster round this core, while everyone else from the village lives in isolated farmhouses in the surrounding woods and fields. Aunt Hilda knew almost all the families there; most were related and many were involved in long-running disputes with one another. Mostly, we just looked across at Stillbach from the opposite slope, the sunny side of the valley, which clear-felling and overgrazing had turned into barren scrubland as far back as the Middle Ages. The annual rainfall where we lived, Aunt Hilda once told me, was about the same as in North Africa. On one of our Sunday excursions, she'd pointed out the pretty mountain fennel and ephedra herbs, which were supposed to stimulate your nervous system. Some chemical derived from ephedra was also used to make hallucinogens, she said. Later, a friend and I had gone looking for ephedra plants, but drew a blank.

When you looked over at Stillbach, rising behind the village you could see the Stillbacher Horn, and off to the left a line of glaciers fringing the mountain ridge; yet on our side of the valley you were standing on a piece of ground that could just as well have been in Southern

Europe. Maybe Mrs Manente, who'd grown up surrounded by woods on the northern slope in Stillbach, had had her whole outlook shaped by the constant view of the dry steppe over on the far side of the valley. Had the sight, day after day, of our arid slopes made her yearn for the South? Was that why she'd left home?

It struck me that she'd sometimes make mistakes in German, for example with verbs like *arbeiten*, which she wrongly stressed on the second syllable. Even as the word left her mouth, she'd furrow her brow as though she sensed something wasn't quite right.

I'd occasionally see her sitting on the terrace, with her head resting against the wall, her eyes shut and her mouth slightly agape. Even at midday she seemed to be exhausted, though she'd spent the whole morning delegating jobs.

Someone called my name. Startled, I spun round and, losing my balance, grasped at an oleander branch to steady myself, but quickly let it go again when I realised it wouldn't bear my weight. The voice was unfamiliar. As I made my way to the main entrance, where it had come from, I passed a wooden chair I hadn't spotted before in the undergrowth, all overgrown with ivy but otherwise undamaged.

'The cook's looking for you,' said Paul from the top of the entrance steps, 'she's in the kitchen.' He was wearing a pair of dark suit trousers, a grey shirt and a white clerical collar.

I didn't have the courage to ask why he sometimes wore the dog collar, but at other times went around in jeans and a T-shirt. Was he some kind of priest-in-training, who was allowed to slip into civvies when he was off duty?

'What does she want?'

'Signora Manente isn't feeling well; you'll have to serve the guests,' Paul replied. He leapt down the three steps to the garden path in a single bound, leaving behind a dark skid-mark on the gravel. 'See you later,' he said and smiled. Halfway to the garden gate, he turned round to look at me again.

In the kitchen, Cocola was busy chopping *frittate* up into small pieces. On the sideboard were two salamis and an unsliced piece of *prosciutto crudo*. She asked me whether I knew how to operate the slicer.

'I'll give it a go,' I said, pulling on an apron.

'Antonella's vanished; she must have known I needed her. Any idea where's she got to?'

'No.'

'No, no – not like that.' She snatched the piece of ham from my hand and cut off the rind.

'Is Mrs Manente ill, then?' I asked.

'Start with the salami, it's easier to cut. But you've got to peel the skin off first. And not so thick as that slice there – no-one wants to eat that.'

Mum never bought salami, not because it was unhealthy but because cured sausage reminded her of my father. He was particularly partial to mule salami: originally, all salami contained donkey and mule meat, and the very thought of it made my mother feel queasy. She swore blind that salami came from knackered army mules, though in fact it had long been made from beef and pork only.

'She's having trouble with a slipped disc…No, too thin! Much too thin!' Cocola adjusted the blade on the machine. 'She really should go to a health spa, but who'd run the hotel? Francesco's a *fannullone*, a good-for-nothing. In the end, this place'll just wither on the vine.'

We worked side by side in silence for a while; all you could hear was the ticking of the kitchen clock. Ada never wasted any time on personal chit-chat. For her, silence had something permanent about it, like she was no longer alive, and only her work had any real durability, outstripping her defunct personal life.

Ada was punctual, clean and industrious – the stereotypical German, in fact. She couldn't help telling you how to do something better, even when you were doing it exactly the same as her. I'd never seen her satisfied with anything.

'Are you from Rome?' I asked.

She was busy fishing eggs out of a pan of boiling water and putting them on a plate. She glanced up briefly like she'd forgotten to do something. She seemed to be slotting my question into the running order of her kitchen routine, as though even incidental conversation had to run to a strict timetable.

'Yes,' she replied.

'You're quite handy really, aren't you?' Cocola said after a while. Her face disappeared behind a cloud of steam as she poured the egg water away. 'Actually, we never have any problems with you German girls.'

'My father's Italian,' I said.

'Then be thankful that you don't seem to have inherited much from him.' Saying this, she fixed me with an even more pointed stare than usual. 'Emma didn't mention that. She told me you'd been brought up by your mother. That you were a widow's daughter.'

'A widow? Where'd she get that from? My parents separated before I was even born. No, I've got a father all right. Somewhere. He remarried.'

'*Donnaiolo,*' muttered Cocola under her breath: 'skirt chaser'.

The *antipasti* were all done; I put them in the cool room. It was time to summon the guests.

17

Emma was lying on a deckchair behind the house, with her eyes wide open, gazing at the sky. The small clutch of dark clouds that had appeared above the hotel roof half an hour before had gradually dispersed and shrunk. One had a pronounced wavy underside and a sort of brindled look about it. Though Emma often watched clouds, it had never occurred to her before that these ephemeral formations were quite unique and that you'd never spot the same cloud twice.

Steg had led Emma out into the garden, draping her left arm over his shoulders to try to hold her upright. Her back pains had spread down to her legs and it seemed to her that she was dragging her left one. Steg appeared oblivious to this – all he'd said was that she looked pale and overworked.

After finding Emma in his bathroom, he'd run down to reception, looked up Doctor Franceschini's number in the phone book and, despite his rudimentary Italian, succeeded in getting his message across. An hour later, the doctor duly appeared at the garden gate and rang the bell. Franceschini had been the GP of Emma's parents-in-law and had also been in attendance when Remo passed away. Despite his age, he kept up his practice because he dreaded boredom. When people asked him why he didn't retire, he always replied that life at home with his wife was like watching paint dry. Illnesses, he claimed, existed to stave off monotony – without them, and all the other bigger or smaller catastrophes we suffer in a lifetime, we'd scarcely be able to close our mouths for yawning. Emma liked Franceschini, even though he always came out with the same old patter about boredom and didn't seem to notice that his repetitiveness had itself become rather tedious.

Steg retired to the corridor when the doctor began examining Emma. For his part, Franceschini discreetly overlooked the fact that Emma Manente was in a stranger's bed and not in her own apartment.

Emma, though, immediately launched into an explanation. Franceschini just approached her bedside, laughed and said conspiratorially: 'Pretty or plain, they all get married.'

From the very first time they'd met here in Rome – in those days Emma was still a chambermaid working for the Manentes – Doctor Franceschini had noticed a striking resemblance between Emma and the actress Laura Nucci, who'd been in the film *Belle o brutte, si sposan tutte*. It had been released the same year Emma left the Scabellos in Venice and came to Rome. Years later, someone in the Anima spread the rumour that the German SS officer Erich Priebke had had an affair with the fascist diva, and Emma, who at that point hadn't seen Nucci either in the flesh or on screen and had no idea what the actress even looked like, still felt secretly flattered.

Nucci was only three years older than Emma.

The sun was setting behind the palms. A feeling of languor spreading through Emma's body made her feel almost euphoric. The jab was clearly having an effect.

She remembered seeing somewhere that Nucci had taken another supporting role in a thriller; they must have just completed shooting when she read the report. In the movie, Nucci played the part of a witch. How idiotic. Thrillers weren't Emma's thing for a start, and she also steered clear of any films set in Venice. She didn't want to be reminded of the Scabellos, especially the lady of the house, who'd insisted on helping her iron shirts; she was adamant that it took two people tugging on the collars to get them back into shape.

The Scabello woman had even forbidden her to use the washboard, forcing Emma to scrub the washing with her bare hands, because the Signora was worried the board might damage her precious enamelled bathtub. In those days, depending on the weather conditions, the fetid smell of the drains would seep up into the house through the outflow pipe. The only thing capable of masking that rank stench was the chlorine in the bleach.

Remo tried inviting Emma to Venice once. 'I'm happy to go anywhere with you,' she replied, 'just not there.' She never, ever wanted to run across that Scabello woman again, who'd been too mean even to let her have a cup of coffee.

The job at the Scabellos that Emma had hated the most, though, was cleaning the carpets with turpentine. The smell of it remained with her for years after. Even so, some of the domestics in Venice at that time had it even worse than she did. One had to clean all fourteen rooms in the villa every day without fail, even if nobody had set foot in them. Another had to take the dirty laundry to a washhouse three blocks away and lug it back again all on her own when it was soaking wet and heavy. In winter, the washing froze stiff and she could barely prise her fingers free from the icy zinc washtub.

But Maria, who'd left Stillbach at the same time as Emma, had really fallen on her feet; in Rome, she ended up working for Gina Lollobrigida. Sure, she had to put in long hours when the actress held receptions at home, but she hadn't had to suffer a tight-fisted and moody employer like Signora Scabello. One time – at a Sunday coffee morning at the Anima, as Emma recalled – Maria told her about meeting Grace Kelly, who'd turned up with Prince Rainier. On another occasion, she'd met Vittorio Gassman and Alberto Sordi; Emma remembered Sordi as the man who'd done the Italian voiceover for Oliver Hardy.

Stories like that cut no ice back home in Stillbach. The only *Gina* Emma's father knew was the neighbour's cow, while her mother immediately started worrying about Maria's moral well-being: 'She shouldn't be hob-nobbing with those sorts of people,' she said disapprovingly.

But soon enough, Emma lost the chance to regale them with such tales, anyway; all contact was broken off in the Fifties and even the trickle of letters that her mother wrote her straight after the war dried up after Emma stopped sending money back home. In any case, as Remo's wife, she wasn't earning anymore; she was accepted, even if not hugely respected, as Signora Manente, had brought up Franz and, after his birth, had also suffered two miscarriages. 'Try to make peace with your family,' Doctor Franceschini advised her at the time, 'maybe it'll help ease the complications with your pregnancies.' The second miscarriage was preceded by violent shivering and stomach pains; her womb, Emma recalled, had become inflamed and turned septic. All the while Franz, who was then five years old, clutched his mother's hand tightly and refused to let go; eighteen months before, after her first miscarriage, they'd whisked her off to hospital and he was terrified she wouldn't come back.

'D'you think she's finally got it through that thick skull of hers that that Roman bloke's not right for her?' Emma's older brother reportedly said to their cousin when he heard the news. Her cousin was always careful to tone down the family's worst excesses: Emma was pretty sure he hadn't said 'Roman bloke', but had used some term like 'spaghetti-eater', 'dago', 'eyetie' or 'wop'.

Later, her cousin tried to persuade one of the many nephews from Stillbach that Emma had acquired in the interim to go and visit her in Rome, but Emma scotched the plan – 'Kids shouldn't have to patch up what their parents have broken' – and that was the end of it. Emma's older brother was one of those diehard Stillbachers who made a point of waving their passport out of the car window at the Chiusa di Salorno Narrows whenever they were driving south to Trento or Verona – a defiant gesture designed to show that they were entering a foreign country. As well as flaunting his credentials at non-existent border guards there, her brother also refused point-blank to speak a word of Italian to the real officials at the Brenner and Resia Passes when he went to Austria. In the mid-Fifties, he'd served an apprenticeship as a hydraulic engineer in Schwäbisch Gmünd and after completing his master's diploma had come back to Stillbach to start his own business. After holidaying in Stillbach and seeing for themselves the desperate lack of job prospects for young people from South Tyrol, ethnic Germans who'd been driven out of the Sudetenland in 1945 and fetched up in Swabia were happy to take on lads from Stillbach as apprentices. After the war, all the public service jobs had gone to Italians. But fortunately help was at hand from Germany, the Land of the Economic Miracle.

It'd been the same story at the Hotel Manente, thought Emma, only no Sudeten Germans ever set foot down here; they preferred visiting the regions inhabited by their oppressed German-speaking comrades.

Emma called to mind a comrade-in-arms of Johann's who'd once paid a surprise visit to the hotel. He'd come down to Rome on the thirtieth anniversary of the partisan attack, but couldn't bring himself to walk down the Via Rasella. Instead, he stopped at the end of the road and peered from a distance at the spot where the outrage had occurred.

Later, he explained that what had happened there had overshadowed his whole life in peacetime. 'You don't just come home from a war and forget about it. You fall into a state of limbo and that's when the nightmares really take hold. Over and over again.' Perhaps it was for the best that Johann had been spared all that, he added.

'Well, I was certainly spared him,' Emma had snapped back bitterly when he'd said that, 'and spared my family, too.' And I was spared Stillbach as well, she now thought.

She didn't dare shift from her prone position. How long had she been lying here motionless in the garden? Where had Steg gone? How would the cook manage to get dinner together without her?

She longed for Steg to be sitting beside her, holding her hand. She swallowed hard. It felt as though something had lodged itself in her throat.

That time, she'd just upped and fled from Johann's old comrade, leaving him standing there in the garden. He had a nice life, a wife and three kids, a house and a carpentry business; he hadn't even lost so much as a finger in the war. And he kept going on about how he took his family on holiday every year to Lake Wörth in Carinthia and how he'd bought himself a Mercedes.

Before he checked out, the carpenter had left a note at reception, wishing her all the best and signed only with his initials. Maybe, Emma thought, the shallow little man had finally understood that a full name implied that you'd also led a full life.

18

Mrs Manente had two parallel vertical creases, running up from the bridge of her nose and ending mid-way up her forehead, that looked like the sketch of a road. Apparently there are sections of motorway like that on Sicily, which just stop in the middle of nowhere. Aunt Hilda told me that public money had been illegally siphoned off and eventually just dried up. There was something unfinished about Mrs M, too. Perhaps it was her contradictory appearance that gave this impression. She had delicate facial features but at the same time big, strong hands – likewise a small head set on broad shoulders.

I was pleased she was ill, though it meant I'd already had to run up to her rooms twice, once with a cup of tea and this time with a bowl of beef consommé.

There was a little shrine with a crucifix in the corner of her lounge. One half of the room was occupied by a dark brown leather sofa, two leather chairs and a glass-topped table, while the other contained a painted wooden chest and a corner bench-and-chair suite made from stone pine. The room measured about 40 square metres, so these two completely mismatched pieces of décor weren't hard up against one another, but even so, there they were occupying the same space without any shelving or plants between them. There were cushions on the pine chairs and corner settle, covered with a fabric that I'd often seen used for curtains. It looked like it was embroidered, but in fact it was machine-made and printed with a pattern of alpine roses and gentians.

Aunt Hilda, I recalled, had been taught how to do linen embroidery as a girl; all her sheets, pillowcases and duvet covers had the initials of her maiden name on them. I wondered whether Mrs Manente had had the money and time to make herself a trousseau, too.

'Put the soup down on the chest.' As though in slow-motion, the proprietress rose with a painful groan from one of the leather chairs. I rushed over to help her, but she shooed me away with a flapping hand gesture that meant she was perfectly capable of getting up by herself. 'Don't go thinking it's holiday time now,' she said. 'The mattresses in the vacant rooms need turning and airing, for one thing. Antonella knows how to do it; ask her. Plus you can both get on with cleaning the blinds as of tomorrow.'

I was standing next to the chest with the tray in my hands, uncertain whether I should go or stay. Outside, it was beginning to get dark; the light-coloured curtains, half-pulled, were reflecting in the windows, making one section of the pane appear like it was made of opaque glass.

I wouldn't have put it past Mrs Manente to polish the bottoms of the table legs, comb the fringes on the rugs and dismantle the leather chairs on a daily basis in her hunt for every last speck of dust. What did she imagine we'd get up to? Loaf about in the guests' rooms reading their newspapers, just because she was stuck in bed up here for a while? Sure, sometimes I'd skimped a bit on cleaning this or that bathroom, so I could retire to the loos and snatch a bit of downtime for myself, reading one of those little paperbacks of Chekhov's *The Man in a Case* or Turgenev's *First Love* that fitted so neatly into my pinafore pocket. Even so, I was lucky if I could get more than ten or at most twenty minutes' reading time in any one afternoon.

I moved towards the door, wishing Mrs M a speedy recovery.

'Wait,' she commanded.

Had I been mistaken? Was she about to give me a tip? She slumped down on a chair. A stone pine suite in the centre of Rome, whatever next? Weren't those traditional wood carvings from Val Gardena made from the same wood?

Mrs Manente paused. Maybe she'd sat down too suddenly; her face was contorted with pain.

'Would you ask Herr Steg to come up and see me?' she said. She leant forward, rubbing the palm of her hand over the base of her spine several times and closing her eyes. 'I'd like to express my gratitude.'

Up on the second floor, I knocked once on Steg's door and, getting no response, waited a while before trying again. I was just about to leave when he finally opened up. He was wearing a flimsy bathrobe, with the belt only loosely tied, revealing his bare legs and a large expanse of hairy torso. I wondered whether he was aware that his stripy silk dressing gown was slipping open and that I could already see that he didn't have any underwear on. Maybe I'd woken him and he was still half asleep.

'Gratitude?' Steg chuckled when I passed on the message and grabbed my hand. 'Now, I wouldn't mind if *you* showed me a bit of gratitude.' Saying this, he tried to pull me into the room. 'Don't worry, I'm not going to hurt you. I'll be nice.'

I wrenched myself free. He stepped back and pulled the door to so that just his head was peeping through the crack. 'Only joking!' he called after me.

I took the tray back to the kitchen, wondering whether to tell Cocola about what had happened, but decided against it. Anyway, the cook was deep in conversation with the couple from Room 30, who were gushing about their trip to Ostia Antica, going on about everything from the grand houses and the mosaics to the Roman public latrines and fishmongers' shops. 'You can still see the pond where they kept fresh fish for sale,' I heard the woman say. She was wearing a dainty little gold watch; the strap was buried in the roll of fat around her wrist.

Cocola nodded at me briefly, then waved me away.

A wind had got up in the garden. The gravel path was shining white.

From the open windows of the dining room came a low murmur of voices. I caught the sound of a woman laughing – it sounded like the long drawn-out noise of the brakes on railway wagons as they were shunted around the marshalling yard in Bologna. Even as a child, I was thrilled at the thought of going to Italian stations, without really knowing where this feeling came from, only that it had something to do with the pale stone benches and the drinking fountains.

Did Mrs M plan on having a cosy little tête-à-tete with Steg in the pine snug of her living room? Hadn't she noticed that he didn't fancy her?

I could hear a cat miaowing in a corner of the garden; I went looking for it, treading softly so as not to alarm the animal. When I thought I'd got close, I crouched down and tried enticing it with some cat-like noises. The evening breeze stirred the leaves and twigs and cooled my sweaty face. But there was no sign of the cat.

'Capponi,' said a man's voice, 'you need to call "Capponi" for her to come.'

Startled, I shot to my feet – and so did the cat, which had been lying low just a few metres from me behind a bush. It shot off in the direction of the laundry block.

The man appeared from behind a palm tree and rummaged in his pockets for cigarettes.

'What are you doing here?' I asked.

Paul laughed: 'More to the point, what are *you* doing here?'

As the flame from his lighter momentarily lit up his neck and face, I noticed he wasn't wearing the clerical collar that he'd had on a few hours before.

'What was the cat's name again?'

'Capponi,' Paul said.

'Never heard of it before.'

'Mrs Manente doesn't like cats, maybe that's why she chose that name. Cigarette?'

I shook my head.

'The cat's pretty ugly. There's a tom too, called "Rosario".' By now, Paul was standing right next to me. I could make out his silhouette, his broad shoulders and sometimes, when he took a drag on his cigarette, his chin, mouth and lips.

'Are you studying theology?'

'What, because of the collar? Suits me, don't you think?' Paul chuckled. 'No, history.'

A twig snapped beneath my foot. It made me nervous not being able to see where I was treading.

'I pay my way through college by working as a tour guide,' Paul went on, 'trouble is, I'm not officially licensed, so I pass myself off as a priest showing his flock around Rome. Shall we sit down on the bench over there?'

'Don't other priests come up and talk to you? What do you do if that happens?'

'Ah, I've got myself a cover story prepared. But I haven't had to use it yet.'

'Does Mrs M know what you're up to?'

'Absolutely. She points guests in my direction in return for a ten percent cut of my takings,' Paul replied.

'God, she never misses a trick, does she?'

'It's a fair trade-off.'

I followed Paul across the garden. The bench was behind the overgrown wooden shed where all the broken sunshade stands and table bases and empty crates were piled up. I reflected that nature had its own way of making things tidy, by simply covering all this unsightly junk with ivy by and by. On the one hand, there was Mrs M homing in on every last limescale mark on the tiles and forcing us to scrub the washbasins and baths until they gleamed, and yet here was the end of the garden slowly turning into a junkyard.

'Watch out, keep to the left there,' warned Paul, catching hold of my forearm and steering me to one side. Looking down, I noticed a square, reflective surface about the size of a manhole cover. 'You can get down into the Catacombs through that,' he explained.

'You mean, you can fall into the Catacombs if you're not watching your step?'

'Yeah, you're better off using the entrance in St Agnes,' agreed Paul. Sitting down on the bench, he stretched his legs and leant back against the shed wall, which bowed inwards slightly. The bench itself was just a single, narrow, uncomfortable plank, which rocked every time you moved. There was room for two more people between us.

Paul had been in Rome for six months; originally, he was just meant to be spending one term abroad, but he'd extended his stay. He told me about his family back in Vienna, some longstanding connection with Rome that he didn't go into, and the university, which the police had been crawling all over in their hunt for suspects following Moro's murder. One of his fellow students had been interrogated for two hours, just because he'd had a book by Toni Negri on him.

I hadn't a clue who this Negri was. A member of the Red Brigades, maybe? I didn't have the courage to ask.

It was a bright new dawn for Italy, Paul claimed. A last, the country had a populist president who'd been in the Resistance. When he went abroad, Pertini always flew as an ordinary Alitalia passenger and paid the fare out of his own pocket. He'd also told his chauffeur to ditch the peaked cap and white gloves.

'It's a start, at least,' said Paul.

I wanted to tell him about Steg, and Antonella's night-time forays, but he didn't give me a chance.

19

Emma turned down the TV for fear of missing Steg's knock. Had Ines managed to find him? Maybe it hadn't been such a good idea to send the girl. She had a fresh face, unmarked by disappointment and bitter experience, and that made her the target of unwelcome attention. Then again, there was a two generation age gap between her and Steg.

Emma swivelled the leather chair to face the open window; way off in the garden she could hear voices, but only indistinctly, as the leaves were rustling in the wind. Probably guests stretching their legs after dinner before retiring.

Emma had never forgotten that young woman she'd spotted all those years ago – the war was still on then – creeping across the garden, an emaciated, scrawny figure. Emma had stood, half-hidden behind a curtain, and watched as she first rattled at the garden gate and then shinned over the wall. When she jumped down, it looked to Emma for all the world like a rag-doll flopping down into the yard.

At that time, Emma had left the hotel on a couple of occasions, once to go to the Anima for Mass and another time to scout round the black market for food. Everywhere, she'd come across people who were just as forlorn as she was, with their clothes hanging limply off their shrunken frames.

In times of famine, Emma knew from her mother, combs suddenly become ravening beasts, tearing out your hair in thick clumps. Perhaps the strange woman had just given birth, maybe that was why she looked so thin and pale; there were dark shadows under her eyes and only thin wisps of hair on her scalp. Emma still had a vivid memory of the back of her head as she knocked rotting persimmons off the tree with a broom handle and then fell on the fruit, gobbling it down. Presumably the woman had clambered over the wall in the hope of finding hens in the shed, but they'd all been taken to Trevignano by the Manentes, save one that was now kept under lock and key in a utility room in the laundry block. At the time, Emma was living alone with just the single hen and her own fear and even found herself scared of this woman, who was only a weedy half-pint and clearly didn't even have enough money for the thin gruel they dished out at the Vatican. But there'd been something truly spooky about her sunken eyes. She'd seemed utterly fearless and hadn't glanced around, not even once.

Old Mr Manente had arranged for the wall to be topped with broken glass where it faced the road, but the workman doing the job failed to turn up one day and never reappeared, so the boundary at the back of the garden remained unprotected. Later, someone told the Manentes that their odd-job brickie had gone back to Quarticciolo, which in those days was nothing but a few mud huts and shacks with no running water, to join the Hunchback's partisan unit. The Hunchback was a good-looking guerrilla leader with an unfortunate physical deformity. Though he'd only just turned seventeen, he was supposed to have carried out several successful raids on food convoys supplying the German garrison. And unlike his fellow partisans, he wasn't in the habit of selling on the bread and grain he'd seized from the Germans on the black market, but gave it away to the city's poor and needy instead.

Emma took her vanity case off the sideboard and got out her hand mirror to check her lipstick wasn't smudged. The magnifying side of the mirror was face-up as she extracted it and she recoiled at the sudden sight of her wrinkles and drooping eyelids. No point in complaining, though, when there was no-one there to hear her. If Cocola had been there, she'd surely have cheered her up by listing all the regular guests of Emma's age who looked far worse than she did.

Now Emma suddenly found herself wishing that Ines hadn't passed her message on to Steg; it crossed her mind to call after the girl to intercept her at the last minute. Emma stood up and extinguished the main light, switching on the standard lamp instead, which bathed everything in a much softer light. In the glow it cast, not only the edges of the furniture seemed less harsh, but her skin also looked smoother. The analgesic was beginning to wear off and with every step she took Emma could feel sharp pains shooting down her back into her left thigh. Ignoring Doctor Franceschini's orders to repeat the dose only after a couple of hours at the earliest, she reached for the packet of painkillers and took one.

Pertini appeared on the TV screen. The President had been paying a state visit to Pope Paul VI at his summer residence in Castel Gandolfo. The next thing on was a trailer, with the pop singer Rita Pavone announcing her return to showbiz and telling viewers she'd be going round Italian discos to find the country's very own John Travolta and his dream dance partner. *Sunday Night Fever?* Emma shook her head – had she misheard something? She got up to turn the sound up again when there was a knock at the door. Instead of opening up right away, she stood there stock still, as petrified as the time when an artillery barrage had landed near the hotel. The shells had crashed through the walls of several neighbouring houses and ploughed up the road surface.

'Just a moment!' She fixed her hair, smoothed down her skirt and quickly ran her finger round the edges of her lips and examined it; good – no lipstick smudges.

Steg's face wore a grumpy look as though someone had interrupted him in the middle of an important task.

Emma invited him in; she had a bottle of wine ready. 'I hope I didn't disturb you,' she said.

He sat down on the leather sofa. 'Such a vision of loveliness can disturb me anytime she likes.'

'You're too kind,' replied Emma. She thanked him for his help and told him about Doctor Franceschini, who'd always been good to her, not like some of the others – 'He never made me feel like I didn't belong here,' she went on. 'You can well imagine how out of place I felt down here to begin with. There wasn't a single car in Stillbach back in 1938, let alone a lift. The first couple of weeks, I didn't dare use it. I ran myself ragged going up and down the stairs, till the cook took me by the hand and showed me it was safe.' She laughed, clinked glasses with Steg, toasted Rome, and then added: 'Good health to both of us!' He took a sip, rolling it round his mouth like he was at a wine-tasting, then swigged back the remainder in one. Emma refilled his glass.

Steg wondered who 'the others' might be who'd made Emma feel so unwelcome. He picked up the wine bottle and scrutinised the label. 'Colli della Sabina,' he read. 'Don't know it. I had some of the white from Zagarolo the other day, though. That was good.' Seemingly forgetting his original question, he clicked his tongue. 'Nice place you've got here,' he said, surveying the room.

'They always used to call me *crucchetta*,' Emma picked up the thread again. 'On the one hand, they invited us down here because we didn't ask much and worked hard, but on the other they spent all their time taking the mickey out of Northerners.'

'What was that word again?'

'*Crucchetta*. They still call Germans *crucchi* nowadays, don't ask me what it means, I'm still not entirely sure.' Emma paused to take a sip of wine. 'All I know is that it isn't very nice.' She recalled how she'd once mistakenly said *tette* instead of *tetti*, so while she thought she was talking about 'roofs', all the while she'd been saying 'breasts'. So much snow on the breasts! It had snowed in Rome that winter, a rare event that brought tears to Emma's eyes out of sheer joy and homesickness for Stillbach. And then she'd gone and dropped a clanger like that!

Una barzelletta della nostra crucchetta – 'Our little Kraut girl's joke' – old Mr Manente exclaimed in delight, and dined out on the story for weeks after.

'Mind you,' Emma went on, 'I knew a cook who worked for a rich jeweller in the Via Sistina. One time, the mistress sent her out to buy some *capelli d'angelo*.'

'Angel's...' Steg, halfway through his second glass, groped for the translation: '...hats?'

'No, not "hats", "hair". "Angel's Hair." It's that fine spun-glass stuff you use to decorate Christmas trees. You must know it.' Emma looked at Steg's hands, wrapped round his glass like he was warming himself on it. Did he always drink so fast? 'Anyway, the cook was gone for hours, until she finally tracked down some Angel's Hair in a stationer's. And all the while what the jeweller's wife was really after was the other sort of "Angel's Hair" – you know, the thin pasta for soup!'

Steg didn't get it immediately, but then began laughing, guffawing so loudly that Emma couldn't help but join in.

'Hair for putting in your soup! Only the Italians would come up with that,' chortled Steg, then launched into his own anecdote. His wife, who'd taken an evening class in Italian and was keen to try out her new language skills in every hotel on the Adriatic coast, had once got really annoyed because the chambermaids in one place had left the balcony doors open. 'You see, she hated – um, what are mosquitoes called in Italian again?'

'*Zanzare*,' said Emma.

'Exactly! So, down she goes to reception and complains about all the *melanzane* on the ceiling.'

'Which I can quite understand. I don't like aubergines either.'

Emma fetched another bottle. Was there still a Frau Steg, she wondered? But if so, how come he always visited Rome on his own?

Now I'll try sitting down next to him on the sofa, she thought.

She pushed the fresh bottle towards Steg, invited him to help himself and as she did so, brushed against his forearm as if by chance. The very thought of deliberately touching a man in that way would once have horrified Emma, but the drugs combined with the wine now made her cast off her inhibitions. She was past caring what Steg thought of her. By this time, she'd also downed two glasses and was telling Steg about Franz; his travels and his political speeches. She said she read the paper every day because she dreaded finding a photo of her son. Not that she imagined he had any sort of direct contact with the terrorists, but it was enough in this day and age just to voice your sympathies in public. She talked about Remo's malignant tumour and the way his illness had begun with him having problems with coordination, which she'd put down to him drinking too much – 'Absurd,' she said, 'because Remo hardly indulged at all' – and about his final weeks, when he'd been unable to speak, because in the end the brain tumour had destroyed his speech faculty, too. She also recounted her misfortunes with men in general and told him that, after everything that had gone wrong in her life, she thought she really deserved a bit of luck. She told him all about Johann, too. That it wasn't true what everyone said. He wasn't a Nazi, he'd even thought about opting for Italy rather than the German Reich in the plebiscite. 'Perhaps that had something to do with me as well,' Emma said, 'you see, I was in Rome by then. But his father forced him to vote for Hitler. Vowed he'd disinherit him if he didn't choose the Third Reich.'

Emma shifted closer to Steg, close enough to feel the warmth of his body.

'And what about your wife?' Steg didn't recoil, which pleased Emma, but neither did he move closer. In fact, he didn't even reply.

Emma tried again. 'Your wife? Is she still alive?'

The voices of the guests in the garden had ebbed away and even the traffic noise on the Via Nomentana had died down. Steg's breathing, Emma now realised, was deep and regular. He was fast asleep.

20

Paul had gone into the hotel to fetch a couple of beers. There were animal-like scrabblings in the undergrowth near the shed. I froze, then gave a violent start when a bird suddenly screeched. I thought about the labyrinthine passages of the St Agnes Catacombs spreading under my feet, and about how I was sitting just a few metres away from dead bodies. The network of passageways, Paul told me, had been excavated by specialist tunnellers, who'd carted the earth they dug out up to the surface through ventilation shafts, using baskets and sacks. The makeshift cover we'd passed on our way to the shed hid one of these shafts; in former times, they'd been left open to let light and air into the burial chambers. 'There are no coffins down there,' Paul said, 'the poor couldn't afford them. It must have stunk to high heaven when it was in use.'

By now, it was completely dark; in the next few days I really wanted us to try to shift the cover and take a peek down into the necropolis. Maybe we'd even be able to fit a narrow ladder through the opening, take a torch and climb down to have a look around at least part of the Catacomb complex. Was that why so many houses round here had such big gardens, because this second city underground stopped people sinking any foundations for new buildings?

'There are some Jewish Catacombs along the Appian Way, too,' Paul said, before abruptly returning to the subject of the new president. He said he was astonished that I, a native of South Tyrol, should know so little about its fascist and national-socialist past.

I told him that we'd skimmed over the Second World War in just two lessons at school. I'd never really understood, for instance, why the Germans had occupied Rome after the Italian surrender.

Ke-wick! It was the same bird I'd heard before. Was it up on the shed roof?

Our teacher had painted the Germans as welcome protectors of the Pope, a safeguard against the spread of Communism. Naturally, he hadn't told us about how this 'aid mission' had played out on the ground.

Paul came back with a bottle of lemonade soda he'd had up in his room; no beer – the kitchen was closed.

The soda was warm and flat.

'And do you have any idea who Saragat was?' he asked.

'He was president once, wasn't he?'

'Well done!'

Every inch the teacher, I thought.

'Saragat was a member of the Resistance. Like Pertini. They were both betrayed and arrested by the SS.' Paul told me he'd prefer not to go into detail right now about what happened in the cellar of the German Embassy in the Villa Wolkonsky and in the Gestapo head-quarters in the Via Tasso. 'Shame to spoil such a nice evening,' he said, but then went on to mention an officer called Erich Priebke, who was notorious for working over prisoners with knuckle-dusters.

'And where is he now?'

'No idea. Probably escaped. Like loads of others. Maybe he's living under an assumed name, who knows?' In the silence that followed, I sensed Paul was eyeing me up, but under the cover of darkness I couldn't be absolutely sure. He made no attempt to move closer, in any event. Paul appeared to be one of those people who couldn't do two things at once. When he was speaking, he took no notice of things around him and if he stopped to look at you, he seemed incapable of continuing with his narrative.

'Pertini,' he said at length, 'was interrogated as well. They threatened to kill him, but he still didn't crack.'

'But he got away –'

'That's right; he was freed in a partisan raid. And now here he is, President of Italy – amazing. His younger brother died in Flossenbürg concentration camp, though.'

I'd heard about a deserter who'd survived a stretch in Flossenbürg. The man had refused to fight for the Germans in 1944 because he was an Italian citizen. He'd gone into hiding in the woods below the Stillbacher Horn until the Nazis dragged his family off to an internment camp at Bolzano.

Aunt Hilda had taken a real shine to this man, whom she'd met for the first time at one of the talks he used to give about his wartime exploits. Every year, she'd buy a pair of the felt slippers he made for a living. Over the years, we kept getting these crudely finished but warm slippers as presents; my mother alone had four pairs.

'I've heard of Flossenbürg,' I said, relieved I was able to say something that didn't make me sound like some naïve schoolgirl. 'A deserter from our area was forced to work in a quarry there until the war ended. He turned himself in because the Nazis arrested his family.'

Ke...Ke-wick! Paul didn't jump; he didn't even turn around. Perhaps he was just pretending not to have heard the noisy bird directly above our heads.

'They sentenced him to ten years' hard labour. Luckily, eighteen months later it was all over,' I said.

Paul's face showed no emotion. He swigged thirstily from the bottle; every time he took it from his lips, a sour lemony smell drifted over.

'Lucky for him, maybe,' Paul said after a moment, 'but not for millions of others. It made all the difference if you gave yourself up.'

'How do you mean?'

'Well, he could always have stayed holed up in the woods. They didn't actually kill family members in most cases. It was just a way of putting pressure on dissidents.'

We sat there next to one another for a while in silence. I found the sound of the leaves rustling in the wind calming. It reminded me a bit of the Boston ivy round Aunt Hilda's balcony back home blowing in the breeze.

'And Manente's first love – was he a Nazi or not?'

'I don't know anything about him,' Paul replied slowly. 'She only mentioned her late husband to me once, in passing. She was almost in tears when she spoke his name.'

That didn't necessarily mean anything, I thought. My Mum got a bit weepy too whenever my Dad came up in conversation, but only out of rage and disappointment.

'Who was this guy, then?'

'I don't really know much, either. Antonella told me that Mrs Manente was originally engaged to a Nazi. She said he'd been killed in a partisan attack here in the city, but that afterwards – at least, that's what Antonella reckons – she married the Manentes' son for money.'

Paul laughed: 'A true Nazi camp-follower would never marry an Italian.'

'She was pregnant, though.'

'I see. Even so, a committed German nationalist would never have gone out with an Italian, you can bet your bottom dollar. In 1941, the Nazi Party even thought about outlawing marriages between Germans and Italians. And in the autumn of 1944 – I've just been studying this, as it happens – Martin Bormann announced that marriages or any carnal relations with Italians tainted the purity of the German race and were to be avoided at all costs. The Italians were mere Latins, you see, not Teutons.'

It sounded to me like he was trotting out his exam answer.

'And there was a German Lieutenant-General – I've forgotten his name for the moment – who always referred to Italians as *die Herren*

Cazzolini – 'the gentlemen with the little pricks.' He found the Croatians much more racially acceptable. Von Horstenau, that was his name. Came from Braunau too, like Hitler.'

'And how do we know this Remo wasn't a fascist himself?'

'No, you're definitely barking up the wrong tree there. First, the Manentes weren't fascists, I know that for a fact. They were devout Catholic monarchists. And for another thing, the Germans pretty much spurned the fascists after the Italian surrender. In actual fact, the Nazis had always had serious misgivings about Italy. The Latin race was too weak and effete for them.'

'The self same reason why German women on holiday find them so attractive nowadays.'

'D'you reckon?' Paul looked at me. 'And does that include you?'

'I'm not here on holiday. And anyway, I'm an Italian citizen.'

Paul said nothing for a few moments.

'That doesn't answer the question. Do you find the Italians attractive?' he finally asked quietly.

'Depends who you mean by "the Italians". The squat little bald blokes selling newspapers on the Via Nomentana? Or Vittorio Gassman?'

'You're forgetting Marcello Mastroianni,' Paul said.

'Not my type.'

'What about me, then? Am I your type?'

'With the dog collar or without?' I teased him.

'Oh, with, naturally,' Paul laughed. After a brief pause, he suddenly asked me if I found him boring.

'Why do you ask?'

'Just because.' He fell silent, apparently sunk in thought, then added: 'I've got a girlfriend, you see, and she finds all this history stuff of mine too much sometimes. She's jealous of my obsession with the past.'

21

A fly had drowned in Steg's wine. Emma noticed it as she was about to raise his glass to her lips. He was still asleep and she had no desire to wake him. As long as he didn't stir from his slumbers, he couldn't leave her flat.

From the bottom of the garden came the *Ke–wick* call of a tawny owl. Emma had once seen a buzzard dispatch a mouse with a swift bite to the neck. That had been in the hills above Stillbach – foraging for mushrooms one time, she'd sat down on a tree stump to take a breather and ended up sitting there a long while thinking about Johann.

It was good that tawny owls were back in Rome. The two feral cats were useless hunters these days; a constant diet of titbits from guests had turned them into lazy beasts.

Emma studied Steg's face; the small, long-healed scar under his chin and his wine-flushed – or were they sleep-flushed? – cheeks. Bending down close to him, from his creased neck she thought she caught a faint whiff of the aftershave she'd discovered in his bathroom. She couldn't imagine anything nicer than having Steg all to herself, breathing in his scent and counting the white hairs sprouting from his nostrils. Emma gave a little excited titter; for the first time in ages, she got the sensation that time was standing still, that she didn't have to run to catch up with it, that something from her former life had returned. There was just the faintest hint of Stillbach in the air.

She pressed up close to Steg, carefully so as not to wake him, and nestled her head against his shoulder. Emma's body seemed to fall in with the rhythm of Steg's breathing, and all at once a feeling of peace and serenity overtook her. In that instant, even the furnishings in the room, which she'd left unchanged since Remo's death, seemed to rock gently like the boats she remembered from Venice all those years ago. The lagoon could be as calm as a millpond, without a breath of wind, yet still the prows of the gondolas went on nodding to one another.

Emma closed her eyes for a moment, yet even in the dark, clouds of bright colour kept spinning behind her eyelids, as if in slow motion. Steg curled up and rolled over to rest against Emma. There was a pleasing weight to his body. His left hand started convulsively patting his crumpled trousers like he was searching for something.

The stone pine chairs also seemed to have taken on a life of their own, rocking back and forth. Emma clutched at her temples, as if suddenly gripped by a powerful urge to keep a tight hold of her head. Maybe there was something wrong with the transmission, making the images flicker like when a thunderstorm dislodged the aerial from its proper position. A fit of the silent giggles washed over Emma; her shoulders heaved, she could barely contain herself. Feeling Steg's hand touch her own, she flinched. The shock sobered her up. Had he done it deliberately? She froze, fearful that this new intimacy of his might turn out to be a mirage. His hand was resting there, sure, but it wasn't squeezing hers. Perhaps he was dreaming and was touching someone else in his dream. Did he have a lover in Ischl? Maybe she'd just left him and he had made up that story about building work going on at the guesthouse as a pretext for staying here and seeking solace in Emma's arms?

What am I thinking of, though? Just look at me: the owner of a budget hotel. Uneducated. Way too old. Any minute now, I'll start sweating. Emma leant over to see if Steg was still asleep. His eyes were closed, certainly. Her darling professor. He could come and live here with her. She'd teach him Italian. And they could go on trips together to

Stillbach. And go walking; through the mixed woods to the belt of conifers and then on up to the Stillbacher Horn. They'd take cheese in their rucksack. Not *pecorino* or *gorgonzola* or *taleggio*, but some Alpine cheeses and a bit of smoked sausage too. And a good bottle of red.

Latterly, Emma had noticed that she couldn't remember some of the names of the farms round Stillbach anymore, and that her visual memory wasn't as reliable as it had once been. For so long, she'd had clear mental images of all the houses and barns in Stillbach, but now they'd begun to blur into impressions of other, unfamiliar houses from places she'd never set foot in. A few weeks back, she'd even had to dig out a written note to check when her eldest brother's birthday was. Not that she planned to ring him or anything; she'd just been trying to retrieve a few basic bits of information.

Steg's hand was that of an old person; liver-spotted and with the nail on his index finger all ragged-looking and thicker than the rest. And his veins were so prominent and blue that they seemed like rivers on a map. Emma longed to kiss Steg's hand, but to do that she'd have to move her own, extracting it from under his.

Glancing round the room, the feeling began to grow in her that all the objects – the vases, the newspaper racks, the vanity mirror on the table, the fruit bowls, even the bottle opener – weren't the same ones that had been there a few hours ago, because everything she was looking at now, she was seeing through Steg's eyes. The most familiar things no longer seemed to belong there. They grew blurry, losing their sharp contours. Nor did it help if she closed her eyes; in the darkness, the world really started to go badly out of kilter.

I shouldn't have had anything to drink or taken that second painkiller, she thought. Emma's heart didn't seem to be beating normally either and her breathing was erratic, which alarmed her.

Although she was sitting down, it felt to her like she was losing her balance. She cut a ridiculous figure; she was ashamed of her desires, especially now they'd become public knowledge. What would that Ines think of her? By now, Cocola would surely have heard about her invit-ing Steg up to her apartment, as well. How could she have got herself into this mess? Steg must have been pretty drunk when he arrived. His touching her was purely accidental, not deliberate, that much was clear to her now. She pulled her hand away from his and got up slowly. Steg slumped over to one side like a heavy sack, then woke with a start, rubbing his eyes and shooting to his feet so abruptly that the frame of the glass table clattered noisily as he caught it with his leg.

'Oh, how embarrassing!' he said, clutching at Emma's arm and grip-ping it tight.

She groped around for something to say, but everything that came to mind seemed banal, just as banal as saying nothing at all. Was he unsteady on his feet? Or was it her getting giddy again?

'No matter,' said Emma, 'nothing happened.'

Steg pulled her towards him and buried his face in her neck. She clung fast to him and for a moment or two they stood there rooted to the spot, between the sofa and the table, before collapsing back, still entwined, onto the leather sofa. Steg unbuttoned the top of her blouse and started planting kisses on her cleavage and fumbling with her bra. She tugged his shirt up and stroked his back, which felt smooth, if a bit sweaty from the heat.

'My head's swimming,' gasped Emma, 'I've had too much to drink.'

'I really like you,' Steg murmured in reply.

To see him more clearly, Emma would have to have put on her glasses. On his last visit, Franz had told her she should get a chain and hang them round her neck so she wouldn't have to keep hunting around for them. Emma had always found elderly ladies with spec-tacles dangling on their bosoms from a cord faintly absurd. They reminded her of the dummies that people hung round their babies' necks, another stupid habit. After all, men didn't go around with pipes or lighters bouncing off their chests.

She was amazed she could still get aroused. Steg's breath wasn't anything to write home about, true. He must have put away some beers before he'd come over to see her. But it didn't really bother her; he was a good kisser.

Emma couldn't quite believe she was letting it happen. After Remo, there'd been a whole procession of male guests who'd made advances, sending her flowers, writing her love letters, but none had ever been granted access to her flat.

No, no, I can't, she thought. She began waving her right hand like she was trying to shoo away a fly.

At the same time, though, she really wanted Steg to stay. Then she wouldn't need to be fearful at night and the shadows and shapes that morphed into such unsettling apparitions in the dark would suddenly be dispelled – or maybe she wouldn't even see them in the first place. It'd be like when Remo was –

Oh God no, not that image, anything but that. But it was no good. She'd conjured up the spirit of her dead husband, and not just him, either. The shades of all the people still alive and whom she hadn't thought about for ages were suddenly there in the room with her. Remo sat down beside her – how could this be happening? – and shook his head. *Che fai?* – 'What do you think you're doing?' And her sisters were there, too, whispering disapprovingly to one another.

Did Steg say something? Emma could feel his teeth nibbling at her ear lobe. She felt deeply ashamed in front of her sisters and remembered the time Remo and she had first kissed in the lift. Johann had been dead and buried two months when it happened. 'Thank your lucky stars he was killed instantly,' her cousin told her later. Another recruit from a village just outside Stillbach had survived the blast, but was hideously maimed. He had only just got married when he was called up. When he came back home to his wife, he was missing an eye and the whole of his upper body was mangled beyond recognition.

'Please, just shut up,' Emma had told her cousin down the line.

22

Negri, von Horstenau, Priebke – with all these names buzzing round my head, I took my leave of Paul and headed back to my room. I thought about Mrs Manente and how she'd invited Steg up to her apartment. What was she after? Shouldn't I let her know he was sniffing round me? And why hadn't I confided in Paul? Surely I'd feel safer now if I had.

'Did you see how the soldiers were ogling her? And their wolf-whistling and cat-calls!' Mum was furious when Aunt Hilda spoke up in favour of my Rome trip: 'If the *militari* up here are so out of control, what do you think they'll be like down South?' Admittedly, she calmed down a bit after I promised her I'd get my hair cut before I left and put a ring on my finger. She'd surely never imagined that I'd be having to beat off advances from an elderly professor, though.

What if Steg was lying in wait for me now in the ironing room? Or if he'd spotted that Antonella had gone out on the town again?

I ran back into the garden, looking for Paul, all the way to the shed, but he'd left. The windows in the part of the hotel where Mrs Manente's flat was were still lit. One was open, and behind it the curtains billowed in the wind. I heard voices but couldn't make out what they were saying. They were so indistinct they could just as well have been coming from one of the rooms on the top floor. Lots of the guests slept with their windows open and went on talking after they'd switched off the lights. Room 30 had its windows on this side of the building; maybe

I was hearing the couple who'd come back from Ostia Antica, perhaps the wife was still going on about the pool for fresh fish or the amazingly well-preserved mosaic supposedly showing a dolphin with an octopus in its mouth, or the man was chuckling over his latrine anecdote. Earlier, he'd buttonholed Ada Cocola and told her about a toilet called the Paterculus that had apparently once existed near the Forum. One time, a Roman poet by the name of Vacerra waited there all day, not through some pressing need to empty his bowels, but because he hoped to wangle a dinner invitation from a rich patron using the facilities. 'All the man wanted to do was eat, for heaven's sake!' exclaimed the man from Room 30, and went on to wax lyrical about all the poor, starving Roman poets who, according to him, had to spend their time hanging around public conveniences just to try to find a patron. As I listened in, I had a moment's panic that the guy might have seen me sitting on one of the hotel loos reading my paperback, but he was clearly only concerned with regaling Cocola with his funny story. He kept touching his wife's arm as though he wanted her to confirm what he was saying and she duly obliged, nodding at him and laughing loudly.

I wondered whether to climb the persimmon tree, which would give me a good view into Mrs Manente's flat, but I was wearing sandals with smooth soles that weren't suitable. And if I attempted it barefoot, I was worried I'd get a splinter. The instant I thought of that, my old German mistress came to mind, who would always correct my Southern dialect word for splinter into its 'proper' High German equivalent.

Yesterday, Mrs M pressed the key to the roof terrace into my hand and told me I could sunbathe there in my free time if I wanted to. There was even a tap in one corner with a hose for cooling down, but she swore me to secrecy as far as guests were concerned. She didn't want the Germans finding out about it.

I called out Paul's name, but straight away an angry voice shouted 'Quiet!' from one of the windows, causing me to dart behind the persimmon until I was sure the coast was clear. At least it wasn't the proprietress; I'd have instantly recognised her odd pronunciation of the word. All the years she'd spent in Rome hadn't just left their mark on her clothes and the way she wore her hair, but on the way she pronounced certain words. I'd even once heard her refer to Hermann Steg as 'Ermann'.

When I thought of the inn at Stillbach – the only place there that offered accommodation – and the rancid smell in the bar, which probably came from a combination of greasy fried food and the landlord's unwashed clothes, it seemed to me that our proprietress was hell-bent on banishing all such smells that reminded her of Stillbach. 'You should wash your hair more often,' she'd instructed Gianni only today, 'it reeks of cooking fat.'

We had to change our pinafores daily. Mrs Manente had an eagle eye for stains and was obsessive about airing the place on a regular basis to get rid of the smell of *varecchina*, which I really liked, as the bleach in it made me think of swimming pools.

'I can't wash it every day,' Gianni objected, 'there's eight of us at home and there's not enough water to go round.' The proprietress stopped on her way out of the kitchen door and replied: 'OK, then – you can use the girls' shower from now on.'

'And clean it too,' Antonella called after her.

When Mrs M had disappeared, Antonella sidled over to me at the sink. 'Boys all wank in the shower, see, and I for one don't want to be treading in it,' she announced. Gianni was struck dumb at this and fled into the cool room. 'Mimmo's always wanking,' Antonella whispered to me, 'and I bet since he met you, he's thinking of you when he's at it. Did you ever stop to think about how many bucketloads of cum might have been shed in your honour?'

The lights in Manente's apartment went out and the sudden descent into complete darkness startled me. Only a single window on the top storey remained lit, but it was too high up to illuminate the garden. I groped my way back to the entrance and sat down on the marble steps, which shone white as snow in the inky blackness. Maybe Paul had popped out again to the Via Nomentana to buy cigarettes.

I thought about our tiny apartment in the Fanfani box, where Mum was no doubt already asleep at this very moment. As a child, I used to love hiding in cardboard boxes as big as a washing machine. I got them from an electrical shop nearby and dragged them back to the flat, and although I wasn't supposed to touch it, I'd fetch the Stanley knife and cut windows in them and pin up scraps of fabric as curtains. I even painted the inside walls. I lived in the boxes alongside my dolls and cuddly animal toys, who'd sometimes shout and bark at me and sometimes praise me and cuddle up to me, while my Mum went out to be the breadwinner. In those days, she worked in the warehouse of the local fruit growers' cooperative sorting apples in the autumn, while in the spring and summer she helped out on the building sites where they were putting up new holiday homes for Germans, carting away rubble and scraping mortar off floor tiles.

'You're a big girl now,' she said one day, before leaving me all on my own for the first time. Then again, I wasn't really on my own, I had all my talking toys and my puppets and my make-believe friends who came with me to the kitchen and sat on the sofa next to me. I was a latchkey kid, but one key would never have been enough for me, I'd always have hankered after more boxes inside the box, more opportunities to hide myself away.

I shut my eyes tight. When I opened them again, the lower lids felt cool. I was getting more than a little spooked now. Together, the dark night and my vague imaginings combined to conjure up sinister forebodings, try as I might to keep a lid on them. Another *Ke-wick!* call gave me the willies so badly that I leapt to my feet. No cardboard box here, let alone a Fanfani box. Trying to get back into my room, I missed the door handle completely at first.

Once I was back in my room at last, I locked the door twice to make sure and left the key in the lock. I was trembling and breathless.

If Steg started fiddling with the lock, the key would fall to the ground and wake me up. And Antonella, I was sure, would have no qualms about rousing me when she came back and found she couldn't get in.

Cazzolini – today was the first time I'd ever heard that expression. I couldn't get off to sleep. I kept thinking about Paul's account of the Nazis doing their utmost to block marriages between Germans and Italians. There'd been a girl called Orthhild at my school, whose father threatened to show her the door if she ever went out with an Italian.

And then my Mum, flying in the face of prejudice, had gone and brought one back home. A *Cazzolino*, a 'little prick'. As if size really mattered, anyway. By all accounts, my Dad was a good lover, that wasn't why the relationship had foundered – Mum had said as much to her several times, Aunt Hilda once told me.

Hearing a soft knock at the door, I dug my nails into the bedsheet and froze. It was so quiet I could hear my own breathing. *Negroid influences.* The only Italians the Nazis accepted, and even then only grudgingly, were the Germanised race from the North. 'You lot, in other words,' Paul said with a laugh. 'Southerners were all Negroes and Arabs in their book.' I ran my hand over my nose and traced the outline of my mouth with the tip of my index finger.

The noise didn't recur. To give the sheets a chance to cool, I rolled over to the far side of the bed, pressing my back against the wall. Right now, I longed to be back home or at Aunt Hilda's. At night there, cool mountain air streamed into the bedroom; here it was stuffy and airless, like a closed railway compartment.

Antonella still hadn't come back. I hoped nothing had happened to her. I closed my eyes, then opened them again straight away, thinking I'd seen a light. But all around me was unrelieved darkness.

If only I'd listened to Mum. Maybe it'd been a mistake not to keep my word; I should have got my hair cut like I promised.

The room smelt musty and I badly wanted to go to the loo, but I didn't dare venture out into the corridor.

Paul had overawed me with his knowledge; I'd scarcely got a word in edgeways. No, come to think of it, 'Negroid infiltration' was the phrase he'd used, not 'influences'. As ever, I could rely 100 percent on my short-term memory; I could recall every last detail of our time together. The way his front teeth were almost perfectly aligned, except for the left central incisor, which was pushed back ever so slightly. I noticed it every time he flicked his lighter, and each time he lifted the cigarette up to his mouth to take a drag I waited for him to exhale so I could catch a glimpse of it again.

23

A huge throng of people had come out onto the streets – some bare-foot, some in their nightshirts – and there was a cacophony of yelling, laughter and dancing. 'Long live freedom!' – 'Long live Garibaldi!' – 'Down with the fascist lackeys!' Emma stood at the gate, her right hand clutching the bars. A few pages came fluttering down from a window of the house opposite; a woman was sitting on a ledge on the third floor, ripping up books. But now the house was no longer the one opposite; it had changed, expanding and growing wider like it was made of rubber. Emma was jostled by a man carrying a portrait of Mussolini, which he hurled to the ground and trampled on. Another was trying to set posters alight, but the wind kept blowing out the matches before he could put them to the paper. On the posters, Emma now noticed, were the familiar faces of people she'd seen before; pictures of parish councillors, churchgoers and pub regulars from Stillbach.

Although she'd stuck her fingers in her ears, she could still hear the people out on the street, bellowing 'Foreigners out!' and 'Down with Mussolini!' She shut the gate and ducked back into the garden, which was densely planted with small-leaved limes, cypresses and thorny caper bushes. There was a smell of burning in the air, but when Emma turned round, the fire she could see blazing just outside the gate was giving off no smoke. Flailing about with her arms and cough-ing, she retreated into the house, closing several doors and windows and even securing the shutters. The man waiting for Emma in one of the rooms looked like old Mr Manente; he was standing in the corner of the lounge and staring down at the record player, from which only a scratching sound emerged. As Emma drew closer, she could see that the needle was touching the groove of the LP but wasn't advancing. In the same instant, she felt as though her feet were rooted to the floor, so firmly she couldn't move them. And she still had loads more windows to close. The man nodded at Emma and pointed at the record player. She took hold of the pick-up arm, lifted it up carefully and swung it over, but as soon as she let it go, it dropped back down onto the record again. She repeated the action several times, always with the same result.

'There must be something wrong with the counterbalance,' said the man.

Now there were more and more arms swinging from the edge to the middle of the LP and it was all that Emma could do to keep the pick-up heads away from the playing surface. Whenever any of the needles came into contact with the grooves, a deafening crackling ensued.

When Emma opened her eyes, the first thing she thought about was her father-in-law, sitting in the lounge at news time and calling out: 'Did you hear that? They're talking about "His Majesty the Emperor" again, not just plain "His Majesty"!' A new government under His Excellency Pietro Badoglio had just been appointed.

The sheet on the other side of the bed was rucked up and the pillow was squashed. Someone had been there – Steg. My beloved Hermann. Emma ran her hand over the mattress, shifted over to the far side and sniffed the sheets, trying to pick up his smell. Was he regretting what had happened? Had he just gone to the bathroom or left the apartment?

'Hermann?' she called. As she walked into the lounge, her gaze fell on the corner of the room with the record player, which she hadn't used for a long time now. She remembered the time when Remo had rushed the son of some regular guests from Ludwigsburg to hospital in the middle of the night when he'd contracted a fever. The following year, by way of thanks for Remo's mercy dash, the Ludwigsburgers had brought him this portable record player, a Loewe; they also told him about a new model by the same company that you could install in your car. Of course, Remo had to go straight out and buy this gadget, which set him back 1,000 deutschmarks. He dreamt of cruising along the coast road with Emma and Franz, listening to music. The record player was in the blue Fiat 850 for a whole fortnight; Remo never did get to the coast. The one trip he did make was into the city centre, where he parked near Termini Station to pick up some new guests. By the time he got back to the car, someone had smashed the side window and stolen the little record player.

'Hermann?' Maybe he was on the toilet.

His trousers were gone from the sofa.

My misfortune really began when Mussolini was overthrown, thought Emma. I didn't have any reason to celebrate then, but I celebrated with the others all the same, sitting out in the garden with the Manentes and their friends. The day after the new administration was announced, a cousin of old Mr Manente had donated half a suckling pig: 'Now my son's going to be able to come home from exile.' How could his son have been so stupid as to call Mussolini an *idiota* in public? He'd been sent into *confino* in the far South without further ado. Antifascists were packed off to miserable little holes in the back of beyond, where they were lucky if they got enough to keep body and soul together. Just like in Stillbach.

'Hermann?' No, he must have left the flat, and hadn't even left a note. I should have realised this would just be a one-night stand, thought Emma.

She slumped down on the corner settle. The stone pine suddenly struck her as far too light in colour; it was completely out of place in the room.

It was still early, seven at the latest. Time to close the windows. The traffic noise had already begun; pretty soon, the heat of the day would dispel the modicum of coolness that the night wind had blown in.

Emma couldn't bring herself to get up; she just stared at the open windows. She'd always done what was expected of her. She'd stayed in Rome the whole time. And even when she did get away briefly, she was never really able to put any distance between herself and this city. She couldn't stop thinking about the hotel. Even on the day of her mother's funeral, she'd tried calling Rome several times to check with Cocola that everything was fine. There were only two telephones in Stillbach then, one at the inn and the other at the mayor's house. Unable to get through for an entire morning, Emma had got it into her head that the landlord was deliberately cutting her off. 'That's absurd,' her cousin had said when she'd told her, 'why would he want to stop you ringing? Because you married an Italian?' She'd reassured her that the landlord, like most people in the village, was more interested in making money.

After so many years, Emma had been forced to recognise that she was losing the language of her childhood; that every now and then, at the inn or out on the street, she'd pick up words she hadn't heard since she left for Rome. During those days of mourning in Stillbach, she felt she'd rediscovered something she hadn't been looking for but which she'd missed all the same. So delighted was she at hearing these unfamiliar words again that she'd burst into tears at the inn. The waitress had thought she was crying for her dead mother and had come up to Emma to squeeze her hand and offer her condolences.

Emma wondered where all her energy had gone. She looked out of the windows, which were still open. It would have been such a comfort to her now if Hermann had got up and closed the shutters, and then returned to her across the semi-lit room and held her in his arms. Sitting there with her eyes closed, Emma gave a violent start when a fly landed on her hand; for a second, she thought it might be him touching her.

The din of the street brought her back to her senses. She didn't know which she found worse: the roar of motorbikes and scooters or the honking of cars and lorries. Hermann reckoned Rome had always been a noisy place, with tub-thumping religious zealots, money changers and match sellers on every street corner. To get some sleep, you needed money. In Ancient Rome, wealthy people managed to get away from the noise of hammering workmen and the raucous cries of street hawkers by having large gardens. 'Quite a bit bigger than yours,' Hermann told her.

Emma was intrigued by what Steg got up to when he wasn't in Rome. But she hadn't found out a thing, because he wouldn't stop talking about 'his Rome', banging on about the gloomy, draughty little bathhouses and the large *Thermae* built by Nero and Agrippa, where men and women bathed communally, in the nude. They were loud places, filled with groaning weightlifters and attendants vying to strigil the dirt, sweat and hairs off bathers' bodies. Plus, of course, Roman bathhouses had been places of commerce, where voracious customers could get anything their hearts desired. The more Hermann told her, the more insignificant Emma seemed to herself, with her vague reminiscences of Stillbach and the humdrum of all the years she'd spent working in Rome.

At least she could console herself that there was no ring on Hermann's finger, but then again he might just be one of those men who took their rings off when they went abroad, or maybe he'd given it up during one of those drives to raise German war finances.

No, that can't be right, Emma thought, he's an Austrian.

She'd still been living in Stillbach when the Italian state began asking people to donate their jewellery to fund the war in Abyssinia – Mussolini's bit of adventurism in Africa, which Johann had been called up for, too. Who wanted to be shipped off there? Afterwards, word had gone round Stillbach that when the conscripts were being put on trains at the station in Bolzano, some of them struck up the

Horst Wessel song in protest. A friend of Johann's fled, just in time, over the Swiss border, but Johann hadn't had the gumption to do the same. The Abyssinian War didn't warrant the name – the Ethiopian troops didn't have any boots and had fought on horseback with lances, while Mussolini had given his generals free rein to drop mustard-gas bombs. 'They just gassed and slaughtered them at will,' Johann reported, 'the Abyssinians didn't even know what an aircraft was. And the Italian cardinals, including that Roncalli, gave the operation their blessing.'

'Why didn't you just go back home in 1939 like most of the German-speaking servant girls?' Hermann asked her during the night. Emma hadn't been able to come up with a good answer. *Well,* she thought, *I'd only just arrived in Rome then, for one thing, and I was enjoying having a room all to myself and a decent income after my experiences at the Scabellos. Why would I have wanted to go back to South Tyrol and enrol in the Reich Labour Service?*

Emma stood up now and closed the shutters. Her back pains had subsided. She took a shower and put on a light, floaty dress, whose colour reminded her of unripe ears of rye growing in the fields south of Stillbach in the late spring.

24

Antonella didn't come back to the hotel that night. She hadn't mentioned a boyfriend to me, but even so I thought she must have slept over at some man's place and I was waiting for her to show up at any minute. Peering at the water stains and smears of toothpaste on our washbasin mirror, I realised it was her turn to scrub the front steps today, a chore that needed to be done before breakfast. Around a quarter past seven, I filled a bucket with hot water, poured in some *varecchina* and made my way to the entrance. I thought about my school friends, who'd still be asleep at this hour and then be spending the whole day at the swimming baths, and about the two farmers' daughters in our class whose fathers had got European subsidies just because their productive apple orchards higher up the valley counted as hill farms, and the surgeon's daughter and the two lawyers' sons who, when school broke up for the summer, still hadn't decided where to spend their vacations. Would it be Lake Garda? Or England? 'What?' they'd gasped when I told them what I was doing, 'You're going to Rome? On your own? Wish we were!'

After a while, my fingers had turned to prunes and my knees were aching. I was scrubbing the marble steps hard to remove all the sticky soft-drink splashes, bird droppings and stubborn brown marks left by stubbed-out cigarette butts when I was startled by someone clearing their throat right behind me. It was Steg, who'd crept up without me noticing and been standing there, who knows for how long, watching me work.

'Are you always so jumpy?'

I shot to my feet. I didn't like kneeling in front of him. 'Only when I see you,' I answered.

Steg clapped his hands in glee. 'Oh-ho, you're quick on the draw, I like that.'

Actually, I thought, my comebacks are normally about as prompt as Italian trains. Steg muttered something in Latin, which I didn't understand. As I put the bucket down at the end of the steps, he translated it for me: 'The more one looks – You are a jealous pinafore!' He carried on up the still-wet steps and stopped in front of the door. '*Sordide niveo corpore pulvis abi!* Vile dust, away from her snowy body! A touch of sun would do you good. Will you accompany me to the Temple of Venus?'

'Not a chance,' I replied, chucking the sodden cloth onto the steps. Water splashed everywhere.

'A bit more of a sense of humour,' he called back as he went in, 'and a bit less water in your mop!'

Glancing up at one of the windows, I saw Mrs Manente's face. She'd been eavesdropping and ducked back behind the curtain when she saw that I'd spotted her.

A couple of minutes later she was standing right in front of me: 'I'd take Mr Steg's advice to heart if I were you.'

'I don't understand.'

'You know exactly what I mean. And you can leave Paul alone while you're about it.'

I dried my fingers on my pinafore.

'He's here to study,' she went on, 'not to have a fling with some chambermaid.' She cast an eye over the gravel path and pointed at some leaves that the evening breeze had blown off the trees. 'You can pick those up, too,' she said, and I thought of the white gravel shining in the moonlight, which still bore the imprints of Paul's feet at this early hour. Soon, they'd be erased by the footsteps of departing guests.

'Where's Antonella, then? There's no-one in the kitchen. Shouldn't that be your job?'

'She'll be along any moment.'

An hour passed – in the meantime, I'd dusted the lobby and prepared breakfast for the guests – and still Antonella hadn't appeared. She hadn't phoned or sent anyone by with a message, either. Had she been caught fishing for coins?

The proprietress was sitting next to Cocola in the kitchen, drinking coffee. Ada was telling her that she'd found another litre of milk was off when it was delivered. 'The producers blame the distributors; they say they turn the refrigeration off at night.'

'Get Gianni to take it back,' Mrs M replied.

'No use, they won't give us another one. The distributors say it's the producers' fault.'

'And they blame the cows, I'll bet.' Mrs Manente got up. 'Fortunately, the cows can't talk, or they'd try to pin it on the grass.'

'The Pope's ill,' said Cocola at length. She jabbed her finger at the report in *Il Messaggero*. 'Maybe the new President isn't to his liking.' She sipped her coffee absentmindedly, forgetting to put the cup back down on the table.

The proprietress shot me a sharp look when she saw me standing there. I glanced down but saw that my pinafore was spotless and no buttons were missing.

'Still no sign?'

'No.'

'Didn't she spend the night in your room?'

I didn't respond.

'That's enough of an answer for me,' said Mrs Manente. 'I'll have to let her parents know.'

'She might still turn up.'

'Can you manage on your own, or should I get Gianni to help you? I certainly can't be…'

'Is your back any better?' I interrupted her. The thought of cleaning Steg's room on my own filled me with dread. I couldn't do it if he was there, come what may; I'd have to wait until I was sure he'd gone out. And even then, I'd take precautions, like locking the door from inside.

'Sure, the tablets seem to be working,' she replied, massaging her back like she was trying to find the place that had hurt.

Ada Cocola still had her nose buried in the newspaper and was giving brief running digests of some stories: Aldo Moro's kidnappers were believed to have held him captive in the suburb of Focene; in Turin a woman had flung boiling oil in her unfaithful husband's face; the high-jumper Sara Simeoni had cleared two metres. Cocola looked up. 'Two metres and one centimetre, to be precise.'

I drank my coffee standing up, ate just half a *rosetta* with a bit of butter on and left the kitchen. Behind me, I heard Cocola say to Mrs M: 'Berlinguer's accusing the Socialists of wanting to destroy the Left. But he's the real villain of the piece.'

Each floor of the hotel had a small closet which, as well as storing cleaning materials, also contained a built-in chest for fresh laundry. I deliberately kicked the door of the chest, dropped my keys on the floor and slammed the closet door – not once but twice – to rouse the guests so I could get on with cleaning their rooms. In my first few days there, I'd felt sorry for the guests, I'd even asked Antonella to keep the noise down. 'They've got to get up right now,' she told me, 'otherwise Cocola hits the roof. She says she must have all the breakfast stuff cleared away by eleven.' Plus, any sleepy-heads just ate into our free time.

I pushed the pile of clean sheets to one side and reached for the open packet of biscuits. Antonella kept a little stash of sweet goodies behind the bed linen. I'd just settled down on the floor, with my back leaning against the closet door and pulled out my paperback to read a couple of pages, when I suddenly felt someone trying to get in. I quickly hid my book under a bucket but had trouble swallowing the rest of the biscuit. As I opened the door, some of it went down the wrong way and I began to choke, gasping and waving my arms about, causing Paul to reel back in alarm.

'Do I really look that awful?' he asked jokingly. He followed me back into the closet, where I'd gone to find a bottle of water, which I knew Antonella had left by the cleaning materials two days ago. Paul slapped me on the back and as I recovered, wiping the tears from my eyes, I realised that he'd left his right hand resting there. I offered him a biscuit, but he just took the box from me and put it down on the linen pile. For a moment, I thought he was going to kiss me, but then he picked up the packet of biscuits again, turning it this way and that like he was searching for the list of ingredients.

'One of the key people behind the attack in the Via Rasella was a woman called *Capponi*,' he said.

'What attack?' I thought of Antonella and her sympathies for the *Brigate Rosse*. What was her family name again? I knew I'd heard the name *Capponi* somewhere before. At a loss what to say, I simply replied: 'Antonella never came back to our room last night.'

Paul looked at me. 'What, you've never heard of the Via Rasella?' he shook his head in astonishment. 'You must have, surely?' He took a biscuit and took a bite, but didn't chew it. Looking at his face, I noticed the impression of crumpled bedsheets on his left cheek. 'It was a bomb attack against a battalion of Nazis. The next day, in revenge, they executed ten Italians for every one German killed. All of them innocent civilians. Don't you remember: the cat – ?' Paul's right cheek looked noticeably fatter; he still wasn't eating the biscuit.

'The cat in the garden was called *Capponi*,' he continued.

'You mean Mrs Manente named the cat after a female assassin? Aren't you reading too much into it? Couldn't there have been somebody else she once knew who was called that? A cheeky guest, maybe? Or one who tried to get her claws into Remo?' I offered Paul another biscuit, but he declined. '*Capponi, capuni* – isn't there a fish called something like that?'

Paul was giving me a pitying smile.

'So… maybe the cat stinks like a fish? Or that kind of fish has got a blunt, round head and the ugly cat's head reminded Manente of it?' I floundered, then changed tack: 'Not wearing your collar, then? No guided tours today, Reverend?'

'No, not today.' Paul stepped out into the corridor. 'It's very loyal and touching of you to try to explain it away. But haven't you heard Manente going on about Pertini? She hates our new president.'

'Yes, I s'pose – whenever she's chatting with Cocola about him, she calls him the "Carnation President". And she can't stand carnations, not even as table decoration. Even though they last for ages.'

'He was a *partigiano* too, see. Maybe Antonella's right and Mrs M really was engaged to a Nazi who was killed here in Rome.' As he spoke, Paul kept fiddling nervously with the doorknob.

'I know some more juicy titbits about her, too. Antonella – '

'Yeah, what about Antonella? Where'd she get to last night?'

'No idea. Manente's going to tell her parents.'

'Maybe she just overslept and she's lying in the arms of one of the guests right now?'

'I don't think so.'

'Maybe they'll walk in on us like that?'

As he moved to touch me, I dodged his advance by bending down to pick up the cleaning bucket. 'Not me, they won't,' I replied. I squeezed past him and strode down the corridor, leaving him standing by the closet.

25

Emma had positioned herself in the kitchen in such a way as to get a clear view of every guest as they came into the dining room for breakfast. She was only half-listening to Cocola, who was telling her about more arrests, including a man from the suburb of Magliana, who'd had contact with the Red Brigades' printer. Even now, more than two months after the death of Aldo Moro, crowds of supporters and mourners still flocked to the Via Fani and the Via Caetani to pay their last respects to the dead politician by leaving wreaths of flowers, posters and little handwritten messages. She'd been along there, too, Ada said.

Emma was relieved that the man they'd arrested came from Magliana and not from the Via Nomentana and that her son's name wasn't among those terror suspects listed in the paper. And when Ada went on to say 'If you ask me, they should string up all these terrorists,' Emma tried not to listen; secretly, she sympathised with her cook, but was fearful that one of the ropes might end up being put round Franz's neck. No sooner had she thought this, though, than her suspicions struck her as absurd. Sure, Franz travelled a lot and only called infrequently, but what did that signify? Emma chided herself silently for being an unjust and stupid mother, gulped down the rest of her coffee and set off for reception to telephone Antonella's parents and ask where she was.

Emma really wished she had someone she could call up to enquire about the whereabouts of her own son. She thought about the untidy girl from Trieste whom Franz had once brought home with him, but the only thing she could remember about her was her surname, Rizzo. It somehow seemed to chime in with her wild, frizzy hair, but it was an extremely common name the length and breadth of Italy, so it'd be pointless trying to find her in the phone book. In fact, the girl from Trieste, Emma discovered during that Christmas visit, turned out not to be from Trieste at all. The thing was, she'd kept on going back there to support that doctor who'd advocated closing all the lunatic asylums and releasing the inmates, so her friends – Franz called them 'comrades' – had come up with the nickname 'the girl from Trieste' for her. Now it alarmed Emma that she'd never got to learn the girl's first name and that even Franz had called her *Triestina*. Perhaps she was part of the underground, like so many others in the headlines right now, and was on the run.

Emma rang the contact number she'd been given by Antonella, but was met with silence, not even an engaged tone. The line appeared to be dead. She wondered whether she'd got the wrong number or if Antonella's brother hadn't paid the bill. So how was this Mimmo supposed to survive if he couldn't even take telephone orders for bread?

What if something had happened to Antonella?

The rectangle of reflected sunlight on the wall above the reception desk had already shifted nearer the door and was quivering slightly. Emma stepped outside and gazed up into the treetops, among which floated little blue islands of sky. She shut her eyes and imagined that Steg had come up silently behind her and wished her a good morning. If they were in Stillbach now, they'd both be out on the balcony of her guestroom looking over at the far side of the valley, those Southern-looking slopes, whose forests had once been chopped down to help build the city of Venice. She had it from several reliable sources that slash-and-burn farming was to blame, but she stuck to her story that the river down in the valley had once been navigable and that they'd clear-felled the entire stand of timber over there and floated rafts of logs downstream to the

Lagoon. Just before leaving Venice, she accused Signora Scabello and her Venetian forbears of ruining the landscape of her homeland. Even now, she said, villages in the valley floor were threatened by mudslides as a result. The Scabello woman just scoffed at her: 'Problem is, you've got too many goats and sheep grazing up there.'

Nobody kept herds of goats anymore, Emma thought at the time, not even the farmer at the Nörderhof. Johann's third eldest brother had stayed in South Tyrol after '39 and gone on to fight alongside the Italians. In the autumn of 1943, when Italy withdrew from the war, he didn't see any reason why he should take up arms and fight for the Wehrmacht. So, when all the ethnic Germans were called up, he absconded and went into hiding in the woods. For weeks, he managed to scratch out a meagre existence, breaking into alpine chalets and hunting lodges and eating the scraps of food his little sister collected and hid for him in one of the remote caves under the Stillbacher Horn. But then the snows came and his sister couldn't get any more provisions to him, as the Germans would have spotted her tracks. Their farm didn't have a herd of goats that she could have driven up the track to obscure her suspicious footprints.

It was only after the war ended that Emma got to hear the story of this brother, who'd also ultimately gone to live in Switzerland, eight years after Johann's rebellious friend. It seems the brother came back to Stillbach briefly after the war, but his own father and brothers attacked him for being a 'coward' and a 'deserter', so he'd upped sticks, turned his back on the Nörderhof for good and gone to start a new life in a remote valley in the east of the country.

Emma's gaze strayed to the windows; almost all of them were closed. She could never have slept in a stuffy room like that. Even when she'd still been just a chambermaid here, she'd flung open all the doors and windows to let some fresh air in.

Looking at the individual windows, Emma recalled the outdoor larder, a kind of crate made of wire mesh, which her father had hung like a birdcage out of the window on the shady side of the kitchen. Strange, because they hadn't had much to keep cool back then; still less after Emma's money from Rome dried up. Even after she got married, she continued sending money back to Stillbach until her savings were all used up. Only then did her father start criticising her for marrying Remo. He didn't say what it was about his son-in-law that he didn't like; fact is, he couldn't have, as he never bothered to get to know him. After her father made such scathing comments about her marriage and her child, Emma had thought more than once about going up to Stillbach unannounced and in front of them all, filling the outdoor larder with cheeses and hams. It would have been sweet revenge for her to see the weight of all that food bending the wire mesh and slowly dragging the cage right off the window ledge.

The one time when her father might have had a chance to get to know Remo, he'd stalked off and not come back before the evening. Her brothers made themselves scarce then, too. Emma and her husband had been in Switzerland on a belated honeymoon. They'd been staying with distant relatives of Remo's mother in Bellinzona, but had left there in good time to make a detour to Stillbach. It'd been Emma who'd pressed for them to leave that pretty little town in Ticino with its castles and battlements because she wanted to spend a few days of their all-too-brief holiday with her family and had hoped that things would be alright now after all that time.

True, there hadn't been any open hostility when they turned up, it was just that her mother was the only person there. She was pleasant enough to Remo, but at the same time she left them in no doubt that they should clear off again straight away. She hadn't laid the kitchen table. When they left, her mother didn't even shake Remo's hand; all she did was dodge back behind the kitchen door, dip her fingers in the holy water dish and, standing on the threshold, wave a slapdash sign of the cross in the air. The holy water didn't even touch Emma and Remo's foreheads, but instead splashed on the flagstone floor.

Afterwards, although it was already late, Remo was keen to drive straight down to Verona without a break. To try to reassure Emma, he kept putting his hand on her thigh, and just before they reached the Chiusa di Salorno Narrows, that invisible frontier between two peoples, he'd pointed up at a bright patch in the sky and said: 'Your father has to share that light with us, whether he likes it or not. Even if he chooses to look away.'

When Emma came back to reception, the rectangle of sunlight was still trembling on the wall. She went over to the window opposite where the light was shining in to try to close it more firmly, but it wasn't well enough insulated and the sashes kept moving in the constant stream of air blowing through the building.

Such ingratitude. And now it was Franz who took all this financial support for granted. She didn't even know what he was using the money for. She worried what he'd say to Hermann Steg. Would he snub him? Steg might even become the cause of a permanent rift between them. No, he'll stay in touch with me if only for the money, thought Emma.

The morning was in full swing by now and the walls were reverberating with the hum of the street. Emma thought about looking in on the dining room. Perhaps Hermann would be having his breakfast already. But if she ran into him when Cocola was present and used the familiar form of address, Ada would immediately twig there was something going on between them. On reflection, better wait for him in reception.

In her head, she ran through a few breezy greetings, but none of them seemed quite right. 'Sleep well?' – 'Catch you later?' – 'Can I invite you for lunch?' – 'Is there anything you need?' She was ashamed of her lack of facility with language. Last night, Steg had reeled off an epigram by heart and Emma hadn't even known who it was by. She was breathing faster and sweating a little. She put it down to the side effects of the painkillers that Doctor Franceschini had given her.

She spent some time sorting out old invoices, totalled up the bill for a couple who were leaving later that day, phoned the wholesale greengrocer and butcher and arranged a delivery of mineral water. Each task seemed to merge into the next; latterly it seemed to Emma that there was no clear sequence of events any more, as though everything was becoming totally intertwined. And this inevitably led her to think of Stillbach and Rome together, each going on with its separate life, her brothers ploughing the fields while she stood here behind the reception desk and how – here she glanced at her watch – in just a minute the church clock there would be striking the quarter-hour. Everything there was still as it always had been, since time immemorial.

At that moment, Steg came down the staircase and behind him followed Ines. He was laughing.

Emma leapt up, snagging the hem of her dress on a drawer she'd left open when putting the invoices away. She called Steg's name, but he didn't turn around.

26

I could see from the way she walked, her drooping shoulders and her tousled hair, that Antonella had stayed up all night. If I hadn't happened to glance out into the garden from the window of one of the guests' rooms, I'd have missed her return. I dropped what I was doing and dashed downstairs. Who of all people should I run into but Steg, who was standing in the stairwell with his arms outstretched like a policeman, blocking my way. Because he could hear other guests getting ready to leave their rooms he backed off, though, laughing his head off like he'd taken complete leave of his senses.

Pausing for a moment, he said: 'Mrs Manente was looking for you.' I used the opportunity to dodge past him and took the final few steps in a single leap. Antonella was right outside the back door to the garden as I opened it. She hung her head disconsolately and her blue mascara was smudged, like she'd been slapped in the face. All the pent-up anger I felt towards her for leaving me to do all the work evaporated instantly at the sight of her.

'What's the matter?' I asked.

'Not here,' she replied.

'No, tell me now. You know I've got to get back upstairs and finish the beds.'

In response, she gave a brief shrug and pushed past me into our room, where she flung herself on the bed and buried her face in the pillow.

I stayed standing in the doorway, thinking about all the rooms and corridors that still had to be cleaned, and about Manente, who'd no doubt be coming to look for me if I didn't get back to work soon.

'He'll kill me. My brother's gonna kill me.'

'What, did they catch you? Were you fishing coins –'

She sat up. 'Oh, not that again. Change the record, will you? – No, I got arrested.' Antonella scraped her fingers through her hair several times. Her fringe was sticking out in all directions. Suddenly, she leapt up, stripped off her outer clothes and put on her pinafore.

I could smell her BO from the door.

'Manente'll go spare. I never bothered registering myself as employed. If they come here – '

'What are you on about?'

She looked down at the floor and started buttoning up her pinafore, but missed the lower buttonhole, so that the pinny sat all skewiff. 'We're campaigning to get Paragraph 194 properly enforced,' she explained, looking up at me.

'You've buttoned it up wrong,' I said.

'You haven't got a clue what Paragraph 194 is, have you?' she said, ignoring me. 'What planet do you live on?' She scraped at her hair again, sat down on the chair, which was covered with underwear and clothes, and swore: '*Merda, merda, merda.* That shouldn't have happened. I was too slow. I should have run faster. But the cops didn't pick me up right outside, I'd got a block away before they collared me.'

'Did you –'

'Look, no-one obeys the law in this country. No-one, understand? We're living in a Catholic fascist state where termination's supposedly legal, but you've still got to go to some back-street abortionist to have it done, like in the Middle Ages. All we're asking is for abortions to be done properly in clinics or hospitals.'

'And how are you going about it, exactly?'

'Look, don't come all high and mighty with me. What would you do? – nothing, I'll bet. Does Manente know I didn't come back last night?'

'Presumably.'

'What's that s'posed to mean? Does she know or doesn't she? Did you rat on me?'

'I didn't say anything, she just noticed you hadn't come back, alright?'

'You're lying.' Antonella came up to me; I stepped aside to let her pass. 'You're not being straight with me,' she said.

'Oh, just leave me out of your little dramas, I've had enough,' I snapped back, turning on my heel and leaving the room. The lift was down in the basement, so I took it to avoid running into the proprietress. It juddered its way up, creaking and rattling so badly I was afraid it would come to a grinding halt.

I started with Steg's room. I figured Mrs M must have buttonholed him, or he'd be having his breakfast and wouldn't be able to pester me. His bed wasn't rucked up much; I just smoothed the undersheet flat. The bathroom was a quick job, too. Steg hadn't showered, or maybe the water droplets had just dried off by now. He must have used a lot of aftershave, though – its minty, sweet smell permeated the bathroom and the bedroom.

I skipped dusting and just straightened up the chairs and the bedside carpet. Before leaving, I leafed through Steg's books. On a note stuck into a volume of poetry, he'd jotted down various dishes: *rampant rocket, mackerel garnished with rue leaves, sow's udder served in a tuna marinade*, and next to them the note: *Entrées for dinner*. The book underneath had lots of small Post-it notes sticking out of it; one of them marked a passage where a poet was complaining that people had lost all interest in politics and only wanted *panem et circenses*. Further on, Steg had underlined a sentence that reminded me of his remark to me earlier that morning: 'You're a jealous dress to hide such lovely legs…' I closed the book: *Roman Poets of Antiquity*. How come Steg didn't read any works by living authors?

All of a sudden I heard footsteps and Antonella's voice: 'What are you doing starting here? We're supposed to start on the third floor and work our way down –'

'What's your problem? It's not like you do anything else Mrs M tells you to.'

I wondered if Paul had gone already. The moment I thought it, my stomach went into a knot and my face felt much hotter than normal.

'So,' I asked, 'How do you go about persuading doctors to carry out abortions? By slashing their car tyres?'

'Good idea,' said Antonella. 'Do you really want to know, though? Can you keep your mouth shut? No, actually I don't trust you.' She made to leave.

I went after her. 'Look,' I said, 'it's not my choice to be sharing a room with you. If the boss asks whether you were there overnight or not, I can't lie to her. So I thought it better to say nothing.'

Antonella was standing by the window in the corridor and pressing her finger against the putty like she was testing if it had hardened yet. In fact, it had become brittle over the years and started to flake away from the lower part of the frame.

'So how did you avoid a grilling?'

'I didn't have to. She's preoccupied with Steg at the moment. God knows what she sees in him. All she said was that she'd speak to me later.'

We went up to the top floor and cleaned the rooms in silence. I kept asking myself the whole time what on earth Antonella had done. Had she just gone out with a couple of mates to stick up illegal posters, or was it something more serious?

I wouldn't have put it past her to smash windows or spray revolutionary slogans up on hospitals. I figured anyone who had the brass face to fish money out of the Trevi Fountain from under the noses of hundreds of tourists wouldn't baulk at damaging public property.

A couple of days before, she'd stood in front of the wardrobe mirror with her fist clenched, winked at me and chanted '*La lotta continua!* The struggle goes on!' At the time, I'd thought she was joking. I wondered if the guy who'd thrown the screwed-up note into our room was involved in all this. What if some group of grown-up militants were using her for their own ends?

Then again, it was none of my business. I spent the morning cleaning tooth mugs, polishing tables and making windows sparkle. Occasionally, in magazines and newspapers that guests had left in the waste bin, I caught sight of headlines saying that Christina Onassis was planning to marry Sergei Kanzov, that 10 million Italians were once again sitting in traffic jams now the holidays had started and that the world's first test-tube baby Louise Brown, 'The Child who Came in from the Cold', had been born.

I couldn't get a peep out of Antonella. I asked her once to chuck me over the floor cloth but she didn't hear me. Another time, the clean hand towels were missing; when I pointed this out to her, she just looked at me. There was an anxious expression on her face and she was squinting slightly. But it could just have been that she was tired after her sleepless night, and the sunlight and the humid air we let into the rooms to get rid of the sleep and bathroom smells were bothering her.

At lunchtime, Antonella disappeared to our room. She said she wasn't really hungry, but asked me to bring her a bit of fruit. 'Tell Manente I'm lovesick. Tell her – no, on second thoughts, don't tell her anything.' As I left the room, Antonella was lying back on the bed with her face turned to the wall.

After lunch, I got myself a towel from the ironing room and went up onto the roof terrace for the first time. There was no sunshade there. The terrace was flanked on the short sides by low walls, while the long sides were protected by a white-painted, wrought-iron balustrade, which let a cooling breeze blow through, but also exposed you to the neighbours' gazes.

To get up to the terrace, you ascended a spiral staircase that ended in a kind of roofed hut. I had trouble opening the thin steel door. From up here on the roof, the umbrella pines looked like soft, wave-like clouds and the garden took on the appearance of an impenetrable primeval forest. There was no sign of the wooden shed where I'd had my liaisons with Paul.

I looked down on deserted lower roof terraces, on flat roofs with TV aerials blown askew by the wind, on balconies with folding tables and deckchairs, and on blue and black plastic sheets covering all kinds of household items that had no place in the house anymore.

After a while, I stripped down to my knickers and lay on the ground with my face in the shade of the half-open steel door. I couldn't stand being in the sun for long. I turned on the tap to the left of the stairs and hosed myself down. Beneath me, a puddle formed, which, when I dabbled my feet in it, sounded like someone smacking their lips.

There were hardly any cars on the Via Nomentana. The faint swooshing I could hear was a mixture of city noises, its inner workings and public face, which began to flicker up here under the blazing sun. I lay on the wet roof and, gazing up at the sky, saw the sea, its surface just starting to ripple in the suddenly freshening wind. I heard the cries of children playing and beach flags fluttering. When I closed my eyes, I could feel the individual drops of water evaporating off my skin. It was as though *coriandoli* – bright confetti – was falling from the sky and landing on me.

I'd stood up to spray myself again when I heard whistles coming from one of the balconies of the palazzo opposite. The man continued to draw attention to himself even after I'd sat down and covered my breasts with the hand towel. He must have been using his fingers to make the sound, as the whistles were so piercing they scared a flock of doves off the roof.

Now, the sky was just sky, and the water droplets tickled so irritatingly I brushed them off my skin. I packed up my things and left the terrace.

27

Hermann Steg had almost breezed past Emma like nothing had happened between them. But then, first thing that morning, he'd made amends by coming and chatting to her at the reception desk. Emma immediately rushed off to the kitchen to fetch two cappuccinos and some fresh rolls. No-one had ever been allowed to breakfast in the lobby before; Hermann had stayed there for a whole hour, without even wanting to sit down.

He asked Emma whether she didn't ever feel homesick for Stillbach after all the years she'd spent in the South.

That was all the invitation Emma needed. She told him how her heart still beat a little faster whenever she saw cars with South Tyrol number plates. And how tears always came to her eyes on winter strolls along the seashore at Ostia, because the crunching sound the mussel shells made as she trod on them reminded her of the crump of snow underfoot and the grey-white landscapes of home, which she'd never liked when she was there but found herself longing for ever since. How sometimes, when she was alone, she'd talk to herself in Stillbach dialect. How she'd once brought a bunch of grass home from a country walk and dried it up on the roof terrace, just so she could enjoy the smell of hay again, and how disappointed she had been when it failed to release the aromas of herbs and bitter almonds that she'd always associated with dried grass. How occasionally, in St Peter's Square, she thought she recognised people from her region from their posture and the way they walked, with their knees buckled and their backs bent from heavy manual labour in the fields and woods, and how she'd once called out 'Dad!' to someone on the Piazza del Popolo – a small, non-descript, grey-haired man who turned out not to be her father after all.

I don't know how I could ever have imagined he'd come and visit me in Rome, thought Emma. She was sitting now in her favourite chair next to the terrace door, with a cushion wedged between the back and the armrest, and studying her legs; the shadows of the oleander leaves played across the mass of spider veins that had formed just above her ankles.

When Emma went back home one time around Easter, she'd smeared some mud on her slip-ons so her father wouldn't see that they were new. Even so, he'd noticed the shoes because her sisters kept looking at her feet. He asked her whether she'd forgotten how they lived up here in Stillbach.

'Perhaps he was afraid the new shoes would take his daughter even further away from him,' Hermann said when she related this incident to him.

Emma now admitted to herself that, although she'd felt pangs of homesickness now and again, it had never become a gnawing, painful obsession, a fixation so deep-seated that she would have staked everything on going back. After Remo died, she could have sold the hotel and left Rome with Franz, but a single winter trip back to Stillbach, a single turn round the icy cemetery and a visit to the family home had been enough to remind her how much the hotel and the mild Roman climate meant to her.

Homesickness – that was something for soldiers. It was what Johann and his Italian comrades had clung to when they'd been out in Ethiopia. This nostalgia had fuelled their daydreams and their thirst for stories, which all turned on their native villages and hometowns, which so few of them had left voluntarily.

Emma had still been in Stillbach when she had heard a friend of her brother talking about the victims of mustard gas and how there were no doctors or drugs to hand to treat them in remote parts of Abyssinia. Mustard gas, he explained, burned your skin down to the bone, causing blisters and weeping sores and making you temporarily blind because your eyelids became swollen. He said he was just a driver who had had to move trucks over the country's sand and mud tracks and jungle trails. He passed around a snapshot of a bare-breasted 'pretty Negress', but quickly put it back in his trouser pocket when Emma's mother came in.

A few months after Emma had visited the Lady General to get work down south and had already terminated her employment with Signor Scabello, a Roman column had been erected in Bolzano, under the patronage of Prince Umberto of Savoy, to commemorate all those who'd lost their lives fighting for Mussolini's colonial empire in Africa. Speeches and reports on the day of its unveiling proclaimed that the glorious war dead had strengthened the bond between the northern territory on the Brenner Pass and the 'great motherland of Rome'. Johann had not forgotten that the very first time he'd ever had a square meal was when the Italians, who occupied the region after the First World War, arrived with pasta, chestnuts and rice in their backpacks. Unlike many others in Stillbach, he never used racist terms for Italians and was infuriated by these bombastic festivities: 'The fascists should be ashamed of themselves, celebrating that "victory".' As far as he was concerned, the 'great motherland of Rome' had spawned a race of cowards, who had unleashed poison gas and flamethrowers on a handful of horsemen and tribal warriors armed only with spears.

In the first few months after his return from Africa, Johann had managed to convince Emma that he'd only been responsible for building roads and laying on running water. Gradually, though, she had come to doubt this version of events, especially after Johann got drunk at the last Stillbach Harvest Festival they attended together and told her about his recurring nightmares. At night in his bed in Stillbach, he dreamt that he was surrounded by Abyssinian hyenas and jackals, who would tear him to pieces like the Ethiopians had been torn to pieces by hand grenades. That was the only party Emma ever saw Johann drunk at. He'd staggered around among the assembled guests, telling them how provisions like rice and rusks had fallen like manna from Heaven in Africa. Those Eyetie idiots, he shouted, had dropped supplies to them without using parachutes. They'd had to scrabble around on their hands and knees picking up the rice, grain by grain. He kept knocking back wine and babbling names Emma had never heard of.

As soon as he came back from the Abyssinian War, Johann had walked to the chapel on the edge of the wood with Emma to give thanks to the Virgin Mary for his safe return. But as it turned out, the Queen of Heaven wasn't content to let him stay in Stillbach, but sent him off to war once more.

Good Luck has only ever got one hand on the rudder, thought Emma. Best if you learn to swim yourself, Remo once advised her.

Emma watched Ines wiping off the garden furniture with a damp cloth, so that the guests, who would be coming out onto the terrace for a nap or an aperitif any time now, would find their seats and loungers spotless.

With her eyes closed, Emma could tell from the sounds Ines made whether she was wiping the chairs or dawdling. She could hear exactly when the girl paused, got up from her crouched position and looked down the garden. She was also wise to the fact that Ines deliberately shifted one of the plastic chairs around with her foot to make out that she was working hard.

'Keep at it, girl!' Emma called out, without opening her eyes. Though she thought it several times, what she really wanted to say, but didn't, was 'Why don't you just clear off?' She wanted to avoid having to share Hermann, whom she had been waiting for the whole time, with Ines.

That morning, she had asked him what he'd done during the war, but he'd only given evasive answers, mentioning his basic training in Innsbruck before changing the subject to Rio Silenzio, which he had never visited.

There was something else that was news to Hermann, too. Long before the fascists seized power, an Italian named Ettore Tolomei had begun translating all the German place names in South Tyrol, because he regarded the watershed on the main ridge of the Alps as the natural frontier between the two cultures. He made it his life's work to get this little leftover piece of the Habsburg monarchy incorporated into the Kingdom of Italy. As she recounted all this to Hermann, Emma felt on a par with him for the very first time. 'That bungler translated Linsberg as "Monte Luigi" – and who knows, when it came to Still-bach, he probably thought the first part meant 'style' rather than 'still' before someone put him wise.' At this, Hermann took Emma's hand and reassured her that *Rio Stile* would have been a far more appropri-ate name for her home village than *Rio Silenzio*, but because the couple from Room 30 came up to reception to hand in their key, he quickly let her hand go again. Neither he nor Emma made any reference to the night they had spent together.

'By the way, where's Antonella?' Emma asked, getting up and going over to the balustrade to check on the clothes lines.

'She's not feeling well,' Ines told her.

'What's up, then? Is she ill?'

'I don't know. She's just lying on the bed and saying nothing.'

Emma turned around. 'Tell her to come to the kitchen at six,' she said. She straightened a lounger and used her index finger to push an ashtray gingerly to the middle of a table. 'OK, you can stop wiping down and take the sheets in. They must be dry by now. And when you've done that you can make a start on the ironing.'

Right, now Hermann can turn up any time he likes, thought Emma. She went back to her place and slipped off her sandals.

But Steg didn't appear. He didn't even take up his usual spot under the tree to read his book in peace. Emma would have loved to have talked some more about Tolomei – for instance, how he had wanted to remove the statues of the Austrian Empress Sissi and the poet Walther von der Vogelweide. And he was convinced that he was the first person to climb the Klockerkarkopf, which was nonsense, of course, as someone else had got to the summit years before him. Still, he had the temerity to claim it as the northernmost peak in Italy – the Vetta d'Italia – and decades later, the fascists honoured Tolomei's 'achievement' by ennobling him as the *Conte della Vetta*, the 'Count of the Peak'. In any event, he'd got it wrong, as Italy's northernmost peak was actually the Westliche Zwillingsköpfl, a few kilometres to the west. They should really have called him Count Heights of Arrogance, since only such a complete idiot could have hit on the idea of shipping off 2,000 South Tyrolean farmers to Ethiopia, a scheme that thankfully never came to anything. But they had sent her Johann to Africa – no, on second thoughts, Emma didn't want to talk about that. *My Johann.*

She got up and walked over to the balustrade again. *All your memories are left hanging in the air*, she thought. She watched Ines as she folded the washing and put it in the basket.

28

I put off going to the kitchen to avoid the row between Antonella and Mrs M. Gianni had also made himself scarce. I came across him behind the hotel, pointlessly rearranging drinks crates that had already been stacked once. Gianni was the lightning conductor for everyone else's bad moods, but by now was a dab hand at disappearing in good time.

We polished off the washing up together and then went into the garden. He offered me a cigarette. I declined, fearful that Mrs Manente would see me and report back to Aunt Hilda that I smoked. Instead, I asked him to give me one for later. He pressed the whole pack on me. Try as I might, I couldn't get him to take them back; he held his arms behind his back and grinned at me.

'Just so as you know,' I told him, 'I don't mind you using our shower.'

Gianni hooked his thumbs into his trouser pockets and thrust his hips forward.

'You want to watch out for Antonella,' he said, letting out little puffs of smoke.

'How come?'

'No reason, really,' he answered. He chewed his lips; it made it look like he was trying to eat the words he'd just spoken. 'Her brother's an arsehole.'

'What, Mimmo?'

Gianni nodded. 'He's bad news for girls.'

'Do you know him, then?'

'He hangs around waiting for Antonella sometimes.' Gianni finished his cigarette, stubbed it out on the ground with his foot and buried the butt beneath the gravel. He shook a few stones out of his sandals. 'If the boss sacks Antonella, I can help you do the rooms.'

'You reckon she's going to give her the boot? I don't. Who'd work in the kitchen, in that case?'

'I could manage both, no problem,' said Gianni. He stood staring at me in silence for a while. Then, suddenly, he launched himself forward, planted a swift, clumsy kiss on my lips and dashed off to his scooter without a backward glance.

In truth, it was more of a peck than a kiss. On the back of the football top he was wearing, I read the name *Paolo Rossi*.

Only when he reached the gate did he slow down. He looked back at me and with a laugh, called out: 'See you tomorrow!'

I strolled round the garden and halted at the fountain. The longer I stood in front of the leprous statuette and gazed at the figure's face, the more I could see of its contours. In the soft evening light, its features seemed to grow animated, like a real person's face.

My fingernails were dull from doing the pots and pans, and the cuticles were split. I dipped one arm, then the other, into the water, enjoying the coolness and looked over at the false acacia trees flanking the washhouse. In the spring, the scent of their heavy blossoms must have wafted up into all the rooms. Now, their regularly spaced leaves were being shaken by droves of sparrows landing on their furrowed branches and taking off again.

I'd be off to university in a year. Aunt Hilda had promised to pay for three weeks' holiday if I passed my school-leaving exams. Finally, I'd get to enjoy a proper summer – a summer that wouldn't be entirely occupied with looking after small children, clearing restaurant tables or cleaning hotel rooms, like the past few years. I'd revel in a blissful few weeks when I wasn't at someone's beck and call. There would be no-one to interrupt my reading. And the days would be mine to spend as I liked. And one day, my whole life would belong to me, that 'better life' that Mum always talked about when she came home, dog-tired, from the fruit growers' cooperative warehouse, with the noise of the automatic sorting mechanism still ringing in her ears. All the apple names like *Morgenduft, Jonagold, Kalterer Böhmer* and *Golden Delicious* sounded so alien to me here, and in that other, better life, I swore the only place I'd ever encounter these apples would be by chance, on some foreign market stall.

'Are you following me?' I asked, lifting my arms out of the water; opposite me, on the far side of the fountain, stood Steg, clutching a book covered in newspaper.

'*Tu mihi sola places!*' Steg replied, giving a loud laugh and dipping his left hand into the water. He opened and closed it like a mouth snapping at prey. The goldfish scattered.

I shook my arms to dry them quicker. I really ought to have had my hair cut short and put on a wedding ring, I thought. But that wouldn't have done any good in Steg's case; even the blackest goddesses of the Underworld, snake-haired and grimacing grotesquely, would have struck him less as vile hags and more as potential conquests.

'You can't honestly think I'll do you any harm, can you?' he asked.

The 'nice' things you have in mind are bad enough, I thought.

'Have you got a boyfriend?'

'None of your business.' I've got to get away from here, I thought. 'What about you? Aren't you married, Mr Steg?'

'If I was, do you think I'd be here on my own?' Smiling, he took a step towards me. 'Hang on, you've got –'

As I dodged away from him, his outstretched fingers brushed my breasts.

Instinctively, I dipped the flat of my hand into the fountain like a shovel and scooped it up, drenching him with water.

Steg's face was soaking wet and his shirt and book were liberally splashed, too. He wiped his forehead and eyes with the back of his hand.

'Oops, sorry,' I said.

I ran back into the house, chuckling to myself.

Passing the kitchen, I saw Cocola and Manente sitting at the table. They were busy working out the shopping rota and the menus for the next few days and took no notice of me. They'd set Antonella to work cutting out all the rotten bits from a load of apples, pears and bananas and dicing them up to make a fruit salad. When she saw me, she pulled a face behind their backs and made a stabbing motion with her knife at the proprietress.

I hurried back to our room. There was a screwed-up piece of paper near the wardrobe, but there was no message on it. I heard footsteps on the gravel path and hid myself behind the wardrobe door, but they didn't come any closer. Presumably, Steg had gone back up to his room to change his wet shirt.

As I stripped off, I noticed a ladybird on my pinafore. Was that what Steg had been trying to draw my attention to? No – no excuses: after all, he'd said '*Tu mihi sola places*' to me.

I wondered why, with all the jerky movements I'd made, the ladybird hadn't flown off. Perhaps it had only landed on my pinny in the stairwell.

My hair smelt of the frying and steaming smells of the kitchen. After showering, I lay down on the bed to read, but then decided to go out into the garden with a pack of biscuits and a bottle of water before Antonella came back.

On the way to the shed, I stopped by the square manhole cover. Using a broken branch, I scraped it clear of earth and weeds and ripped away the mat of ivy tendrils that was growing over it. I took hold of the metal cover and tried to lift it, but failed. There was no lock to be seen, so I couldn't understand why the cover, which was only a metre square at most, wouldn't budge. Even so, I couldn't have climbed down into the hole without a ladder and a torch.

Hearing voices, I dived for cover behind a caper bush. It was some guests walking down the main path; most never deviated from this well-tended strip of gravel.

Although it was already getting dark, it was still humid. I carried on to the shed and lay down on the bench. I kept having to swat midges. Smoking one of Gianni's cigarettes kept them at bay for a while. My heart was beating faster. Was I hoping Paul would show up?

There was a rustling in the bushes. The cat, probably. I took a cookie from the packet. The noise in my head as I ate the crisp, buttery biscuit was just like the sound my climbing boots had made when I crossed the compacted crystalline snow on the Höchstberg. I'd only been up that far the one time, with Aunt Hilda. Coming down from the mountain, I was so exhausted I was on the verge of tears. We stayed overnight in an alpine refuge hut; all the snoring in the dormitory kept me awake until the small hours.

One of the cats crept past. It went to sit down at a safe distance on the well-worn path leading from the shed to the back of the fountain and stared at me. In the dark, I couldn't make out whether it was Capponi or Rosario. Only when it was satisfied I wasn't about to move did it start licking its paws.

The sky was alive with stars. I even spotted the Evening Star, shining above the crown of a palm tree. I had no idea if Paul was coming or not. If he did, I'd tell him about what happened with Steg today and about Gianni's peck. I'd ask him to take me down into the Catacombs. Just the once. And I'd –

Oh, what the hell. I sprung to my feet. The cat leapt aside and vanished into the undergrowth.

There and then I decided to go and knock on Paul's door and ask him to come out into the garden with me. And if he wasn't there, I'd stick a note in his door.

29

If only it hadn't been such a pain finding new staff, Emma would have fired Antonella on the spot. Suburban brat – bolshie like that partisan who'd refused to give away the state president's hiding place.

Antonella just said she was sorry she'd turned up late, but didn't explain why. Emma laid into her, trying to impress upon her that because she was still a minor, she couldn't just do as she pleased. Antonella's only response was to shrug her shoulders and go on shelling walnuts.

Whenever Emma saw walnuts, she couldn't help but think of that woman from the Anima who'd worked in the kitchen of the German ambassador Mackensen. She had had to prepare a banquet for Mussolini and other high-ranking fascists. The job had entailed shelling lots of walnuts. Some of them, the woman explained, had proven really hard to crack, so she popped them into her mouth and broke them with her teeth. As she crunched away, she was thinking, so what? The only person who eats walnuts is *Il Duce*, anyway.

Emma remembered the occasion well. They had all met up at the Anima to play cards and have a tombola, and some *Wehrmacht* soldiers and two Swiss Guards had also been present there in the recreation room. 'What's that?' one of the German soldiers called out when he overheard the woman's story, 'you had the *Duce*'s nuts in your mouth?' and he fell about laughing.

Emma couldn't recall the woman's name any more; the last time she'd seen her was in the summer of 1943, talking excitedly about the bombing raid on San Lorenzo. She said she'd been standing on the terrace of the Villa Wolkonsky and had been utterly transfixed by the sky turning blacker and blacker with debris until another member of the embassy staff had dragged her away and led her down to the air-raid shelter.

Though Emma had always rather envied the woman, because she had a Diplomatic Corps pass that entitled her to free public transport around Rome, in the end she was relieved to be living at the Manentes. For one thing, she didn't suddenly find herself out of work, nor did she have to flee for her life to avoid being stoned by an angry Italian mob, like all the officially registered *Reich* Germans had done at the end of the war.

While most of the other domestic servants and nannies that she'd got to know in the Anima hurried along to the German Consulate in 1939 to vote for the Third Reich, Emma had remained an Italian citizen. Even Rome hadn't been immune at that time from the intensive propaganda campaign for the Führer, which her cousin kept talking about for years after. In Stillbach, people who voted to stay part of Italy were decried as 'old women' or 'pimps' and accused of being in league with the Italian fascists. There was even talk of forcibly resettling them in Ethiopia or Sicily.

One time, Emma had been harangued in church by a woman who, when the plebiscite was announced, summarily handed in her notice with her Italian employer and went to work for a German officer. But women like her had soon returned to their home villages and then emigrated over the Brenner or Reschen Passes into the German Reich, sparing Emma any further unpleasantness.

Old Mr Manente, bless him, had set her mind at ease. He reassured her that the authorities wouldn't force a mountain-dweller – a *montanara* – like Emma to go and earn her living on a fishing boat, any more than they'd transplant a Sicilian shepherd who'd never seen snow in his life to a farm in the Alps. All that was just propaganda and scaremongering.

Mr Manente was a nice old boy – later, despite her background, he had no qualms whatsoever about accepting her as his daughter-in-law. Emma didn't want to fall out with him. Even so, at the time she was sorely tempted to tell him a few home truths about what his compatriots had been doing to hers for the past two decades. How fascists from all over Italy had flooded into the North to try to Italianise it. That there was no comparison between the Italians 'down here' and the zealots and fascist interlopers 'up there'. She also longed to ask him how he and his fellow Italians would feel if the boot had been on the other foot and they had suddenly been forced to attend German-speaking schools and register with German authorities, and he'd had to change his name from Umberto Manente to Hubert Bleiber. Or what his reaction would be to being exiled, at the slightest sign of insubordination, to the far east of Austria or East Frisia.

Though Emma's father had voted for the German Reich, in the end he didn't emigrate there. The poorest hovels in Stillbach were still a lot better than the conditions the emigrants were faced with when they got over the border. So much was clear even to him, the man who'd named the first pigs he bought with the money Emma sent back after the fascist prefect Mastromattei and the hated provincial secretary Tallarigo. After the war, Emma heard, there'd even been an Adolf in her father's barn, though it was a bull, at least.

When Emma thought back now to the world of her childhood, she always pictured a model railway landscape. Glued to a green hillside, Stillbach was a cluster of little houses that all looked the same. Time's a great leveller, she thought. All pictures ultimately fade to yellow.

In actual fact, she couldn't have cared less where Antonella spent her nights. What really riled her was the girl's stubbornness and her cheeky riposte: 'I don't have to take any lessons from you when half your staff are illegals.'

Emma had given Antonella the choice when she started work. Right from the off, her brother, whom Emma had dealt with, had been against a regular employment contract, as that would mean his sister earning less. And Antonella had said a casual arrangement would be fine by her. But now here she was, coming over all holier-than-thou. Emma had even gone behind Mimmo's back and offered to register Antonella as an hourly-paid worker, but she'd turned her down. She'd also snubbed Emma's suggestion that she should learn German twice weekly in her free time. She'd sooner learn Arabic than that Nazi language, was her curt reply.

When Hitler and Mussolini had been close confederates, there'd been a positive mania in Italy for learning German. The papers were full of small ads offering jobs to girls with good language skills. All of a sudden, girls from the North were expected to teach their employers' children the Classical German of Goethe, while they themselves were herded into fascist schools and forced to speak Italian. But by the time Emma took up her post in Rome, this fashion was on the wane, after the first cracks began to appear in the relationship between the Axis dictators.

Nevertheless, old Mr Manente had been all ears, memorising the odd polite German phrase, while Remo enrolled himself with a retired grammar school teacher for two years to learn German, 'so I can understand what my wife's saying to my son.'

Although Emma tried for years to speak German with Franz, he insisted on answering in Italian, until finally Emma too started to become more comfortable with Italian. At first, it seemed like moving into a furnished apartment, but she gradually managed to put her individual stamp on this other language. Remo loved the way she spoke it; he was fascinated by her logical and analytical approach to its superficial sing-song cadences. Emma herself never found Italian a superficial language, although its tendency to beat about the bush would always remain alien to her.

Steg lay low for the rest of the day. Emma caught herself checking the same bill three times and automatically reaching for the booking register, though she didn't need to consult it. There was nothing more to be done at reception. Emma was tired but didn't want to turn in before seeing Hermann. She was still seething about Antonella; she seemed so powerless to do anything about her.

Today Emma had noticed that moss had begun to grow in the gutters on the shady side of the hotel, that the roots of the huge plane tree were beginning to lift up the flagstones in front of the laundry block and that some of the indoor tiling was cracking. Also, it must have been ages since the main gate was repainted, as the ironwork was starting to rust near the ground. Who was supposed to do all these odd jobs? Steg had only ever had to deal with paperwork, thought Emma, she couldn't picture him with a paint scraper in his hands. Even so, it would be a big help to her if Hermann could just be there to deal with workmen and oversee the gardener. Staff were more inclined to listen to a man. Who knows, Antonella might even fall into line.

Emma slipped off her sandals, feeling the cool terrace floor beneath her feet, which were swollen from lots of standing around and rushing about. She tiptoed over to the sofa, sat down and examined the balls of her feet. Ines had mopped the terrace earlier; there was scarcely a speck of dust to be seen on her feet.

The little piece of sky that Emma could see from the sofa was midnight blue. Barely an hour ago the clouds, those greedy gobblers of light, had been glowing orange with the setting sun before they were dispelled by the evening breeze. Emma stared up at the ceiling light and thought of her father, who had always badgered the family about saving light. When the mayor of Stillbach had more streetlights installed, so that not just the extremities of roads or paths were lit, but the whole village was illuminated, her father had marched along to the municipal office to complain about the shameful waste of energy. 'Do some people need to count the spiders and beetles on their outside walls, then?' he'd asked. He'd also, in all seriousness, put forward the idea of turning off the streetlights when there was a full moon. Perhaps, Emma mused, he'd actually had a romantic streak. She was jolted from her reverie by the familiar clatter and bang of the lift lurching into motion as someone summoned it from upstairs.

30

'Sorry, I don't know where the time's gone to today,' said Paul. Apparently, he'd almost missed seeing my note. He came up to me as I was leaving the hotel by the back door and kissed me on the cheek. My face felt flushed. I turned away from him and bent down to try to fix my sandal strap; the prong was bent and kept slipping out of the hole.

'Let's go and eat,' he said, 'my treat – I hope you haven't eaten already.'

'Only a couple of biscuits.' I wondered how he thought of me – a lonely chambermaid, a keen student, or some scatterbrained bed-hopper who'd be easy prey? Paul seemed to be studying my every movement, making me nervous and self-conscious. My sandals suddenly seemed clunky and ugly. Why hadn't I got myself some more stylish little slingbacks? And why I was so ignorant about history?

We travelled several stops on the bus, then walked a stretch to a restaurant near Porta Pia. The tables were laid with white tablecloths and the waiters were dressed in dark suits. I could hardly wait to hide my feet under the table.

Paul confided that he'd done well on tips today.

Two of the waiters couldn't agree on where they should seat us, even though the whole of the front of the restaurant was empty.

Paul ordered a bottle of wine and only checked afterwards whether that was okay with me.

There had been this story that had done the rounds for weeks in our class about a boy who'd slept with a girl from school. Apparently, he'd said afterwards: 'Well, she didn't object, so I just went ahead and did it.'

'Why are you shaking your head?' Paul asked.

'I can't tell you,' I answered, 'just remembering something.'

'You're too young for reminiscences.'

'Quite right.' I took the menu that the waiter proffered me. He looked askance at us when Paul laughed.

'So,' I asked, 'how come you got so many tips today? Do your groups donate to the Church without realising you're not a priest?'

'No, it's 'cause I'm good at what I do – honestly.'

'I bet you really look the part – like some high-minded seminarian.'

'If they only knew I was quarter-Jewish.' He tore a piece of bread in half, sprinkled salt on it and popped it into his mouth.

'So what did you do today?'

'Oh, just the usual round: the Palazzo Corsini, the Palazzo Doria Pamphili and the Palazzo Farnese. Bit of a slog, to tell you the truth.'

'I really like the façade of the Farnese,' I chipped in, 'even though the windows are different on each floor.'

'Already done the High Renaissance for Art History, then, have we?'

Embarrassed, I kept quiet.

Paul reached for my hand and gave it a squeeze; then when the waiter reappeared ordered the same for both of us. That was something I had okayed beforehand.

Most of the dishes were unfamiliar to me, especially the meat and fish specialities. At home, on Fridays, we'd sometimes have *sgombri* – mackerel preserved in oil – which you could buy loose at the grocer's. Like the spreadable chocolate we used to buy, they came in a large, round tin.

During the pasta course, Paul told me about his childhood in Vienna, his secondary education at the famous Stubenbastei grammar school, and later – we'd been served our main courses by this time – went on to talk about his Roman grandfather, who'd escaped deportation in October 1943 by fleeing to the countryside. He'd taken refuge in a monastery, Paul said. Alongside Denmark, Italy could boast the highest proportion of Jewish survivors. Unlike in Austria, there had never been a tradition of anti-Semitism in Italy, because the state had been founded by anti-clerical liberals. Besides, he said, he found it liberating to discover how little of that typical Austrian subservience to authority was evident in Italy: 'I admire the Italians' skill at sidestepping rules and regulations.'

We were already on our second bottle when Paul suddenly let his fork drop noisily on his plate and summoned the waiter. He'd found a fly under his lemon slice, he announced in a loud voice; a hush fell over the conversations at the surrounding tables and the other diners craned their necks to look at us. You save up for weeks to splash out on an expensive meal to treat your girlfriend on her birthday, Paul complained, only to find *this* – here, he pointed at the fat, black shape on his plate and grimaced. The waiter bowed, apologised and picked up the plate. He tried to reassure Paul that the fly must have got onto the plate while they were eating.

'Come off it,' Paul replied, 'there isn't a fly in the world strong enough to push its way under a slice of lemon – not even one that was trying to commit suicide.'

The couple sitting to my left burst out laughing and nodded their approval. I cringed with embarrassment and stared at my lap. The shadows of the carnations in the little red flower vase on the table cast a shadow as sharp as a scissor cut across the white tablecloth.

'I'll bring you a fresh main course,' said the waiter.

'Forget it – I've lost my appetite,' replied Paul, 'and so has my girlfriend.'

A second waiter, evidently higher up the pecking order, appeared at our table and promised to sort things out. Saying he'd go and speak to the chef straight away, he disappeared into the kitchen and returned to tell us that there would, of course, be no charge for our meal.

We ate the *ricotta* ice cream the restaurant brought us, finished the rest of the wine and left the place at around 11 o'clock.

'Wasn't easy catching a fly today,' Paul said on the bus home. Though there was plenty of standing room, we were standing toe-to-toe and hanging on to the roof straps. Our upper bodies bumped against one another now and then.

'The trick is,' he continued, 'never to go back to the same restaurant, plus you've got to make sure the ones you do go to aren't too near to one another, just in case the waiters or chefs were to compare notes. And they've got to be popular and pricey places – it's not worth kicking up a stink in simple *trattorie.*'

'Are you saying you deliberately put the fly under your lemon?'

'No, of course not – I'm kidding you!' laughed Paul, 'but it'd be a brilliant idea, wouldn't it? Still, we've only had to pay for the wine.'

Aunt Hilda once found a tiny snail, still alive, in a salad she was eating at the inn in Stillbach. By way of apology, the landlord gave her a free dessert and a glass of Jägermeister. I couldn't work out whether Paul was telling the truth now or if he really had put the fly on the plate on purpose. After all, he did go around the city posing as a priest.

When we got off the bus, he put his arm round my shoulder for a moment, like he was shielding me from the automatic closing door.

Some flowers were giving off a scent when we entered the garden. We walked towards the entrance, slowing our pace the closer we came to the marble steps.

'I really want to see the Catacombs,' I whispered.

'Aren't you frightened?'

'Well, I'm not planning on roaming around down there. I just wanted to have a quick look.'

'I'll get my torch,' Paul said, 'wait for me by the laundry block.'

The brick-mounted trough outside the washhouse felt warm to the touch, as though the sun had only just gone down. I probed my teeth with my tongue to dislodge any residual scraps of food. Pity I didn't have any chewing gum with me. I sniffed my armpits and smoothed down my skirt.

I began to feel the effect of the wine; I skidded on the gravel path and only just stopped myself from falling over by grabbing hold of the ivy tendrils growing over the low brickwork around the trough. That was the South for you – wherever I lunged, there was dense vegetation.

Over dinner, Paul had told me that the landscape of Rome had remained essentially the same as it had been at the end of the Roman Empire, while other regions of Italy had gone downhill fast. As soon as people stopped working the land, the plains reverted to swamps and the fire-cleared forests became choked with scrub. Mussolini had the Pontine Marshes drained and purged of malaria, Paul claimed, precisely in order to demonstrate Rome's greatness. His mention of marshes called to mind the tufts of grass I'd seen growing out of the guttering on the roof terrace and trembling in the wind.

Paul came down again, carrying not just a torch but also a special type of ladder that the proprietress must have ordered from Stillbach, as I'd only ever seen them being used before by apple pickers up there. The ladder had just a single stringer, with short rungs wedged and glued into it.

'Where'd you find that?'

'Behind the shed,' Paul said, 'it's been there for ages.'

'Not too long, I hope.'

After several attempts, we managed to lever off the manhole cover. Paul shone his torch down into the hole before lowering the ladder.

'Who's going first?'

'I will,' replied Paul.

The dancing light of the torch made me feel giddy. Paul was holding it and the ladder in one hand and guiding me down with the other. My knees started to go wobbly, so I jumped down the last few rungs and landed in his arms. We stood there like that for a while in the cool subterranean passage. The cone of light from the torch illuminated several wall niches, all of them empty.

'Looks like a stone couchette,' I joked.

Paul felt for my face and kissed the tip of my nose. 'Even in death,' he whispered, 'they wanted to journey together into the Afterlife.'

31

It was a bright, moonlit night. The few clouds in the sky looked like pedestrians ambling between heaven and earth. Some clustered together, forming little groups. Was Johann up there? And Remo too, for that matter – even though he hadn't been much of a believer? He only used to go to church with Emma on major feast days. What really mattered, he told her, was how you lived your life and the respect and consideration you showed others. Prayers, he maintained, were just short-term solutions for relieving stress.

Not that all the 'Our Fathers' and 'Hail Marys' that Emma had said during her pregnancies had brought her much in the way of relief. She'd gone along to the Church of Sant'Agnese a couple of times. But who was she supposed to talk to there? Nobody knew about the child she was carrying. And in those days, anyway, people were all wrapped up in their own misery. Emma even began to think that God the Father was only really bothered about the fate of his Only-Begotten Son and had abandoned his human flock.

In her own mind, Emma had resolved to entrust her baby to the care of the *Opera Nazionale Maternità e Infanzia* – the fascist organisation that promoted the institution of motherhood and looked after the welfare of infants. She wouldn't go back to Stillbach, that was for sure. Even a state institution was preferable to having to face her father's recriminations and the village gossip.

She couldn't possibly have ever imagined being taken into the bosom of the Manente family. Right from the beginning, they'd presented her with a strong, intact family unit – not one of those seedy arrangements where a widower would offer the other half of the matrimonial bed to a new domestic servant he'd just taken on. All kinds of extraordinary things had gone on back then. *Di tutti i colori.*

Yes, Fate had got up to some rare old tricks, alright.

Though Emma had her hair cut short and wore sensible patent leather shoes, she still felt like she was running around in pigtails and clogs. Looking in the mirror, it had taken her a long time to stop primping so obsessively and to start seeing herself as the woman who Remo wanted to spend the rest of his life with. She guessed he'd only started to entertain the idea of taking her as his wife when he learnt about her pregnancy. He'd surely have followed his parents' wish for a more suitable match if there hadn't already been a child on the way.

'Don't take any notice of what other people say,' Remo always used to say to Emma when she'd been upset by someone claiming that she'd hoodwinked the Manentes.

'What if the kid isn't Remo's?' she'd once overheard old Mrs Manente say when she happened to pass beneath an open window. But the only other person's it could conceivably have been had been blown to pieces by the partisans – and Emma had never slept with Johann. The only people who were put up at hotels like the Bernini, the Ambasciatori, the Excelsior and so on were the wives and lovers of the Nazi élite. Some general or other had even set up his headquarters at the Hotel Flora. The bigwigs lost no time in commandeering the smartest villas and throwing lavish parties in their ballrooms and banqueting suites. They even laid on appropriate entertainment in the city at large, with the Barberini cinema showing German films twice a week. The pleasure of these little soirées had ended abruptly when a man on a bicycle opened fire on the soldiers and officers as they streamed out one evening. That had been just a few months before Johann's death. The reason Emma could remember it so vividly was because the German High Command reacted by banning everyone from riding a bike and threatening to shoot on sight anyone who disobeyed. Mälzer had just taken over as the Wehrmacht commandant in Rome; he was rumoured, even in the Anima, to be a heavy drinker and was prone to issuing shoot-to-kill orders. After the attack in the Via Rasella, he'd really had a field day. The so-called 'King of Rome' had avenged her Johann alright, but what good had it done Emma?

For years after, she'd tormented herself for not having given in to Johann's urging her to sleep with him. She refused to go to some fleabitten hotel with him. 'We've waited long enough already,' she told him, 'so it won't do any harm to wait a bit longer.' Johann had respected her wish; they'd wait until they were back in Stillbach.

Oh, to Hell with Stillbach.

Now all the stars were twinkling in the sky, sparkling and shimmering. Emma didn't even notice that she was suddenly clapping her hands for joy and gyrating her hips like someone was playing music for her. She felt a bit like that time she'd gone along with Franz to the political rally.

Hermann would be back soon. She'd waited an eternity at reception for him today. He'd broken his usual routine by going out for an evening stroll. There was so much that wasn't his usual routine, he'd replied when Emma quizzed him, looking deep into her eyes. And now he'd gone downstairs to get them a couple of bedspreads and some pillows. *You can keep all the fancy hotels in the Via Veneto*, thought Emma. *This is real heaven, gazing up at the night sky from the terrace that I really should use more often.*

From many of the surrounding windows came the flickering blue light of TV screens. On his last visit, Franz had complained that Emma still had the old black-and-white set in her living room. 'Splash out a bit on yourself, Mum, for heaven's sake!' he'd said to her. But it was all the same to Emma what colour tie the newsreader was wearing.

Hermann reappeared on the terrace, out of breath. 'Ran into that student of yours just now…Quite the night owl,' he gasped. Emma couldn't help but call to mind that recent guest from Berlin, who confided in her that she tested out her prospective lovers in the stairwell at home. Anyone who made it up to her flat on the fourth floor without too much difficulty was likely to be pretty handy in the sack, too. The rest disqualified themselves. The woman from Berlin had come to Rome on her own.

Hermann laid out the bedspreads on the ground. 'Must be quite well off, that young man. Otherwise he couldn't afford to stay in a hotel.'

Emma lay down gingerly, fearful of putting her back out again. 'His grandparents came here on holiday once. His room's very small, anyhow, I couldn't really let it to a proper guest. And I'm pleased he does his guided tours – saves me from being pestered all the time by the *guide turistiche*.'

'Oho, the Grand Lady even keeps her own *cicerone*,' said Hermann, kissing her lightly on the mouth.

How beautiful it was up here on the roof at night. The warm air lay on Emma like a light cotton blanket, which no-one was tugging on. For a while, she felt safe and secure. Hermann pushed up her skirt and began stroking between her legs. The noise of the traffic on the Via Nomentana was transformed into the babbling sound of a mountain stream and the sky seemed suddenly so near. Only the roar of a powerful motorbike disturbed her reverie, momentarily reminding her of all the reckless bikers on the roads, including Franz. As Hermann struggled to undo the small buttons on her blouse, Emma was thinking about her son. She pictured him tearing down the motorway. In a tunnel, of all places, the travel bag he'd strapped to the back of his bike fell off one time; it contained his wallet and identity card. Just the thought of him stopping beyond the flyover somewhere between Florence and Bologna on a stretch of motorway that had no hard shoulder and walking back into the poorly lit tunnel to retrieve his belongings set her heart racing. If only she could be sure where Franz was now and that he was alright. She thought about all the patches of oil on the roads, the potholes and the lorries. She hoped he wasn't riding too fast. All of a sudden, an image came into her head of those crazy bikers who rode over the Reschen Pass from Austria to the South Tyrol at weekends; their thrill was to blast down the Stillbach mountain road, leaning fast into the hairpin bends with their knees grazing the tarmac. If Franz…

She shifted slightly away from Hermann, who responded by sliding back towards her and stroking her breasts. He was still out of breath and wheezing so loudly that Emma began to get worried. On the other hand, she was pleased that he'd hurried up to the terrace to be with her.

Presently, it started to get uncomfortable lying on the roof. Whoever laid the tiles up here hadn't bothered using a spirit level. The mastic sealant had begun to come away in places and the little chips of mortar that had worked loose felt like sharp stones under the bedspread. Emma seemed to recall that old Mr Manente had got an unskilled labourer to do the job; the man had friends in the Hunchback's partisan unit, like that odd-job bricklayer who'd cemented broken glass into a section of the garden wall. Franz had already been born when old Mr M had the roof terrace done. When he was a small child, she'd never gone up there with Franz. And later, she'd kept the key to the terrace hidden away from him, because she was frightened he'd clamber over the balustrade or the low walls or climb up too high on the roof.

Hermann had a son, too; he was younger than Franz and worked as a hairdresser in the centre of Innsbruck. Hermann only mentioned him in passing. He took after his mother, he said, and then promptly changed the subject. Emma didn't like to ask what that similarity with his mother might be. With one hand, she fumbled with Hermann's flies, finally managing with some difficulty to pull down the zip. Everything beneath was soft and warm. His head was resting on her stomach and his hands were kneading her breasts. He seemed not to hear her when she hissed sharply 'Not so rough!' and only stopped when she took hold of his wrists.

'What, not in the mood?'

'It's my back,' Emma said, though in actual fact it wasn't troubling her right then. 'And what about your wife – does she know that you – '

Hermann sat up. 'My wife lives seven hundred and seventy kilometres away. Isn't that far enough for you?'

In the darkness, Emma couldn't make out his expression.

'Oh, change the record, will you?' he murmured to himself.

He stood up, went over to the balustrade, peered over the edge, though there was nothing to see except the dark silhouettes of pines, palms and planes. He zipped up his flies and tucked his shirt into his trousers.

'Oh and another thing,' he said, 'I had some cash in my room. It's disappeared.'

Emma rose to her feet, almost tripping over the tangle of bedspreads. 'That's impossible!' she exclaimed.

'I couldn't believe it either,' said Hermann, 'it's more than four thousand schillings.'

'You left that kind of money in your room?'

'I've never had any problems before.'

I should have left some cash lying around various places to see if the girls picked it up and handed it in to me or pocketed it, Emma thought. Now it was too late. 'Have you looked everywhere it might be?' she asked Steg.

'Of course.' He took a few steps towards the terrace door, but then thought better of it and came back to hug Emma.

32

When I woke up, my arm was dangling over the side of the bed and my fingertips were touching the floor. It was six in the morning. Paul had rolled over to face the wall. In the half-light, his shoulder blades looked like they'd been hewn out of stone. I thought of Greek and Roman statues, though I'd scarcely seen one for real. I slid out of bed, taking care not to wake Paul. I was moving in slow motion, but still the parquet flooring creaked with every step I took. No matter; Paul went on sleeping undisturbed. I bent over him and looked at his long eyelashes. His mouth was half-open and he was dribbling.

I stood motionless in the middle of Paul's room. The refuse lorry was crawling up the Via Nomentana; I could hear the grey aluminium wheelie bins being hoisted up into the truck, emptied and trundled back in front of the house gates. From somewhere came the sound of roller blinds being opened.

I couldn't bring myself to leave the room. I stared at the narrow bed and the little table underneath the window, which was covered in books, journals, notepads and slips of paper. Under the table was an Olivetti typewriter with paper already in the roller. I picked up a book at random, flicked through it and read some of the notes Paul had jotted in the top margin: *cover-up of irreconcilable differences; they claimed to be active, but masked their inactivity with a fog of pseudo-active phrases and resolutions; delaying tactics; August 1942 – orders were circumvented – Ciano and Mussolini appeared unconcerned at this. A calculated move? (In the event of a separate peace with the Allies, did they hope for special treatment if they refused to support the Nazis in their extermination of the Jews?).* On the next page, he'd written: *Ring Mum, Birthday!*

How could Paul make any sense of this chaotic clutter?

He'd scribbled down the times of various tours he was due to take on a page torn from a newspaper: *6.8: 11 o'clock Palazzo Farnese; 7.8: Pensioners' group from Lüneberg – start: 10 o'clock at the Trevi Fountain, tour to last till 1 p.m. Contact: Signora Romanelli 222 18 11.*

There were even some paperback editions of Pavese, Ginzburg and Morante stacked on top of the hot water boiler under the sink. At the bottom of this pile, I discovered a slim volume entitled *Volterra*. How did Paul come to know about Franz Tumler, a writer from my part of the world? I'd have loved to ask him, but I had to get out of here before Antonella woke up and Manente began her daily tour of inspection.

I reached for my clothes and dragged on my T-shirt. I looked down at Paul once more and kissed his earlobes. He stretched, flailing his arm about behind him, but grasping at thin air.

'I've got to go.'

Paul looked at me through sleep-narrowed eyes. 'Just ten more minutes. Come on. Please.' He frowned, looking at me as I put my clothes on, and then took them off again. He smiled.

After getting dressed for a second time, I left the room. My hair was still ruffled from sleeping and my eyeliner was smudged.

Carrying my sandals, I crept out into the stairwell and stopped to listen. Satisfied no-one was about, I nipped down the stairs as fast as I could, wetting my finger with spit as I went to try to clean the last vestiges of black mascara off my eyelids.

Near the entrance it smelt of fresh bread. Cocola had begun her working day already. I could hear her talking. I guessed she was on the phone, because I couldn't hear anyone else's voice. At first, from what she was saying, I thought her father must have died, then she said: 'That's right, last night. Terrible. No. He was ill. In Castel Gandolfo.'

I made it to my room without being spotted. I tried to be as quiet as I could and wondered whether I should lie down on the bed and pretend to be asleep. But no sooner had I shut the door behind me, with a barely audible click, than Antonella woke up. She dragged her fingers through her hair, which was sticking up at the back, and glanced at her watch.

'The Pope's dead,' I said.

'Shit – that'll really put the cat among the pigeons.' She trained her beady eye on me. 'Out on the tiles, eh? Which room number?'

I opened the wardrobe, reached for a white pinafore and checked the label. It was the right size.

'Come on, who's the lucky guy? Bet you made his night.'

Actually, I'd have loved to know if Paul was happy. Can you be happy when you've just betrayed your girlfriend? Hadn't he mentioned a girlfriend, who was jealous of his obsession with the past? Had he meant just a female friend or his girlfriend?

'We sat up talking,' I replied.

'Doesn't look like that to me.' Antonella stood up and switched on the cassette player. 'You can crash out for half an hour if you like. It's my turn to do the front steps this morning.'

Antonella clearly only listened to the outside world. Inwardly, she seemed to be deaf. If there wasn't noise going on around her, she had to make some. She rummaged in the wardrobe, pulled out a crumpled T-shirt and her pinny and put them on the chair. 'The kraut'll go spare again if she notices I've forgotten to iron my things. *Churmann discipline!* she mimicked, giving a Nazi salute.

'You're overegging it. Mrs M would never have gone out with an Italian if she'd been a committed national socialist. Manente may have lots of faults, but being a Nazi isn't one of them. Paul told me as much.'

'Paolo – what does he know? He's got no idea. He's just a bookworm.' She picked up some tweezers and started plucking her eyebrows, then glanced at her watch again and quickly rubbed a flannel over her armpits. 'People'll ditch their beliefs for money and status.'

'You might,' I said, turning down the music. 'Do you really think money's that important to the boss?'

'If it wasn't, she'd pay us more.' Antonella slipped on her pinafore and left the room without putting on any make-up.

I flaked out on the bed. My heart was beating faster and faster; I put my hand over it.

It had been a good decision to come down here, I told myself. I just had to watch out that Mrs Manente didn't catch me with Paul.

'I really like you,' Paul had told me. Was that the truth?

I thought about his pale skin and the little moles and freckles I'd kissed. There had been so many they made me think of constellations.

Paul had dropped off to sleep quickly without saying much to me. He had slept without moving a muscle or making the slightest sound until, quite suddenly, he started snoring, as if his body was revving up to full speed to replay his dreams like a film. Behind his gently flickering eyelids, images went racing by, fragments of the day just gone and memories of past times. Mum was convinced that dreams are the dustbin of our minds. I regretted not being able to see inside Paul's head like some invisible deity. In all likelihood, though, I would have made as little of his dreams as I had of the notes in his book.

As for me, the instant I awoke from my catnap, my dreams were as vivid to me as the images in a picture book that someone had quickly flicked through the pages of, before clapping it shut and putting it aside on a table. All that remained in my recollection were dark intimations of equally dark passageways, which immediately became confused with my memories of last night's descent into the Catacombs.

I heard footsteps on the gravel; probably some early riser stretching his legs in the garden. Maybe it was Steg. But it could just as well have been another guest who had woken prematurely and come down too soon for breakfast.

I got up and dragged my tired body to the bathroom. I took a hot shower, then turned it to cold. I put on my pinny and lay back down on the bed with my wet hair wrapped in a towel and began dozing. I couldn't bear the thought that my time here in Rome would come to an end before long, and with it the intimacy between me and Paul. In this state between sleep and waking, I imagined us sharing a little attic flat in Trastevere, full of books. From our roof terrace you could look over the roofs of all the surrounding houses and see the Gianicolo hill behind us and in the distance the white Victor Emmanuel monument shining out above a sea of predominantly grey and brown buildings. I saw our little abode as a shimmering oasis of happiness, with wisteria climbing up the walls, and started daydreaming about nights of love followed by a lavish *al fresco* breakfast. I dropped off and, after being woken briefly by the sound of someone talking in the garden, snoozed some more until Antonella flung open the door. 'Manente wants to speak to you, right now. The old bag's foaming at the mouth.'

I quickly dried my hair and tied it up because it was still damp and tousled. When I bent down to pick up the hairbrush I'd dropped, little silver spots danced before my eyes and the floor seemed to sway. I had to brace myself and take several deep breaths to overcome my dizziness.

I started wondering whether Mrs M had seen me earlier. Or if Antonella had ratted on me. I wouldn't have put it past her. Perhaps she still didn't believe that I hadn't dropped the screwed-up note on purpose and that I didn't have any idea who had thrown it into the room or what was written on it.

The sound of some voices drifted out of the dining room; most of the guests were still asleep, though. When I entered the kitchen, Cocola fell silent and looked at me. Gianni, who had just that instant started working, lowered his gaze and concentrated hard on buttoning up his apron.

'The boss wants to see you in her flat,' said Cocola, pointing up at the ceiling with the bread knife, as though Mrs Manente's living room was directly above the kitchen.

As I turned to go, I heard the cook say to Gianni: 'These German girls aren't a patch on what they used to be.'

33

In February 1938, the Scabellos had been on the lookout for a house-maid because Emma's predecessor had apparently stolen a can of corned beef and a tube of shoe polish. The Scabellos set great store by well-polished shoes. Emma had had to treat Signor Scabello's shoes with one brand of shoe cream and his wife's with another. Signora Scabello was an avid reader of the *Gazzettino* and kept cuttings of adverts for a whole range of luxury creams and lotions.

Back in Stillbach shoes were cleaned with a coarse brush, sometimes with the addition of a smear of pig fat. Emma was perplexed by the Scabello woman's palaver with her shoes. Also, she was at a loss to understand why the former housemaid, who supposedly came from Mestre, would have purloined shoe polish. On one occasion, when she and Remo had been watching TV and a commercial had come on showing a German polishing his car, he turned to her and said: 'Now you know why you were always having to polish shoes at the Scabellos'. Shoes are to Venetians what cars are to other people.'

But what were a can of meat and a tube of shoe cream compared to four thousand schillings? Emma shook her head at the thought, despite there being no-one else in the room.

Hermann hadn't stayed over last night; she had hoped he would come to her flat with her and that she'd fall asleep in his arms. It seemed to Emma like he was blaming her somehow for the theft. The money, Hermann said, had still been there yesterday morning. He had tucked it under the cover of one of his books.

'Perhaps you took the book out into the garden with you? Could the notes have slipped out?'

'Absolutely not.'

Even so, first thing that morning, Emma had gone round the garden to check and found that someone had opened the manhole cover down into the Catacombs. The evidence was fresh – the ivy uprooted, and the earth they had scraped away to expose the hinges still damp.

Old Mrs Manente had always given the hole a wide berth; she always meant to have it bricked up or welded shut to make sure the dead never emerged from it. But even though the entrance was on the Manentes' private property, it wasn't allowed. If Remo's mother had still been alive today, she would surely have linked the disturbed manhole cover with the Pope's death.

Maybe someone had gone down there to hide the stolen cash in the Catacombs.

Antonella swore blind to Emma that she hadn't been in Steg's room the day before, because – Emma remembered it clearly now – she had been too late coming in to work.

Ines was the only person who'd had access to Steg's room, Antonella said. Emma didn't like the way she tried to cast suspicion on Ines, but then again, the little Italian – whom she thought perfectly capable of plenty of things, including a theft of this order – did seem like she was telling the truth this time.

Emma's stomach was aching. After Steg left the terrace, she had sat there a while longer and finished the wine. She'd never been up there on her own at night before. Once she had given up all hope of Hermann coming back, she stood up, went over to the balustrade and, slamming her hand down repeatedly on it, burst into tears.

I look really done in, she thought as she stood now in front of the wardrobe mirror. She pinched her cheeks and using her fingertips, pushed the skin back towards her ears to tauten it. Her tongue seemed to be coated in fur. After every meal involving wine, Signora Scabello had always drunk a glass of water with a sachet of antacid powder dissolved in it. The tongue was the mirror of the stomach, she always said, and liked to do an occasional tongue-test on her staff. She once prescribed the antacid powder to the nanny because she said her tongue looked dirty, too unclean for her children to see at any rate. 'But I don't show the children my tongue,' the *bambinaia* had objected.

May the Pope rest in peace, Emma thought, and lit a candle. I've already outlived so many of the people around me. But a bit of me has died alongside them. And in the meantime: hunger. My boy. The hotel.

She crossed herself and looked out into the garden at the myrtles, the bindweed and the false acacias.

Why did the Pope have to go and die right then, when everything was in uproar in the hotel? When Emma had left Venice for Rome, her mother had been relieved, because she believed that people who lived in the Eternal City were under the Pope's personal protection. Or at least that of his guardian angels. Emma wondered whether she still thought that after what happened to Johann. Or after Emma married Remo. So who was there to look after Emma now? She felt sick to her stomach with rage. Rage at Steg. And at the girl. And even a bit at the Pope, who had condemned her to a hotel full of pilgrims and mourning Christians. She would have to buy in some more cutlery. There weren't enough forks or knives. The only things the guests didn't nick were the spoons.

At the Scabellos', the domestics weren't even allowed to use the same cutlery, Emma now recalled, but the same was also true of some farmhouses in Stillbach. Their neighbour, for instance, had treated her younger brother like a serf and only allowed him to eat after the family had finished their meal, at a separate table in a corner of the room and with his own set of crockery. Emma's mother had always hated that kind of person. But her father was a strong believer in the survival of the fittest and thought it was all part of the divine scheme of things.

The Manentes hadn't made any distinction between their staff and their own family. In their eyes, the only person worthy of special reverence was the King, but when Victor Emmanuel II was awarded the highest fascist military honour, when he was named Marshal of Italy alongside the Duce, the House of Savoy was never spoken of in the household again, not even by Remo's parents. They were so disillusioned with the royal family's political misjudgement that old Mrs Manente even banned alpine violets from the hotel, on the grounds that they were one of Queen Elena's favourite flowers. Only when the King stripped Mussolini of all his official posts was the embargo on mentioning members of the royal family lifted.

How sad and horrified Remo's mother had been when, soon after, the Nazis arrested Princess Mafalda. At the time, her children were living in the sanctuary of the Vatican with Cardinal Montini, the future Pope who'd just died. The Princess had thought her marriage to that national socialist prince from Hesse would guarantee her safety during the German occupation of Rome, but she had been lured under false pretences to the German Embassy, taken into custody and spirited away to Bolzano. She was held at the internment camp there before being transferred to Buchenwald, where she was killed in an American bombing raid. Hitler had had her deported because her father and his family had sought refuge with the Allies. Poor Princess Mafalda. For years afterwards, Remo's mother had set a vase with fresh flowers in front of Mafalda's portrait. When she eventually died, Remo had the picture removed. But Emma could still remember the young woman's face, her sensual mouth and her large, dark eyes that were set a little too far apart.

Emma opened the drawer with the medicines in it and searched for a dyspepsia tablet. She paced up and down the living room and looked anxiously at the clock. Where had the girl got to? If Emma was to believe Steg, then the only person who could have taken the money was Ines. What was she supposed to do with her now? There was no

question of calling the *carabinieri*. If they turned up here in their uni-
forms, it would only harm the business and unsettle the guests.

One of the Anima women from the Thirties once told her employer's little boy that Mussolini was a nasty man who was leading the
country into ruin. That same evening, the boy repeated this to his
parents. The woman was summarily carted off and locked up for three
months and also had to pay a five-hundred lire fine. Nowadays, it
seemed, girls could steal four thousand schillings and get off scot-free.
It just wouldn't do. Emma wouldn't stand for it, even if Ines did come
from near Stillbach and Emma had never had anything but good experiences with girls from her home region. This time though, it seemed
her cousin in South Tyrol hadn't done her homework thoroughly
enough.

She asked herself what Ines might want the money for. If such a thing
had happened when Emma was in service, she might have understood
it – back then, everyone was dirt poor and the more money you sent
home the better you were loved. You would have done anything just
for a little glimmer of appreciation. Many of the women who worked
away from home didn't realise that their wages were being used to pay
off their fathers' debts and that the farmland which their fathers had
purchased on credit would go on to be inherited, lock stock and barrel,
by their brothers. 'The closed farm' was never anything other than a
form of legalised exploitation. Who could have blamed these women
if they'd secretly salted away some of the money they earnt for themselves, or if they'd pocketed a bit of illicit cash now and then? But the
simple fact was, they were all much too scared to have ever done that.

So, for years on end, Emma had sent all her wages back home. Her
own sisters envied her for having such a swish job. But all she'd been,
at least at the beginning, was a clumsy and nervous second-string
housewife who was obliged to work fifteen-hour days. And she'd had a
gap between her two front top incisors – as a result, the rumour went
around back home that if you had teeth like that, you would become

quite the globetrotter. Old Mrs Manente got hold of some little rubber bands for her, which Emma used to put on her teeth at night to pull them closer together. Slowly, the gap narrowed and finally disappeared altogether.

There was a knock at the door. Outside stood Ines; there was something strange about her hair.

'How could you have left your room looking like that?' Emma said.

34

I dragged my suitcase behind me, my eyes burning with tears. Two women standing at the bus stop with bulging net shopping bags stared at me. At least I'd had a chance to shower; and I'd never have to dust the radiators any more, or rub the water marks off mirrors, or breathe in all those cream cleanser fumes, or fold the loo roll into little chevrons. And I'd be spared having to rinse out the insides of flower vases, which gave off that stench of rotting vegetation that turned my stomach, or wipe finger marks and greasy smudges off the window panes, or dispose of the guests' condoms and porn mags. I didn't have to do anything anymore.

At first, I ran into a side street, not knowing what I should do next. I looked at the street sign, reading over and over again the unfamiliar name Via Cheren, which sounded so strange and un-Italian. I walked on to the Via Nomentana, desperately hoping I would run into Paul, so he could console me. But he never appeared and I didn't have the nerve to go back and ask to see him, or even to ring up and ask to speak to him. Manente would have realised straight away who was calling and refused to put me through.

That frigid bitch. That cow.

I bet her husband had never seen her naked. When she conceived her son, she must have been wearing one of those modesty nighties with a coitus-vent let into it.

I tried turning my face away from the women, but couldn't sustain it for long. I had to keep watch on the gate into the Hotel Manente's garden. All the while, the two women wouldn't stop staring at me.

If I still wanted to catch a train back up to Bolzano, I really should get along to the station rather than hang around here any longer. I suddenly became fearful about what I'd do when night fell, though it was still morning. I could see myself dragging my suitcase around the city centre somewhere, my footsteps dogged by predatory Romans.

When the bus came, I got on without asking where it was going. The driver seemed to be in a hurry; he accelerated and braked so hard that passengers who were standing were flung about. As we proceeded, a group of English girls grew louder and louder with every passing stop, their giggles and shrieks drowning out the locals' conversations, who turned round to glare indignantly at the pale-skinned tourists. The girls were standing in the aisle of the bus, without holding on, and waiting for the driver to hit the brakes; whenever he did and they touched a fellow passenger instead of grabbing hold of a seat back or hanging strap, the entire group erupted into gales of laughter.

I sat in the back row and looked out of the window, trying in vain to focus on anything on the kerbside as the bus sped onwards. For fractions of a second, I would catch sight of the roots of trees that had burst their way through tarmac or lifted up paving stones, or glimpse Paul's face on imaginary billboards or behind the wheel of oncoming cars. Time and again, I tried refocusing my gaze so as to fix on something, but this something was torn away from me so fast that I often couldn't even be sure of what I'd seen. Was that a lemon-yellow Fiat 126 I'd seen parked on someone's driveway? A deckchair folded up and leant against a fence? And had there been a flock of birds perched on that twisted TV aerial I'd just caught sight of, or was it just shreds of paper and plastic bags? My restless eyes filled with tears once more, as though they were trying to flush out of me the thing I couldn't comprehend.

I had to change again to get to the station. At the kiosk next to the bus stop, I bought myself a copy of the *Messaggero*. *Il Papa è morte*. The headlines in all the papers announced the death of the Pope. I laughed at the thought that the Hotel Manente would soon be booked solid and the proprietress would have to try to cope with just a single, unreliable chambermaid and kitchen assistant to help her. Four thousand schillings. I had no idea how many lire that was. I didn't even know what Austrian banknotes looked like.

The newspaper wrinkled under my fingertips. I was sweating profusely, but it seemed to me like my whole body was weeping. What would Aunt Hilda make of all this? Would she believe me?

After my conversation with the proprietress, I went back to our room to pack my things. Antonella had been standing in the door of the kitchen, watching me. I could have sworn she was smirking.

The second bus drove through empty streets; most Romans were on holiday at the coast or in the countryside at this time of year. My suitcase was wedged between my legs and I was clutching my shoulder bag tightly to my chest, like I was carrying a whole summer's wages in it. In fact, Manente hadn't even paid me what was owing. 'Four thousand schillings,' she shouted after me, 'is more than enough.'

Aunt Hilda once had a job as a secretary at a prominent building firm and had gone to the bank one time to pick up the wages for twelve bricklayers. Before driving off in her Citroën Dyane, she'd put the leather bag with the money on the car roof while she did up a button on her blouse that had come undone. Only when she got out did she realise the bag was missing. It was all because of that loose button, she told me, that she came to be the parish secretary of Stillbach and was only earning half her former salary. The only way to get on in life, she said, was to be completely shameless.

So, I'd taken her advice and appropriated Antonella's stash of coins. I hoped there was enough cash for the ticket back home; it struck me there were too many foreign coins in the box. I couldn't use them to pay at the ticket booth, nor would I find a bank willing to change all the US dollar and Deutschmark coins into lire.

In front of Termini Station, I looked for a quiet place where I could sort through my haul of coins. Tourists kept coming and standing next to me. And when a beggar woman spotted how much small change I had, she ran off and reappeared with a gaggle of scruffy children who laid siege to me. I fled first to the porch at the front of the station, where the taxi ranks are, and then to the ticket office in the main hall. The man behind the counter waited patiently while I painstakingly counted out the coins from the box, one by one, until I had the right fare for a one-way ticket to Bolzano. Behind me, a tall, thin Italian man observed this pantomime with his eyes wide open in astonishment and the corners of his mouth turned down.

I still had an hour before my train left – not enough time to head off into the city centre in search of Paul. Besides, I couldn't remember when Paul's next guided tour was scheduled for. I pictured his hand-written notes in the margin of the *Repubblica* and even recalled the name *Romanelli*, but for the life of me couldn't remember when his tour with the pensioners' group was due to start. Also, in my confusion, I was no longer sure whether they were meeting at the Trevi Fountain or somewhere else. Maybe it was for the best anyway that I didn't see him in my present state.

And what if he didn't believe me either?

I hunched over my bag so nobody could see my face.

When I'd calmed down a bit, I sat in the station bar and drank a mineral water. As I leafed through *Il Messaggero*, my eye was caught by a short article about a group of feminists who had lobbed Molotov cocktails into an outpatient clinic in Monteverde. In other cities in Italy, too, like Cagliari and Trieste, there had been demonstrations against the medical profession. The women were demanding that doctors carry out legal abortions.

Monteverde... It was only just beyond Trastevere – was that where Antonella had been two nights ago? Perhaps this was the struggle the *indiani metropolitani* she so admired were engaged in. If the *carabinieri* had set up a roadblock and identity check near the scene of the crime and clocked her, maybe she was frightened they would link her to this attack and pick her up. '*Merda, merda, merda.* That shouldn't have happened.' – that was what she'd said. And that she'd been too slow. Could the note I picked up off the floor have had some important information on it? It was even possible Antonella had supplied the Molotovs.

I would have loved to confront her now and ask her how the doctors were supposed to do their jobs if their clinics were reduced to charred shells.

All of a sudden, I longed to see Paul so much that the newsprint started swimming before my eyes as the tears welled up again. Or perhaps it was just out of sheer rage at Manente. I hid my face behind the paper, but the proprietress's voice wouldn't stop echoing in my head. So insistently that I couldn't concentrate any more on what I was reading. I had stood there, thunderstruck, in her two-room apartment and said nothing in my defence. I had been transfixed by the two parallel vertical creases running up from the bridge of her nose, which seemed to draw closer together with every sentence she spoke.

From a certain point on, I'd stopped listening to what she was saying altogether and retreated from her, stepping back slowly from the brown leather sofa in the direction of the stone pine corner suite.

The trains arriving from the South were all delayed. The loudspeakers crackled and swallowed several words.

Gradually, I found I could concentrate on reading again. The number of people living on their own had increased sharply, apparently. Louise Brown was doing well. Pertini had taken over only two of the rooms – an office and a dining room measuring four metres square – out of the almost two thousand at his disposal in the Quirinal Palace. Someone suspected international terrorism was behind Aldo Moro's assassination.

Antonella had probably done nothing worse than hand out a few leaflets. And swiped four thousands schillings, most likely.

1978

As I stood up and headed towards the platform, a young man accosted me; he kept pace alongside until I'd boarded the express, but stopped short of pursuing me into the carriage. I hadn't noticed, but after a while, he sidled along the platform until he located my compartment. As the train pulled away, he banged his fist against the window.

I stuck out my tongue, but he just laughed.

2009

Every time the aircraft commenced its descent, the clouds became denser, forming a viscous mass that the plane found impossible to penetrate. The man sitting beside Clara blessed the passengers; his dog collar had slipped off-centre.

'I want to get down,' Clara announced. She unclipped her seatbelt and went forward to the cockpit. A conference was going on in the galley as she passed; the co-pilot was all for attempting a landing.

'That's impossible, we're in heaven!' shouted one of the stewardesses. By now, the passenger with the skewiff collar had also left his seat in the cabin and was tugging at the cockpit door. 'We're not in heaven,' Clara told the steward-ess, 'can't you see that?'

The crew leapt on the man at the cockpit door. Clara was relieved to find she wasn't alone; among all these unfamiliar faces there was at least someone she knew, if only in passing. 'Let Herr Vogel go!' she commanded.

While all this pushing and shoving was going on, the aircraft touched down and took off again – not once, but twice – before banking steeply and ploughing headlong into the amorphous mass, which nobody could fathom the source of.

The cabin windows suddenly whited out, like in a snowstorm. The pilot tried to make an announcement; all Clara could hear was a whistling, then a quiet voice intermittently drowned out by the passengers screams, saying: '*Atteraggio di fortuna riuscito*, We've made a successful crash landing.' Then she was already outside the aircraft, standing on a wide-open expanse that no-one before her appeared to have set foot on. Paul was walking silently beside her, but kept on sinking up to his knees in the dense morass; both of them had their eyes fixed

259

on the cloud beneath their feet, searching for an opening. Clara had never seen such whiteness before, one with no gradations or reflections.

'I want to get down,' repeated Clara. The aircraft was already a tiny speck receding into the distance when they finally found the hole.

'Looks like an ice hole,' said Paul, 'only with no water in it.' They were standing next to one another, peering down into the depths. Her life was down there at the far end of this hole, which had opened up, colourfully and inexplicably, in the middle of the featureless cloud-field.

'I want to get down,' Clara heard herself saying.

The walls around her were painted a subtle shade of blue. If only I could speak with Paul, she thought.

She was exhausted from lack of sleep. After reading the first few pages of Ines's manuscript, she had left the hotel again and taken the novel with her to find a quiet bar. 'You just don't get it, do you?' Ines had once said to her: 'What you're looking for doesn't exist here.' At the time, they had been dashing around the Termini Station neighbourhood, searching for a café without any loud music where they could read.

The bar Clara had found last night, not far from the hotel, had high tables and uncomfortable stools, but the guy behind the counter had been kind enough to switch on an extra light so Clara wouldn't strain her pretty eyes, and served her an espresso, even though he was already cleaning up the coffee machine for the night when she walked in.

Business was slow; after ordering their drinks, most customers took them outside so they could smoke. Initially, the music in the bar had bothered Clara, but soon she was so immersed in the text that she didn't even notice the barman, who had been standing right next to her for some time. He gave a chuckle when she suddenly looked up at him in alarm.

'What do you want?' Clara blurted out. That's what he was about to ask *her*, he replied. He guessed it must be a love story she was so engrossed in.

'It's the story of my friend.'

Now it was six in the morning and Clara had a headache. She lay on the bed, naked, fanning herself with the folded cover sheet of the manuscript. After she'd told him about Ines, the barman with the salt-and-pepper crewcut had given her a *grappa* on the house. The next round had been on Clara and the third on Gianni – and so on, until Clara began to feel unwell and took her leave at around two o'clock. Just before she left, she asked the barman whether he had worked in a hotel on the Via Nomentana in the late Seventies.

'What makes you think that?'

'Because my friend knew a kitchen assistant called Gianni.'

He shook his head and after a brief pause asked her: 'Would you like me to walk you back to your hotel?'

'I'm just fine on my own, thanks.'

'Me too. We can walk together, then.'

She'd even found it an effort laughing at his little pleasantry. As soon as she got back to her room, she was sick. After that, she sobered up instantly and felt refreshed enough to read the manuscript right through to the end.

Clara couldn't understand how Ines could have written all those pages without telling anyone. Perhaps she had decided not to say anything until she found a publisher. Had she planned on publishing the novel, then? Was it even complete?

I really ought to get some rest, she thought, I've got a tough day ahead. She calculated how many hours there were before she was due to meet Paul. As always when she tried to force herself to go to sleep, she only achieved the opposite. Just the thought that Claus or Gesine might ring in two or three hours' time put her on edge.

Clara was a little put out that she wasn't mentioned in the manuscript. The only thing from their past that Ines had included was their hunt for ephedra plants. In actual fact, she had been the one who had told Ines about this rare plant – along with wild liquorice, the sun star and spiked speedwell, none of which appeared in the text. Ines hadn't even been able to tell a berberis from a juniper.

And why had Ines hushed up the fact that she, too, was from Stillbach, from the same dump as Emma and Johann and Clara herself and all the others? *I hadn't been to Stillbach very often*. What a joke; she had grown up there, in one of those three-storey *INA-Case* on the outskirts of the village, where only Italian incomers and families on welfare lived. Nor was Stillbach as small as Ines described it. It even had a small industrial zone and its own fruit-growers' collective. In truth, Clara was irritated by several passages, but what annoyed her most was that Ines was no longer alive. That wasn't the way to die. You didn't just drop everything, leave things hanging like that and pass on a whole heap of unanswered questions. Clara reached for the cover sheet, screwed it up angrily in a ball and flung it across the room. No sooner had she done so, though, than she sprang out of bed, picked it up, unfolded it and tried to smooth it flat.

Her head was thumping. She looked for an aspirin, drank some water straight from the tap because she had forgotten to bring an extra bottle of mineral water up to her room, and lay back down again. For a moment it seemed to Clara as though she was in the Hotel Manente and that she would only have to go over to the window to look down into the garden. She was startled, when she got up again to fetch her laptop, by the sight of an Esso sign in the distance.

Clara had never heard of this *Anima*; searching the Internet, she discovered that the church was home to the German Pontifical College in Rome and a hospice for German pilgrims. The German and Austrian Conferences of Catholic Bishops were jointly responsible for running it. Clearly, the Santa Maria dell'Anima had long been an elite training establishment for those seeking a career in the higher echelons of the Church, a stepping-stone for those on the way to the very top. The Anima ran special courses in canon law and moral theology, but also provided pastoral care for all the German-speaking Catholics in Rome.

Did Emma keep going there even after her marriage to Remo? What did the German national church at that time think about mixed marriages? Did it, too, find Croats more racially acceptable than those *Herren Cazzolini*?

Clara couldn't ring Paul this early in the morning, so she dropped him an e-mail instead: *Just imagine, Ines even mentioned the suicide of my emotionally disturbed aunt and her lemon-yellow Fiat 126, a colour we always poked fun at. But my aunt didn't kill herself over an affair. She'd learnt quite by chance that she wasn't the daughter of a gentleman farmer from Stillbach, like she'd always thought, but of a* carabinieri. *Why didn't Ines write about that? That would have been more interesting than this tale of jealousy. She certainly hasn't pulled any punches where other people from Stillbach are concerned.*

Once she'd begun, Clara couldn't stop typing. Did Paul know about the Anima? If so, was it true that German domestics working in Rome used to meet there? And could you really get down into the Catacombs from the garden of the Hotel Manente? She also thought about asking Paul whether he remembered kissing Ines there for the first time – but decided it was too personal a question and deleted the sentence. She signed off rather abruptly – *See you tomorrow at eleven, but I'll be at Ines's flat well before then* – and jumped out of bed. I can't get back to sleep now, anyhow, she thought, I'll go over there straight away.

Paul sat perched on the edge of the bed, watching the young archaeologist grind her teeth. Julia's jaw made some quite alarming noises. Funny, he thought, her teeth didn't seem at all worn. Presumably, the girl had no idea what went on in her mouth. Or was it his presence exerting some terrible emotional pressure on her?

They hadn't slept together. Penetration was *so* last century, she said and laughed. She would only consent to coming back to his flat, she told him, if he promised to lay off all that bump-and-grind stuff.

'And don't go expecting any trout-sex from me, either.'

'*Trout-sex?*'

'You know, faked orgasms. Female trout have a habit of quivering and panting without actually laying any eggs. They make the males randy by pretending to be randy themselves.'

'No worries. Nobody's ever managed to put one over on me in that department,' Paul reassured her. How ridiculous – you could tell from the contractions in a woman's pelvis whether she was having an orgasm or not.

'Oh, I see I'm dealing with a sensitive man!'

So, all she had let him do was perform cunnilingus on her and bring himself off at the same time. Now he would really rather Julia left. He didn't fancy having to make small talk over breakfast. Besides, he never felt comfortable in his own skin in the morning, when he looked even more crumpled than the night before. He'd already played the attentive listener the previous evening.

Julia was studying in Innsbruck, but had grown up in Sterzing. Paul was astonished at her command of Ancient Greek and Latin, and how much she knew about Ancient Rome. The first thing she'd said on walking into Paul's flat after their bar-crawl was *Quasi homo tandem habitare coepi* – 'Now at last I can live like a human being'. She'd been so tipsy she'd clung on to the door frame, her body swaying from side to side, and crossed her legs: 'Otherwise I'll piss myself laughing.'

Still snorting with suppressed laughter, she told him it was a quotation from Nero, who had supposedly said it when his opulent 'Domus Aurea' palace was completed in Rome. Paul conceded that his apartment wasn't exactly a palace.

'But really, 900 Euros a month for this – forgive me – this hole?'

She seemed to be fast asleep. Paul stood up, went over to his desk and booted up his computer. He checked his e-mails: *AVA* – the *Agenzia Viaggi Alternativi* – was asking whether he also offered guided daytrips to Anzio and Monte Cassino. A tour group of German veterans wanted to go back there and see where they had fought.

Christ, that was all he needed, thought Paul – taking a load of ex-paratroopers on a pilgrimage to the Benedictine monastery at Monte Cassino. Even though he could have used the extra cash – to upgrade his 'hole' to a proper flat – he decided to decline the offer. Still, he would have been interested to learn how the old boys recalled the long months they had spent holding the Gustav Line, whether they still talked about their resoluteness and their morale, or claimed that they'd had the remains of St Benedict of Nursia and all the important artworks in the monastery – by Titian, Raphael and Leonardo da Vinci – transferred to Castel Sant'Angelo in Rome to save them from the Allied bombardment. He would also have loved to ask them if they remembered packing off some of the monastery's artworks to the salt mines at Altaussee and whether they still maintained they'd saved these treasures rather than plundered them.

The Red Poppies on Monte Cassino. Paul had no idea why this song had popped into his head. He couldn't even remember the context in which he had first heard it.

Julia groaned and rolled onto her side. The sound of grinding teeth had stopped. Paul looked at her half-open mouth.

As he was looking at Julia, he thought of the many long, tender mornings he'd spent with Marianne. They had often stayed in bed until midday. Marianne had loved it when he entered her while she was still sleeping and fucked her awake.

Sex without penetration – was that in vogue now, then? In the cold light of day, he couldn't understand why he'd brought Julia back to the flat. He must have found her attractive in some way. But the fact remained he was meeting Clara today. Ah yes, Clara: she had a family. Since the break-up of his relationship with Marianne, the only women Paul had been with were neurotic singles or married women looking for a bit on the side. Women whose husbands had gone off sex entirely, or who preferred those *veline* – the TV quiz show hostesses who wore hot pants and skimpy tops and smiled at the camera all the time, so beloved of Italy's Prime Minister that he crammed his television channels with them. And because these Italian Mr Averages never met an Elena Barolo or a Giorgia Palmas in the flesh, the country was now full of wannabe *veline* with botoxed lips and tightened eyelids, bimbos who would have given their eyeteeth to earn a living taking their clothes off if only they'd had the figures of those cuties on the TV. 'Even their names, for Christ's sake!' Marianne once fulminated: *Microfonine* – 'little microphone' – or *Letterine,* 'little letter'. By now, Paul had been living in Italy for so long that linguistic inanities like this failed to surprise him.

He almost missed seeing Clara's message. He groped around for his reading glasses, which he'd had for several months now but rarely used. What a long e-mail she'd written. He began to feel uneasy.

Clara had finished reading the manuscript. So, Ines really had compiled her *multi-volume work*, not just talked about it, like that friend of Marianne's who apparently still preferred daydreaming about being a novelist and basking in imaginary success rather than knuckling down to the business of writing. Vienna was full of such hypersensitive women novelists and poets.

It was entirely possible, Paul supposed, that German domestic staff had met in the Anima. Sunday Mass had once been an important component of social life, after all. He wondered if Ines had included the Austrian bishop Alois Hudal in her book.

Not long ago, on his way back from the Caffè della Pace, Paul happened to walk past the Santa Maria dell'Anima. He had stuck his nose into the church, and just inside the door found a leaflet telling him a bit about the 600-year history of the building. One interesting fact was that, during the French Revolution, the Anima had been sacked and horses stabled in the sacristy. But no mention whatever of the crimes of Bishop Alois Hudal. The Pontifical College was founded in 1859, and the hospice for pilgrims opened in 1954 – between those two dates, there was a yawning gap.

The morning light came and went in the room, making Julia's hair look as though someone was switching it on and off; just a moment ago, it had been dazzlingly bright. It was probably best he woke Julia now, then he could meet up with Clara a bit sooner than arranged and cast an eye over Ines's manuscript himself.

An archaeologist; Paul shook his head disapprovingly. Her future career would be spent poring over soil samples, animal bones and stomach contents, from which she would piece together the way people once lived. Far better to be on the track of war criminals and those who had helped them evade justice – that Hudal for instance, who as rector of the seminary had provided Nazis with false papers from South Tyrol. In the twinkling of an eye, they were transformed into simple German-speaking Italians, above all suspicion. Shame, then, that some of them had been stupid enough to start bawling German marching songs as they were embarking for South America, so that even the easygoing *carabinieri*, who had been prepared to turn two blind eyes to what was going on, must have felt they were being taken for a ride and began to take a closer look at their papers. That was how the supposed South Tyrolean Helmut Gregor – the pseudonym adopted by Dr Josef Mengele – came to be detained briefly in Genoa.

Alongside the historical leaflet in the vestibule was the parish newsletter; Paul hadn't bothered taking a copy, since all it contained were the times of services and some contact details, but now he recalled that there had also been mention of a craft circle that met in the parish hall. Suddenly it seemed only too plausible to him that the German-speaking domestic servants should have met up in the Anima; he pictured Franz Stangl, whom Hudal had briefly found a job for in the library of the Collegium Germanicum in 1948, joking with the girls and women as they sat knitting and sewing in the hall. Women who among their circle of family or friends may well have known someone handicapped who had never returned from the Hartheim Castle euthanasia institute, because Stangl had organised their 'mercy killing', as Nazi ideology dictated.

When Stangl turned up at the Anima, Paul imagined, he would have been a handsome forty-year-old with slightly greying temples and a distinguished-looking receding hairline. He had spent his time diligently cataloguing books before leaving for Brazil, via Syria, on a Red Cross passport. 'My conscience is clear,' he allegedly said on his deathbed, though he did admit that, as a concentration camp commandant, he had witnessed the murder of four hundred thousand people at Sobibór and Treblinka. Stangl could never have made it across the Brenner Pass to Sterzing so easily without the help of old SS comrades from South Tyrol. And if it hadn't been for Simon Wiesenthal's efforts, in all likelihood he wouldn't have been tracked down as quickly as he was.

It had just turned eight. No point answering Clara's questions now. No doubt she'd already be at Ines's flat and would have turned off the Internet access on her iPhone to avoid incurring the steep roaming charges.

Paul got up and made coffee. He'd forgotten Julia's surname. He hoped it wasn't something like Stötter or even Schwammberger, but when all was said and done he really couldn't have cared less.

He thought about Ines's flat and how much work Clara anticipated to make it tidy. The desk was covered in slips of paper; Ines had left notes all over the place, on paper napkins, train tickets and envelopes, even on the margins of her city map of Rome. He knew this *modus operandi* only too well. He had once had to rummage through every last scrap of paper he'd put out for recycling in search of a flyer he had roughed out the plan of an essay on.

Paul could readily understand why Ines had chosen to fabricate this tale of jealousy rather than go into the real interethnic conflict in Clara's aunt's family. To retain credibility in a novel, you had to steer clear of the insanities of real life.

*

Clara was still shaking; she had arrived at Ines's apartment and put the key in the door, only to find that it wasn't locked. The previous night, she had taken care to double lock it, even trying the door handle afterwards to make absolutely sure.

Her first thought was to wait for Paul and kill time by strolling round the neighbourhood, but because it was still so early she decided to confront her fear and step inside. Perhaps she had been wrong about last night and, flustered by Paul's presence, had mistakenly turned the key one way and then the other, leaving it unlocked.

'Please, no cause for alarm,' said the man who loomed up in the hallway as she pushed open the door, 'I really should have asked your permission, but as I happened to be in the neighbourhood anyway, I thought I'd drop by the flat to say goodbye to the place, to Ines…'

'But you… you've –' She was about to say 'broken in', but the man pre-empted her by extending his hand in greeting: 'I'm Francesco Manente. We spoke on the phone.'

'How come you have a key?'

He explained that he and Ines had been an item for several months.

Clara walked through the flat, quickly checking to see that everything was still where it should be. So, the initial 'F' in Ines's organiser had stood for Francesco, as she'd thought. Her Wednesday lover.

They sat facing one another, Clara with her arms folded over her chest to conceal her shaking hands. Here he was then, in the flesh – the communist who had abandoned his mother in the summer of 1978 and whom Ines hadn't even given a walk-on part in her novel. But even though he must have been past sixty, Clara took an instant shine to him. An atypical Italian, she thought: broad shoulders, tall, and he hadn't run to fat in middle age, either. Plus he still had a full head of hair.

'I thought as much,' Clara replied, 'Ines noted down all the times she met you in her organiser, except for the last few months –'

'We stopped seeing one another,' Francesco interjected. He looked down at his fingernails, like he was about to file them.

'Why, if you don't mind my asking?'

'Actually, I do mind.'

'Did she want more from you?'

'Oh, right – you're asking anyway,' he smiled. 'No,' he continued, 'she wasn't the possessive type.' Clara noticed that Francesco kept on glancing over at the writing desk. Had he come here looking for something?

They talked about Ines's sudden death, and Francesco told Clara how devastated he had been at the news, so distraught that he'd shut himself in the bathroom and wept.

'Why the bathroom?'

'I'm married, with two sons. Now you'll think badly –'

'I'm not here to judge you.'

'I lied to you on the phone,' he said presently, 'I knew Ines from way back, more than thirty years ago. She once worked in my mother's hotel.'

'In 1978.'

'That's right. You know all about that, then?'

'I just know she was in Rome at the time.'

'We met one another very briefly that summer. Then we lost touch for decades until we ran into each other again at the care home.'

So the novel version was a fabrication, thought Clara, but then why should it mirror the truth anyhow? The only strange thing was that Ines should have taken the names from real life. That wasn't like her. Maybe she just hadn't had time to change them. If Clara got the novel published, she would have to disguise the family names at least. On reflection, she'd better alter the place names as well.

'I'll just get myself a glass of water, if that's okay with you.'

While Francesco went off to the kitchen, Clara stretched her legs. For instance, she could change the name *Scabello* to *Scattolin*, 'little box'. And what would be a good speaking name to replace *Manente*? *Robustelli*, 'burly', maybe?

At school, Ines and Clara had had a German teacher one year called Norbert Hahn, who they hated because of his penchant for nationalistic, folksy German doggerel. Translating his surname into Italian – *gallo* – they had been delighted to discover a place called Strangolagalli, which people popularly thought meant 'wring the cockerel's neck'. For years after, they mentally banished everyone they didn't approve of to this small town, which they knew nothing about except that it was in the Ciociaria district just south of Rome. They had been watching Vittorio De Sica's film of Alberto Moravia's novel *La Ciociaria*, and had looked in an atlas to see exactly where the hilly region of Ciociaria was, and that was when they came across the town whose name probably had nothing whatsoever to do with strangling chickens.

Clara had been forced to sit through De Sica's film three times because Ines had a crush on Sophia Loren. If Clara remembered rightly, Loren was originally meant to play the part of Rosetta, but because Anna Magnani refused to play Loren's mother Cesira, Loren herself had taken on the role of the young widow, and Magnani had dropped out of the film entirely.

There was a faint roaring sound. Clara wondered whether it was the traffic, or maybe the air conditioning or an extractor fan. Francesco came back in and handed her a glass of water.

'Do you hear that?'

'What?'

'That noise like a babbling brook.'

'Oh, it's the computer.'

'You switched on Ines's laptop?'

'Don't worry, I didn't manage to guess the password.'

'Huh, that's rich! How dare you? You're way out of line, you know.' Clara could feel her face glowing with anger. 'I really ought to throw you out, right now.'

'Oh, come on! I've got a key to the flat. Do you really think Ines would have given me it if she didn't trust me? I've let myself in here any number of times to wait for her.'

Clara had always shut her eyes to the reality of people leading double lives like that. Could that be why Ines had never told her about Francesco?

Francesco sat down. 'I don't want to jeopardise my marriage.'

In his shoes, thought Clara, would I even still bother to say that about Claus?

'How could I know whether or not you'd sent all my letters to Ines to my home address – or post back the books I'd given her?' Francesco went on, shifting uneasily on his chair. 'My wife already suspects...'

There was definitely something not quite right about the guy. 'So, why didn't you see Ines in the final few weeks? Did you argue?' she asked.

He crossed his legs, looked at his left knee and massaged it briefly. 'You really are persistent, aren't you? Look, Ines had the wrong idea about my mother. I wasn't prepared to stand for that. But don't go thinking I'm some kind of mummy's boy just because I talk about her a lot.' He took a sip of water and put his glass down on the floor. 'Mum's a simple woman – she even learnt dancing by practising with a chair. And she enjoyed meeting up with other women who spoke German, but that didn't make her a Nazi.'

'Is that what Ines said?'

'Ultimately she accused my mother of going to the Anima and meeting the worst kind of Nazi there. The Anima –'

'I know what it is.'

'Then I don't need to spell it out. You could get coffee and cake there for fifty *Centesimi*. Wouldn't you have gone there if you'd been her? Mum was really homesick when she first came here. It's only natural she should want to seek out other people from home. Honestly, do you think my mother would have stayed in Rome if she'd been a loyal follower of the Führer?'

'Well, for a while you could be more German in Rome than in South Tyrol; the Italian fascists really came down hard on the populace up there.'

'In the Twenties, maybe, but my Mum wasn't here at that time. Do you come from the same region, then?'

Clara nodded.

'What, from Stillbach?'

'Yes. But I've been living in Vienna for some years now.'

'Mum once told me about a friend of hers who was shut up, night and day, in her employers' villa. She ended up hanging herself. Maybe that wouldn't have happened if they had only allowed her to go to the Anima on Sundays.' Francesco stood up and went over to the window. 'My father never felt at ease going there with her. He was a jealous man – and the place was full of handsome Swiss Guards, and any number of male students. But at least he understood that she needed to go there. It was only Ines…' He turned around to look at Clara. 'I must be getting back to the hotel now. Do me a favour and delete all the e-mails between me and Ines, will you?'

'I can't promise that, but you have my word that nothing will ever appear on your wife's computer.'

'I'd prefer it if you binned them. Have you –' He checked himself for a moment. 'Have you read Ines's writings?'

'Some of them, yes.'

'Please don't believe everything she says. That's not my mother.' He walked over to the door. 'You know, you really shouldn't get involved with people who write. Everything gets recorded. That's not healthy. Every prejudice. I don't know what Ines had against my mother. She was a wonderful person. She never told my grandparents that she'd had to learn German in secret as a kid up in South Tyrol, in an underground school. And, believe me, my grandmother could be quite unpleasant to her. She had always imagined my father would make a far better match, not marry some lowly chambermaid. But my mother was a canny woman, and she never kicked against the goad.' He looked down into the street, then back at Clara. 'She never let on to anyone in our family how truly dreadfully the Italians behaved up in Stillbach.'

Why was he going on about his mother again? Clara also got to her feet, and accompanied him to the front door.

'I'm sorry I let myself in without telling you first. I loved Ines. We had a great time together until that – no, I wouldn't say it was a row, more a difference of opinion. She's – She was so stubborn, so opinionated. Ines claimed we had cats in the garden. I can tell you, there were never any cats in the hotel garden. My mother wouldn't allow it. If one even strayed into the grounds, she was after it with the hose. Why am I telling you all this, though? It's really not important. You know –' Francesco's hand was already on the door handle, 'it's terrible that Ines and I never got the chance to talk things over.'

'The key,' Clara cut him short, 'I want you to give me your door key.'

Francesco patted his trouser pockets and pulled out the key. 'There you go. Will I see you again before you leave?'

Clara didn't respond. He was already out in the stairwell, and Clara made to shut the door when Francesco suddenly turned back and wedged his foot in the gap. 'Look, please don't be angry with me,' he pleaded, 'I know I should have asked you first.'

'All right,' was all Clara said in reply.

He had only gone over to the bed to wake Julia, but as he approached, she pulled him down, slipped under the sheet and took his cock in her mouth. The more she sucked and licked at it, the more he thought of her ban on penetration and their conversation the previous night about trout-sex. He closed his eyes and tried to immerse himself in his fantasies, but it was no good. 'I'm sorry,' he said, pulling away, 'let's just leave it.'

Julia untangled herself from the sheet, looked at him silently and sat on the edge of the bed. 'Is it different – I mean, what's it like when you're older? Do you do it less often?'

That was all he needed now, for her to start talking about sex. He stood up and pulled on his boxer shorts. 'Yeah, most of all, you lose the urge to analyse it,' he said, picking up the packet of coffee on the table and snipping the corner off.

Julia disappeared into the bathroom; a moment later, he heard the shower start running. All he had in the cupboard was evaporated milk and breadsticks. No problem, Paul thought, I'll invite her to breakfast in the bar, then I'll be shot of her all the sooner.

For God's sake, what had he been thinking? He calculated that short of some unforeseen mishap, he would die a quarter of a century before Julia, and was suddenly shocked at their difference in age. When he and Marianne had been together, he'd always mocked ill-assorted couples – those wheezing old guys in discos, or the white-haired skaters on the Danube Island, puffing to keep up with their 20-year-old girlfriends – and now here he was in the same predicament. 'What's it like when you're older?' Ouch! he thought, as he slipped on a pair of light chinos.

He looked out of the window; a fine day in prospect. He smiled: no, he wasn't ready for the knacker's yard quite yet. He thought of Marianne, who had once compared the half-moon over the Aegean to an orange segment and had accused Paul of having lost his sense of fun, of just being happy for its own sake.

Paul replied drily that happiness was being able to forget; but unfortunately his line of work made that impossible.

What was Clara's Hemingway quotation again? *'Happiness is good health and a bad memory'*. Set against the background of some of his letters, Hemingway's definition took on a rather hollow ring. *'We have a very jolly and gay life, full of deads...'* he wrote when he was with US troops after the Normandy Landings. Paul stood in front of his bookshelves and pulled out an old copy of *Focus* magazine; he had marked the place he was looking for and found the passage straight away.

Emerging from the bathroom, Julia came and stood by his side; her hair was dripping wet. 'What are you reading? I want to hear,' she said.

'One time I killed a very snotty SS kraut who, when I told him I would kill him unless he revealed what his escape route signs were, said: You will not kill me, the kraut stated. Because you are afraid to and because you are a race of mongrel degenerates. Besides, it is against the Geneva Convention. What a mistake you made, brother, I told him and shot him three times in the belly fast and then, when he went down on his knees, shot him on the topside so his brains came out of his mouth or I guess it was his nose.'

'That's disgusting.' Julia slipped off the towel that had been covering her breasts and pubic hair and used it dry her hair.

'Guess who wrote that.'

'Some sicko, I suppose.'

'Hemingway.'

'He must have made it up.'

'Not a bit of it – it's from a letter he wrote to his publisher, Charles Scribner, in August 1949. Five years after he was in Normandy. Do you want a coffee?'

She nodded. 'Was he prosecuted, then? I mean, it's clearly a war crime, what he did.'

'A commission held an inquiry but acquitted him. But even in a more recent report, there's talk of Hemingway making up a lot of what he recorded. They've got it easy, writers. They can write the truth and pass it off as fiction. There's also another letter he wrote after the event where he claims to have killed 122 Germans.'

'That's laying it on a bit thick.' She ruffled her hair and tugged it into place with her fingers.

Paul could smell his deodorant on her. 'I haven't got any sugar, I'm afraid, just evaporated milk.'

'That's fine by me.'

'So, what are you up to today?'

'The Circus Maximus. Ancient Romans loved going there because the seating wasn't segregated by sex, like in the theatres.' She slipped on her bra. 'Plus the area was full of brothels.'

'Where even the Empress used to ply –'

'Messalina, that's right. Every man's fantasy. When she was working in the brothel, she used the name Lycisca and hid her dark hair under a blonde wig. The brazen hussy, who got her kicks by "soaking up all the battering" of clients' cocks – at least, that's what Juvenal claimed.'

'Funny how times change, isn't it? Now it's the state screwing us. Honestly, though, for someone so young, you know some pretty filthy stuff.'

'"Generation Porno", don't you know?' Julia replied, lifting her arm and sniffing her armpit to check that her T-shirt was still fresh enough. She laughed: 'You don't really think that, do you?'

'Well –'

'Look, it's all so much nonsense. The first time I slept with a man, I was seventeen. My best friend even waited 'til she was nineteen. There have always been some girls who mature early. My mum was at school with a girl who got pregnant at fourteen.'

'That couldn't happen to you, at least,' said Paul tartly.

'Hey! Who rattled your cage?'

Paul shrugged his shoulders and turned off the gas under the coffee. 'Just takes some getting used to, that's all.' He poured two cups of espresso. 'You can't blame Messalina for playing away, though. Claudius was thirty-five years older than her. Apparently, he was a frail old man with a limp even when they got married. He had a facial tic and stuttered. So he didn't even have the saving grace of the gift of the gab.'

'Yeah, he drew the short straw, all right. I knew he was quite a bit older, but I'd forgotten all the gory details.' She smiled at Paul. 'And how about you – what are you doing with your day?'

'I'm helping a lady friend of mine clear out a flat. Then, in the afternoon, I'm giving a lecture to some private-school pupils. The state schools won't stump up for that kind of thing.'

'On the "Wolf Girl"?'

'"Wolf Girl"?'

'*Lay*cisca. It was her nickname.'

'Heaven forbid! No, it's about another kind of wolf, actually, one with two 'f's – Karl Wolff: he was the most senior SS general in Italy.'

'So what will you tell them?'

'Oh, the usual stuff. I'll give them a general rundown of German war crimes in Italy. They will lap that up. The kids see it as some kind of action film in words, and the older teachers nod their heads in agreement. After the lecture, they often come up to me and tell me that Italian Fascism wasn't half as bad as Nazism.'

'Well, that's true, isn't it? There's a case for saying modern Italy couldn't even have come into existence without Fascism, isn't there?'

'Huh – some modernity! As a woman, you would have had to stay at home ironing black shirts and reading *La brava domestica*.' Unable to find his lighter, Paul lit a cigarette from the stove. 'And the Pontine Marshes would've been drained sometime, even without Mussolini. The whole of Western Europe experienced an upswing after the Great Depression, that wasn't just down to the fascists. Anyhow, are you going back to your hotel now or straight to the Circus Maximus? Do you know the way from here?'

As Paul looked up the bus connections for Julia, she sat on the sofa, sipping her coffee and staring at him.

'What's up,' he said, noticing her, 'did I snore in the night?'

'Not that I heard – by the way, your talk yesterday was really good. I liked the way you torpedoed our tour organiser's enthusiasm for Italian football.'

'I really didn't mean to. After all, Italy's the only European country to have won the World Cup four times, and they still play a beautiful game.'

'That's not how you made it sound.'

Paul jotted down the buses for Julia on a slip of paper and handed it to her. 'It's just that I can't stand these blowhards who get all aerated about the Prime Minister but are still really gung-ho about all things Italian. They should be routinely forced to take a long, hard look at everyday life in this country, and ask themselves why it's failed to come to terms with its past.'

'Sounds like the title of a dissertation,' said Julia, putting her cup down.

'Oh, you know what I mean.'

'It's nothing new, what you're proposing; Bachmann tried it already.'

'The thing is, in Germany any kind of fascistic posturing is still being exposed for what it is, and condemned; all Nazi insignia are banned there. But in Italy, it's become an accepted part of public life, not to say a new marketing opportunity, even.'

'Now you're exaggerating.'

'You think so? Just go and visit Mussolini's birthplace at Predappio – there's a museum there exhibiting the trousers and boots he was wearing when he was strung up. Or go on a bit further to the Morosini Villa at Carpena – the whole place is one big shrine full of Duce memorabilia. Or drive out to Rieti province; if you look out of the car on the road out of Antrodoco you'll see a hillside where the trees have been planted to spell out the word DUX: it's visible for miles around. Then imagine someone planting firs in a German forest in the shape of a swastika, or having a restaurant chef appear in the dining room wearing an apron emblazoned with Hitler's face.'

'There would be a public outcry.'

'Dead right – it's different here, though. Most Italians see Mussolini as some kind of swashbuckler who loved children and seduced women. And when he wanted rid of his lovers, there's nothing he wouldn't stoop to. For instance, he never acknowledged his first wife Ida Dalser in public, even though she was the mother of his son. When she started to cause trouble, he had her locked up in

psychiatric hospitals, first in Pergine Valsugana and then on the island of San Cle-
mente in the Venice lagoon. But when she and Mussolini were together, she'd
sold her thriving beauty salon in Milan to support him financially when he fell
on hard times after being ousted as the editor of the Socialist Party newspaper
Avanti. Their son also died in an asylum in the early 1940s, a few years after his
mother. He wasted away from malnutrition, so they said.'

'I'm impressed.' Julia put her espresso cup in the sink.

'What, when I can't even recall what the son was called? – I'm also struggling to remember the name of the newspaper Mussolini founded with Dalser's
money before he joined up in 1915. All gone, like it's been wiped clean from
my memory.' Paul tugged at his earlobes, unscrewed the espresso machine and
rinsed it under the tap. He thought first of Ines, and then of Clara and what she'd
said on the phone: 'You feature in it, you know.'

Maybe Ines's manuscript would help jog his memory and remind him at long
last what they had done together.

After Francesco had gone, Clara sat down at Ines's desk and stared at her books,
without touching them. She imagined them speaking to her, telling her when
Ines had last opened them, which passage she had re-read and what she had
been thinking about at the time. But all she could see were the blank Post-it
notes stuck between the pages. *Like Swallows Leaving the Nest: South Tyrolean
Domestic Servants in Italian Cities: 1920–1960* ran the title of one volume. The
dust jacket showed ten women assembled for a group photo – young women
with friendly faces, happy even. They must have been in their twenties, or
at most their early thirties, when the picture was taken; a few of them were
wearing modish cloche hats.

Clara wondered whether Emma Manente might be one of them.

She leant back, and cast her eye over all the books, magazines, pens and
postcards lying on the desk. Despite her friendship with Ines, Clara felt like an
interloper in this room, because she was seeing most of the objects in it, keep-
sakes that Ines must surely have regarded as significant mementoes of her life,
for the first time.

After sitting there motionless for a while just scanning the room, she finally picked up the book on domestic servants and began leafing through it. A section of photos showed images of Christmas at a monastery in the Via Panizza in Milan, the Segafredo family from Bologna and their domestic staff and celebrations for Shrove Tuesday and St Nicholas' Day at the Anima in Rome. None of the men or women in the photos were identified. In one, Clara fleetingly thought she recognised her grandmother's sister, but the more she looked at the dark-haired woman in fancy dress, behind whose back St Nicholas could be seen pulling a present out of his sack, the less it seemed likely it was her great-aunt. After all, it was well known in the family that she'd never left Stillbach. The picture also showed the flag of the South Tyrolean Homeland Association hanging above a radiator, the heraldic eagle partially obscured by St Nicholas's mitre. On closer inspection, it almost looked like the bird and the shining cross on the mitre were getting married.

Clara put the book down and closed her eyes. Just because Ines was dead didn't give her the right to go poking about. She felt like someone about to violate a taboo. On the other hand, there was no getting round the fact that death certificates permitted you to invade other people's private spaces.

She pulled out her mobile to call Claus. He was already at the hospital.

'You don't have to ring every day, you know,' said Claus, 'Gesine's well – we're two grown-ups and we're getting on just fine.'

'Do you think I'm pestering you, then?'

'Look, I really can't talk now, darling.'

After Claus had rung off, Clara heard the whooshing of Ines's laptop again. It made her think of the foaming spray of a waterfall, the dark, deeply eroded stone where the torrent came crashing down, where the billion droplets reassembled and came momentarily to rest before flowing ever onwards.

She turned to the computer. For her wallpaper, Ines had chosen a picture of Stillbach Mere, with the trees around its shore reflected in its glassy surface. Only at a second glance did Clara notice a head in the water, but she couldn't make out who the swimmer was. She suddenly recalled that North Germans called a small pond a *Laken*, while a large lake was a *Meer*, and that a colleague of Claus's, a young intern who had grown up in the Lüneburg Heath area, always called Lake Neusiedl the *Neusiedler Meer*. He also called a bucket an *Eimer* rather than a *Kübel*, a cushion a *Kissen* rather than a *Polster*, and a stairwell a *Treppenhaus*, not a *Stiegenhaus*.

It struck Clara that Ines had mainly used Austrian words and formulations in her manuscript, but that whenever she visited Vienna she had always insisted on ordering hot chocolate with cream as *Kakao mit Sahne* rather than using the Viennese phrase *heiße Schockolade mit Schlagobers*. 'I'm not going to suck up to the Austrians,' she once wrote to Clara, after a critic accused her of pandering to the West German market by using the word *Sahne* in one of her early radio plays. Anyway, it wasn't easy pigeonholing the German they used in Stillbach, Ines said in the same letter: there, *Karotten* grew alongside the *Erdäpfelacker*, but equally, *Gelbe Rüben* could grow alongside the *Kartoffelfeld* – while crisps were always referred to by the Italian *patatine*. Yes, the Stillbach dialect fell firmly between two stools, a place where it felt safe and comfortable. The Austrian monarchy, Italian Fascism with its proscription of the German language, and finally schoolbooks and tourists from Germany had all left their mark on it.

With a lump in her throat, Clara stood up and started pacing up and down the room. Pausing for a moment to look out of the window, she noticed the morning was already well advanced.

Grief makes everything dull, she reflected. Although the sun was shining, nothing seemed to have any sparkle about it. Then again, perhaps it was only her tears that were spoiling the view.

I'm determined not to be the person Ines saw in me any longer, thought Clara.

'If anything should happen to me, I'm making you responsible for looking after Gesine,' she'd told Ines when she came to Vienna for Gesine's christening.

'Nothing's going to happen to you,' replied Ines, as she cradled the baby in her arms.

The longer Clara paced, the louder the computer seemed to her, though it could just have been her headache, which amplified the slightest sound. So she sat down and tried pressing keys at random. She thought of Ines's hands opening and closing the laptop only a few days ago. One of the letters on the keypad had become illegible, no doubt through repeated heavy use; it was just like Ines to have left the little black plastic square like that and not written over it or replaced it.

Ines had entered her own first name as her user name, but what on earth could her password be? Why hadn't Clara thought to ask the aunt in Stillbach for the dates of birth of all of Ines's closest relatives?

She typed it Gesine's birthday – anything was worth a try – and realised with a start that she'd gained access.

You were always being warned not to use the names of relatives, friends, lovers or pets, or your nearest and dearests' birthdays or addresses as your password – but Ines had ignored all this advice and plumped for her godchild's birthday. She clearly hadn't set much store by data security.

For years on end, Clara recalled, Ines had come to Vienna and only spent time with Gesine. Her friend hadn't visited any exhibitions or gone to concerts, but instead had taken the little girl to the Museum of Childhood or the funfair on the Prater. Only when Gesine reached eleven or twelve did Ines resume her old habits and start going to the cinema or the theatre again in the evening, and spending the day visiting libraries and museums. Her favourite haunt was the *Kunsthistorisches Museum*, which housed Lorenzo Lotto's painting *Portrait of a Young Man with a Lamp*, which she particularly loved because of its striking resemblance to a photo of her aunt in her youth. There was another picture in the same gallery, by the Spanish painter Antonio de Pereda, which Ines was also fascinated by. Clara couldn't call its title to mind; all she remembered was an angel standing behind a table, pointing with his right index finger at a globe and the inscription NIL OMNE next to an hourglass: 'Everything is nothing'.

Clara opened several drawers in search of a paper tissue. She wondered if the day would ever come when she would stop getting upset at the memories of Ines. Or when the memories wouldn't even arise in the first place.

Clara opened Ines's files and began avidly reading her notes:

— Emma Manente saw an S-shaped sofa for the first time and couldn't understand the point of it until someone explained to her that it was a love-seat, which allowed the woman to sit on one side and the man on the other and for them to talk to one another without having to turn their heads all the time.

— Old Mr Manente never deducted the cost of plates and glasses that Emma broke from her wages.

— Emma once had a ravenous appetite and ate everything that was left in a pot. She only realised after she'd finished that the food wasn't cooked.

— At home in Stillbach, the bed linen was only changed every six weeks, but in Rome it was every two to three weeks.

— The first time Emma saw sandals with cork soles was when Cocola got herself a pair. At first, she didn't dare take off her thick stockings and slip her bare feet into the shoes.

— A woman in the Anima once claimed she had lost her job with the Levi family in 1938 because they'd fled to Switzerland.

— Another domestic servant simply vanished overnight. Weeks later, Emma heard in the Anima that the woman had written a letter home criticising the fascists. The censor intercepted her mail and she was forced to get out of Italy within three days.

Had Ines found these snippets a bit weak, or was it simply that she hadn't had time to work them into the novel? Some of the anecdotes were familiar to Clara.

She skimmed through another set of notes and read that the German nationals who had had to flee from the Allied advance had barricaded the windows of their cars with mattresses for fear of partisan attacks. She also learnt that Emma could get by on very little sleep, a trait she shared with the Duce. *The nights were black, as black as the fascists' shirts and trousers, and the windows were blacked out due to the air-raid precautions*, ran one passage. Below it was a note: *Francesco owes his existence to Johann's death.*

Paul drank another half-cup of coffee with Julia in the bar on the Viale Trastevere before she got on her tram.

'So, that's that, then?'

'If that's the way you want it.'

She laughed. In the corner of her mouth, there was still a residue of icing sugar from the *cornetto* she'd eaten for breakfast.

'That's what I like about you older men – there's rarely a dull moment with you.' Saying this, she planted a kiss on his cheek. 'Shame we don't live in the same town. I'd have loved to hear more about your patriotic Jews.'

Earlier, he'd forgotten to mention Umberto Terracini, who alongside Gramsci, Togliatti and Tasca was one of the founder members of the Communist Party. Now, after Julia had already departed, it suddenly occurred to him that Count Cavour had also had a Jewish private secretary, and that even the Dante Alighieri Society had been founded by a Jewess. Jews everywhere.

It really bothered Paul that he had such trouble retrieving facts. Nowadays, more often than not, key details only came to him long after he needed them. On the other hand, certain humdrum things triggered mental loops: for instance, whenever Paul read the word *Lavazza*, he couldn't help thinking of the Turin private banker named *Ovazza*, a Jew who had thrown in his lot with the fascists and carried out an arson attack on the offices of the magazine *Israel* in Florence, just to prove his political credentials. Plenty of Jews had taken part in Mussolini's March on Rome – but that hadn't been enough to save them all.

Lavazza – Ovazza. How could he put an end to these involuntary associations, and stop himself endlessly revisiting the same recollections? He found it irritating the way certain thoughts and memories of particular things or even words lodged in his brain, so he could no longer disengage them from one another. Perhaps it was a ploy of an aging memory – hanging past events on pegs from everyday life in order to stop you forgetting them so quickly.

Ettore Ovazza and his wife, son and daughter had taken refuge in Switzerland. The son was sent on ahead with a sizable portion of the family assets, which he was to deposit safely in a Swiss account, but the Germans seized him at the Swiss border, interrogated him and finally put him to death. All out of pure greed. A few days later, the rest of the family, whose hideaway – in a school cellar in Intra in the Valle d'Aosta – the son had divulged under torture, were all executed. Their bodies were cremated in the furnace of the school's boiler-room.

Paul had even tried switching to another brand of coffee to dispel these auto-matic associations with the fate of the Ovazzas, but it was no good. Drinking *Illy* or *Kimbo* of a morning instead of *Lavazza oro* only served to remind him of what he was so eager to forget.

When the Ovazzas fled in October 1943, the Leibstandarte–SS Adolf Hitler, under the command of Gottfried Meir, an SS Obersturmbannführer from Carin-thia, was stationed in the region around Lake Maggiore. Meir, on whose direct orders the family was shot, was acquitted by a court in Graz in the 1950s due to lack of evidence. Soon after, though, he was sentenced to life imprisonment by a military tribunal in Turin, but Austria refused to extradite Meir, who by that time was a headmaster.

After taking his leave of Julia, Paul went back to the flat, did the washing-up and tidied away the worst of the mess. After a long search, he found the number of Signor Casagrande, who had helped him when he last moved house. Then he got a taxi downtown, but got out after a few hundred metres because the traffic was gridlocked.

He debated whether he should bring Clara some flowers or something sweet by way of condolence. Or maybe even a book.

Lifting his hand up to scratch his nose, Paul caught the scent of Julia on his fingers. It had felt good lying next to a warm body last night. He had woken around four, gone to the window and smoked a cigarette. He had always been incapable of just lying there wide awake, staring into the darkness, feeling the time tick by, not knowing how late it was, how long he'd already been awake or whether he'd drop off again. Normally, he would switch on the radio or read, but out of consideration for Julia, this time he got up straight away to avoid dis-turbing her with his tossing and turning.

As they were drinking their coffee, he had asked her whether she'd been dreaming; not that she could remember, she replied.

Him neither, he answered, though it was a lie. He didn't feel like telling her about his ex-wife. In his dream, he'd gazed into Marianne's pale, anaemic face and had been amazed that she'd kept staring straight ahead even when he started pulling faces at her. In the end, he had been roused from sleep by his own violent facial contortions; on waking, he pressed his aching cheeks and forehead in alarm.

The bus, he suddenly realised, was already close to where Ines's flat was; just three more stops.

He got off and bought a box of pralines in a confectioner's; Marianne had always been mad about them. He originally thought about getting Clara some *Baci* but decided that the picture of entwined lovers on the blue box might seem a bit presumptuous. Not only that – each individual chocolate came wrapped in a love note. Besides, he wouldn't be able to resist telling Clara that *Baci* were invented in 1922, the same year as Mussolini's March on Rome, and then he could see himself going on about Hitler's plans to organise a similar march on Berlin, which came to nothing after the failure of the Munich Beer Hall Putsch in the autumn of 1923.

The kind of theatrical and violent actions that Mussolini staged just didn't chime in with the German legalistic mindset, thought Paul.

So, if the conversation turned to *Baci*, maybe he'd better stop himself veering off on this historical tangent and stick to telling her about the self-mythologising of the firm that made them. For instance, the story of Luisa Spagnoli, their supposed inventor. She was a successful businesswoman who started a chain of fashion shops, still widespread throughout Italy. One day, Spagnoli hit on the idea of coating hazelnuts with chocolate and on the brilliant notion of wrapping them in little *billets-doux*. She had sent them to her string of young lovers. When the firm Perugina started manufacturing *Baci*, they retained the idea, printing literary quotations and popular sayings on the wrappers.

It took a long time for Paul to find the right bell. The entrance to the flats was open to the sun and rain, and many of the handwritten name tags had faded.

Clara was waiting in the doorway; she shook his hand, thanked him for keeping his promise to come, and for the *Gianduiotti*, and led him into the kitchen.

'Cup of coffee?'

He hesitated, and sat down: 'I'd prefer water, thanks.'

She launched straight into telling him about the manuscript and Emma

Manente, who had come to Rome in the 1930s dressed in clogs – every inch the uneducated country girl.

Paul thought Clara was looking tired; there were dark rings under her eyes and she cleared her throat repeatedly, or let her sentences trail off. Her cheeks grew redder as she talked, and he had to stop himself becoming mesmerised by her facial expressions and losing the thread of what she was saying.

He interrupted her only once, to explain the role of the Anima in the Second World War.

She nodded. 'Ah, now I understand,' she said, without explaining exactly what it was she'd understood.

All the while, he was waiting for Clara to tell him about the passages where he got a mention – but she kept on about the hotel, listing the staff, and describing the roof terrace where Paul – he was certain – had never been, in fact had never even known existed. She concluded with a rundown of the old lady's family circumstances, and her relations in Stillbach, of whom Clara knew just one, and then only slightly. 'She had an older brother,' she said, 'he's been dead for some years now. He got quite high-up in a separatist party that doesn't let any Italians join. Ines described him as one of those people who waved their passports out of the car window where the German- and Italian-speaking areas of the region met, even though there was no frontier there. 'He thought that abroad began at the Chiusa di Salorno Narrows.' She went on to explain that he wanted South Tyrol to secede from the rest of Italy.

'And what then? Annexation by Austria?'

'No, the idea was for it to become a state in its own right.'

'Where you'd need proof of Aryan ancestry, no doubt?'

'That would be difficult,' said Clara, 'there's been too much intermarrying with the *Cazzolini*.'

'Lieutenant-General Edmund Glaise von Horstenau,' muttered Paul.

'What's that?'

'He used to call the Italians *Herren Cazzolini* or just *Cazzi*.'

'Oh, yes – so he was a real person?'

'Absolutely. German attitudes changed from the spring of 1941. They drew a very clear distinction between the Germanized Italians in the north and the inferior Negroid race in the south. The blows of fate, so ran the narrative, had caused the Italians to become weak and supine but made the Germans tough, strong and resolute. The plan was to do away with these *esseri inferiori*, these 'lower beings', as quickly as possible.' Paul lifted his glass of water, but didn't drink. 'As early as '41, Hitler claimed the Latin race had gained an undeserved position of power but was now ripe for suppression. In his eyes, there was only one European power, and that was the German Reich.' He put the glass down again, and stared at Clara. 'How did you know about the *Cazzolini*, though?'

Clara laughed. 'For a moment, while you were talking there, I felt like I was a character in the manuscript. We're not sitting in the hotel garden, though, we're in Ines's flat. And –', she said, flicking her hair out of her eyes, 'I'm not Ines.'

'But I'm *Paul*? I mean – I'm still *Paul* in the novel, am I?'

They worked steadily for two hours. Paul looked through the piles of books in Ines's library and put aside signed copies or any containing notes in a corner of the room; these were part of the estate and would be taken back to Stillbach, at least for now, until a buyer could be found for Ines's papers. While he was busy with that, Clara went through most of the drawers and boxes. Now she was sitting at the laptop, with Outlook open, and skimming through Ines's e-mails from the past few weeks and months. They were mostly work-related messages, translation queries, confirmations of appointments, and requests for royalty payments – hardly anything personal. Ines had sent off sections of the manuscript to a publisher in Frankfurt, but – as far as Clara could see – hadn't had a reply yet.

Then Clara spotted an e-mail that she had written to Ines, complaining about her marriage and talking about possibly making a fresh start. Here in Rome, sitting at Ines's computer, her own words seemed utterly alien to her, but at the same time, she was shocked at their frankness. When I write, she thought, I'm insightful and clever, but in real life I fight shy of my own skill with words. She looked over at Paul and suddenly felt a great sense of intimacy. Sitting there, buried in a book, he didn't notice her. He briefly stroked his brow and then carried on reading.

'Can I get you another glass of water?'

Paul looked up. 'I didn't know the Argentinian President spent several months in Merano.'

'Isn't it that woman called Kirchner in charge nowadays?'

'Yes. I'm talking about Perón, though.' He flicked on through the book, but kept his finger marking the page. 'Water – sorry, is that what you said? – No, actually, I'd really like that coffee now.'

'Was Perón there on holiday, then?'

'No, it says here that he was on a training course for the Argentine military organised by the Italian Army in late 1939.'

Paul followed Clara into the tiny kitchen and watched as she pressed the coffee down into the espresso filter with a teaspoon. 'Perón was a great admirer of Mussolini,' he continued, 'and I understand he'd already made some important contacts within the Italian armed forces. It wasn't only Nazis who fled to Argentina after the war, but several high-ranking Italian fascists, too, including Mussolini's son Vittorio.'

'I wonder why Ines was gathering all this information,' said Clara.

'Well, she was planning something with it all, that much is clear – look at this,' Paul passed her the book. The flyleaf was covered with a list of handwritten headwords with page references: *Ethnic Germans, p.19; Swiss bank accounts p.56; Barbie, p.102; Priebke, p.156; rebaptism, p.166; Anima, p.117; Red Cross, p.118; monasteries in the South Tyrol, p.161; Lana, p.162,* and so on.

Lana? The name rang a bell with Clara. Hadn't that novelist Sabine Gruber, who now lived in Vienna, grown up there? Clara had recently got hold of one of her books, because Venice played a central part in it. But Gruber hadn't recounted any actual Venetian love affairs, as it turned out, so the book was of no use for Clara's research. Unless she was very much mistaken, Ines had even been friends with Gruber very briefly.

'Should I go and get some more milk?' asked Paul.

'Not for me, thanks.' Clara sat down and turned to page 162. On 1 December 1945, she read, *carabinieri* stormed the monastery of the Teutonic Order in Lana, seizing not only many fugitive soldiers and collaborators from

Germany, France, Czechoslovakia and Croatia, but also a quantity of weapons, cars and cash to the value of fifteen million lire. In the course of the raid, various precious artworks also came to light, stolen by the Tyrolean *Gauleiter* Franz Hofer.

Monasteries, Clara learnt as she read on, had for the most part been safe havens where fugitives from justice, and especially Nazi war criminals, were able to hole up with impunity. But in the case of Lana, the Allied authorities had been able to obtain a search warrant.

Perhaps Ines had only noted down the goings on in this monastery in order to tell Sabine Gruber about them at some stage? But in truth Clara wasn't especially interested in all that stuff.

She stood up again, handed the book back to Paul, and fell back to thinking about her own e-mail, and its self-pitying tone. She had wittered on about how Claus didn't seem to notice her anymore and had lost all interest in sex. Not even an egg-white salad had helped, she'd written. At the time, she had been researching Casanova's love affairs with various Venetian nuns. The great lover had chopped up the whites of boiled eggs into tiny pieces and marinated them in olive oil and herb vinegar to boost his virility. Clara once tried replicating the dish for Claus – admittedly not with Tuscan olive oil, but an even more aromatic variety from Apulia – but it had done no good.

Was Paul single, she wondered. Did he not have time for a relationship, or was he just keeping it quiet? Clara stole a sideways glance at him. He had returned to his book.

Emma Manente and her love for Hermann Steg came into her mind. I should have asked Francesco whether there was anyone else in his mother's life after his father died, she thought. Also whether he remembered money going missing from the hotel in the summer of 1978. And if he knew what became of that Antonella girl.

Had she, like so many others, settled down after a wild youth, got married and had kids?

'I'm sorry,' Paul said, putting his book aside on the sideboard, 'it's very rude of me to be reading all the time.'

We're even about the same height, thought Clara, looking down at her feet in her flat sandals.

'Do you have any children?' It was meant to sound casual, but it came out far too strident. Perhaps it was just the size of the kitchen that made her voice sound so loud.

'No – I was in a long relationship with a woman who couldn't have kids. Then again, I didn't have any children with other women who weren't barren. So I suppose it's mainly down to me.' He shrugged his shoulders. 'Because I don't know what it's like to have children, I can't say whether it was a mistake not to have had any.'

Yes, it is a mistake, thought Clara, but didn't say it. No other questions came to mind, at least none that she dared voice.

The coffee machine gave a gurgle. Ines had the old Bialetti *caffettiera* from her student days. If it wasn't used for any length of time, the coffee tasted bitter. When it boiled, it sprayed little specks of coffee over the top of the hob and its enamel cover; she couldn't tell which of them were fresh and which had been there for ages.

Clara poured two small cups of espresso and filled two glasses with cold water. As she passed Paul his glass, a few drops fell onto the hot hob. Two tiny droplets gyrated on the hotplate before evaporating.

'It's strange reading your own e-mails on Ines's computer,' said Clara.

Paul looked at her, taking small sips of his coffee.

'I sound so certain in them. But the truth is, I'm cowardly and indecisive.'

'Aren't we all?' said Paul.

'Ines wasn't. She lived out her dreams.'

Paul made a sweeping gesture with his hand: 'So this was her dream, was it?'

'You mean this shabby flat? Money wasn't important to her.'

'Mine looks much the same.' He put his cup down on the windowsill and fished for the pack of cigarettes in his shirt pocket. 'Ines was probably even more uncompromising than me, though.'

'Yes, she was that, too. But unlike me, she always knew where and how she wanted to live.'

'You can't know that for sure.'

'No. Yes. That is —'

Paul smiled. 'She wanted to live in Rome, and she got to do that, fine. But did she always want to go to bed at night just with books and magazines?'

I could say the same about myself, thought Clara. Quickly, she responded: 'Look, there were plenty of men in Ines's life – one of them was here earlier, Francesco –'

'Aha.'

Clara told Paul about the good-looking older man who had let himself into Ines's flat unbidden, and how she and he had fallen out – and about the young Francesco in the manuscript, a wastrel who couldn't even be bothered to check he had enough coins to hand when he called his mother.

'He didn't give the impression of being some sensitive intellectual,' Clara went on, 'I should have thrown him out straight away. He had a bloody nerve just barging his way into Ines's flat like that.'

'What was he after?'

'Well, when I came in, the laptop was switched on – but he didn't know the password.'

'Looks like he wanted to delete something.'

'Yeah, his private e-mails to Ines, in case they got into the wrong hands.'

'I don't buy that. May I?' said Paul, pointing at his cigarette. Getting a nod, he opened the window. 'Ines described him as a communist, right? So he's probably still labouring under the delusion that Italy liberated itself. Pertini was always going on about how Italy was a product of anti-Fascism, that it was the bedrock of the constitution and the Italian Republic. Of course, that's just a nice, cosy myth. And everyone was happy to go along with it. So much so that even the worst fascists thought of themselves as resistance fighters.'

Clara told Paul about the lectures that Francesco supposedly delivered in 1978, at the *Feste de l'Unità*.

'I was there, too,' said Paul, blowing smoke out of the window. 'Those were just harmless, nostalgic folk festivals. I imagine Francesco, just like lots of others, got swept along by the whole left-wing culture. And part of that culture involves commemorating the massacre of Germans.'

'What – you can cheerfully stand there and say that?'

'Wait, let me finish.' He took two more drags of his cigarette before stubbing it out. 'They harped on about the evil Germans – who did commit some appalling atrocities, there's no getting round it – but then they also used the German war crimes in Marzabotto or the Ardeatine Caves to exonerate Italy from its fascist complicity.'

'That's far too simplistic an explanation, surely.'

'Fact is, some connections are so straightforward and self-evident, they hurt.' Paul looked straight into Clara's eyes, so intently that she couldn't bear his gaze and had to turn away to refill her water glass.

'Look,' he continued, 'Francesco's mother lost her first love in the partisan attack in the Via Rasella – you said that yourself earlier.'

'If it's true, though. The story's there in the manuscript, right enough. But I'm beginning to suspect that Ines made it up. This Francesco has spent his entire life trying to paint his mother as an anti-Nazi; I'd even go so far as to say he has a mother complex,' said Clara.

'But it doesn't matter whether it's true or not, don't you see? It's intolerable for Francesco, whatever. His own mother was on the side of the perpetrators. In his eyes, she became the wicked *tedesca*. And he can't go on whitewashing her actions indefinitely. One day, the whole house of cards will come crashing down. I've no idea whether Francesco's still politically active these days, or what party he's in, but it seems his whole world view was shaken to the core by the way Ines portrayed his mother.'

Paul was lying on the sofa reading the manuscript that Clara had handed him.

'Read it for yourself,' she had said.

Although he was well aware that memories always recast themselves in the act of being recalled, he caught himself believing everything that was written on these sheets of A4, and taking all the things he'd said back in 1978, which Ines surely must have twisted and spun, at face value. He even started underlining some words and jotting questions in the margin. After a while he put the pencil down on the floor and began chuckling at his own credulity. 'You really got me…' he said under his breath.

2009

'What's that?' said Clara.

'Oh, nothing,' Paul replied.

All of a sudden he was hit by a wave of tiredness. It was comforting knowing Clara was in this room, in this flat with him. He laid the manuscript on his chest and closed his eyes.

Earlier, she went out and got in bread, ham, cheese and something to drink from the nearest supermarket. After eating, they had both gone back to their tasks, until Paul could contain his curiosity no longer. 'So, are you going to tell me what Ines thought of me?' he asked Clara. In lieu of an answer, she had passed him the manuscript.

He had galloped through the first seventy pages.

What was so embarrassing, he wondered, to make Clara reticent about discussing his part in the novel? The white priest's collar he used to wear when conducting tours? Could it be that Clara was a devout believer? He very much doubted it.

This Antonella had been a member of the Communist Party and idolised Berlinguer, but at the same time she sympathised with the *indiani metropolitani*. How was that supposed to work? No-one in the CP would have had anything to do with those anarchists, whose specialities were occupying houses and staging 'happenings', and who shunned any formal political structures or coherent programmes.

Keep your mouth shut, though, Paul told himself. Don't tell Clara about this contradiction. In fact, say nothing at all from now on. You talk too much anyhow.

When he opened his eyes again, he saw Clara sitting with her back to him on a wobbly wooden chair and rummaging in a box. Paul thought about her neck, and how he'd like to brush her hair aside and bury his face in it.

I'm sure I didn't sleep with Ines, I would have remembered that, he thought. But there was still a nagging doubt. He picked up the manuscript again and looked at the clock. The school was expecting him in an hour. He toyed with the idea of cancelling the lecture, something he had never done before. Last night's lack of sleep way was affecting his concentration, and he kept having to break off from reading.

293

Clara had made herself comfortable in the meantime. She was lying on a blanket – he'd offered her the sofa, but she had declined – and was reading a book.

Paul made out he was having a nap, but all the time kept listening for her to lift her hand to turn the page. But whenever he opened his eyes a crack to look over in her direction, she was staring at the same page. Either she was reading it over and over again because she, too, couldn't concentrate, or she'd stopped reading and was staring into space, her eyes drifting over the letters and the white spaces as she slipped into drowsiness, oblivious to everything around her, including him.

He realised he was getting agitated.

Suddenly their eyes met and Clara gave him a little smile before returning to her book.

'Just dreadful,' she said after a while, 'I can't read this stuff any longer.' Raising her voice, she intoned: '...*do you know of any other place in the world which is capable, at certain moments, of stimulating the human life force and heightening all desires to fever pitch...?*'

'None other than this place,' said Paul, affecting a tone of pathos.

They both laughed.

'So what place is he talking about?'

Clara held up her copy of D'Annunzio's novel *The Flame of Life*.

Paul thought of Hemingway, who had also been one of the fascist poet's admirers in the Twenties, and who had even been convinced that the new opposition after Mussolini's March on Rome should be led by the 'fearless speechifier' D'Annunzio. But in reality D'Annunzio couldn't stand the Duce, and had only feigned his friendship with him. All he wanted to do was to exert influence on Mussolini.

'It was him who warned Mussolini about Hitler,' said Paul.

'That's right,' said Clara, 'he called the infamous meeting between the two dictators – in 1937, I think – a 'ruin'. In all honesty, I'd never have credited D'Annunzio with so much insight.'

'When you're done with your D'Annunzio–Duse love story, though, who are you going to write about next?'

'If only I knew. Marlene Dietrich and Erich Maria Remarque, maybe. Or some fictional pair of lovers from one of the countless novels set in Venice. Mind you, that wouldn't exactly thrill my readers. Everything's got to seem real, even if it's a fake.'

'Is that why Ines kept people's real names in the novel?'

'Did she, though? I'm in no position to judge. I only know Mrs Manente, because she's from Stillbach. Her name really is Emma. And of course I know Stillbach itself – that's real. And then there's you.'

'I haven't got that far,' said Paul, drumming his fingers on the manuscript, 'to the bit where I'm mentioned, I mean.'

'But you appear right at the beginning.'

'Do I?' He stood up, and glanced at his watch again. 'I really must go. Shall we see one another later? Should I come back here?'

'If you'd like to.'

'Very much so.'

Before Paul left, Clara showed him a photo that had been in an envelope with some others.

'That's her,' she said.

'Who?'

'Emma Manente. In 2008.'

Paul looked at Clara's hands, which were trembling slightly.

'And here's the address of the old people's home.' She pointed to a sticker on the back of the photo. 'I'd be fascinated to know whether this Johann really existed.'

'Why not go there and ask her yourself?'

'Do you think I should? What about all the stuff I still need to do here?'

Clara walked to the door with Paul.

'It'll keep,' he said.

In the stairwell, Paul kicked himself for not giving her a parting kiss on the cheek. But by the time he was down on the street, he was telling himself not to be such a bloody idiot.

No way you want to get yourself entangled in a love triangle.

So, keep your paws off her.

And don't get drunk this evening.

He got on the bus.

On the way to the private school, he felt a sudden great longing for Mari-anne. She had been his safe haven, his point of fixity; he hadn't had to constantly reinvent himself in her presence. She knew everything about him: the words he hadn't been able to pronounce as a child, his family circumstances, and all his personal likes and dislikes. She had put up with his impatience and pig-headed-ness, and knew just how to deal with him. When he'd been with her, he had still been able to envisage a future together, even though she was ill. Together, they had mapped out the years they would still have with one another, dreaming of a little house up in the Waldviertel, where they would be able to retreat in the summer, sometime, who knew when? But then this Beppe bloke put his oar in – a plump, misshapen man full of all the passions that Paul couldn't muster any more, even if he'd wanted to.

As he changed and boarded a tram, he mused that Ines had had the last word with this novel of hers. It was irrelevant what had happened or would still happen, or what Francesco thought or what his mother had gone through – anyone who had already read the manuscript or who had yet to work their way through it, wouldn't be able to contradict Ines. They would just have to sit there helplessly as readers and take in what she had written. That's what Francesco's visit that morning had been about, Paul felt sure – an attempt to overcome this sense of impotence.

'You've always got to have the last word, haven't you?' Paul's mother once yelled angrily at him; he was fifteen and still at school, and she'd just slapped his mouth. Writers remained children all their lives; the only difference was that, as adults, they had found a way of having the last word.

And Ines's mouth was now safely under the earth for all eternity.

Before calling the taxi to go to the care home, Clara looked at various films on YouTube under the search term *Via Rasella*. One documentary clip included an interview with one of the key figures who had masterminded the ambush, Carla

Capponi. Now an old woman, she was shown preparing dinner in a kitchen with blue and white tiles, lifting the lid of a pot to stir something, and talking about the preparations for the attack as she did so.

She said she had got little sleep the night before in their hideout in the cellar of a house on the Via Marc Aurelio; they had spent most of that evening getting the dustcart containing the bomb ready.

Clara replayed the film several times; she was transfixed by this woman and her mundane tasks and how she kept chatting away the whole time like she was talking about a new recipe she wanted to try.

The way Carla Capponi moved around her kitchen and the almost cheerful manner in which she described the preparations for the bombing were so polished that Clara kept scrolling back, time and again, to the beginning of the film to see if there wasn't just one jarring moment in this perfectly choreographed performance that might betray a flicker of doubt on Capponi's part.

But Clara could find nothing. There wasn't even a hint of uncertainty in Capponi's commentary, either. She didn't miss a beat, and her voice never wavered. It was as if the thirty-three soldiers, the two innocent civilian passers-by and the 335 victims of the Nazi massacre in the tufa caves the following day had never even perished.

In all honesty, Clara hadn't expected a show of remorse from the old lady, who had fought under the codename *Elena* – after all, she and her husband Rosario Bentivegna and all the other brave communists had been involved in a bitter struggle against a brutal regime; even so, she had hoped that there might be something ineffable in the innermost being of this Signora Capponi that would yield some insight into her true nature. At the very least, she'd thought that the former resistance fighter might have chosen a more appropriate location for reminiscing about her part in the bombing – a quiet corner of a living room or a fixed camera angle somewhere out in the open – instead of pottering round the kitchen stirring pans.

A swift Internet search revealed that as a Communist Party MP, Capponi had been honoured many years later for her part in the anti-fascist struggle with a gold medal for military valour. She had also given many interviews and written a book about her exploits entitled *Con cuore di donna*, 'With the Heart of a Woman'.

But Clara hadn't found any evidence of that heart in the YouTube clip.

The four men sitting on a wooden bench outside the old people's home looked over inquisitively as Clara stepped out of the taxi. Perhaps they were expecting visitors. One of them held his middle and index fingers up to his lips; it only dawned on Clara the second time she looked that he was asking for a cigarette. She shook her head by way of saying sorry and made for the entrance.

The women's ward, a nurse informed her, was on the first floor. The stairwell was decorated with pictures of mountains and coastal scenes, which reminded Clara of her honeymoon with Claus. They had gone down to Ravello and marvelled at the panorama from the *Terrazza dell'Infinito* of the Villa Cimbrone, convinced that their love would be as limitless as the view from up there. The many famous people who had visited this eyrie before them – passionate couples like Greta Garbo and the conductor Leopold Stokowski, or Duse and D'Annunzio – seemed to Clara and Claus to be like godparents to their own love. At the time, Clara knew nothing of the poet's serial infidelity. But after the diva's death in faraway Pittsburgh on Easter Monday 1924, D'Annunzio asked Mussolini to have his former muse's body flown back to Italy and publicly announced: 'The woman I was never worthy of has died.'

Clara found Emma Manente asleep in a chair in the residents' lounge. She pulled up a seat next to her and sat down to wait. The air conditioning was turned up too high; Clara felt freezing. The other old ladies sitting around the bare room, which was permeated by indefinable cooking smells, looked over at her.

Clara began to wonder whether any of them had been in the resistance, laying out caltrops or cutting telephone lines like that Capponi woman. Who knows, perhaps the lady with the navy-blue trousers and the white T-shirt, sitting by the door in her wheelchair, had once been a guerrilla? Maybe a member of a partisan group like the GAP, who, like Carla Capponi, had had to sleep in a different place every night and who had had to sever all ties with her family to ensure her safety? Perhaps the woman had also gone to wash at the public bathhouse, had couriered secret messages and smuggled weapons across the city, and taken part in attacks on military headquarters and important transport hubs? Or, when all was said and done, had she *only* been the wife of a fascist collaborator? A 'hero's mother' and the 'guard and pillar of her family', to use the fascist formulation?

Capponi, Clara recalled, had protested against the discrimination that women faced. The men of the GAP resistance group grabbed the best guns for themselves, leaving the women with all sorts of old rubbish for weapons. Even under the communists there was no equality, thought Clara. There would never be equality.

She'd had enough of almost eighteen years of looking after Gesine. Claus had been allowed to pursue his career. Now it was time for Clara to start looking out for herself. If it wasn't already too late, that is.

How should I address Mrs Manente? In Stillbach dialect, or Italian?

Sleep and life had left so many traces on her face, thought Clara as she looked at the dozing Emma. So much confusion. Age scribbles out your facial features.

Clara's gaze lighted on Emma's hands, on the deep furrows on her fingertips, which looked like the tread on car tyres. She had read somewhere that people's fingerprints formed in the fourth month of their mother's pregnancy, and that some of the furrows and grooves were genetically determined, while the rest came about as a result of the pressure and the position of the embryo in the womb.

But looking again at Emma, Clara noticed that there were still definite traces of Stillbach about her.

Her size, for one thing; none of the Italian women in the room had such long legs. Despite the fact that Emma Manente was sitting slumped in a chair and snoring gently, she still cut an imposing figure. Her white hair was still full, and growing profusely in all directions.

'Mrs Manente?'

'Shake her! You've got to shake her. She sleeps the whole day. And when she's not sleeping, she's trying to run off,' piped up the woman in the wheelchair, nodding as she spoke as if to confirm what she was saying. 'I'm Mrs Dallapiazza.' She raised her right hand in greeting. 'Dallapiazza.'

Amplatz in German, thought Clara. There had been a family called Amplatz in Stillbach who had been forced to change their name to Dallapiazza in the fascist period. The fascists had even turned William Shakespeare into Guglielmo Scuotilancia. Even D'Annunzio had got in on the act and changed 'Hip, hip, hooray!' into the Ancient Roman battle cry *Eja, eja alalà*! because 'hooray' didn't sound Italian enough to him.

'My name's Burger,' replied Clara, 'I'm originally from the same village as Mrs Manente.'

'Mrs Dallapiazza,' the woman in the wheelchair repeated, nodding a second and third time. 'Dallapiazza,' she said again.

Clara stroked Mrs M's arm, but she didn't stir. Only when she pinched the skin on her arm lightly did she open her eyes.

'Oh, Ines. What a nice surprise –' She wetted her lips with her tongue and stretched her arms.

'I'm not Ines. I'm Clara.'

Emma Manente leant forward and stroked Clara's hair.

'You're not Ines? Of course you're Ines,' she said, slapping her thigh to emphasise the point.

'She calls everyone Ines,' called Signora Dallapiazza. 'Even Mariella.' She nodded. 'Everyone. Everyone. Even the manager. Manager.'

Dallapiazza pazza, thought Clara – Dallapiazza the crazy woman. She can't help repeating the last word of every sentence. Like the mountain nymph Echo.

Emma Manente suddenly grew agitated, fidgeting about on the chair, moving her lips like she was chewing on something or kneading her words and trying to give them some form. But no sound emerged.

'Mrs Manente, I'm from Stillbach. Can you hear me? From Stillbach. Do you remember Stillbach?'

Clara made to take Emma's hand, but she pulled it away, then stared fixedly in the direction of the door, saying nothing. After a while, she suddenly stood up.

'Let's go,' she said. 'Let's go to the hotel. I know where the money is.' She began tottering, so Clara linked arms with her to support her. She was afraid she'd fall over.

What money, thought Clara. 'I haven't come about money,' she told Emma.

Mrs M stopped in her tracks. 'Yes, yes, I know. I'm sorry. I spotted it too late. But we're friends again now, aren't we? I made sure you were compensated, though, didn't I?'

Clara nodded, though she had no idea what the old lady was talking about. Emma kept tugging her towards the door.

'There she goes, rushing off again,' said Signora Dallapiazza. 'You must call Mariella. Mariella.'

Out in the corridor, Clara tried to stop Mrs M by standing in her way. 'Why don't we go and sit in the garden for a bit? – Do you remember Johann? Johann from Stillbach?'

Emma turned her head and looked inquiringly at Clara, as though her thoughts were hanging like pictures on a gallery wall and all she had to do was stare intently at them before offering an opinion.

'Johann,' Clara tried again. 'He was killed in the Via Rasella. You two were engaged, weren't you?'

'I know where it is,' said Mrs M, 'Room 34 – that's it!'

Paul took the last three steps in a single bound, and only just managed to stop himself from stumbling and falling over by grasping the banister. The schoolboy in the second row had not only looked like a miniature version of Mayor Gianni Alemanno, he had talked like him, too: he kept on returning to the question of the country's internal security, and tried to steer the discussion away from historical themes.

'Thing is,' the boy said, 'you're an arch-Leftie,' after Paul had delivered his lecture on the Italian *Resistenza,* which had once been one of the strongest resistance movements in the whole of Western Europe. It had been a broad church, Paul said, comprising not only socialists and communists, but also Christian Democrats, monarchists and republicans. 'What nonsense,' the boy challenged him, 'why don't you admit that the *Resistenza* wanted to turn Italy into a Soviet republic?' He went on to claim that surrender had spelt the end of the motherland, and of Italy as an independent nation.

Paul was familiar with this line of argument. There were now an increasing number of historians who were prepared to take issue with the anti-fascist interpretation of the country's past. They were in the Prime Minister's inner circle and peddled their views on the many TV channels and in the newspapers he owned. They argued that the resistance movement had been an unrepresentative minority, whose actions had split Italy. And the communists' sole aim had been a dictatorship of the proletariat. In fact, the entire *Resistenza* phenomenon was nothing other than ideological self-justification by the Left.

Even the smell of schools made Paul feel queasy – once out in the open, he took a deep breath. He looked around for a bar. The sky was cloudless. He could really use a drink now.

It was only logical that the schoolboy should have condemned the partisans for the bomb attack in the Via Rasella. If only they'd given themselves up after the outrage, he seriously suggested, the massacre in the caves would never have happened. Plus, the soldiers they'd murdered were innocent *Altoatesini*, South Tyroleans. At this point, another pupil interrupted him, calling him a revisionist and a fascist. This provoked some laughter in the back rows. At this, the teacher – he must have been in his late twenties, and had minimal teaching experience, having only completed his degree in Bologna two years earlier – looked over at Paul for a response.

It was true, Paul conceded, that there were some innocent victims among those killed in the blast – South Tyroleans who prior to this had fought for the Kingdom of Italy, and had served in Ethiopia. But unfortunately other sections of the Bolzano Regiment comprised diehard Nazis, who had massacred civilians in the Val Biois and Belluno in the summer of 1944. 'They did it out of pure frustration,' he added, 'because their campaign against the partisans was going badly. They torched entire villages. These were brutal revenge attacks directed at the civilian population.'

Paul went into the nearest bar and ordered a glass of white wine. When it came, the pinot grigio wasn't cold enough. He was looking forward to seeing Clara again, and tried to take the edge off his nervous anticipation with a second glass.

He found a message from Julia on his iPhone: *How are you fixed this evening?*

Your last chance. That's the way it always went, he thought: you finally get yourself a date, and it clashes with another one.

The only times Paul had gone out on the town in the past few weeks had been with Lorenzo; they'd crawled round various bars and usually ended up drinking too much and slagging off the films and historical documentaries they'd watched recently. Lorenzo had been trying to write an essay on the subject for months, but hadn't got beyond the first couple of pages. But these programmes produced by the state broadcaster RAI weren't by any means the first to trot out the familiar litany that evil had only come into the world with the Nazis, and that the Italians had always been innocent victims. The Germans were still being saddled with sole responsibility for the massacre at the Ardeatine Caves, for instance, even though the notorious fascist Pietro Koch – whose brilliantined hair was always plastered to his head, making him look like he'd been out in the rain – had been instrumental in drawing up the execution list. As was Pietro Caruso, the Italian Chief of Police at the time. Koch supplied thirty names, while the state police head contributed twenty. One of those selected by Koch was the young police lieutenant Maurizio Giglio, who had already been so badly tortured at the Gestapo HQ in the Via Tasso that he couldn't walk. His silence saved the lives of a dozen partisans and an American secret service officer he'd been in contact with. What was his codename again?

'Give me one more glass, would you?' he asked the barman. I'd never have had the strength to keep quiet, he thought. I'd have given in after the first fingernail they pulled out. *Cervo*, 'Stag' – that was the name, I remember now. Pictures of Giglio reminded Paul of Franz Kafka: in honour of what Kafka's surname meant in Czech, Paul would have given Giglio the codename *taccola*, 'jackdaw'.

Sorry, can't make it tonight, he texted to Julia, *bon voyage! Paul V.* Then he thought better of it, deleted the text and called her.

She was already in *Trans Tiberim*, she said when she picked up, laughing. Trastevere, once the home of tanneries and fulling mills with their stench of urine. Not far from his apartment, in other words.

Was that a sly dig about the state of his flat, he wondered. He didn't rise to the bait. His little studio flat, his *monolocale*, wasn't all that bad.

So how had his school visit gone, she wanted to know.

Well, Paul told her, the rift running through Italian society ran right through that classroom, too. 'But let's talk about something else, shall we?' he said.

'Sounds like you had an uphill struggle.'

'Dead right. You should be happy you deal in flints and bones – they don't answer back.'

'Maybe I'll be down in Rome again sometime,' she said and paused, then added, 'Right, I must go now. You take care.'

'And you stick to your guns. No trout-sex!'

He paid the barman and left.

It was still too early to go back to Ines's flat. Clara would most likely still be at the old people's home. He decided to drive back to the Viale Trastevere, take a shower and put on a clean shirt.

Walking in the front door of his block soon after, he heard noises coming from the workshop and went out into the yard. The young mechanic was kneeling on the ground and removing the engine cover and chrome trim from a Lambretta.

'Hi, Signor Vogel, how's things?' He stood up, wiped his hands on his jeans and ran them through his hair, which he had spiked up with liberal amounts of gel. Behind him the courtyard was strewn with dismantled engine guards from Vespas and sundry two-stroke engines and leather seats.

'You don't by any chance have a Vespa 125 you could lend me for a couple of days, do you?' Paul asked him.

'You really ought to buy one, you know,' replied the mechanic, 'taxi fares don't half mount up these days.' He winked at Paul with his left eye.

'You're not wrong – I had a Lambretta just like that thirty years ago,' said Paul, pointing at the dismantled scooter.

'Yeah, they're all well and good, but it takes me half an hour just to change the carburettor on them. Now, Piaggios are a lovely bit of engineering by comparison – everything's easily accessible. In retrospect, I guess we should be glad the Allies flattened the Piaggio aircraft works, otherwise the company wouldn't have had to go looking for something new to manufacture after the war.'

'Piaggio made planes, then?'

'Didn't you know? Yeah, the Vespa engine was originally designed as a starter motor for aircraft during the war.'

'How come you're so surprised I didn't know that?'

'Well, it's your line of work, isn't it? My cousin says you know everything there is to know about the Second World War.' He reached for a packet of Gauloises and offered Paul one before lighting up himself.

'Your cousin?'

'You gave a talk at her school once.' Saying this, the lad turned round and tugged at a plastic tarpaulin, unveiling three Vespas. 'I can let you have the spinach-green one,' he said.

'Not very pretty though, is it?'

'Oh, how can you say that! All Vespas are beautiful! Just look at the flowing curves, the slimline frame —' he said, caressing the headlight.

'Haven't you got anything in white or red?'

'No, honestly, you really should take the green one, it's indestructible, it'll even start in the rain. The others are all a bit temperamental. I mean, I *could* fix up the light blue one there for you at a pinch, but I'd need a bit more time.'

'Fair enough, then, I'll take the green one. And —' here he lowered his voice, 'maybe you can let me have some of your *greenery* as well?'

The young mechanic looked at him, frowned, then nodded.

'And I'll need a spare helmet, too.'

'Size?'

'No idea. Not too small, anyhow.' His business concluded, Paul disappeared upstairs.

He put new sheets on the bed, vacuumed the lounge and, after having his shower, cleaned round the bathroom. Again, the boy in the second row came to mind, who had defended Mussolini's Abyssinia escapade as a 'civilizing mission'. The young man had been precociously, frighteningly bright — his classmates could only counter what he had to say with platitudes. He had sounded for all the world like Gianfranco Fini, when he'd still been Berlusconi's foreign minister and had praised the state of Somalia, Ethiopia and Libya under Italian colonial rule. Fini, of course, omitted to mention Mussolini's use of weapons of mass destruction, or the concentration camps at Nocra and Danane. As far as many Italians were concerned, these wars were great African adventures, and they still believed Italian troops had been there to help the natives improve their countries' infrastructure. And they were free to indulge their colonial nostalgia through all the street names and monuments in Italy relating to this era, which had never been removed.

Paul had once organised a showing of Giuliano Montaldo's movie *Tempo di uccidere* in a high school. It starred Nicolas Cage as an Italian lieutenant in Ethiopia who accidentally kills a native woman and is tormented by feelings of guilt, but the pupils found the film boring. One of the girls said she thought Enio Flaiano, who wrote the novel it was based on, was a much better screenwriter than an author. After all, he had three Oscar nominations for Best Screenplay for his work on Fellini's films *La dolce vita*, *I Vitelloni,* and *8 1/2*, whereas nobody mentioned his novel *Tempo di uccidere*, 'The Short Cut', anymore. Once again, Paul felt he was left looking like some failed professional nostalgist.

He dashed out of the house again, got some money out of a cash machine and went to the corner shop, where he bought wine, milk, goat's cheese, Parma ham, white bread, two honey melons and a kilo of beefsteak tomatoes.

Then he went to pay for his weed and the deposit on the scooter. He took his bags of groceries upstairs, washed his face again, dabbed on a little Le Male aftershave, took his black crash helmet from the cupboard and left the apartment. The Vespa was waiting there on the pavement for him, with the spare helmet in the foot-well.

Emma Manente had dozed off on the garden bench after starting to tell Clara about Johann. She said she'd felt like an alien in Rome at first, she hadn't fitted in; for one thing, she felt so much bigger than everyone else. She'd tried desperately not to stand out. 'Over time, you just blend into the background,' she said in a lucid moment. 'When Johann was transferred to Rome, I crept out of my hole again. I prettied myself up and made an effort for him. And that's when Remo spotted me for the first time, though I'd been working in the hotel for years. Italians only take notice of a woman when she's put on her glad rags.'

Clara watched Emma as she slept. She had learnt from Sister Mariella that Mrs Manente only had the occasional visitor. Apart from her son dropping by pretty regularly, there was just that other woman, Ines she was called, who spoke German with the old lady. 'But she hasn't shown up this week,' Mariella said.

On their way to the garden, Mrs M's talk had been rambling; it seemed to Clara she was confusing her wartime memories with life in the hotel kitchen; she went on about some soldiers trying to flee in trucks on badly damaged roads, and being tossed about on the benches like pancakes in a greased frying pan.

As soon as Clara and Emma emerged from the dark stairwell into the bright afternoon sun, the old lady started talking about fluorescent balls and light spots and then about nights so dark 'that even your eyes didn't seem to work.' Now, she went on, nothing at all worked anymore, not her legs or her ears, let alone her eyes.

'But you can see me fine now, can't you, Mrs Manente?'

Emma had burst out laughing at this, but then pulled a face that almost looked close to tears.

Signora Manente had gone walkabout three times already, Sister Mariella informed her, once in her nightdress and another time in her dressing gown. The first time a policeman had brought her back, but on the second and third occasions, one of the residents had gone after her and summoned help. She had the constitution of an ox, the nurse said, you could tell she'd grown up in the mountains. 'We used to strap her into her bed, but we're not allowed to do that anymore. So please take care she doesn't do a runner.'

So, thought Clara, Emma's legs would work well enough if only her brain could tell her what her legs wanted.

Emma was surprisingly light on her feet, unlike most of the care home residents who shuffled about like they were wearing lead-soled shoes.

If you realised that you were becoming confused in your own mind about time, did you start running to try to escape the confusion? Or was it simply that as an old lady, Emma felt somehow rejuvenated by running away from the home?

Clara also asked about Antonella, but Emma just sat there motionless on the bench, saying nothing.

'And what about Mimmo? Does the name Mimmo ring any bells?'

Again there was no reply; she just rocked her head to and fro like she was trying to jog her memories into life.

'Who's that, then?' she asked finally.

'Antonella's brother.'

'I've got two brothers, too.' Gradually, she subsided on the bench, slumping into a lying position.

They aren't allowed to tie the old people down, thought Clara, but it's still okay to drug them up to the eyeballs. She lifted up Emma's dangling arm and laid it on the bench.

Back on the staircase, Mrs M had stopped and listened intently every time Clara uttered the word *Stillbach*.

'Can you still remember the inn in Stillbach, Mrs Manente? Or the church? Or your family?'

'Oh, that just won't do!' said Emma in reply. And then she had gone on to talk about her mother's legs and how she used to rub arnica schnapps into them.

'Your mother's long dead, isn't she?'

'Long dead,' repeated Emma. 'I'm okay, though, I don't have to cut the corn anymore.'

When they reached the door out into the garden, Mrs M stopped again and clutched Clara's arm. 'You can swim in the mere now.'

'Of course you can.'

As Emma was sleeping, Clara noticed two men sitting in the shade at the far end of the garden having a heated argument. One of them suddenly stood up and brandished his walking-stick in the air. Then he turned around and strode towards Clara.

Standing in front of her, he pointed back at the other old man with his stick. 'Can you tell him that communists don't exist anymore? He won't believe me.'

'Well, the Communist Party's finished, that's for sure. But I'm sure there are still communists.'

'Look here, if there were still any communists, there'd be a Communist Party too,' said the man, thumping his stick on the ground.

'She's always running off,' said the man suddenly, pointing the tip of his stick at Emma's slippers. Clara noticed there were dried-in coffee stains on them.

'Bodies in the cellar,' Emma murmured, without opening her eyes.

'What did she say?' said the man.

If Clara hadn't stepped between them, the man would have bent down so close to Emma that he would have toppled over onto her. His legs were unsteady, and rather than supporting himself on his stick, he was using it as an extension of his arm.

There was no flicker of movement in Emma's face. She still seemed to be fast asleep.

'The Russians didn't like the aristocrat,' said the man.

'What aristocrat?'

'Berlinguer. They ruined everything. They had their fingers in every pie you can think of. And the Salò people, too.'

Clara thought how lively the old man's eyes looked, without noticing that someone had approached the bench from the other side.

'So it *is* you! You get all agitated about me letting myself into Ines's flat, yet here you are meddling in my private life.'

Clara stood up and offered Francesco her hand.

'I'm sorry, I didn't mean to disturb you,' said the old man. 'It's rude to bore a lovely lady with politics.' He paused for a moment before correcting himself: '*Two* lovely ladies, I should say.'

Clara fancied she saw a smile flicker across Emma's face.

'*Mammina*, are you awake?' Francesco asked.

'*Bello o brutti si sposan tutti*,' said Emma.

The old man shook his head, gave a wink with his left eye and returned to his bench, where the other residents were waiting for him.

'You mean *Belle o brutte si sposan tutte*, Mamma.'

'Whatever you say.'

Baffled, Francesco shot Clara a questioning look.

'We were chatting about Stillbach just now.'

'That's not good for her,' hissed Francesco *sotto voce*. 'What are you doing here anyway? Are you planning on carrying on Ines's work? Squeezing my mother dry and spreading lies about her?'

'I can't imagine that Ines –'

'Oh, you can't, can you? Well just try reading what she wrote… Look, my mother wasn't engaged to a Nazi. She had nothing to do with those jackbooted Germans goose-stepping down the Via Rasella – who the partisans were quite right to blow up. The Germans lost nothing here in Rome. They occupied our country when there was a power vacuum and terrorized civilians. It's perfectly understandable that some people weren't prepared to just stand idly by and wait for the Allies to liberate us.'

In the meantime, Emma had stood up and, without a word, wandered away from the bench in the direction of the pine trees at the end of the garden.

'Your mother has got a right to tell her own story.'

'Her own, absolutely. But not one that's been put in her mouth by some delusional woman from Stillbach.'

'And how would you know what her own story is?'

'I've got to go and look after my mother now. Francesco turned around to intercept his *mammina* before she strayed too far. Before leaving, he added a parting shot to Clara: 'I don't want you going public with all this.'

'With what? The manuscript?'

'Yes, exactly. My mother loved my father. She stayed here of her own free will. Out of love, pure and simple. It wasn't some dramatic life-or-death decision like Ines paints it. And that bloke Steg never existed either. Mum, wait!'

'What if I were to change the names of all the people and places?'

Francesco gave a shrug. 'You'll know best what you can get away with. But I'll have my lawyers go over it with a fine-tooth comb, you can be sure of that.'

'Bye bye, Ines!' called Mrs Manente when Clara waved farewell to her.

Paul had forgotten the sensation of riding a scooter. With its souped-up engine, the green Vespa didn't make the usual puttering and buzzing sound, but emitted a clattering roar. It seemed like it was trying to take off from the tarmac.

He had to make a conscious effort to keep his eyes on the road. Glancing up as he sped along, he caught sight of a stone angel here, a domed roof there, a young man in a singlet leaning out of a window to have a smoke, and a woman watching the world go by beneath her balcony. Whenever Paul approached a crossroads where the lights were against him, he weaved the 125 between the stationary cars and pulled up in front of the lead vehicle in order to make a quick getaway.

The further he rode, the more the city changed: the house colours looked like they'd been freshly mixed, the rows of houses took on a different aspect and the light, which was gradually starting to fade to dusk, seemed to blur the appearance of things, so that even crumbling old façades looked as smooth as porous skin photographed through a soft-focus lens.

The young mechanic had come out front to see Paul off, pointing out missing cobbles in the alleyway and other rough bits of paving to look out for, and had also given him a spare lock, which Paul could now feel pressing into his back through the saddle pannier.

He would be there any minute now. His shirt billowed in the slipstream as he turned into Ines's street. A car hard on his tail honked at him as he suddenly slowed right down. As he stopped to manoeuvre the scooter back into a space, the driver, who had also had to brake sharply, roared past him with screeching tyres.

When Clara opened the door, Paul could hear a man's voice in the background. His first thought was that she had a visitor, but he was relieved to see no-one. Perhaps she'd switched on the radio.

Clara didn't notice the two helmets Paul was carrying.

'I've found some tape recordings,' she said, disappearing into Ines's bedroom.

'. . .no, I don't remember exactly. It must have been after Moro's murder sometime. All of a sudden, she was flush with readies. I wanted to know where she'd got them, but she wouldn't tell me, not even when I threatened to go to the police. 'And what if I won it in the lottery?' she said; that was plain stupid – she didn't even know how to fill out a ticket. And it didn't square with her rigid anti-capitalist stance, anyhow.

She kept on disappearing places. One time, she said she'd gone to see some friends in Turin for a few days, another time it turned out she'd spent a week in Paris.'

Paul stood in the doorway, looking at Ines's bed. On it was a cassette player from the 1990s and next to it Clara, hunched over with her chin cupped in her right hand. She had fitted the CASIO recorder with an extension lead plugged into a socket in the hallway. Paul had almost tripped over it when he came into the flat.

Clara stopped the tape and pointed at an open cardboard box. She'd found it under the bed, she said, and told him to take a look.

In the box, Paul found several small DAT-format cassettes. He recalled that they had come on the market about twenty years ago and that he'd occasionally used them himself for interviews.

'Can you make any sense of this for me?' Clara quickly rewound and pressed the 'Play' button again. '*– friends in Turin for a few days, another time it turned out she'd spent a week in Paris.*

'*I don't know how she got caught up in that business. Sure, we were a communist family; her grandfather was sent to a work camp by the Germans, and her grandmother always kept her Party Membership card on the bedside table. But her father wasn't involved at all; he wasn't even openly sympathetic. It was too much of an effort for him to have any political convictions. He never dreamt of the revolution, I can assure you.*

'*So, why her? What did she hope to gain from it? She might just as well have approached the Mafia. At least they'd have protected her, whereas the communists hung her out to dry.*

'*So, the upshot was that she didn't have a normal life anymore – it was all opponents and opposition, alternative lifestyles and down with the state. A shit life, in other words.*

'*She didn't just have some bee in her bonnet, though, she bought into a whole crazy ideology and started to see herself as the Chosen One. But in actual fact she was stigmatised; her grandfather's scars were her undoing.*

'*You see, she adopted his scars as her own. She thought she could use the hydrogen peroxide that her granddad was forced to produce in the Schickert camp for rocket motors and U-boat turbines to fuel her own hatred as well.'*

'That was at Bad Lauterberg,' Paul chipped in, 'in the Harz Mountains, if I remember correctly.'

Clara stopped the tape and looked at him.

'It's nothing, sorry. Carry on.'

'I should have seen the warning signs from way back; she attacked her employers for being fascists just because they didn't go around hurling Molotov cocktails at antenatal clinics. Everyone was a fascist in her eyes, even those who signed up to the Historic Compromise. Although she'd agreed with Berlinguer's idea of Eurocommunism at the start, she suddenly changed tack and condemned any communists who were in favour of a compromise as traitors, because they'd got involved with the Christian Democrats and deviated from the path of true socialism.

'I was still in contact with her when she was working at that hotel in the Via Nomentana. That's where it all began. She was still a Party member at that stage, but was searching around for new directions. She even flirted briefly with those anarchists who staged happenings, the indiani metropolitani.

'At the time, I thought she'd be better off finding her own political feet first. But then others stepped in and decided for her.

'I've no idea whether she actually killed anyone; maybe she was just a courier who carried forged documents, or channelled money to activists who'd gone underground. It's possible she didn't even know what was in the packages and envelopes she handed over to strangers.

'Perhaps she had to die because they were afraid she might know something. But given how forgetful she was generally, I doubt she retained anything. When she used to help out in the bakery, the takings never tallied; she was always mixing up the price per kilo for rosette *with that for* ciabatte.

'You know, Ines, there's not much I can tell you about her, in truth. The one thing I'm absolutely certain of, though, is that the accident was no accident. But even if I'd been able to prove that someone had tampered with her car, it wouldn't have done any good. All I'd have done is put my own life in danger. The people behind it occupy all the positions of power and have ways of ensuring your silence.

'In fact, this whole insane business of violent opposition was only cooked up to break the power of the Communist Party. I can't believe she didn't realise that! If only she'd twigged she wasn't manning some barricade, but was caught in the crossfire! Terrorism by the Left played right into the hands of the fascists she so loathed – in fact, they may well have been funding it all along; how could she not have seen that?'

Clara switched off the cassette player. 'So, do you think they murdered her?'

'Murdered who?'

'This Antonella, the girl they're talking about. There's no name on the tape, but I'm assuming the interview's with Mimmo, her brother. Or what do you reckon?' She stood up; her T-shirt was crumpled.

'How was your school visit?' Clara asked, catching her foot in the extension lead. She just managed to catch the cassette player in time.

Paul ignored her question. 'Well, they could well have killed her, but I honestly don't know enough to say for sure. Certainly, lots of people around then died in traffic accidents. But some resurfaced under assumed names. It could be that she's still alive and well and living in Buenos Aires with a new identity.'

'What, she's in Argentina too, you think? So where did she get all that money Mimmo mentions at the beginning?'

'No idea – bank robberies? Not from fishing in the Trevi Fountain, that's for sure.'

'I'll listen to the rest later,' said Clara. Now, finally, she spotted the helmets. 'Oh, you came here by motorbike, did you? Why the two helmets?'

'One for you, one for me. And it's only a Vespa.'

'Not a chance. How do I know you're not from the secret service, and that you're not planning to spirit me away somewhere and bump me off?' She squeezed past Paul; he could smell her perfume.

'Maybe you could start a new life somewhere afterwards,' Paul quipped.

'Do you mean in the Here and Now, or the Hereafter?'

'I'd much prefer the Here and Now.'

She stopped and looked into his eyes.

This is where I kiss her, Paul thought, I've got to kiss her. But before he could act, she had turned away and gone into the kitchen. 'So, tell me, then. How was it at the school?'

'How was it in the old people's home?'

'No answering a question with a question. I asked first.'

Clara thought about Priebke, the keeper of the list, who had stood at the entrance to the Caves, ticking off the names of all those being brought in for execution. He was also actively involved in the shooting. Everything that Clara had read in the last few hours came back to her. She leant against the wall and looked out of the window but didn't register the passing cars and people.

Originally, the fine volcanic tufa ash mined from the *Fosse Ardeatine* was used in the manufacture of cement. Plenty of it ended up in the monumental buildings the fascists put up all over Rome.

Later, all the galleries and tunnels were backfilled. Along with three hundred and thirty-five dead people of all ages and social classes. The youngest was fifteen, the oldest seventy-four. *It was anything but a legitimate reprisal*, Ines had written. *The retribution meted out there was a brutal act of revenge that rode roughshod over the provisions of the Hague Convention.*

Kappler was faced with the problem of not having enough prisoners on death row, either at Gestapo headquarters or in the other gaols around Rome. His solution was to get the Italian fascist police chiefs to produce their own lists of names, and then topped it up with Jews. A very German solution, thought Clara.

Before Paul's return, and her discovery of the cassette recorder, she had sat at Ines's computer and read through her notes. She couldn't work out whether the descriptions of the first consignments of prisoners from the Regina Coeli prison, who had arrived at the Ardeatine Caves at 15.30, were Ines's own summaries or whether her friend had copied out passages from historical texts.

Kappler had apparently reassured his officers of his full support. He said he realised they faced a difficult task but that it was all for a just cause.

Clara took a sip of water and looked over at Paul, who was reading the manuscript again.

After Priebke had ticked off the names, the prisoners were led down into the dimly lit passages, where they were forced to kneel and were shot in groups of five.

The Germans forced their victims to bow their heads and look to one side – they believed this posture would ensure that the bullet passed through the brain and the top of the skull, killing them instantly.

At one point, the pile of bodies grew so large that traffic into and out of the Caves came to a standstill. So the corpses were simply stacked up and the next batch of prisoners were forced to lie on top of them to be executed, so as to save time.

To make sure they still got the right shooting position, the executioners had to clamber up onto the piles of bodies, too.

Clara began to read out loud: '*Kappler gave his soldiers brandy to steady their nerves, but it only had the effect of spoiling their aim, and they had to fire three or four shots into the backs of the victims' heads. Sometimes, the bullets just passed through their faces, destroying the nose or removing an eye.* But you must know all this stuff.'

Paul laid the manuscript in his lap and looked at Clara. 'Where's all this from?'

'Ines documented everything. *After they'd finished their day's work, Kappler ordered Priebke and the other men to go and have dinner at Gestapo HQ; he said they should get drunk.* Why did Ines write all this material down, though, and then only describe the attack in the Via Rasella?'

'Perhaps she was saving all her research on what happened in the Caves for her next novel,' Paul suggested.

'You can't talk about *saving* in this context. You sound like those doctors who go on about their diagnoses and forget to ask how the patient's feeling.' Clara bit her lower lip. 'Sorry, that's a stupid comparison,' she said, and rushed out of the room. Paul followed her.

'No, it's not stupid,' he said, 'Sometimes I can't see the wood for the trees. I could use a brandy myself. But I drink too much, anyhow,' he said after a moment. 'Your husband could hardly drink brandy, though, otherwise he would anaesthetise himself rather than his patient.'

'My husband?'

'Yes, Claus – he's your husband, isn't he?'

Clara shrugged in response.

'The people they shot in the Caves came from all walks of life,' she said presently, 'cobblers, butchers, street hawkers, printers –'

'– Chemists, lawyers, artists, architects, engineers, industrialists, generals, officers, soldiers, even a priest and many others,' Paul added, 'but what difference does that make?'

'A lot,' replied Clara, 'surely you can see that? It means you can picture real lives behind the statistics.'

'So, you've got to have a profession to have a life?'

Clara didn't respond.

'The daughter of Umberto Scattoni, one of the victims,' began Paul, 'was just thirteen years old when the massacre took place. She visited her father regularly in the Regina Coeli prison and brought him fresh bed linen. That day, she came to the gates as usual and one of these fascists told her, straight to her face, that she could take the stuff straight back, 'cos they'd shot her father and all the others. She fainted on the spot and had to be carried home. To this day, she still suffers from persecution mania. She can't watch the news; she goes berserk if she even hears the word *fascisti*.'

Paul closed his eyes for a moment and rubbed the lids. 'It doesn't stop. It'll never stop,' he went on, 'Scattoni's experiences live on in his daughter. All our experiences live on in us in some shape or form.'

'At root, there's no connection between the attack in the Via Rasella and the people executed in the Caves,' he continued. 'The two groups had nothing to do with one another. Many of the victims were political prisoners, but equally for lots of others, their only crime was being a Jew.'

'I think it's good that Ines kept the two incidents separate. All the indications are that she was going to deal with the perpetrators in her next manuscript.'

'But Johann was a perpetrator, too, wasn't he?' Clara took an apple from the fruit bowl, fetched a knife from the cutlery drawer and started to peel it. Outside, it had already got dark. The noise of peeling sounded like muffled scratching. 'Want some?' she asked.

Paul took the proffered slice of apple and popped it in his mouth.

'People like this Johann could only have risen as high as company sergeant; all the important positions in the Bolzano police battalion were filled by Germans from the Reich, definitely not South Tyroleans – the Reich Germans didn't trust them. Some of them had fought in the Italian Army beforehand.'

'Johann would only have been responsible for security duties, for guarding convoys and German Army installations. So, in that regard, you can actually see him as a victim among the potential perpetrators. Later, you see, some of the survivors from the Via Rasella attack took part in the campaign against the partisans in northern Italy and were implicated in atrocities against civilians.'

'And all for just twelve and a half lire a day,' said Clara, handing Paul another slice of apple.

'Precisely,' said Paul, 'they got two and a half lire more than ordinary Wehrmacht soldiers. Didn't you want to look through Ines's accounts and go to the bank tomorrow, though?'

'Just one more question,' replied Clara, 'weren't the survivors from the Bolzano police battalion involved in the massacre at the Caves? After all, it was their comrades who had been blown to pieces in the Via Rasella.'

'Honestly, you're incorrigible. According to witness statements, Dobrick, the head of the paramilitary police, refused to make his men available for firing-squad duties. His view was that the South Tyrolean police were devout Catholics and mostly older men, and were unsuited to the role, so the SS took over responsibility.'

'So what should I do with the novel manuscript now we've found there was meant to be a sequel that's never going to appear?'

'What, with this?' Paul held up the stack of A4 sheets. 'Just put it with Ines's papers. Or do you know any writers she was in contact with?'

'She obviously knew Sabine Gruber. At least, I found a note of her number,' said Clara.

'Ask her, then.'

'I'm really not sure.'

'Do you want me to call her?'

'Francesco's threatening to set his lawyers on me even before I've found a publisher.'

'Let's cross that bridge when we come to it,' said Paul.

After a pause, he asked her: 'So what did you mean yesterday when you said "It's not just Ines I'm crying about, but that's another story." Who else were you crying about?'

'Maybe I was mourning lost chances…'

'Were there some, then?'

'No, you're quite right. I'm mourning lost chances I never actually had. My sense of responsibility stifled them. I was blinded by devotion to duty and motherly love. And all I've got to show for it now is a stroppy daughter and a husband whose only passion is his job.' Clara turned on the tap and held the knife under the stream. She felt Paul's thigh press against her leg. He had shifted closer. She took a step sideways.

'I want to dive headlong into life again,' said Clara, 'It's like I spend all my time timidly bouncing up and down on a trampoline, never daring to take a proper leap; I'm going nowhere, it's pointless. I really want to spread my wings for once.'

'So how about a spin on the Vespa. Let's get out – we've done enough work for one day,' said Paul, turning off the tap.

'Come on.'

Clara's hands were resting lightly on his waist; she wasn't clinging on to him tightly enough. Because Paul was concerned about her, at first he went quite slowly and braked carefully. But gradually he gained the confidence to pick up speed, which clearly delighted her, as he could hear her laughing.

In the west, the sky still showed faint streaks of red.

It had been a long time since he had met a woman who was comfortable with silence. The botanist, who spent most of her life around plants, had demanded constant attention and conversation from him. She construed every silence as dullness or lack of interest on his part.

Paul and Clara had been together in Ines's flat for hours without him ever getting the impression she was bored with his company.

When they reached the highest hill in the city, Paul pulled over by the kerb.
'Tell me what you'd like to see.'

'Everything,' she said and laughed. 'Just drive anywhere.'

Paul pointed out the Quirinal Palace; he was on the point of informing her that it had once been the summer residence of the Popes, before the kings of Italy and finally the presidents took it over. Instead he blurted out something about fascists standing outside the gates during the Abyssinian War and collecting people's gold coins and jewellery for the war effort. He said it so quickly and breathlessly that Clara asked him if he was alright.

The scratched-up old white helmet really suits her, thought Paul. Other people just looked like that cartoon chicken *Calimero nero* – with his head still stuck in the eggshell – when they wore that kind of thing.

'You should tie your hair back,' he told her, 'the wind can whip it into little knots.'

'I'm really not bothered,' she said, 'just step on it!'

'Is the pannier pressing into your back?'

'No, I can't feel it at all,' said Clara.

Life with Marianne, Paul reflected, had been a bit of a stopgap solution – there had been something transitional about their relationship, like being carried by a Saint Christopher from one bank of love to the other. This willingness to adapt, which he had identified in himself for some time now, had been completely unknown to him previously. Before, he'd attached no importance to surrounding himself with objects that evoked certain memories. He had been happy enough to just muddle along with makeshift arrangements. And now, suddenly, he felt ashamed of his flat. He thought of Julia and how she'd clung to the doorframe and called his apartment a 'dump'. 'Watch out!' he suddenly heard Clara say as he weaved his Vespa between two lines of stationary cars, 'my leg brushed against the bus back there.'

Marianne found this twilight existence strange, but it was precisely its strangeness that appealed to him, this mixture of informality and rootlessness, which always made him feel euphoric because everything was still open and undecided. Open for him, that is, not for Marianne, whose life was constrained by her physical frailty.

Paul felt Clara's hands and arms on his waist. And he fancied he could still catch the scent of her perfume, though the headwind must have been blowing it away from him.

In the distance, the bridge over the Tiber came into view.

Clara could feel the balmy air on her skin. She would never be in Stillbach with Ines again, she thought. They wouldn't ever be able to look out at the far side of the valley again and see the bare slopes there. No more dreams that would carry them out into the world beyond.

When the feeling of being alive begins to grow again…but it was night, and the clouds were hidden from sight.

She thought about all the books in Ines's apartment, and the things that her friend had used for bookmarks: used tickets for buses and museums, strands of hair and pieces of toilet paper. Ines had spent her whole life around books; she'd loved them, but she hadn't revered them. Claus would never have turned the corners of pages over or jotted things in the margins, let alone used highlighter pens to mark passages.

Only once, Clara recalled, had she ever seen Ines cry, and that was when she discovered some books she had stored on a windowsill had become mildewed. It rained heavily in Stillbach, and water must have seeped through the frame.

Some memorable phrases from Ines's notes came into her mind: *the quiet ivy-courtyards, the smooth stone-skin of the statues, and the market women peeling artichokes* – peeling away the stiff leaves until the light-coloured choke itself appears. Clara remembered that in Venice they kept artichoke hearts in sky-blue plastic buckets of water with lemon slices to stop them from turning brown.

Everything here is built on blood, Ines wrote at another point. *On staunched wounds, not on healed ones.* To the half-sentence *Legacy of power*, Ines had added *Legacy of impotence*. Beside this, in brackets, was the name *Emma Manente*. Some notes, Clara thought, read like a distillation of thorough deliberations, while others came across as the random utterances of a meandering mind.

She felt the urge to bury her face in the fabric of Paul's shirt, but the helmet – and not just the helmet – prevented her from doing so.

Clara couldn't remember the last time she'd ridden on a moped. When she'd still been living in Stillbach, she and Ines had sometimes borrowed Aunt Hilda's *Ciao* at the weekends, going off into the countryside, just the two of them, without any crash helmets. They had made Aunt Hilda promise not to tell Ines's mother. In those days, wild red carnations still grew along the banks of the irrigation ditches on the far side of the valley.

Paul parked the Vespa and put the heavy chain-lock around the front wheel. A homeless man was lying in the road between parked cars.

'Are you okay?' Paul asked him.

'Get lost,' the man replied.

'This is where we were yesterday,' Clara said, 'and the old lady's still looking out of the window over there.'

Paul would have loved to ask Clara to come home with him, but his experience with Julia put him off the idea. He was convinced that if Clara had had a seismograph fitted inside her, the device would have registered oscillations that were well off the normal scale. She operated on a higher plane of perception – other people saw the same things she did, but didn't subject them to the same thorough scrutiny. She seemed to transcend the limits of ordinary vision.

Clara wanted another slice of courgette pizza from the *panetteria* they had been to the day before, and then to walk down to the riverbank. But it was just before closing time and the bakery didn't have much left, so she settled for a can of beer and a *pizza bianca*. Paul had the last piece of *focaccia* and two cans of Cola. They wandered out of the Via del Moro towards the Tiber. In an alcove, some candles had been lit beneath a picture of the Virgin Mary; the faithful had also laid bunches of flowers as votive offerings.

'In winter, thousands of starlings roost in the plane trees here,' Paul said to Clara. 'You need an umbrella to fend off their droppings.'

They carried on down the street for a while until they found a flight of steps leading down to the river.

Scraps of paper and other flotsam were caught in the vegetation on the banks from the last high tide; in the evening light they looked like tree decorations.

*

Clara had lost all sense of time. Hours must have elapsed. She had talked about her work, about D'Annunzio's last words – 'I'm so bored' – before his death on the shores of Lake Garda, and about Hemingway's drinking binges and hunting sprees around the Venetian Lagoon. Hemingway had liked nothing better than skulking round the muddy reed-beds and blasting away at partridges, snipe, and pheasants. She told Paul all about Hemingway's dispatches from the 1920s and the young – far too young – impoverished nobleman's daughter he later pursued in Venice, when he was over fifty.

The sky was already getting light. The whole time, Paul had sat next to Clara, saying virtually nothing. He had piped up just once, to tell her that Hemingway had once said that Italy would have become a communist country if only the Reds had had a song to match the fascist hymn *Giovinezza*. Nobody, Hemingway claimed, could go into battle singing the *Internationale*.

Clara didn't tell Paul that she already knew this story. She was surprised at Paul's reticence; he seemed almost shy. Maybe it was because he hadn't had any wine that evening.

She asked him what he'd made of Ines, whether anything about her had struck him as unusual that afternoon in the Galleria Alberto Sordi, but he remained resolutely monosyllabic, just saying that he still couldn't remember what kind of relationship they'd had back then, more than thirty years ago.

'I'm pretty certain there was never anything between us,' he said quietly, 'but when I read the passages about me and Ines in the manuscript, I began to have my doubts. By the way, I Googled the name *Hermann Steg* earlier this afternoon; he was a longstanding board member of the Tyrolean Ancient Philology Society. But I wasn't able to find out whether he's still alive.'

Paul was exhausted and his back hurt from all the sitting down; what he really wanted to do now was to hit the sack. But he couldn't stir himself to get up because he was afraid he'd have to take Clara back to her hotel. About 150 metres away, a girl and boy were lying entwined on a blanket. He stood up, went over to them and asked them if they would sell it to him. 'Are you crazy?' the girl said to her partner when he named a price, 'you should be asking much more.'

Clara saw Paul pulling his wallet out of his jeans. Was he buying cigarettes? The Tiber was flowing by sluggishly, an indefinable shade somewhere between yellow and mud-green. Although the plane trees were casting no shadow as yet, it was already light enough to make out the first colours.

She laughed when he came back. 'You bought the blanket? Let's get out into the countryside, then – the ground's softer there.'

On their way back to the scooter he would have put his arm round her, if they hadn't been chatting about Claus and Gesine, and her husband's job in Vienna General Hospital and her daughter's problems with her schoolwork. It seemed to him that she was filling the silence between them with words that he had banned himself from using. Her keen anticipation of the pine grove they were going to visit was infectious, even though he couldn't understand why she found these trees so attractive. Was it just because they weren't ones that you could climb?

Clara looked up at the clouds, and saw figures and faces in them. How is it that we don't ever see anything mundane like sandcastles, molehills or tables covered in flour in the sky? she asked herself. Is it because we've got used to looking for the dead in the clouds? Because of their constant dissipation and shape-shifting up there?

Had the gauzy fabric of the clouds taken the place of the fabric of meaning, which had become tattered and torn down on Earth?

Stillbach always flowed towards us, either as a stream or as a rivulet, thought Clara. What will become of Stillbach without Ines?

Was Clara dozing? Was she dreaming?

High above her, the pines had opened their umbrellas.

*

After they'd smoked the weed that the lad from the garage had sold him, he slid his hand into hers. Then they rode out to the grounds of the Villa Doria Pamphili.

Clara lay there motionless, gazing up into the blue between the canopies of the pines and singing the praises of the morning coolness in the park. They weren't alone any longer. Several early risers strolled past them, and a woman jogged by; they could hear her heavy breathing.

When Paul admitted he'd paid fifty euros for the blanket, Clara burst out laughing.

She pressed her nose into his shoulder, smelling fresh mint, warm vanilla and lavender. She told him how Emma and Johann's love had become public knowledge in Stillbach. To put an end to all the subterfuge, a friend of Johann's had laid a trail of sawdust in the snow from the Nörderhof to Emma's parents' house.

Good job it's not winter now, thought Clara.

Paul's hand stroked her hair. They were lying close together now, on their stomachs, too tired to sleep, and staring into each other's eyes. Reaching out to caress her neck, his eye was caught by something behind her in the park.

His first thought was that the bald man on the path was a pensioner walking his dog, but then, when the dog turned tail and ran off, he realised that they weren't together. As the old man drew nearer, Paul recognised him.

'I've fallen in love,' he heard Clara say.

She kissed him and he kissed her back, while still trying to keep an eye on the man. In that instant, Paul couldn't help but think of the partisan Palladini, whose genitals Priebke had beaten with a knuckleduster, and the twenty-one-year-old Riccardo Mancini from the Matteotti Brigades, who they had handcuffed, with his hands behind his back, to the door handle. The old man strolling through the park over there had kicked and punched Mancini so savagely that he only came to again when he was back in his cell, to find himself lying in a pool of blood with a broken nose.

*

Clara snuggled up closer to Paul. 'I'm so happy,' she said.

All of a sudden, she pictured the weathervane that sits atop a golden ball on the roof of the Punta della Dogana in Venice – a statue of Fortuna prey to the prevailing winds.

'She turns like a weathercock in the wind.'

'Who does?'

'Fortuna.'

'But there's no wind today,' said Paul.

*

Following the resignation of Horst Köhler as President of the Federal Republic of Germany on 31 May 2010, the far-right National Democratic Party of Germany (NPD) considered putting forward Erich Priebke as its presidential candidate.

Emma Manente died in a nursing home in Rome on 7 January 2011. She was laid to rest alongside her husband Remo Manente in the Campo Verano, the city's largest cemetery.

Glossary

Alemanno, Gianni – (b. 1958 Bari) Mayor of Rome since 2008. A former member of the neofascist *Movimento Sociale Italiano* (MSI; Italian Social Movement), in 1995 he founded the new Social Right Party and later became minister of agriculture in Silvio Berlusconi's second government (2001–6). His victory in the mayoral election was greeted by skinheads chanting '*Duce! Duce!*', though Alemanno claims to have renounced his fascist part.

Altaussee – Located in the Salzkammergut region of Styria in southwestern Austria, Altaussee was the site of extensive salt mine workings, which the Nazis used as a repository for stolen art treasures looted from throughout Europe in World War Two.

Anni di piombo – ('Years of Lead') Period in the social/political history of Italy that lasted from the late 1960s to the early 1980s, and was characterised by upheaval, especially acts of terrorism by opposing left- and right-wing extremist factions. The name may be an allusion to the large number of bullets fired during the unrest.

Badoglio, Pietro – (b. 1871 Grazzano Monferrato; d. 1956 Grazzano Monferrato) Italian marshal and politician. At Mussolini's urging, he was given the title 'Duke of Addis Abeba' in recognition of his victory in the invasion of Ethiopia (1935–6). Badoglio was Italy's first prime minister in the post-fascist era.

Bentivegna, Rosario – (b. 1922; d. 2012) Occupational physician and resistance fighter. As a medical student in Rome, Bentivegna (codename 'Paolo') was one of the key perpetrators of the Via Rasella bomb attack against a German police unit. He later married his fellow partisan and bomb plotter, Carla Capponi.

Berlinguer, Enrico – (b. 1922 Sassari; d. 1984 Padua) General Secretary of the Communist Party of Italy (PCI) from 1972 to 1984. In 1969, he condemned the Warsaw Pact crushing of the Prague Spring as a 'tragedy'. In the general election of 1976, the PCI under Berlinguer gained 34.4 percent of the vote, just 5 percent less than the Christian Democrats (DC). He was an advocate of 'Eurocommunism' (which involved collaboration with bourgeois-liberal and social democratic parties, and a conscious distancing from the notion of the 'dictatorship of the proletariat') and of the 'Historic Compromise' – negotiations began with the DC, but due to the assassination of Aldo Moro, the PCI never got to participate in government.

Bormann, Martin – (b. 1900 Wegeleben; d. 1945 Berlin) Head of the Nazi Party Chancellery and private secretary to Adolf Hitler. A skilled political operative and a virulent anti-Semite, Bormann's closeness to Hitler made him enemies among other members of the Nazi elite. He is believed to have committed suicide during the fall of Berlin to Soviet forces. Though for many years rumours persisted that he had escaped to South America.

Brambilla, Michela – (b. 1967) Italian journalist, politician and heiress to a steel fortune. Elected undersecretary for tourism in Silvio Berlusconi's cabinet in 2008, the following year Brambilla allegedly gave a fascist salute during a ceremony honouring the Carabinieri's paramilitary police division. She denies making the gesture.

Capponi, Carla – (b. 1918; d. 2000) Partisan and member of the Patriotic Action Groups (GAP) guerrilla unit, Capponi helped orchestrate the Via Rasella attack, and later became a member of parliament for the Communist Party.

Caruso, Pietro – (b. 1988; executed Rome, 1944) Fascist and head of the Italian police in 1943–4. Caruso was jointly responsible, with Herbert Kappler, for organising the Ardeatine Caves massacre of 335 Italian civilians in reprisal for the Via Rasella bombing.

Ciano, Gian Galeazzo – (b. 1903 Livorno; d. 1944 Verona) Italian foreign minister 1936–43. Born to an aristocratic family, Ciano married Mussolini's daughter Edda in 1930. After serving in the air force in the invasion of Abyssinia in 1935, he was appointed foreign minister, but on the outbreak of the Second World War became increasingly disaffected with Mussolini's policies, especially his alliance with Nazi Germany. After the Allied invasion of Italy in 1943, Count Ciano and a majority of members of the Fascist Grand Council voted to oust Mussolini as leader. In the ensuing civil war, Ciano was captured by the fascists and executed for treason.

Craxi, Bettino – (b. 1934 Milan; d.2000 Hammamet, Tunisia) General Secretary of the Socialist Party of Italy 1976–1993. Dominated Italian politics in the 1980s and served as prime minister 1983–6.

D'Annunzio, Gabriele – (b. 1863 Pescara; d. 1938 Gardone Riviera; real name Francesco Rapagnetta) Italian novelist, poet, playwright and journalist. An ardent nationalist, he argued for Italy's entry into World War One on the side of the Allies, and volunteered as a pilot in the Italian air force, losing an eye in a flying accident. He supported irredentism, and had a strong influence on the development of Italian fascism, but found himself at odds with Mussolini, unsuccessfully trying to persuade him not to join the Axis with Hitler in 1933. D'Annunzio's erotic novel *Il Fuoco* (*The Flame of Life*, 1900) describes his tempestuous relationship with the actress Eleanora Duse (1858–1924).

Eichmann, Adolf – (b. 1906 Solingen; executed 1962, Ramla, Israel) SS *Obersturnbannführer* and a leading organiser of the Holocaust. Eichmann was appointed by his superior Reinhard Heydrich as Transport Administrator for the 'Final Solution to the Jewish Question', i.e. the mass deportation of Europe's Jews to extermination camps. In 1950, having travelled to Italy, he obtained Red Cross papers with the aid of a Franciscan monk with connections to Bishop Alois Hudal and, posing as one Ricardo Klement, fled to Argentina. Tracked down by the Nazi hunter Simon Wiesenthal, Eichmann was abducted from South America by the Israeli secret service Mossad and put on trial in Jerusalem in 1961. He was found guilty of genocide and hanged.

Fanfani boxes – (Italian – *INA-Case*) State-subsidised workers' housing developments erected from 1949 onwards by the *Istituto Nazionale delle Assicurazioni* (INA: National Institute of Social Security). Their popular name comes from the then-Minister of Labour Amintore Fanfani (1908–99), a leading Christian Democrat politician of the postwar years who championed a series of social and agricultural reforms.

Feste de l'Unità – Festivals organised first by the Communist Party, then by the *Partito Democratico della Sinistra* (Democratic Left Party) and latterly by the *Democratici della Sinistra* (Democrats of the Left) throughout Italy. These festivals are based around cultural events and political discussion forums, but are also social occasions, involving food, drink and dancing.

Fini, Gianfranco – (b. 1952 Bologna) Italian politician; leader of the right-wing *Futuro e libertà* ('Future and Freedom') Party and a former leader of the neofascist MSI. He was deputy prime minister and foreign minister in Silvio Berlusconi's second administration, from 2001 to 2006.

Giglio, Maurizio – (b. 1920 Paris; murdered in 1944) Italian officer and secret agent, who towards the end of the war cooperated with the Americans. After his cover was blown, he was arrested by the Banda Koch (a Fascist militia under the command of Pietro Koch) and handed over to the Germans. Giglio was tortured at Gestapo HQ in Rome's Via Tasso and executed in the Ardeatine Caves massacre on 24 March 1944.

Haider, Jörg – (b. 1950 Bad Goisern; d. 2008 Köttmannsdorf) Austrian far-right politician, and chairman of the Austrian Freedon Party (FPÖ). His charismatic leadership helped the party rise from 5 percent to almost 27 percent of the popular vote, and in 200 the FPÖ entered into a coalition with the Christian Democratic Austrian People's Party. A vehement opponent of immigration, Haider attracted international condemnation for his praise of certain Nazi policies and his anti-Semitic stance. He died in a car crash in 2008.

Hass, Karl – (b. 1912 Kiel; d. 2004 Castel Gandolfo) Appointed an SS *Sturmbannführer* in 1941, Hass was involved in the Ardeatine Caves massacre. He was also responsible for luring Princess Mafalda of Savoy into custody at Gestapo HQ; she later died in Buchenwald concentration camp when it was bombed by the Allies. Hass was declared dead in 1953, whle continuing to live under the maiden name of his Italian wife. After the war, he was actively involved in helping leading Nazis escape justice, but also worked for the United States Army Counterintelligence Corps. He was only made to stand trial in 1998, when he was sentenced to life imprisonment, though this was commuted to house arrest in Castel Gandolfo.

Hudal, Alois – (b. 1885 Graz; d.1963 Rome) Director of the seminary at the German church of Santa Maria dell'Anima from 1923. In June 1933, Hudal was made a bishop. Postwar, he was instrumental in organising a 'rat-run' to South America for Nazi war criminals. He resigned as rector of Santa Maria in 1952.

Indiani metropolitani – (also known as the *movimento del '77*) Autonomous and spontaneous movement, organised by groups of the extraparliamentary left, which called for direct action against the party system and political institutions. Its favoured tactics included house occupation and violent street clashes with the police.

Kappler, Herbert – (b. 1907 Stuttgart; d.1978 Soltau) Head of the German security police in Rome during the occupation. In 1943–4, in his capacity as *Obersturmbannführer*, he was responsible, among other things, for the seizure of Jewish property, the deportation of Rome's Jews, and the massacre in the Ardeatine Caves. After the war, Kappler was sentenced to life imprisonment by an Italian military tribunal, but in the summer of 1977, with his wife's help, he escaped from the Roman military hospital at Celio.

Koch, Pietro – (b. 1918 Benevento; executed 1945, Rome) Italian soldier and leader of the notorious anti-partisan group Banda Koch. Under the protection of Herbert Kappler, Koch's group committed numerous atrocities, and he was given control of his own prisons and torture chambers in Rome, Florence and Milan as the fascists retreated north. He was arrested by the Allies and put to death for his crimes.

Langer, Alexander – (b. 1943 Sterzing; committed suicide in 1995)

German–Italian journalist, peace activist and leftist opposition politician from the South Tyrol/Alto Adige region. Langer was a Green Party member of the European Parliament. He took his own life in Florence, leaving behind a note reading 'Keep on doing the right thing.'

Leone, Giovanni – (b. 1908 Naples; d.2001 Rome) Italian Christian Democrat politician and President of Italy 1971–8. His election to president was the most protracted in the history of the post; he finally had to rely upon the votes of the neofascist *Movimento Sociale Italiano* (MSI). He stepped down after being implicated in the Lockheed Starfighter procurement scandal.

Mengele, Josef – (b. 1911 Günzburg; d. 1979, Bertioga, Brazil) SS officer and chief doctor at the Auschwitz–Birkenau extermination camp. Known as the 'Angel of Death', Mengele is notorious for having conducted appallingly inhumane medical experiments on thousands of Jews, Gypsies and other prisoners from 1943 to 1945. He is thought to have been responsible for the deaths of as many as 400,000 people. After the war, he fled via South Tyrol first to Argentina and then Paraguay. Private and official investigators never managed to track him down, possibly because he lived under the protection of longstanding Paraguayan dictator Alfredo Stroessner.

Monte Cassino – A hill around 80 miles southeast of Rome, and the site of a Benedictine monastery since the 6th century. Monte Cassino was a key stronghold on the German defensive Gustav Line facing the Allied invasion, and was the scene of fierce fighting in January–May 1944, when German paratroops occupied the ruins of the building and held up the Allied advance for over four months.

Moretti, Nanni – (b. 1953 Bruneck, South Tyrol) Italian film director and actor. An avowed leftist, Moretti has been outspoken in his criticism of the corrupt Italian political establishment and especially the right-wing media tycoon and three-times prime minister of Italy, Silvio Berlusconi.

Moro, Aldo – (b. 1916 Maglie; murdered in Rome 1978) Christian Democrat politician and prime minister of Italy 1963–8 and 1974–6. In March 1978, he was kidnapped by the extreme left-wing Red Brigades (*Brigate Rosse*) terrorist organisation and held for 55 days before being killed. His body was found dumped in the boot of a car.

Negri, Toni (Antonio) – (b. 1933 Padua) Italian Neo-Marxist political philosopher and sociologist. He was a founder member of the *Autonomia Operaia* ('Autonomous Workers') group, an extra-parliamentary movement active in the late 1970s.

ONMI – (*Opera Nazionale Maternità e Infanzia*) National agency established in 1925 by Mussolini's fascist regime to oversee maternal and infant welfare. It provided help to mothers (including single mothers), such as free medicines, baby food and childcare centres, but also had a eugenic agenda aimed at the 'active reclamation of the [Italian] race.'

Padre Pio – (b. 1887 Pietrelcina; d. 1968 San Giovanni Rotondo) Capuchin priest who is venerated as a saint by the Roman Catholic Church. He was famous for bearing the stigmata – bleeding in places corresponding to Christ's crucifixion wounds – from 1918 onwards. He was also reputed to experience visions. Though accused by an eminent Catholic academic physician of being a 'self-mutilating psychopath who exploited people's credulity', the Vatican dismissed all objections and he was canonised by Pope John Paul II in 2002.

'Pasquino' – one of the so-called 'talking statues' of Rome, this battered

3rd-century BC statue stands in the city's Piazza Pasquino, and for centuries has been a site for the posting of witty and scurrilous epigrams aimed at politicians or Church dignitaries.

Pertini, Sandro – (b. 1896 Stella/Savona; d. 1990 Rome) Socialist politician and president of Italy 1978–85. One of Italy's most popular statesmen, Pertini was active in the struggle against Fascism and National Socialism in the Second World War, and was arrested, interrogated and tortured on several occasions. He was sentenced to death by the Germans, but freed in a partisan raid.

Priebke, Erich – (b. 1913 Henningsdorf) An SS *Hauptsturmführer*, Priebke was Herbert Kappler's deputy in Rome and played a leading role in the Ardeatine Caves massacre in 1944. After the war, with the assistance of Bishop Alois Hudal and under the assumed name of Otto Pape, he escaped to Bariloche, Argentina, where he lived until he was tracked down by an American journalist in 1994. Extradited to Rome, he was first cleared by a military court in 1996, but two years later re-tried and sentenced to life imprisonment. The sentence was commuted to house arrest, on grounds of ill health, and Priebke still lives in an apartment in the Boccea district in the western suburbs of Rome.

Princess Mafalda of Savoy – (b. 1902 Rome; d. 1944 Buchenwald) The second daughter of King Victor Emmanuel III of Italy (r.1900–46), in 1925 Mafalda married Prince Philipp of Hesse, an early adherent of the National Socialist movement. Hitler was always suspicious of her loyalty to the cause, and when Italy surrendered to the Allies in 1943, she was lured under false pretences to the German High Command in Rome and arrested. After being deported to Germany for questioning, she was interned in Buchenwald concentration camp, where she was killed in an Allied air raid in August 1944.

Roncalli, Angelo Giuseppe – (b. 1881 Sotto il Monte; d. 1963 Rome) Catholic cardinal who was elected as Pope John XXIII in 1958. He was fêted as a popular and innovative pontiff. During the Second World War, he intervened to save Jewish refugee groups from the Nazis, though he stands accused, along with other cardinals during Mussolini's dictatorship, of approving the Italian invasion of Abyssinia, during which chemical weapons were used and other atrocities committed against the Ethiopian people.

Saragat, Giuseppe – (b. 1893 Turin; d. 1988 Rome) Socialist politician and fifth president of the Italian Republic from 1964 to 1971.

Schickert Works – From 1941 to 1945, the Munich-based firm of Otto Schickert & Co. ran a plant producing highly concentrated hydrogen peroxide in the town of Bad Lauterberg in Lower Saxony, Germany. This chemical was used as a fuel for rocket motors and in the turbines of U-boats. The workforce for building and expanding the plant was drawn from its own forced labour camp nearby, whose inmates included Belgians and, increasingly after 1943, Italians. The factory's Italian workers were called 'Badoglios' after the 'turncoat' prime minister Pietro Badoglio, who signed an armistice with the Allies.

Schwammberger, Josef – (b. 1912 Brixen/Bressanone, South Tyrol; d. 2004 Ludwigsburg) SS officer who commanded various labour camps in the Krakow district of occupied Poland in World War Two, where he organised random killings and at least one mass execution of Jewish prisoners. Aided by the 'rat-run', he escaped to Argentina in 1948, but was discovered and extradited to Germany in 1987. He was sentenced to life imprisonment in 1992 and died in prison in 2004.

Sindona, Michele – (b. 1920 Patti, Sicily; d. 1986 Voghera) Italian lawyer and banker. Sindona (known by contemporaries as 'The Shark') was convicted of fraud and money laundering in 1974, and while in prison used his connections to the Mafia and the secret *Propaganda Due* (P2) Masonic lodge to have his opponents murdered. In 1984, he was convicted in the USA of arranging the murder of the liquidator of his banking business, Giorgio Ambrosoli, and sentenced to life imprisonment. Two years later, he was poisoned in his cell at the Voghera maximum security prison by cyanide in his coffee.

Sossi, Mario – (b. 1932 Impera) Italian lawyer. While working as a judge in Genoa, Sossi was kidnapped by the Red Brigades in April 1974, but released after less than a month without any payment of ransom or other concessions.

Stangl, Franz – (b. 1908 Altmünster; d. 1971 Düsseldorf) Superintendent of the SS euthanasia clinic at Hartheim Castle near Linz in Austria. Stangl was appointed by Heinrich Himmler as the first commandant of the extermination camp at Sobibór and later became commandant of the Treblinka camp. In 1943 he was transferred to Italy to organise the campaign against the partisans. Post-war, with Alois Hudal's help, he fled first to Syria and then to Brazil. He was tracked down by Nazi hunter Simon Wiesenthal in 1967 and extradited to West Germany. Stangl was found guilty of murdering 900,000 people and was sentenced to life imprisonment, but died soon afterwards.

Tasca, Angelo – (b. 1892 Moretta; d. 1960 Paris) Italian communist politician and writer. Together with Gramsci, Togliatti and Terracini, he founded the weekly newspaper *L'Ordine Nuovo* ('New Order' 1919–20) in Turin and was a founder member of the Italian Communist Party in 1921.

Terracini, Umberto – (b. 1895 Genoa; d. 1983 Rome) From a Jewish cloth merchant's family in Piedmont, Terracini was a prominent politician and antifascist activist who spent many years in gaol under Mussolini. Co-founder of the Italian Communist Party.

Togliatti, Palmiro – (b. 1893 Genoa; d. 1964 Yalta, Crimea) Leading member of the Italian Communist Party (PCI) from 1921 until its banning five years later by Mussolini. Escaping arrest, he broadcast regularly from Moscow to the antifascist opposition in Italy during the Second World War. General Secretary of the PCI from 1947 to his death; during his leadership it became the country's second largest party.

Tolomei, Ettore – (b. 1865 Rovereto; d. 1952 Rome) Italian nationalist and fascist. A supporter of Italian irredentism, he was the chief proponent of the idea that the Brenner and Reschen passes should be regarded as the country's northernmost boundaries (thus taking in South Tyrol, mainly populated by German speakers). Tolomei was at the forefront of the forced fascist Italianisation of the region from 1923 onwards. One infamous measure was the imposition of Italian place and family names.

Tumler, Franz – (b. 1912 Gries bei Bozen, South Tyrol; d. 1998 Berlin) Austrian writer whose works were strongly redolent of his South Tyrolean homeland. In early life, the folk-oriented nature of his writing led to his embracing many aspects of Nazi ideology; he welcomed the annexation of Austria into the German Third Reich in 1938. After the war, he moved to West Berlin and recanted his former Nazi sympathies.

von Horstenau, Edmund Glaise – (b. 1882 Braunau-am-Inn, Austria; d. 1946 Nuremberg) An Austrian, and subsequently German, army officer, von Horstenau was appointed by Hitler as military overseer of the independent state of Croatia (a Nazi ally in World War Two), where he was shocked by the atrocities of the *Ustase* fascist paramilitaries.

After capture, fearing extradition to Yugoslavia to face a war crimes trial, he committed suicide.

Acknowledgments

Posthumously, I would like to thank my grandmothers Luise Monauni (1918–2008) and Anna Gruber (1909–1995) for their stories; in particular, it was the personal accounts that Grandma Luise gave of her experiences as a domestic servant in a household in Bolzano (Bozen) that prompted me to start investigating the social circumstances of women from South Tyrol in the interwar period, and subsequently led me on to read the interviews of housemaids conducted by Ursula Lüfter, Martha Verdorfer and Adelina Wallnöfer. The studies and findings of these South Tyrolean historians furnished me with some important building blocks for my novel. For further information on the subject, I am much obliged to the historian Leopold Steurer and the historian and political scientist Günther Pallaver.

Moreover, the novel in its present form would never have seen the light of day had it not been for the diverse publications of Eva Gesine Baur, Umberto Gandini, Christian Jansen, Robert Katz, Aram Mattioli, Christoff Neumeister, Alberto Portelli, Gerhard Schreiber, Gerald Steinmacher and Jonathan Steinberg.

I would also like to thank the librarians at the Casa della Memoria e della Storia in Trastevere, Rome, and the staff of both the Biblioteca Nazionale Centrale di Roma and the Biblioteca Nazionale Marciana in Venice for their invaluable help.

I also owe a great debt of gratitude to Johannes Knapp-Menzel for solving my IT problems, Robert Schindel and Anna Brandstätter for their constructive criticism of my draft manuscript, my editor Martin Hielscher for his outstanding collaboration, and Karl-Heinz Ströhle for his patience.

My special thanks are due to the Austrian Cultural Forum in Rome, and especially its director Astrid Harz, for being so welcoming during my stay at the institute, and to the Austrian Federal Ministry for Education, Art and Culture for granting me the Robert Musil memorial bursary from 2009 to 2011 to undertake the writing of this novel.

Non Gridate Piu from *Giuseppe Ungaretti: Selected Poems* (April 2004) reproduced with the kind permission of Carcanet Press Limited and Farrar, Straus and Giroux, LLC.